SIREN

Book One
The Trident Throne
Trilogy

ISLA MELYSIN

SPELLWINGS
PRESS

IslaMelysin.com

"If I have seen further, it is by standing on the shoulders of giants."

Sir Isaac Newton, 1675

Dedicated to all who lift us up.

CONTENTS

Frostvaar
Ember
Skaera
Ruins of Twilight
Solace
Seed of the Binding
Shade
Moon
Ghealach Siorai
Tides
Ardaion
IslaMelysin.com

BOOK ONE: THE TRIDENT THRONE

"The Queen called me a mistake.
Ardaion called me the Heir."

FOREWORD

"In every age, there had been predators," Serena would later say, "but none so feared as the sirens."

Beneath the trees, in the rivers and lakes, in the salt-stung air of the coast, the sirens reigned.

They were not merely beautiful. They were apex predators—Alluring, yes. Lethal, absolutely. Their bodies were born to survive what others could not. They did not learn how to hold power. They were born from it, forged to command it.

Other fae cracked beneath the tides of wild magic. Sirens thrived. They were dominance and yielding in perfect balance, seduction laced with slaughter. They ruled the rivers, the shadowed lakes, the drowned caverns where no other fae dared tread.

Their tribes did not fracture. Their matriarchs were not questioned. Where high fae feuded, sirens bound themselves by ritual, by blood, and by will. A sisterhood. No quarrel outlived their law. No rival withstood their queen's command.

So when the land began to change—when the wellspring grew wild and unchecked—it was the sirens who came prepared. They knew the scent of death in the water.

Sirens do not fear death.

PROLOGUE: THE BINDING

*A*s told beside fire, to daughters meant to remember

Before there were cities. Before marble towers, and glyph-bound scrolls. Before the word "queen" meant anything at all. There was still Ardaion.

But Ardaion was not a realm. Not a nation. It was a wild thing—mountain, ocean, sky, each pulsing with power, untamed and unwatched. Magic did not follow rule. It did not follow reason. It surged. It warped. It killed.

Fae were born in it, from it—tribes of winged and clawed and fanged beings, scattered across land and sea. Some hunted in high passes. Some lived near rivers that boiled. Some swam in waters that sang. They did not call themselves courts. They had no lords, no borders. Only territory, and the blood it cost to keep it.

Yet even these tribes, for all their pride and fury, saw what was coming. The land was weakening. Magic spilled in waves—corrupting the very earth. Children were born wrong. Beasts twisted. Rituals failed. The oldest among them said the land was leaking. That its power was not infinite. That it would break them all, if it was not sealed.

Worse still, others had begun to come. Not fae, not kin. Foreign forces. Invaders. Armies from beyond the sea, fae and human alike, drawn by territory left unguarded, fractured, ripe for conquest. The tribes had no single banner. No unified force. And no one to stop what was already inside the gates.

So, across the plains and mountains, they sent word. A gathering. A great one. Every tribe, even enemies, came. Not all survived the meeting. But the need was greater than the hate.

No fae alive had seen such a thing. Leaders and chiefs were brought forward. The strongest. The purest of line. They were not asked to rule. They were asked to offer themselves—to be the vessel that would bind the wellspring.

The mages—back then little more than blood-sorcerers and storm-tamers—cut the glyphs into stone. Old magic. Dangerous, deadly. No one had done this before. No one would ever do it again.

The ritual began. The land shook. One by one, the chiefs stepped forward. Some begged. Some fought. Some wept. The land rejected them all.

Until another walked the circle barefoot, silent. A siren—black-haired, sea-born, eyes like the storm. She did not speak. She did not bow. For she was a matriarch. She simply stepped forward, and offered her death.

Not power. Not glory. *Her death.*

And the land listened. Accepted her as its avatar, its conduit.

The air changed. The power thickened. She did not fall. She did not burn. She changed.

Body remade. Blood reforged. Her body took in the wellspring—and did not break.

From her shoulders tore wings of light and pure power. Spell-wings, we call them now. Proof. The land had chosen.

Not just her. *Her bloodline.*

That was the First Binding.

The fae did not cheer. They did not fully understand what had been made.

But they felt it. A tether. A shift in the world. From that day forward, magic was tamed and the land had a guardian.

She bore one daughter. That daughter bore another. Each one stronger than the last. Each one tied to the land. Each one able to carry the wellspring's power without dying.

The line of siren queens.

They did not rule because they wanted to. They ruled because the land would not let anyone else.

That was how it began. Not with conquest. But with willing sacrifice.

Civilization did not follow all at once. It took centuries.

But that moment—*that choice*—was the hinge of all Ardaion history.

PART 1: CHILDHOOD

CHAPTER ONE

MAB

Queen Tatiana's death did not halt the realm. It hardened it.

She had been murdered in her own court—by powdered ash wood, finely ground, and slipped into her food. Not a blade. Not a visible wound. Just blood that wouldn't stop. By the time the truth was uncovered, despite the best healers, there was nothing left to do but watch the queen bleed out from within. Jormunder ripped the assassin to pieces with his bare hands.

Mab did not cry. She did not scream. Only silence, and the cold, absolute stillness of purpose. She had always been the heir. Her blood already carried the power of the land. The realm did not wait to ask her if she was ready. And she gave it no reason to.

She took the throne before her mother's body cooled.

Then she ordered the maps brought forward.

The humans had believed that killing the queen would destabilize the Binding—perhaps even break it. They hoped to collapse Ardaion's structure from the inside, to undo the order that had grown over the last several millennia. But all they had done was provoke the wrong heir.

What followed, *Mab's Wrath*, was not a campaign. It was annihilation.

No warnings were issued. No demands for justice were made. She struck where the assassins had come from—human territories that had profited from the plot, hidden those responsible, or turned their eyes away. Coastal towns were drowned or burned. Entire regions vanished beneath spells too old to have names.

There were no survivors where her orders landed. It was not a war. It was a purge. Deliberate, swift, and total. For millennia human mothers would warn misbehaving children that if they didn't listen, Queen Mab would get them.

When the campaign ended, Mab returned to Ghealach Siorai and locked the palace tighter than it had ever been. She had learned from Tatiana and Jormunder alike—how to use silence, how to wait, how to strike only when it mattered most. She did not outburst. She outmaneuvered. And when she moved, it was already too late to stop her.

The courts whispered her name with reverence and caution. The Spider, they called her. She observed from her web. She plotted. And when her trap was set, she pounced with merciless precision.

Yet, for all her control, there was still one thread she had not chosen.

Edric arrived as a military envoy from the Tides Court, assigned to work with Rivarin and Jormunder in the development of the aerial forces. He was Akyist—winged, white-feathered, blue-eyed—and he came from the high sea cliffs where the Akyist had lived for ages above the water fae who nested in the caves below. Their coexistence was long-established: the sky guarded the sea, the sea warned the sky. It was a rhythm older than records.

Edric was not what most expected from a soldier. Though he could fly and fight with the best of them, he spent most of his free time reading. He kept a scribal team at his side, documenting everything from tactical drills to architectural shifts in Ghealach Siorai. He studied glyphwork, toyed with elixirs, and even proposed magical theories to court mages that forced them to rewrite more than one assumption. He was quiet, curious, deliberate. Occasionally mischievous, he could make Mab smile.

He and Rivarin, Mab's younger brother, had begun refining aerial doctrine—training for winged soldiers supporting battle from above. Along with Jormunder and the Lord of Tides, they formalized what became the Valkyrie corps—elite aerial soldiers whose existence reshaped the future of sky warfare.

It was during these years of collaboration that the Binding revealed Edric as Mab's mate.

Edric of the Tides. Akyist. Scholar. Prince Consort.

He became her equal—not in politics, but in presence. Her balance. The one who could speak without fear of reprisal, who could temper her rage without shaming her for it. Edric never tried to rule. He offered clarity. Mab let him offer it.

He could reach her when no one else could. He softened her heart.

And though she never softened her rule, the presence of Edric beside her made it feel unshakable.

Their love came slowly. But it came deeply. It was a match of balance—her fire and his calm. Her vision and his insight. It was not a public affair of fawning or display. But it was real. Real enough that the Binding recognized it. Real enough that the realm did too.

Together, they expanded the reach of the Moon Court—not through fear alone, but through intellect, diplomacy, and vision. And yet the fear never vanished. Mab made sure of that.

Her reign was not one of mercy. But it was one of order. Ardaion thrived beneath her. The courts, now secure in their borders and governments, expanded their cities and refined their traditions. But none dared rival the Moon Court. Because at its center stood a queen with no weakness, a bonded mate who studied everything, and a father who still commanded armies with a glance.

She did not forgive. She did not forget.

And Ardaion would not forget her.

CHAPTER TWO

THE FALL

Part I: The Death

It began, as many endings do, with a silence that felt too still.

The hour was late—the moon high, the palace quiet save for the whisper of silks and the rustle of jasmine vines that climbed the white columns outside the high windows. Queen Mab, swollen with child and unable to sleep, had dismissed her attendants hours ago.

The palace physicians had pleaded with her to rest. The priests had left offerings beneath the balcony, scented oils meant to soothe and protect. But Mab stood alone in the solar that overlooked Ghealach Siorai's glittering night gardens, her arms wrapped under her belly, her gown clinging to sweat-dampened skin.

Her black hair, streaked with crimson and gold, and usually pinned in the regal coils expected of a queen, hung in loose, disheveled waves around her bare shoulders. The moonlight caught on her cheekbones—unpainted for once—and lit the edges of her profile in silver. Her grey-blue eyes, so often hard as polished opal, were dull with the kind of tension that could only come from waiting.

The courier came without sound. He did not announce himself—he could not. The guards had tried to stall him, but Mab had felt his approach. She had turned before he stepped foot on the mosaic tile. She had *known*. Something in their bond, in the pit of her stomach.

He dropped to one knee. Blood on his knuckles. Mud on his boots. His white wings were torn, and his feathers snapped.

"Highness," he said, hoarse. "I bring word—"

She didn't hear the words.

Not really.

Just the name. *Edric.*

And *gone.*

Then—nothing.

The solar detonated.

A siren's scream erupted from Mab's chest so raw it shattered every window in the high wing. Glass rained down across polished floors. Magic rippled outward in an uncontrollable wave that sent every servant within a hundred paces to their knees.

Blood ran from the ears and noses of the nearest guards. The drapes were torn from their rings. Mirrors cracked. One of the statues—an old carving of Queen Morgana—splintered down the center as if it, too, could not bear the sound of Mab's grief.

She did not stop screaming. Not when the guards burst in. Not when the priestesses arrived.

Her scream became an aria of rage and loss, siren-born and ancient—one that did not seduce but *punished*, dragging every soul in the palace into the drowning depths of her despair. Chandeliers shook. The harbor sea drew away from her grief only to rush in again with fury and smash ships in the moorings. Mages shielded the foundation of the Siorai palace itself.

The courier had long since died. Too near the queen. Blood ran from his eyes, nose, ears.

And then—silence.

Too sudden. Too hollow.

Mab stood at the center of the wreckage barefoot, blood dripping from her palm where the broken edge of a glass flute had sliced through her skin. Her hair was caught in her mouth. She did not brush it aside. Her eyes were vacant.

No one dared speak.

Then she turned.

And walked toward the wide, arched balcony, bare feet crunching over the shards leaving bloody footprints of enthralling siren blood in her wake.

Kriesta—Lady of the Shade Court—was the first to move. She was still young then, only two hundred, and not yet hardened by politics or grief. She stepped forward, voice soft and low, her black Dardani wings tucked tight. She was Lady-in-Waiting and pregnant herself, sent to the Siorai palace while the Shade Lord joined the war.

"Mab—don't—"

But the queen didn't stop.

The double doors had already been blasted off their hinges. The wind lifted Mab's hair like a bridal veil as she stepped onto the stone ledge. Mab had not inherited Jormunder's Dardani wings.

Seven stories above the gardens.

The jasmine vines swayed. The moon burned cold above her, bright and full. Far below, the reflecting pools shimmered.

The guards began to rush forward.

"Stop," Kriesta barked, and even they obeyed.

Mab raised her head, arms limp at her sides. Her voice was quiet, raw from the scream-ing. "My mate. I swore to him I'd follow him. That I would always be at his side and he at mine."

There was no tremble. No drama. Just flat certainty.

Kriesta moved slowly now, one foot after the other, careful not to startle her. "He died in the field, Mab. He died defending the line. For the realm. For you. For—"

"For *nothing*," Mab whispered. "He was never meant to be there."

The words sliced more than her scream had.

She hadn't sent him into the front. She'd told him to stay behind. She had *ordered* it. He'd disobeyed. Because he believed in the cause. Because he was a leader. Quiet Edric... soft-spoken but never weak. He was Akyist, a warrior scholar. A poet with the heart of a dragon.

Now he was gone.

The child shifted low in her belly, heavy and insistent. It made her sway slightly. She clutched the stone with one hand, steadying herself.

"I can't do this," she said.

Kriesta did not argue. She simply said: "If you die, the bloodline ends. The Binding breaks. The wellspring fails. Ardaion falls."

Mab stared forward.

"I don't care."

But Kriesta kept going. "Then let her die with you. Let Edric's daughter perish because her mother was too much of a coward to face life without him."

The insult landed like a slap. Mab turned her head, slowly. She bared her fangs and hissed.

Kriesta did not flinch.

"You want to follow him? Fine. But you spit on what he died to protect."

"I *am* what he died to protect!" Mab hissed.

"No," Kriesta said. "*She* is. Your heir. *His* heir."

Mab's hand clenched on the stone rail. The wind howled.

"You don't know what you're saying," Mab said.

"I do. And so do you." Kriesta's voice dropped lower. "He gave you a daughter. You still have something left of him. If you throw yourself from this ledge, all that's left is ash."

Mab swayed again.

The ache was deeper than flesh. Deeper than bone. It lived in her very blood.

Still—she stepped down.

Not because of logic. Not because of loyalty to Ardaion. Not because of the Binding.

But because some small part of her, desperate and shattered, still clung to the illusion that Edric might live on. That the daughter within her might look up one day with his same steady gaze. Might laugh like him. Might smile with that same gentle curve that made Mab forget how brutal the world was.

She stepped down.

And then, Mab began to laugh. Bitter, with an edge of hysteria to it.

A sharp, bitter sound. It cracked and rang through the ruined solar.

"I'll raise him again," she said to no one. "She'll be his mirror. I will see him again. His smile, his eyes, those brave wings. He will come back to me."

Part II: The Birth

The pain came early.

Too early. Too fast. The child wasn't due for another month, and yet Mab's body had turned against her—as if the grief it carried had grown too heavy. Her court had done all they could in the days after Edric's death.

The priestesses had spoken of legacy, of purpose, of the great honor of bringing forth his heir. How he would live on through his daughter. They had told her she would see him again in the child's eyes, that it would be a comfort, that she would carry his memory into the future.

Mab had believed them.

She had twisted their words into something sharper. She had clung to the idea not of comfort, but resurrection. She would see him again—his golden hair, his bronze skin, his feathered wings. The same deep blue eyes that had steadied her for centuries. She imagined a daughter with his gentleness, his quiet strength, his radiant light. His face reborn in her arms.

It was the only reason she hadn't stepped off the balcony three days ago.

When the pain started, she said nothing.

The staff recognized it anyway—the set of her jaw, the sharp flicker of magic pulsing from her skin. The birthing chamber was prepared. Runes flared to life in the walls. Steam filled the air. The High Priestess took her place at Mab's side as if that alone could anchor the realm. Rhythmic chanting began, punctuated with occasional growls and hisses- the ancient sounds of the Mer, the water fae.

Mab didn't speak. She didn't cry out. Her body labored in silence, jaw clenched, breath steady. The only sounds were the quiet orders of the midwives and the slow, tightening creak of the queen's fingers crushing the carved headboard. But her thoughts were on Edric. His daughter would be here soon.

The final contraction came with a wave of dark heat.

And then the child was born.

The midwife caught her, turned her gently, and cleared her airway. Still no sound. No cry, no gasp.

But she was breathing. Eyes open. A fierce glare.

Mab's head shifted on the pillow, sweaty but eager. *Desperate.* She'd stepped off the ledge because this child would give her Edric back. Nothing- not the birthing pain, not the blood- *nothing* mattered but seeing his face again.

The midwife hesitated before lifting the child into view.

There was no golden hair. The infant's was black, wet, and curling already. Her eyes—open far too soon—were not blue but storm-grey. Her skin, instead of bronzed or gold, bore the pale coolness of moonstone. Her wings, already twitching faintly, were leathery. Draconic. Not feathered. Not Akyist.

Nothing of Edric.

Only Jormunder. Only Tatiana. Only *them.*

The queen stared. Hope, maniacal, turning to ash in her mouth.

The silence stretched.

"She is—" the midwife began.

Mab's voice cut her off.

"Take it away."

The woman froze. *It?*

Mab looked around the room, her eyes alighting on one of the priestesses who had told her that Edric would live again in their child. She didn't speak a word but the priestess burst into a mist of blood with the speed of a bubble bursting. She hadn't even had time to cry out.

"She is not his. Not in any way that matters." Her voice had gone flat. Quiet. Dead. "She's a traitor to his memory." She paused, falling into bitter resentment then said, "And my greatest disappointment." She rolled onto her side, turning her back to the infant.

The midwife tried one last, brave time, knowing she might be risking herself, and said "Majesty..."

Mab screamed, furious, "OUT! Take her out! Take it out of this room now or I'll kill both of you. I don't care if it dooms Ardaion. Get out!" She didn't turn back around but a window shattered.

The child was quickly lowered into a basket without further protest. Wrapped in a plain grey cloth. The deep navy and silver ceremonial shawl with the Moon court sigil remained folded on the table beside the queen's bed, untouched. The royal parchment that had been prepared for the birth—the name, the signatures, the blood mark—was left blank.

No name was spoken.

The infant was carried out in silence.

In a chamber two wings away, Kriesta labored through her pain, her attendants fewer and younger. Her mate had not returned from the front. She was sweating and exhausted, barely coherent as the door creaked open and a nursemaid slipped in, whispering the queen's child had come—and been cast aside.

No one knew what to do. Mab's rule was absolute, her rage volatile. She'd already killed a priestess and threatened the child and midwife. But this child was of the Binding, bound to the wellspring, Heir of Ardaion. So they did the only thing they could do- send a rushed message to Jormunder at the front.

Part III: The Bond

The nursemaids took the child from the queen's chamber without delay, carrying her through the eastern corridors while the blood on her skin was still drying. Wrapped in a plain grey swaddle, she made no sound as they moved.

One of the attending girls ran ahead, breathless, into Kriesta's birthing room and relayed the news in a low voice: the queen had refused her child. She'd looked at the newborn and turned her head away. Called her a traitor to her father's memory. Refused to name her. Declared her a disappointment.

Kriesta, already deep in her labor, could not respond. She heard it, and her expression changed, but she was unable to speak through the pain.

She fought through each contraction alone, teeth clenched, breath heaving as magic flickered against the walls in pulsing bursts. Three hours later, with her hands clawing at the bedding and her wings twitching erratically against the stone, she gave a final, guttural cry and delivered her son.

Graye was placed against her chest, red-faced and squalling, his cries sharp in the still room. She clutched him, whispered to him, and pressed her lips to his damp brow. When he had quieted and the nurses had finished tending to him, Kriesta turned to the midwife and asked for the other child. The little princess.

The girl was brought in and laid in the cradle beside Kriesta's cot. Her hair was dark and still damp, her eyes a storm-cloud grey. Her wings, though not yet firmed with muscle, were already distinctively Jormunder's in shape.

Whatever quirk had given Jormunder his draconic wings had passed to his grandchild. But hers were not just black; there was an iridescence like an oil slick, reflecting hues of violet, indigo, and emerald in the fae lights. She was alert, silent, watching the room with an unsettling steadiness. She was not swaddled in silks. No gold pin marked her name. She had none.

Kriesta reached out and brushed her hand along the child's cheek, then shifted her son into the cradle beside her. The two newborns, only three hours apart, nestled against each other without hesitation, one quiet, the other still hiccupping from the force of his earlier crying. They pressed into one another, face to face, Graye's small hands curled near the girl's shoulder.

Kriesta watched them for a long moment, then finally allowed the attendants to guide her to the cleansing room across the hall to be bathed and redressed. Her nurses followed, arms full of linens and tinctures, leaving the chamber empty.

They did not see Jaryk, Lord of the Shade Court, slip through the side door like a shadow. He'd been waiting for his son's birth and had already heard the nursemaids aghast with the queen's rejection of her heir, for the binding was clear- only one daughter would be born to a siren queen. The Heir of Ardaion. Doubly so with the death of Edric.

This child, regardless of Mab's rejection, *was* the princess of the Moon Court, the inheritor of the blood binding, and an infant siren queen. But unwanted, unloved, unguarded. An opportunity for his newborn son.

He moved without sound, without glamour, without need for concealment. No guards saw him. No nurses returned in time to interrupt. His gaze swept the cradle once, twice. Then he stepped toward it and knelt.

The children were sleeping. Still pressed close.

If the Binding one day bound them as mates, the result would be more than power—it would be an heir that combined the Moon Court and Shade Court lines. But even if that did not happen, a blood bond would secure a lasting connection. It would guarantee his son's influence in the court that stood above all others.

The ritual had long since been outlawed, banned by decree after it was discovered that it twisted more than magic. It exchanged a sliver of soul between those it bound. A permanent tether. If one were wounded, the other might feel it. If they were separated too long, the longing would become an ache. Not unbearable, but constant. Insidious. Inescapable.

As strong as the Binding's mate bond, and just as irrevocable.

He withdrew a curved ritual blade from the inner pocket of his cloak, its surface marked with ancient runes for binding, yearning, and permanence. He pricked Graye's finger, then the girl's. Neither woke, he kept them soothed with a pulse of power. He squeezed gently on their pricked fingers, one drop of the princess's blood into Graye's tiny mouth and one drop of Graye's into hers.

Jaryk spoke the words under his breath, low and firm, the old tongue rasping through the air as the spell settled. His Shade magery did not stir the walls or darken the lights. It was precise and subtle, coiled around the spell-like smoke around a blade. No outward effect marked the moment. No wind. No light. But the bond had taken.

Graye and the girl remained asleep, curled together in the cradle, unaware of what had been done.

The lord stood. Straightened his collar. And left through the same shadowed hall, the scent of his magic already fading. By the time Kriesta returned, the room was unchanged. The nursemaids believed nothing had happened.

But the two children were no longer unconnected.

They had been bound—not by chance, nor love, nor fate.

By blood. By soul.

And by ambition.

Part IV: The Heir of Ardaion

The argument echoed through the halls. Everyone heard it. No one intervened.

Jormunder had not waited long after hearing what had happened. The moment the report reached him—of the queen's labor, the birth, and the rejection—he flew back to the Moon Palace with outrage. He landed in the upper courtyard in full armor, still bloodstained from the front lines. The rain hadn't even been cleared from his wings when he stormed into the high chamber where his daughter sat recovering, her face still pale from blood loss.

"You discarded her," he spat, not as a question, but an accusation. "Your own child."

Mab didn't look up from the documents spread across the table. A battle map. Logistics. Anything but the subject at hand.

"She is not my child," she said flatly. "Not truly. She is a mockery of him."

"She is your blood," Jormunder growled. "She bears the Binding. She is the only daughter you will ever have. The Heir to Ardaion."

"She doesn't look like him." Mab's hands curled slightly over the parchment. "Not his hair. Not his eyes. Not his wings. I looked at her and saw only Tatiana. Only *you*."

"And that is reason to cast her aside?" Jormunder's voice rose. "Because she bears her grandmother's face? That child is not a failure, Mab! She is everything you and Edric were meant to create."

"She is *nothing* I wanted! Useless!" Mab hissed. "I do not even know where they took her."

The admission hit harder than a blow. Jormunder stared at her, disbelief sharp behind his eyes. "You didn't even ask?"

"I had nothing to say," Mab said, turning away. "Nothing to give her."

Jormunder stood still for a long moment. When he finally spoke again, his voice was quiet, cold, and deliberate.

"Then she is an orphan."

And he left.

He did not speak again until he reached the lower wing, demanding to know where the child had been placed. His voice had lowered into a growl and his eyes promised dread consequences. The palace aides stammered. Some didn't know. Eventually, one of the guards, shaken from the expression on Jormunder's face, told him she'd been taken to the eastern suite—where Lady Kriesta was recovering with her son.

He reached the doors without waiting for permission. The guards jumped aside.

Inside, the air was warm. The lamplight glowed softly. Kriesta sat near the cradle rocking it slowly. When she noticed the general, she tried to rise, her movements slow from healing. He motioned her to stay seated.

"She's here," Kriesta said. "They didn't know what else to do with her."

Jormunder looked past her.

The two infants lay side by side, their small bodies curled together naturally. His granddaughter was lying on her back, awake. Not crying. Watching the ceiling. Graye's head rested lightly against the girl's. Her small hand had curled into the edge of his blanket.

Jormunder stepped forward.

And stopped.

His heart pounded once, hard, in his chest. His breath caught.

Tatiana. His mate. The shape of the face. The set of the mouth. Those eyes.

The child looked exactly like her. The same grey stare, too knowing by far. The same pale skin. Her hair was damp, but dark and curling already. The resemblance was so exact it hollowed him. His beloved mate's face.

Then he saw the wings. Folded close to her sides but unmistakable in shape—slightly larger than normal, leathery. His own wings, not Mab's. Not Dardani, not Akyist. *Draconic.*

His throat tightened. Not with anger. Not with grief.

He had not expected it to hurt like this.

His legs carried him forward before he thought to move.

The child didn't blink when he leaned down.

She looked at him, bold, assessing, sharp.

Something in his chest cracked open.

He reached down and picked her up carefully, his hands huge compared to her tiny frame. He held her against his chest, cradling her with a precision few thought him capable of, as though she were made of spun glass. The Black Dragon, the undefeated general of the Moon Court, the slayer of kings, bent his head and kissed the child's brow with a gentleness no one in the palace had ever seen from him.

"She didn't even name her," Kriesta said behind him.

He didn't answer at first.

He held her a moment longer.

Then, finally: "Serena."

He looked back down at her. Her eyelids fluttered slightly.

"It means siren in the old tongue."

Kriesta tilted her head. "Siren?"

"She was rejected by her mother," he said, "for looking siren instead of Akyist. Perhaps this name will help her take pride in what she is, rather than shame in what she isn't."

Kriesta stepped closer, watching the way his hand curved around the girl's back.

Jormunder said, "The war still moves. She is the Heir, whether Mab claims her or not. She will be raised at the palace. Trained. Taught. Surrounded by the staff and the best tutors in the realm. And I would ask you to remain, Lady Kriesta. Help raise her. Not as her nursemaid. As her godmother."

Kriesta nodded. "She will not want for care. My son will be like a brother to her."

"She will not want for anything," he said. "She is the Heir, and hope, of Ardaion. One day, she will rule."

With that, the general—the warlord, the weapon forged over nearly three thousand years—held his tiny granddaughter in his arms, and made the first promise she would ever be given: with or without Mab's love, she was still the Princess of the Moon Court, Heir of Ardaion. And by Binding, by tradition, and with his love, she would be raised as such.

The courtiers did not interfere, did not speak out. Mab was lethal in her grief, mercurial, and capable of lashing out with deadly ends. One and all, they decided it was best not to provoke her. After all, though Serena had been rejected emotionally by her mother, her inheritance- *her necessity-* could not be undone.

They reasoned it away over time and it simply became the way things were. Jormunder, as her grandfather, oversaw her upbringing. She was given every due as a royal princess. But she was kept away from Mab at all times.

CHAPTER THREE
MISCHIEF MAKERS

Age 6

The late afternoon sun slanted through the high arched windows of the Moon Palace, gilding the marble hallway in molten gold. Its silence, however, had long since been ruined.

Serena darted left with a triumphant shriek, a wooden ladle gripped tightly in her hand like a sword, her skirts bunched in her fist to free her legs. Graye howled in mock protest as he staggered back, arms flailing, his own stolen ladle up in shaky defense.

"You yield!" Serena declared, striking once, twice, then jabbing for his ribs with gleeful precision.

"Never!" Graye yelped, tripping over his own feet and skidding backward across the polished floor. His heels struck the base of a long sideboard table, heavy and carved from moonwood. His eyes flicked behind him, calculating escape.

"You're cornered," she was breathless, dark hair wild across her face.

He grinned, wiped his sleeve across his cheek, and attempted something dramatic. A spin, a sweep, the kind of dazzling move he'd once seen one of the palace guards perform in the training yard. But his elbow hit the table's edge. The nearest candleholder wobbled, then toppled with a clatter. Wax splashed. The flame licked once, then twice, and caught the hem of the ancient tapestry hanging above.

Both of them froze.

The threadbare silks ignited almost immediately, fire racing up in a ripple of orange and black. Gold embroidery curled into smoke. One of the tassels dropped to the floor in a shower of sparks.

They stared—eyes wide, mouths slightly open—as the fire grew higher, hotter, hungrier.

Then, wordlessly, they turned and *ran*.

Their footsteps echoed like thunder down the corridors. Serena was faster—always faster—and Graye trailed behind, still holding his ladle. Neither looked back. They didn't stop until they reached the kitchens, bursting through the servant entrance red-faced and breathless, sweat clinging to their hairlines.

No one noticed them as they ducked beneath the long work table at the far end, half-covered by linen and shadow. Trays of cooling pastries lined the surfaces above—mooncakes dusted in powdered sugar, still warm and smelling of honey and cinnamon.

They reached up blindly and dragged two down, then three, then more. Sticky fingers tore them open. The honey syrup dripped down their wrists. Crumbs scattered across the stone floor.

They sat with knees drawn up, faces smeared with filling, backs pressed to the table legs. For a while, they said nothing—just the sound of chewing, of licking fingers clean, of trying to breathe quietly through the muffled giggles that kept escaping.

Then Serena muttered, mouth full, "They're going to find it."

Graye swallowed hard. "Probably already have."

She wiped her fingers on her skirt. "We shouldn't have used the good ladles."

"We shouldn't have set the tapestry on fire."

"That too."

Graye picked at a crumb on his shirt. "Do you think it'll burn all the way to the ceiling?"

Serena looked thoughtful, then grim. "I think if it reached the second-story balcony, we'd hear it."

They listened in silence. Somewhere deep in the palace, a bell began to ring. Not an alarm—but close.

They exchanged a look.

Graye muttered, "We're going to die, Sev."

Serena had been "Sev" to Graye since he could speak. Elsibetha, her older cousin, called her "Ser" but it had twisted in Graye's toddler-aged mouth to Sev and the nickname had stuck.

"Not before dinner," Serena said, grabbing another cake.

They chewed quietly for a moment longer, then she added, "Maybe they'll think it was someone else."

"No one else is that stupid."

"Exactly."

Under the scent of singed velvet wafting faintly through the ventilation shafts, they ate another mooncake and waited to be found.

Age 7

The scroll cracked as the scholar unrolled it, flattening the vellum against the lectern with precise fingers. Dust motes swirled in the shaft of afternoon light filtering through the tall, arched windows, illuminating motes of gold in the marble floor beneath their feet. A slight breeze stirred the flame of a nearby candelabra, though it did nothing to relieve the slow, crushing weight of the hour.

"Now, children," the mage intoned, his voice as dry as the brittle scroll in his hands, "it is important to recall the distinction between *innate magical faculties* and *learned disciplines*. One is born to you through blood, the other cultivated by study and repetition. The former, when untrained, can be as volatile as it is potent—particularly in those touched by Binding lineage..."

Serena shifted in her chair, one of the many carved moonwood seats arranged along the long gallery wall of the Hall of Instruction. Her skirts were too stiff with embroidery, her sleeves too tight at the elbows, and the lecture had gone on three hours past its usefulness. She had stopped listening after the second time he'd invoked the phrase *spontaneous combustion*.

Graye sat beside her, his expression carefully blank—until his hand snuck along the bench between them and pinched the underside of her arm.

Hard.

She barely moved. A twitch of her lip. A sharp breath through her nose. She reached across herself with exaggerated nonchalance and returned the favor under the table with the practiced savagery of someone who had played this game for years.

The nursemaids watching from across the room narrowed their eyes but said nothing.

The game had rules.

Don't cry out. Don't get caught. Don't be a baby.

"—affinities may present early in high-blooded fae," the mage continued, utterly unaware. "Especially those born near a wellspring or touched by the Binding itself. These manifestations may appear as elemental responses, minor conjurations, or instinctive reactionary magics during emotional surges. A dangerous and fascinating field, particularly where stormblood and shade-blood intermingle, as in certain hybrid lineages..."

Serena's other hand had curled toward Graye's side, but he'd already shifted out of reach. His pale blue tunic was immaculately pressed; his expression that of a bored princeling who nonetheless knew better than to show it.

The mage finally set the scroll aside.

"That will conclude the day's lecture," he said. "You are dismissed—though I remind you both that your afternoon dance instruction begins within the next quarter bell. Report to the northern ballroom. Master Virell expects an improvement in your posturing during the half-turn sequence of the Spring Waltz."

Graye groaned. Softly. Just enough for Serena to hear.

Serena didn't look at him. She was too busy composing her face into something serene for the benefit of the mage and the ever-watching staff. The minute the door shut behind them, she rolled her eyes so hard she nearly tipped backward.

Graye mimicked the movement with all the grace of a dying fish.

"I'll bet he corrects my wrist again," he muttered as they made their way down the corridor, nursemaids trailing behind like a pair of mild ghosts.

"He always does," Serena smirked. "You hold like a butcher."

"Better than your elbows. You flail."

"I *extend.*"

"You flap."

They turned left past a columned archway and into the main vestibule of the ballroom. The polished stone floor glistened, freshly scrubbed. The windows had been flung open to let in the breeze, and already the music master was tuning strings in the far corner. Master Virell was not yet present, but they could feel him coming.

"I'll lead this time," Graye said, smug.

"You always say that. You never do."

"I forget."

"You panic."

"I panicked once."

"Every time."

They paused outside the ballroom door as a servant crossed the floor ahead of them carrying an armful of practice ribbons.

There was no one else there yet.

For a moment, they leaned against the wall side by side, silent.

They weren't siblings—not truly. Not by blood. But nearly everything else about their lives had been shaped as if they were. Graye, the princeling of Shade, was not technically of the Moon Court. But since the day he had been laid beside the discarded heir in a single shared cradle, since the day Kriesta—his mother and Serena's adoptive guardian—had agreed to raise them together beneath Mab's indifferent eye, that lie had become the truth.

The court didn't speak of it. Not because they didn't know. Because it was safer not to. Even the steward didn't dare mention the arrangement within earshot of the queen. Mab's temper, though rarely displayed these days, was still feared. And whatever her daughter was to become, Mab had made it clear that it would not involve her.

Still, no one could deny Serena's role. She was the Heir of Ardaion, bound to the wellspring through the ancient Binding. She would be queen, eventually. There had never been an heir who wasn't. The Ardaion line ruled until death, and death always came, eventually—by spear, by spell, by fate.

At banquets, rituals, and ceremonies, Mab played her role when she had to. She stood beside Serena in her high robes, placed a hand on her shoulder before an audience, and murmured something civil for the diplomats and the councilors and the guests from distant kingdoms. The moment the doors shut again, the child was escorted away.

But Serena knew the game. She knew what not to say. What not to do. How to avoid the glances, the mistakes, the wrath. Kriesta had ensured her training never faltered. Tutors. Protocol masters. Formal speech. Combat. Magery. All of it, carved into her routine from the moment she could walk. Graye learned with her. Benefitted from her. Laughed and sparred and studied beside her as if he had been born for it. No one dared question it aloud.

The ballroom door opened.

Master Virell stepped inside and clapped once, sharply. His voice rang across the marble floor.

"Positions, please. Show me you remember what you were taught yesterday, and perhaps we'll avoid another wretched display of that 'waltz' you attempted last week."

Serena sighed.

Graye whispered, "You flap."

She elbowed him hard in the ribs and took her place.

Age 7

The kite had no business flying indoors. They both knew it. That was what made it worth doing.

Graye held the spindle of string while Serena ran, trailing the long fabric tail behind her, the breeze from their sprint just enough to keep the red silk lifting, fluttering, and struggling to climb. They shrieked with laughter, bare feet slapping against polished marble, the hem of Serena's overskirt bunched in one hand, Graye shouting instructions from behind with the breathless conviction of a boy who had never once flown a kite properly outdoors.

"Faster—don't let it dip!"

"I *know* that!"

The kite caught a draft as she rounded a corner and surged upward, clipping a chandelier, spinning once, and then bouncing off the edge of a side alcove. The string jerked from Graye's hand. Serena dove to catch it, missed, and skidded into a pedestal just before the turn.

There was a sickening *crack*.

They froze.

The vase that had once stood atop the pedestal—a towering, gold-lacquered relic from the Dardani conquest three thousand years ago—now lay in three perfect pieces on the floor, split down its painted seams like a broken egg. The kite drifted down after it and settled delicately in the ruins.

Graye was the first to speak. "Maybe it wasn't that expensive."

"Jormunder said it was one of a kind."

"...So... not expensive?"

They looked at each other.

And then they ran.

They were found, of course. Not in the moment—by then they had hidden the kite under Serena's wardrobe and each tried to bribe a different page boy into pretending it hadn't happened—but by suppertime, when the vase had been reported and the corridor identified.

The punishment had been swift, formal, and entirely expected: bed without supper. Indecent behavior, unbecoming of court-born children. No respect for relics. No dignity. No remorse.

Neither of them had been particularly remorseful.

Their rooms were across the corridor from one another in the south wing of the palace—far from the Queen's quarters. So far away that Mab would never hear them even if they shouted. Which they sometimes did. It was the wing reserved for quieter dignitaries, visiting scholars, and the occasional favored steward. And Serena, as Mab had long since determined, was none of the above. It was understood that this arrangement kept them out of sight.

That night, their doors were closed early, candles extinguished, and supper trays never brought. The nursemaids did not linger. Serena lay on her side, face to the wall, listening.

Graye appeared at the edge of her bed twelve minutes later, as expected.

"They didn't even yell properly," he whispered, crawling up from the footboard and dragging his blanket with him. "Just sighed and said we were a disgrace."

"Then they called us a menace," Serena whispered back, shifting to make room. "And said we were being raised like stable rats."

"I like rats."

"They're clever."

Graye grinned and rolled to his side, tucking the blanket over his feet.

They were still whispering—half plotting vengeance on the tapestry cleaner who'd snitched about the broken vase, half arguing about whether the kite had actually *flown*—when the bootsteps came.

Graye's eyes widened.

"Go!" Serena hissed.

He flung himself off the side and rolled under her bed as the door opened.

Jormunder stepped inside.

He filled the doorway without effort, still in his field leathers, a fur-lined cloak thrown over one shoulder, the scent of iron and mountain air clinging to him. His long black hair was tied back, and the shadows from the hall caught along the deep ridges of his scarred cheek.

He looked directly at the bed.

"I know you're under there, boy."

Graye held his breath. Serena pressed a fist to her mouth to stifle a laugh.

Jormunder stepped inside and closed the door behind him, the latch clicking softly. Then, without hurrying, he reached into his coat and withdrew two wrapped bundles.

He crouched beside the bed and extended one downward.

Graye took it, sheepish and grinning.

The other he held out to Serena as he sat on the edge of the mattress.

She climbed into his lap without hesitation, tucking her legs up and pressing close against his chest. He smelled like smoke and salt and steel. His hands, callused and massive, settled around her small frame with the practiced care of a man who had never needed to hold something delicate until he had. She didn't squirm. She didn't speak. And as always, his heartstrings pulled at seeing the face of his beloved Tatiana looking back at him.

He unwrapped Serena's bundle—sandwiches, still warm from the outer hearths, and a cloth packet of honeyed oat cookies.

He glanced at the closed door, then at the children.

"If anyone asks," he said, "you ate nothing. You are starving. Pitiful. Weeping."

Graye sat up straighter from under the bed. "Of course, General."

Serena bit into her sandwich and nodded.

He settled in and began the story.

It wasn't the whole truth. Not quite. But it wasn't soft either. He told them about the skirmish outside the western pass, the narrow ledge above the river, the ambush that had gone wrong.

He told them how he'd baited the enemy's image into a miscast that blew a hole through the rock wall, how half a bridge had collapsed under his weight and he'd climbed out on a broken girder with an axe in his teeth. He told them how his lieutenants had thrown fire and smoke until the sky went red, and how one of the enemy's officers lost a hand trying to grapple with him in the mist.

Graye's eyes were huge. Serena grinned, licking honey from her fingers.

It wasn't gentle. But it wasn't cruel. Jormunder knew exactly how much they could take. He knew what amused them. The blood, the grit, the stakes. The taste of real danger was just far enough removed that it thrilled without scarring. And it pleased him more than he'd admit to see them eat it up. He'd huff silent laughter as their imaginations sparked, delighted grins on their faces.

When the story ended, he stood slowly, brushing crumbs from his cloak. Serena leaned her head against his chest one last time before he stepped away.

He didn't look under the bed again.

"Don't get caught with those cookies," he murmured, and that was both warning and permission. A code they understood perfectly.

Then he was gone, boots silent on the stone as the door clicked shut behind him.

In the dim room, they ate the last of the contraband in silence, cheeks sticky, already planning what they'd fly next through the halls.

Age 8

The glen just beyond the palace walls was quiet that afternoon, lit with the soft golden light of late summer and the easy rustle of leaves overhead. The air smelled of grass and water, and the faint sweetness of ripe moss warmed by the sun. The stream chattered softly as it passed between roots and over stones, and for once, the children weren't misbehaving. Not exactly.

Serena lay on her back in the grass, one arm folded behind her head, the other resting on her stomach. Graye was beside her, one booted foot lazily kicking at a fern. The shade from the massive ash tree above them dappled the glade in shifting patterns of green and gold, and they stared up through the canopy, watching clouds drift past in slow procession. They had been unusually reflective that day, content to breathe and speak in low tones instead of shouting or chasing or fencing with stolen kitchenware.

"I think we should run away," Graye announced with a sort of contemplative finality, his eyes squinting at a passing cloud that vaguely resembled a duck with one leg.

Serena didn't move. "You say that every time you get in trouble."

"This time I mean it," he said. "We could go south. Be farmers."

She turned her head slightly, expression dubious. "You want to be a farmer."

"Farmers don't have nannies."

That gave her pause. Valid point.

He continued, warming to the idea. "I'll raise potatoes."

Serena considered the prospect in silence. "Then I want chickens."

"And we need a dog."

"A cat."

A put-upon male sigh. "Fine. Both."

Serena smiled faintly and turned her face back to the sky.

The moment that followed was content, unguarded. Birds flitted above. The sunlight shifted through the leaves.

Then came the low chuff, deep and guttural, followed by the unmistakable scent of animal musk—thick, wild, and predatory.

They froze.

Both rolled onto their bellies in perfect sync, peering around the wide girth of the ash tree.

Across the small stream, head bent to drink, stood a gryphon.

Its massive talons flexed into the muddy bank as it sipped from the cool water, the sunlight glinting off the honeyed gold of its feathered neck. The haunches were leonine, the muscles sleek and coiled beneath the fur. Not marked. Not tame.

Graye's breath caught in his throat. Then he slowly smiled.

"I dare you to ride it."

Serena turned her head just enough to look at him. She hated it when he was smug. He knew it.

He grinned wider. "You won't."

She didn't reply. But her eyes narrowed.

He leaned in, arrogant. "You won't do it."

Her body shifted before he finished the sentence, already lowering herself into a crawl. Her fingers moved silently over dirt and moss as she slithered through the low undergrowth. Graye sat back on his heels, half in disbelief. He hadn't thought she'd try it. No one would. She wouldn't. She *shouldn't.*

But Serena didn't back down from dares. Not to him. Not ever.

She moved with the silent precision of a predator, each step measured and close to the ground. And then, without warning, she bolted from cover. Her hands caught the base of the creature's wing just as it lifted its head. She used the joint to vault upward, her feet bracing against the shoulder, her body rising in one powerful leap.

It would have been impressive if not used for exactly the wrong kind of thing. She swung a leg over and landed across its back, arms flung around its neck, legs cinched tight beneath its shoulders.

The gryphon reared.

Its scream split the glen, a deafening shriek of fury as its wings lashed open. It bucked beneath her, slamming its weight against the ground, talons tearing into the earth as it twisted and writhed. Serena clung to its neck with every ounce of strength she had, her eyes wide, breath locked tight in her throat. Pure terror raced down their bond. Graye was already screaming.

"Jump! Jump, Sev! *Jump and run!*"

She waited for the opening, legs scrambling against the feathers and slick fur as the creature twisted. Then she threw herself sideways, hit the ground with a roll that scraped her elbows raw and scrambled to her feet.

The gryphon struck.

Its claw swept across where she had landed a heartbeat before, its beak snapping toward the space her head had occupied. But she was already moving, legs pounding against the grass, Graye shouting her name as he dragged open the ferns for her to dive into.

The gryphon snarled once more, then launched into the sky, wings shuddering the branches as it vanished into the canopy.

They crouched together in the underbrush, panting, hearts hammering.

Serena looked down first.

Her dress sleeve was shredded. Blood dripped freely from three long, jagged gashes that ran the length of her forearm, red and pulsing and thick. Her hand was already slick with it.

She blinked once, then turned to Graye.

"Graye..it hurts," her voice small, trembling. "And it won't stop bleeding."

He looked at her arm, then back to her, and paled. He didn't hesitate. He pulled off his vest, wrapped it around her arm, and knotted it tightly with his teeth.

"We have to get help," he said, already trying to pull her to her feet. "But not the healers."

Serena nodded once, her face pale. "She'll find out."

That was worse than the gryphon.

They made their way back to the outer wall of the training yard, Serena keeping low behind the armory shed while Graye darted into the Valkyrie ring. Her cousin Elsibetha was in mid-form with two other women, her twin blades flashing in the sunlight. She was older, faster, and already a legend among them despite being only twenty-three. Her wings were tucked, her black hair braided with highlights of plum and indigo, and sweat clinging to her brow.

"Psst," Graye whispered, too softly.

He tried again. "Psst. Elsie."

She turned.

The moment she saw his face, she left the ring without a word. Elsie had long ago assumed the role of big sister and took it seriously.

He led her straight to the shed.

When she caught sight of Serena, hunched behind the crates, blood soaking through the now-crimson vest wrapped around her arm, she swore.

"Fuck, cousin. What the tides did that?!"

Graye pointed. "A gryphon. She rode it." He sounded both grim and proud.

Elsie was letting fly with expletives when Serena's voice cracked with a weak warble and wide eyes as she looked up at her. "Elsie, it hurts... please fix it... don't take me to a healer, they'll tell my mother. Please, Elsie. Help us."

The fear was real now—not from the wound, but from what would follow if the wrong person heard. Elsie fully agreed.

"Come on. Let's get out of sight."

She led them quickly behind the training dummies, yanked open a storage hatch for old practice gear, and shoved a mat to the side so they could sit. She dropped to her knees and unwrapped the vest.

The gashes were worse than she expected. Deep. Ragged. Torn through flesh and past muscle.

She was still cursing under her breath when footsteps approached.

Serena tensed.

Another woman stepped into the narrow gap—taller, older, built like tempered steel.

Serafine.

High fae. Shade Court. Three thousand years old. Shadowdancer, weaponsmaster, legend. She'd been the one who trained Mab and campaigned with Jormunder during Tatiana's reign. She said nothing as she knelt beside them, violet eyes already scanning the wound. Her presence shifted the air—calm, controlled, assessing.

She didn't ask what had happened.

She didn't scold.

Her fingers were already glowing with magic as she rested them lightly over Serena's arm, her mouth murmuring a spell under her breath. The healing was subtle, coaxed rather than forced, the blood slowing under her touch.

"Get her clean clothes," she ordered Elsibetha, without looking up. "Dark ones."

Elsie vanished.

Serafine adjusted her grip, light and steady. "This will leave scars if I don't close it fully. Hold still."

Serena nodded, eyes clenched, breath ragged. Graye stayed beside her, hand on her shoulder.

No one said a word about Mab.

CHAPTER FOUR

THE PARTING

The day was overcast, the sky smothered in heavy grey that pressed low against the towers of the Moon Palace. The war was over, but the world had not returned to peace—only to the quiet, uneasy machinery of courts resuming their patterns. Formal letters. Recall orders. Shifting borders and newly drawn lines.

In the midst of it all, a summons arrived from Shade.

The lord of the court had returned to his seat, and with him came expectation. It was time for Kriesta to resume her role as Lady of Shade. Time for her son to begin the first phase of military training with his mother's kin—the Dardani. Black-winged warriors bred for precision and ferocity. It was tradition. It was duty.

It was also a disaster.

Graye hadn't understood when the letter arrived. He had smiled politely when Kriesta took his hand and gently explained. Kriesta was trying to put on a brave face, a false smile, but her voice trembled with emotion and her eyes were misty with tears. She didn't want to leave the little girl she'd loved like a daughter, and she didn't want to separate the pair. It would be a painful parting, and they'd both be left alone.

He had nodded, even, and swallowed the lump in his throat. But when the moment came, when trunks were packed and servants gathered, when the carriage was brought around and he realized Serena wasn't coming with him—that they would be parted for the first time since the day they were born into the same cradle—he lost control.

He fought the guards.

Kicked, screamed, bit, struck one hard enough to make the man stagger. They tried to hold him, but he wriggled free again and again, throwing himself toward the marble steps where Serena had already been dragged back by her nursemaids.

She was shrieking. Not crying. Not pleading. *Screaming.*

A high, keening sound that made birds burst from the gardens in flight. The air around her shivered. Glass cracked. One of the tall windows above them fractured down its center with a sharp, musical splintering. A vase nearby exploded. A guard's nose began to bleed.

Her magic had answered her.

Her first true siren cry.

Not beautiful. Not entrancing. Raw.

Her voice broke and cracked and broke again, her small body shaking so hard her knees gave out. Graye shouted her name, still clawing toward her even as they lifted him from the floor. His face was streaked with tears and blood from a split lip, his hair clinging to his temples. He reached for her, hands outstretched, begging incoherently.

And then the doors shut between them.

Graye was gone.

Serena screamed until her voice collapsed in on itself and nothing came out at all. They left her in the corridor, marble cold beneath her knees, the wide halls echoing with the memory of her cries. She stayed there long after everyone had left, curled in a fetal position on the marble among the shards of vase. Because it wasn't the only thing that had shattered.

The nannies were terrified of her after they heard about her power awakening. Mages came instead, more equipped to withstand anything the child might do in her grief. They gently Calmed her, the ability of the Solace court. But it wasn't a true calm, and it didn't last beyond getting her to her chambers.

No one could comfort her.

The head cook brought her honey cakes. Her tutors came. One of the court scribes knelt with a book, trying to distract her with the history of dragons. She stared through him like glass.

Finally, someone summoned Elsibetha.

She arrived straight from training, her armor still half-buckled, her hair pinned in the style the Valkyries used on campaign. She found Serena in her bedchamber, curled on her side, eyes open and staring at the wall as if it might change if she stared hard enough.

Elsie sat down beside her.

"Ser," she said gently, "he's coming back."

Serena didn't speak.

Elsie reached for her hand. It was cold.

"You have to eat. You'll make yourself sick."

Still nothing.

Food went untouched. She would not sleep.

When she did collapse from exhaustion, she woke screaming.

Nothing helped.

It was the look in her eyes that did it. Haunted. Hollow. Like someone had reached into her chest and taken something vital, and now she was waiting to stop breathing altogether.

Elsibetha rose and strode out of the room, leather armor creaking. She didn't wait for permission. She didn't follow protocol. She dispatched a private message with magery, the note appearing before Jormunder nearly instantly, as only family correspondence could do.

Jormunder arrived hours later, flown in from a still-smoking border outpost.

He did not stop to rest. He did not remove his armor.

He entered Serena's chamber and stood there, staring at the girl on the bed—so small, so silent, unmoving except for the twitch of her fingers in the sheets.

She did not smile when she saw him. If she even noticed him. Her eyes were empty, glassy.

She did not move.

He knelt beside her, his massive hand resting lightly on her hair.

Then, slowly, he extended himself, his power, and searched. Because of growing fear, a growing rage was creeping up into his intuition, his memories.

Her pulse. Her breath. The hollowness. The refusal to eat. The inability to sleep. The screaming in the night. The physical pain with no cause. Her scream, the shattering glass, the timing of it all. He had seen this before—millennia ago when the ritual had still been whispered among high blood lords. When soulbinding was still performed in secret.

His jaw locked.

He stood, very still, and the walls around him began to tremble. The pressure in the room shifted. The candles flared and bent. The paint along the cornices of the ceiling began to bubble and peel. Cracks spidered across the corner paneling. His golden eyes burned with fury, the heat of it pulsing from him in waves.

"Blood-binding," he snarled, and his voice was low, ragged with rage. "Someone *blood-bound* my granddaughter."

He didn't need to say who did it, and with whom. There was only one candidate. Only one child had been with her since birth. Only one child she was now in agony without. And a scheming father.

The plotting, bald ambition of Jaryk, that *bastard,* who had—without consent, without permission— tethered their souls together in infancy.

He lifted Serena into his arms, careful with her like always, her head falling limply against his shoulder. She didn't even acknowledge him.

And then he turned.

He marched through the palace corridors with the thunder of war in his footsteps, not stopping for guards, not acknowledging the courtiers who scattered before him. He went straight to the queen's wing. The guards at Mab's doors paled and stepped aside.

He kicked the doors open, face full of rage.

Mab looked up from her desk, startled, her gown half-unfastened, her eyes narrowed at the intrusion. She was queen, but she knew her father well enough to know he was on the verge of violence. He was enraged, reeking of outrage and territoriality.

"She is *mine,*" he said before she could speak. "Someone has defiled her blood under your roof."

He laid Serena on the divan, gently. Her head lolled to the side, her eyes unfocused. Mab stared. It had been months since she'd last seen Serena and now the child looked half-dead. Not that Mab cared; it was merely an observation and an annoyance. Serena was the Heir, whether Mab claimed her or not. Her life was tied to the continued existence of Ardaion and its inhabitants.

Jormunder's voice was low, a bass growl on the edges of it that Mab hadn't heard since he was shredding Tatiana's assassin apart with his bare hands.

"She is blood-bound, Mab! And it's *your* fault. You let this happen. You, who would sooner die than let a single insult to your crown pass unanswered? You abandoned your daughter. Your heir. You gave her no name, no shield, no claim—and this is the result."

Mab stood slowly, her expression unreadable.

"Blood-bound?" she asked. Her face was beginning to share traces of Jormunder's indignant rage but for entirely different reasons.

Mab stared at the girl crumpled on the couch—the child who bore her blood, her crown, her inheritance. The child she had rejected from the first breath. Not because of love. Not because of grief. But because her daughter had failed to resemble the man she lost.

Mab's eyes flashed with fury. Not about the pain. Not about the suffering. But the offense. Someone had defied her, someone had thought to manipulate the Spider.

This had happened under her roof. To *her bloodline*. To *the Heir*. Without *her consent*. The disrespect made it unforgivable.

The storm that rose behind her eyes was cold.

"Then we will burn the one who dared it," Mab said, "and any who helped him."

Jormunder didn't thank her. He was already planning retribution with or without her permission. He stood there like a war god carved of stone, arms crossed over his chest, wings flexed behind him.

He was incapable of speech for a moment, caught in a blood rage of his Dardani ancestry, and then he leaned forward, cold, deadly, and growled, "I blame you for this. You will fix this or you will answer to me." She growled back, a low siren hiss and bared fangs. "The insult will not go unpunished. An example must be made."

"And your daughter?"

There was a long pause, where Mab weighed what she genuinely wanted to say against how angry Jormunder was and the reality of the situation- for better or worse, the hated child was the Heir of Ardaion, linked to the Binding.

"The blood bond is irrevocable. She'll suffer without that boy... but it won't kill her." Jormunder growled low in his throat and his wings began to spread that said he was on the fine edge of unleashing his wrath on her. He already knew his granddaughter was going to suffer and was in no mood for Mab's casual callousness.

"I will order that he visit her once a season, for a week. Part of Shade's punishment. They may have a sliver of Serena's soul, but we have a sliver of their heir's soul, too. Let them think on that."

Mab called for her council. Because hell was coming. And it was wearing a crown.

Mab's Retribution

Ordinarily, the Moon Court's retribution against the Shade Court might have called into question how neutral it truly was, and just how powerful the siren queens had become. Under any other circumstances, that kind of swift, brutal, and all-encompassing retaliation would have risked diplomatic fracture or sparked counteraction.

Ultimately, the outrage of the invasion was drowned out by something louder—the furor caused by the other courts realizing for themselves what benefits Shade might have earned for itself in this little coup. Everyone was calculating what it might mean, what Jaryk might have achieved.

No one else had considered it. No one else had acted. Now Shade had dared something momentous. So the rest of the courts looked the other way. They were ultimately all for whatever punishment Mab saw fit to unleash, and if it ended Shade and its power-grasping laddering above them, all the better.

But that didn't mean they were willing to be left out entirely.

Each court began angling for its piece of the princess—subtly, carefully, each trying to claw back some measure of equality, to reestablish their influence and relationships with the future queen. They wanted her presence in their lands, her attention, her goodwill. They wanted visibility. Proximity. Leverage. Each court sent word, quietly, suggesting that the Princess's training might benefit from time in *their* territories. Exposure to their culture, their dialects, and their education. Their sons.

Mab agreed.

She framed it as a component of the expected century of training for any proper royal heir. Serena would spend time in each court—studying their systems, their traditions, their cultures—exposed to their people and reinforcing alliances.

It was framed as refinement, wisdom, and diplomacy. But privately, Mab wished she'd thought of it herself. It would get Serena out of the palace for years at a time. And if the Moon Court gained political favor with every court along the way? All the better.

But the boy would have to come, too, at the appointed intervals.

When it was his time to visit, Graye would be permitted to accompany Serena. But only under strict caveats. Though he had benefited from Serena's royal training at the Moon Court—had been raised with her as her sibling in all but name—he was not to benefit from any further instruction outside its walls.

His presence in other courts was to be tolerated only for the management of the blood bond. He was to be considered, due to his father's transgressions, *persona non grata*.

He would be forbidden from studying at the University or the Mage Tower in Ghealach Siorai—an intentional handicap designed to limit the Shade heir's potential and balance the inequality perceived from his link to the Ardaion heir. He was to have no advanced education as most nobles received, but particularly no advanced magical education. He'd have his innate abilities but no magery, nothing powerful.

Jaryk's punishment was already well underway. The lord's coffers were raided. His most promising mages were taken—absorbed into the Moon Court's Battle Mage ranks. He had been blinded in one eye, and he was going to be forced into retirement as Lord of Shade the moment Graye came of age. A bloodless execution.

This, too, suited Mab.

Removing an ambitious and disrespectful but wily lord, who had raised his son in *her* court, who had dared tie that son to her daughter *without permission*—neutering Shade's political position further only served her ends. It would grant her control over Shade's heir, a puppet lord in the making. If he was shackled to Serena, Mab reasoned, he would not move against her.

For his part, after the dust settled, Jormunder demanded the children be brought back together for a proper farewell. He did not ask. He ordered. No one dared challenge him. He insisted that Serena and Graye be assured they would see each other every few months.

He secured the right for them to write to one another as often as they wished. His fury was still barely cooled. No one questioned the warlord.

Reflection from Serena, age 26

I was born three days after my father died. A month premature.

I never knew him. Not truly. I've seen sketches, oil portraits—read the records of his service, his scholarly writings, the words others wrote when the ache was fresh. But to me, he was never a man. He was an absence. A wound I was expected to fill. A ghost my mother stared through me to see.

They told her I would be his legacy. She twisted that to mean I would be his image. She thought if I emerged from her with his hair, his eyes, his wings, that it might feel like he hadn't died at all.

But I didn't.

I was born with my grandmother's face. With my grandfather's wings. With the shadow of my siren blood rising already in my bones.

And so, in her eyes, I failed.

There are no portraits of my mother holding me. No lullabies. No naming ceremony.

The first time I was held, it was not by her. It was by Kriesta—who had just given birth herself—and then by Jormunder, who looked at me and saw not a disappointment, but a daughter. He named me Serena because it meant siren in the old tongue, and he said I should never be ashamed of what I am. And I never have been.

I was raised by ghosts and giants.

Jormunder, who carved paths through war but held me like spun glass. Elsibetha, who taught me to throw a blade and patch a wound in the same breath. And Graye, who was not my brother, not my cousin, not anything we had a name for—but who was mine.

We shared everything. Cradles. Tutors. Swords stolen from practice racks. Mooncakes eaten under the table. Every lesson learned, every punishment endured, every scheme and scolding and escape. He was always beside me. I never imagined a life where he wouldn't be.

Then he was gone.

I remember that day like a knife remembers flesh. The sound of guards scuffling. My voice broke. The way the magic ripped out of me before I knew what it was—before I understood what I was. I remember the sound of glass shattering. The heat of it. My legs went out from under me.

I remember being left behind.

No one cared that we were children. No one cared that I couldn't breathe without him.

They said I refused food. What they didn't say was that food meant nothing when you felt someone had reached into your chest and taken something you didn't know could be taken. They said I screamed in my sleep. What they didn't say was that I woke up believing he'd died.

And maybe, in some way, part of me had.

That was the blood bond. I didn't know its name then. I didn't know what it meant. Only that it hurt. That it tore. That it made everything too bright, too loud, too wrong. I wanted him near because he belonged near. I had never existed without him. And I had not agreed to suffer in his absence.

But I did.

CHAPTER FIVE
LIVES IN PARALLEL

Serena: The War Camps

A week had passed since the Moon Court forces had returned from the Shade invasion. The palace had resumed its routines—polished floors, endless council meetings, and carefully restructured alliances—but Serena had not. The formal farewell Jormunder had demanded had helped, barely, like a hand pressed over a sucking wound. But Graye was still gone, and Serena was still hollow.

She didn't eat.

Not properly.

She picked at food until her plate was cleared away and the servants gave up trying. She slept fitfully, always alone, and when dreams came, they always ended with screams. Her studies were abandoned. Tutors dismissed, their books closed untouched. She sat in the same window each day, watching the clouds over Siorai's white spires with the kind of stillness that wasn't peace—but grief in a child's frame, calcified.

Jormunder had seen men break under far less.

So he stayed at the palace—reading to her in the gardens, coaxing her to take bites of food during picnics under the flowering trees, carrying her when her legs wouldn't hold up. He who had razed cities and broken siege lines sat beside Serena's bed each night, singing old Dardani war hymns in a voice roughened by age and smoke.

The court called it pining. The warlord called it suffering. And it infuriated him.

He knew the shape of this wound. He had lived it. Tatiana. His rage still kindled when he stared at the corner of her old cloak hanging from his armor rack. Now he recognized it again—grief, that consuming ache—twisting inside a child who could not yet name what it was. She was almost nine, and she was unraveling.

He went to Mab, eyes ringed in sleepless fury. He told her to take Graye back. Let the boy remain at court. Let him be near her again. The child was the only thing keeping Serena alive.

Mab refused without rising from her desk.

She didn't even look at him.

The other courts, she said, would consider the boy a hostage. They would claim the Moon Court was using him for leverage. Political theft. Interference. Or that Shade had been allowed its toe-hold in Siorai. The appearance alone would be enough to shatter decades of treaties.

Then she went back to her letter.

So Jormunder stayed. He began ignoring summons from the front. Messages requesting his presence from other generals went unanswered. The empire could wait. Serena could not. He read to her in her room. Held honey-dipped fruit to her lips until she ate enough to keep her upright. She still didn't laugh. Still didn't speak much. But she let him braid her hair. She let him sit beside her when the dreams came.

He would not let her go cold. Not like this.

The Dardani did not value girls like boys. That had always been their way. But Jormunder had spent his life in service to the siren queens of Ardaion. He had seen what true power was—not in brute strength, but in cunning, in will, in presence. And this child... this girl with Tatiana's face and her blood singing with rage and sorrow... she was worth every campaign he'd ever fought.

He knew what she was going through.

After days of coaxing and watching her fade anyway, he returned to Mab again, this time burning with restrained fury. He asked to take his granddaughter with him. For a change of scenery. For a reason to rise in the morning. For something to focus her mind, if not her heart.

"I want to take her with me. To the army camps."

At first, Mab laughed. Mab didn't look up from the scrolls she was reading.

"She's a child," she said flatly.

"She's dying," he growled.

"She's pining."

"She's suffering."

"Children survive worse."

"She's the Heir of Ardaion."

Finally, Mab looked up.

Her gaze was cold. Tired. Empty in the way only grief left behind for centuries could make a person.

"I survived Edric's death. She can survive a boy."

"She won't."

Mab stared for a long moment. Then she shrugged once, slow and deliberate.

The nannies had been filing their reports. The tutors. The courtiers. She was tired of hearing it. Tired of the disruption. And tired of a daughter she had never wanted slipping quietly into some dramatic decline that might force her hand.

She leaned back in her chair, gave a shrug, and said, "If you get her too-near a battle and she dies, so does Ardaion."

It wasn't a refusal; it was a reminder. If he failed, it would be his burden to bear.

Jormunder said nothing. He bowed and left the room.

Mab, in a moment of amused cruelty, forbade him to take nannies or maids. No nursemaids, no attendants. If he wanted to haul a child into his war camps, he would do it without help.

Jormunder accepted the terms.

The next morning, the warlord of the Moon Court left Ghealach Siorai, but not alone. Her dresses had been replaced by leathers sized down for her little frame, patched and reinforced. Her hair was kept in a single braid, the only style he could manage on his own.

He kept Serena in his command tent. Fed her from his own table. Tucked her bedroll near his cot. When he met with commanders, he sat her on his knee and pointed out the movement of troops on the map. He began teaching her flanking patterns with carved wooden pieces. He told her war stories before bed—filtered only slightly for gore. She listened. Quiet at first, eyes dull. But she listened.

He commissioned a little wooden training sword. Dardani-style, shaped like his own. Had it wrapped in leather for her grip. Began teaching her how to hold it. How to stand.

The commanders began to expect her in the briefings.

She sat beside visiting scholars forced to continue her education in the shade of the supply tents, tutors adjusting their lectures to avoid the sound of hammering from the forges nearby. She memorized battlefield topography before she could recite her lineage. She learned to eat what the soldiers ate, to rise when the war horns blew, to march to the cookfires with ash on her boots and sun on her face.

She became the camp's pet, and not in a way anyone laughed at.

She was the Ardaion heir. Marked by power. A revered bloodline. But she was also a little girl- dusty, scowling, hair tied back in Jormunder's braids- watching them with solemn eyes and a heavy heart.

They taught her things no court would have allowed. How to polish plate and sharpen steel. How to sing bawdy drinking songs she wasn't supposed to know. How to swear in four languages.

They respected her. Adopted her.

Slowly, quietly, she began to come back.

Graye: The Dardani

Things were not much easier for Graye.

He felt the separation physically. Not just the ache of loss, not just the confusion of being yanked from the only life he'd ever known, but a deep, crawling pain beneath the skin—like something tethered inside him was being pulled taut and slowly fraying. He'd never known silence like that before. He'd never *felt* it in his teeth.

And he was caught, from the first day, between two parents.

Kriesta's rage about the blood-bond had been volcanic. Quiet, but volcanic. She hadn't screamed, hadn't thrown things, but her presence became a blade. She looked at Jaryk—her mate, Graye's father—as though she could gut him with her eyes alone. What he'd done to their son without telling her, without her consent, without any thought to the cost... It repulsed her. She didn't hide that from Graye.

But Jaryk hadn't learned his lesson. He hadn't burned the way he should have.

Because in his mind, the bond had worked. His son was still tied to the princess. Shade's toe was still in the door.

So he licked his wounds, unrepentant. He watched and waited. He still had plans. And while Mab might think to use Graye as a future puppet—an heir to Shade bound to her daughter, docile and grateful—Jaryk whispered other visions.

He told Graye, quietly, carefully, that one day he'd be strong enough to make the world right. He'd see Serena during her court visits, walk the palaces, study the other courts, and learn what Mab was too blind to hide. That his training with the Dardani would give him the strength Mab feared. That one day, he could be more than a tethered princeling—he could be king.

With Serena beside him. With Shade restored. With Jaryk at his back.

Kriesta heard enough to be sickened.

She didn't fight Jaryk directly. She knew better. But she pulled Graye away—early, and without warning. He was going to get Graye killed.

She took him to her homeland in the mountains of Ember, away from Jaryk and away from Mab. She brought him there to begin the traditional training and rites of passage that all Dardani males endure. She stayed in Ember, too, leaving Jaryk to his ambitions in Shade.

The Dardani did not train boys with gentleness. They did not speak of fairness, soft landings, or care. Training was survival. Long hours. Freezing winters, scorching summers. Bloodied knuckles and raw feet. They drilled through sleet and ash.

Ember was a land of sparse forests, black cliffs, and places where molten rock oozed like glowing rivers. They believed in cleansing by fire. When it came to training young males, they smelted them down to remove the slag, leaving only iron warriors.

Graye was nine.

He had come from a palace of white marble and glass-smooth floors, with tutors who spoke a dozen dialects and meals served under silver domes. He had read more books than the other boys knew existed. He had been educated, polished, fluent in court customs and politics, and eloquent. He had danced and dined with the Heir of Ardaion and had stories told to him by the great Jormunder.

The other boys hated him for it.

They mocked him for his past, called him a traitor's son, and said he thought he was better than them. They beat him behind the barracks, filled his boots with crushed nettle, pissed on his cloak while he slept. They stole his rations, his better gear, anything of use. Every act of cruelty was a lesson in humiliation.

Yet even in this new personal hell, there were concessions. Because the fae are never free from politics. The generals of Ember weren't blind, nor their Lord, Aegin. If Serena was to visit Ember, as agreed by Mab, to build bridges and learn their ways, then having the Shade heir in their grasp became leverage. Twenty years of training him wasn't about forming a soldier. It was about forming *allegiance*.

If Graye could be shaped—if he grew up loyal not to his father but to Ember, if he disavowed Jaryk and declared a new loyalty—then Ember would have a claim on his influence with the Moon Court.

Leverage with Shade. A tie to the princess.

They didn't need to love him. They didn't even need him whole.

They just needed him close. Sharpened. Durable. And—eventually—*theirs*.

Letter from Serena to Graye, age 9

Written in uneven ink, blotted in one corner with what might be grease or dried soup. The handwriting is elegant for a nine-year-old, thanks to exasperated tutors, with some words underlined three times for emphasis. She refers to Jormunder as *Atta*, the high fae honorific meaning grandfather.

Hi.

We moved camps again. This one's in a valley and there are these boulders the size of wagons and I got to climb one but Atta said "Not during formation hours," which means he didn't say no, just not right now. He's teaching me to fly a bit. He makes me exercise my wings and my back hurts every day but one day I'm going to jump off those boulders and fly.

I got a new map scroll from one of the quartermasters and I'm learning how to read the troop sigils. The horse head means cavalry and the ones with the sunburst are mage units. I asked what the one shaped like a cow turd was and Atta said "That's the enemy," which I think was a joke. But I remember where he put the flanks last time and why he kept the river behind us—so no one could sneak up. I think that's called a natural barrier, or it's just called smart.

Atta tells me battle stories every night before sleep and he always makes the bloodiest part right when I'm under the blanket so I can imagine it better. One had a soldier who lost an ear and didn't notice until he tried to comb his hair and the comb slipped. I laughed so hard I choked and tea came out my nose.

I got my own sword. It's wooden, but it's heavy and I already hit one of the training posts and didn't drop it. I'm going to name it. Maybe Bloodcleaver. Or Elsie's Big Mouth.

The soldiers taught me how to swear but said I wasn't allowed to use it in front of generals or anyone who does court things. My favorite one is "May your cock rot off and feed the snails." They call me Little General and I sit on Atta's knee during morning meetings. I asked a question last time and no one laughed. Not even the crusty one with the missing eye.

Are you okay? I heard the Ember boys don't like you but they're stupid. You're faster than they are and better at reading. If they pick on you again just say "I'll make boots from your skin" in a really calm voice and they'll probably cry.

Write me back fast or I'll call Atta and have him invade you personally. I mean it.

Princess Serena of Ardaion (Little General, First of Her Name, Slayer of Soup Bowls, Hero of Rock Climbing)

Reply from Graye to Serena, age 9

The ink is darker and neater, the paper folded very precisely, though there's a smudge near the bottom where a dirty thumbprint got pressed into the edge. A few creases suggest it was refolded multiple times before being sent. The writing is smaller, and a bit sloppier.

Hi.

I read your letter under my bunk with a candle stub and got yelled at for being awake. And maybe able to read, too. Worth it.

The map stuff is real. They use different colors for different courts and if there's a dotted line between two units it means someone's about to get ambushed. I watched them set up a whole campaign route last week. They make me move the sigil pieces and hit the back of my head if I do something stupid. They call me Princeling sometimes but it's an insult because of what my father did.

My hands are all scraped and I've got bruises on both knees and one on my shoulder from a training stave. The Dardani don't like talking but they respect you if you don't whine. I didn't. It's like playing Don't Be a Baby with you.

We learned how to break a hold and use a knee for leverage. I got one of the older boys in the stomach and he threw up on the stones. Next time I'll aim for his balls. The other boys are used to fighting but they're making sure I learn fast.

They made us do drills in the river two days ago. It was so cold I couldn't feel my toes, but I didn't fall in. One of the others did and a leech got on his neck. He screamed. I pretended it wasn't funny but it was. I know what you mean about wing practice. My back hurts too. But one day we'll fly together.

I miss the mooncakes. And the soup. I miss your laugh. And your dumb face.

When I see you in a few weeks at the Moon Palace, have a plan. A real one. We'll sneak into the library again or convince Atta to let us walk the outer walls. You're going to show me your sword and I'll tell you the name of the one I'm getting when they let me have one. Probably Moonfang. Or Leech's Revenge.

Don't get caught saying that snail thing to a royal. But I'm going to use it too.

Write me again. I keep your letters under my pillow.

—Graye

P.S. Only I get to call you Sev.

Letter from Serena to Graye, age 11

Written in tidy script with careful spelling, but with uneven spacing where she got excited. A smudge of something sticky—likely jam—is in the corner.

Dear Graye,

Our camp is still near that old watchtower. There's a cliff, but I'm not allowed near it unless Atta's with me. He said if I fall, he's not climbing down after me, but I think he would.

Atta said it was time I stop only listening at the morning briefings and help him think, so he told me to show the commanders what I would do on the battle map. Everyone in the tent was watching. This morning I moved the archers and the mage lines and said why I'd put them near the ridge, and one of the commanders said "Smart."

I don't always get it right. Sometimes I forget things, and Atta shows me the better way, but sometimes I guess what he was going to do, and he says things like "That's my shining star" so I know he's proud.

I've been practicing flying more. Only short flights. I'm not allowed to go too high yet. But I can fly in circles above the camp. One time I crashed into a tent. One time I used it during wrestling, but the trainer said my wing bones weren't strong enough to try buffeting yet.

I really, really miss you. It's not the same when you're not here. When you come back, can we spar behind the barracks? I want to show you my new hold. It works on full-grown soldiers if you do it fast enough.

Write me back. Tell me what you're learning. I like hearing about your training even if it sounds awful.

Always your Sev

P.S. I still have the little stone you gave me before you left. It's in my boot. I think it's lucky.

P.P.S. One of the cooks taught me a curse in the Frost Court dialect. I'll teach you next time.

Reply from Graye to Serena, age 11

The paper is rough and dented along the edges. His writing is hard-pressed and uneven, like his hands are still sore. There's dried dirt at the bottom fold, and something that looks like blood on the corner, smudged with a thumb.

Sev,

Yeah, I'm still alive. They took us out in the wilderness and I couldn't send the letter for a few days. It was really cold and we only had sleep sacks.

We did ten sword drills in a row this morning. My shoulders felt like they were falling off. One boy dropped his and the commander made him run with it tied to his back. I didn't drop mine. Kade says I look stiff but better than last month.

Me, Rhune, and Kade caught a rabbit. We tracked it before breakfast, trapped it, and skinned it behind the mess tent. We ate it fast before the other boys came around. Left the bones by the fire pit so nobody would know.

You'd like Kade. He laughed really hard when I told him the gryphon story. Rhune's still quiet. Half-Shade. The others give him trouble for it, just like me. He doesn't say much but he stays, and he's smart. That's enough.

Thanks for the birthday gifts. I have to hide them because the other boys want to burn them but I found this ledge on a cliff nearby and you can only see it if you're flying right by it, so I keep them there in a waterproof bag. I loved the book on military strategy and when I was reading it, I found that story about Atta. I miss his stories. It sounds better when he tells it.

I miss seeing your stupid face. I'll be there in three weeks but it feels like forever. Can you imagine if these Ember boys saw me dancing with you? Father keeps scheming and trying to order my mother back to Shade but she keeps telling him no. She's going to stay in Ember with me but I don't get to see her except once a month. The Dardani say mothers make boys weak.

Let's fly over the lake together when we get back to the Palace. It'll be covered in ice and we can slide on it.

*—**Graye***

CHAPTER SIX

VISITS AND IN-BETWEEN

Age 11

The sky above the lake was glass—wide, pale, and breathless in the early hush of winter. No snow had fallen yet, but the air bit like knives, and the shallow breaths of two children puffed white in their wake as they soared above the treeline. The lake spread below them, frozen over in a long silver sheet edged with rushes and frost-laced stone. It looked solid.

Graye whooped as he tilted into a low glide. "Bet I reach the center first!"

"You won't!" Serena called back, wind whipping her hair loose from its braid. Her wings pumped harder, slicing the air with every powerful beat—broad, ridged, leathery wings like Jormunder's, edged with a bumpy nub on each that would one day sprout claws. Her shoulders burned. The chill made her teeth ache. But she didn't slow.

They weren't supposed to be out this far.

But the lake called to them. Open, still, and glittering beneath the sky. It *looked* frozen. Looked perfect. They were eleven, aching to prove they could fly farther than anyone thought they could, then skate back.

Graye reached the center first.

His boots thudded against the ice with a heavy landing that skidded him a dozen feet. He shouted with delight, arms out for balance, his black feathered wings trailing behind him in dark arcs. "I win!"

Serena landed seconds later, less graceful, her feet slipping out from under her as she tried to brake. She caught herself with one hand, breathless. "That doesn't count! I was right behind you."

He spun once in place, boots scraping frost. "Still counts."

They laughed—exhausted, red-cheeked, giddy with cold and flight and triumph.

The ice beneath them groaned.

Neither heard it at first.

Graye grinned and skated a slow circle, wings tucked loosely at his back. Serena stepped forward, brushing frost from her gloves, watching the faint mist curl from their lips.

He skated further ahead, boot-blades slicing long arcs through the thin crust of frost. The ice crackled faintly underfoot, a spiderweb of sound beneath the glittering surface.

Then—

A crack like lightning.

The lake opened.

One moment, he was grinning. The next, the ice beneath him fractured with a sickening snap, and he dropped like a stone.

The water swallowed him whole.

"Graye!"

Serena surged forward, skidding to her knees. She flung herself flat, belly-down on the ice to distribute her weight, fingers scrabbling toward the jagged hole. The cold bit straight through her cloak. She couldn't see him at first—just the shattered ring where the ice had collapsed, the dark circle of water already trying to smooth itself over.

Then movement.

He surfaced, gasping, thrashing, wings dragging him down like leaden anchors. The wet feathers caught the current and pulled him sideways. He tried to grip the edge of the ice, but his fingers slipped. His nails scraped uselessly across the frozen rim. He kept being pulled under, the wings a cold, dead weight.

"S–Sev—" he choked, gurgling as water flooded his mouth. "I can't—"

She sobbed once, a sharp, animal sound, and crawled forward inch by inch. The ice groaned beneath her. Cracked. Her fingertips were blue. Her wings shook.

He slipped again.

"Stop moving!" she begged, voice cracking, tears running down her face. "Don't—don't move, I'm coming, I'm right here—"

Another lurch and she was sliding into the water herself, her belly plunging beneath the ice shelf, the shock of it knocking the breath from her lungs. Her legs kicked wildly, boots dragging against nothing.

She grabbed his wrist.

He seized her forearm, his fingers like claws extended in blind panic.

But he was heavier. His wings were soaked through, dragging both of them down. The cold ate into her muscles. Her vision blurred.

Her other hand slapped the ice.

"Let go," she whispered to the water. "Please let go..."

The lake didn't care.

It held him fast.

"Let him go!" she screamed, shrill in panic, her voice breaking.

And then something *shifted.*

The water stilled.

In her throat, something ancient rose—not magic she had learned, not anything taught. Instinct, deep, and absolute, surged upward like a breath held too long.

She bared her teeth.

Her voice dropped into a register, low, the edge of a growl and hiss to it, and filled with absolute dominion.

"Release him."

The water answered.

It *shoved.*

Graye exploded upward, ejected from the lake like a fish breaching the surface, his wings flung back, limbs flailing. He landed on the ice with a bone-rattling crack, coughing up water in heaving gasps. Serena, half in and half out of the hole clawed at the edge, dragging herself up with a final grunt and collapsing beside him.

They lay there, chests heaving, limbs trembling, breath turning to mist in the air.

Neither spoke.

Graye's lips were blue. Serena's fingers wouldn't close.

Their clothes clung in frozen sheets, crackling with rime. Their wings steamed faintly in the cold, his too sodden to fold properly, hers lacking insulation which was now sucking away her body heat.

It took long minutes before Serena stirred. She tried to rise. Failed. Tried again.

"Up," she rasped. "We have to get off the ice."

Graye made a sound—something between a nod and a whimper.

They crawled, not walked, toward the shoreline. Wings dragging, wet hair freezing, teeth clacking.

At the tree line, their legs buckled. They collapsed onto the frozen mud, panting.

And then—shouts.

A blur of motion.

Serena's guard, cloaked in blue and black, dropped beside them with a burst of wind. He didn't speak. Just thrust his palms into the frozen ground and summoned fae-fire with a word. The flames flared high, hot, gold, and blue, burning without smoke.

He pulled Serena close, stripped off her soaked cloak, and wrapped her in his own. Did the same for Graye.

Then he barked into the shadows.

"Find Elsibetha. Now. Don't tell the queen."

The wind howled through the trees.

The flames licked higher.

Serena, still shivering against the guard's chest, blinked once at the lake and whispered, dazed, "It listened..."

An hour later....

The fire cracked softly in the hearth, casting golden light across the polished stone and flickering along the fur rug where they sat, knees touching. Serena's wet clothes had long since been stripped away, replaced by a heavy wool tunic and a velvet wrap thick enough to drown her to her chin. Graye wore one of Jormunder's old nightshirts, the hem too long and the sleeves rolled twice.

They were warm now—finally—but still pink-cheeked and raw-eyed from the cold that had nearly killed them. Serena's dark hair hung in wet strings of inky black.

A tray of food lay between them. Roasted root vegetables, soft rolls with melting honey butter, thick slices of cured meat, and mugs of tea sweetened with sugared lemon peel. Elsibetha had sent it herself, with a look that said *tell no one,* before disappearing again in her shadow-dancer's silence. The guard had vanished as well. No lectures. No punishments. Only blankets, fire, and food.

They'd eaten in silence at first. Shivering too hard to chew. Too tired to speak. But the color had come back slowly. The tremors passed. And now—

Serena was grinning.

Graye's hands moved as he spoke, animated and dramatic, a roll still half-eaten in one fist. "So Kade bet me I couldn't sneak a full satchel of ember root past the drill master's tent—and not just that, I had to drop it in Rhune's cot without him noticing."

Serena snorted, a crumb escaping the corner of her mouth. "You're insane."

"Exactly! So I blinked," he said proudly, puffing his chest.

"You *can't* blink yet."

"I tried," he admitted, eyes sparkling. "I sort of... fell sideways into the tent flap. Nearly broke my ankle on his stupid bedpost. But Rhune didn't wake up, so I dropped the satchel *right* in his boots."

She bit her knuckle to keep from laughing. "Did it work?"

"Oh, it worked. By morning, his boots had caught fire inside. Just little flames at first, like angry campfire spirits. He tried to put one on, yelped, and kicked it off. Hit Kade in the face with it."

Serena burst into laughter, the sound curling like smoke around the high-vaulted room. "Serves him right!"

"It gets better," Graye grinned, reaching for another slice of meat. "Rhune thought it was Kade's fault, so he chased him halfway across the barracks—barefoot—shouting something about *'pride of the Shade'* while holding a pillow like it was a war banner."

Serena wheezed.

Graye leaned back against the couch with a satisfied smirk. "I just watched. From the roof."

"Of course," she huffed, voice still warm with laughter. "That's what I'd do, too."

He tilted his chin. "One day I'll be a legend."

"You're already infamous."

Their laughter softened, trailing off into quiet. The fire popped again. Outside the window, the last light of day was fading into snow-blind dusk. Serena reached for her tea, letting the steam brush her face.

"You scared me," she said quietly, eyes on the fire.

Graye didn't answer at first. Then softly: "You scared me too."

She looked at him then—truly looked- the way she'd met the Queen's gaze, Jormunder's gaze on the day of her birth, with solemn stormy sea-grey eyes that seemed to know too much. His dark hair had dried into messy waves. His green eyes, bright and quick, were softer now. His hands still trembled a little when he brought the cup to his lips.

"You almost drowned," she whispered.

"I know."

She stared down at her fingers. "But the water listened. I told it to let go, and it did."

He nodded slowly. "Yeah. I felt it. Like something shoved me up."

They sat in silence a while longer, firelight flickering across their faces.

Then Serena reached out and nudged his foot with hers. "Don't do that again."

"Don't let me go alone next time."

"Deal."

She tore a hunk of roll in half and handed it to him, then said "Whenever. Wherever. Always."

He grinned, a bit roguish, "always," before popping the roll into his mouth.

A week later...

The three of them were crammed onto a half-sawn log near the edge of the Dardani mess ring, steam from the breakfast pots still curling into the cold air. Graye had arrived late the night before, boots caked in frozen mud, cloak half torn and eyes rimmed red from the wind. Kade hadn't even let him finish eating before the questions started.

"So?" Kade asked, elbows on his knees, cheeks still pink from drills. "Did she show you the spell tower this time? Or the place with all the weird potions?"

Graye was busy tearing the skin off a chunk of smoked hare with his teeth. He shook his head and said around the mouthful, "Didn't go near the tower. But we flew over the gardens and went out to the lake."

Kade whistled. "The *lake*? Thought you weren't allowed out of the grounds."

Graye grinned, wiping his hand on his cloak. "We're not. Doesn't stop us."

Rhune sat a little off to the side, his posture neater than either of them, a half-finished roll in his lap. He didn't interrupt, but he was listening, his head tilted slightly like he was filing away details. Kade didn't notice. He was already jabbing Graye in the ribs.

"Come on—what'd you *do* out there?"

"We raced over the ice," Graye said. "Thought it was frozen all the way through but it wasn't. I fell in."

Kade's eyes widened. "You fell in the *lake*?" He was half concerned, half amused.

Graye smirked. "Barely. She pulled me out."

"Wait—you're saying the princess of all Ardaion jumped in a frozen lake to save you?"

"No," Graye said, frowning as he picked at the edge of his sleeve. "She crawled across the ice. Nearly fell in too. But she grabbed me, and then—" he hesitated, glancing at Rhune, who hadn't looked away. "—it was like the water just... spit me out."

Kade squinted. "What do you mean, spit you out?"

"I don't know. I couldn't hold on, my wings were soaked, and I was sinking. And then suddenly I was back on the ice. Not swimming. Not climbing. Just... out."

Kade leaned back, clearly turning it into something bigger in his head already. "Bet it was a spell. One of those siren things."

Graye shrugged. "Maybe. We didn't talk about it."

"Was she mad?" Kade asked, grinning. "Did she cry?"

"She *almost* cried," Graye said with exaggerated but defensive pride. "But only for a second. She's brave."

That made Kade laugh, bumping shoulders with him. "Stars. No wonder the other boys hate you. You get to go visit a *siren princess* who casts water magic and drags you out of a frozen lake. Who also happens to be Jormunder's granddaughter!"

"She's not like that," Graye muttered. "She's just... Sev. She's my best friend. She still punches me when I steal her food."

Kade snorted. "Fair. I'd punch you too."

They both turned as Rhune finally spoke. His voice was quiet but clear. "What does she look like?"

Kade blinked. "Does it matter? She made the lake spit him out."

Graye chewed for a second, then shrugged. "Dark hair. Grey eyes. She's usually smiling, or rolling her eyes. When she's mad she doesn't yell much. She gets quiet and stares at you like she wants you to burst into flames." He said that last part with a slight grin, appreciating his poetic license.

"Tall?" Rhune asked.

"Same as us, more or less. Her wings are big though. She's got dragon wings like Jormunder. They're bigger than mine and they kind of shine. Like a rainbow."

Rhune nodded once, not commenting. His fingers tapped lightly against the bread in his hand.

"She can't fly far yet," Graye added. "But she lands really good, doesn't trip. And she's got two nubs on her wings. I think she's going to have claws like Jormunder."

"She smart?" Rhune asked.

Graye laughed. "Scary smart. Her tutors make her translate old languages and solve puzzles. She already reads battle maps. She said in one of her letters that Jormunder started making her explain her strategies to the army commanders. I think he's training her to be like him."

Kade looked half impressed, half horrified. "I didn't even know there were *maps* that weren't pictures. Do you think she was scared?"

Graye snorted. "That's because you think reading isn't as important as swords. And no, she said Jormunder was proud of her and one of the commanders called her clever."

Kade grinned and leaned back, arms stretched behind him on the log. "Still think the best part's that she nearly drowned to save your scrawny ass."

"I'm not scrawny," Graye muttered.

"Sure you're not."

Rhune didn't say anything more, but his eyes lingered on Graye a moment longer, then shifted to the fire.

Age 13

The snow lay thick along the terrace rails, soft and silent as spilled silk. A veil of pale frost clung to the moonstone windowpanes, dulling the light outside and casting Serena's room in a hush of silvered blue. Inside, it was warm—faint firelight flickering in the hearth, scented with lavender and pine.

The high arched ceiling echoed faintly with their voices, softened by velvet curtains and stacks of books. Serena's formal gown for the ball hung from a carved stand by the wardrobe—silver and smoke-blue silk, open-backed to accommodate her wings. She hadn't put it on yet.

Graye lounged on the rug, legs crossed, one elbow braced against a floor cushion. His sleeves were rolled up, shirt half-wrinkled from disuse, boots off, ink staining the side of one thumb. He held a piece of thick parchment in one hand and a charcoal stylus in the other, the middle of a crooked glyph scratched over the surface.

"That looks like a broken cow," Serena said dryly, glancing up from her notes.

"It's the right shape," he insisted, tilting the page. "Look—loop, tail, counterstroke."

"Not if the loop bulges like that," rising from her spot by the hearth and moving to sit beside him. She was barefoot, her feet nearly silent on the stone. She smelled faintly of rose oil and steel polish. "It's not meant to *sag*. That's a healing rune."

He groaned, flopping onto his back and tossing the paper aside. "I should be waltzing through this place with a drink in my hand, not studying runes like some hunched scribe."

"You'll be waltzing in twenty minutes," she said. "And you're not going to open your mouth in front of a Frostvaar noble until you stop saying 'Vëlkandar' like it means 'barrel.' It means 'honor.' *Barrel* is 'vëklanda.' You'll insult the entire delegation."

Graye gave her a sideways look, a smile tugging at the corner of his mouth. "Who decided those two words should be one syllable apart?"

"The Frostvaari did," Serena smirked, snatching a clean sheet and settling beside him, legs folded neatly under her. "And you're going to speak it well enough to keep up with me. Now—try again."

He huffed, sat up, and repeated slowly, "Vël-kan-dar."

"Better. Sharpen the R, and soften the E. You want to sound cold, not drunk."

He mock-saluted her. "Yes, *Princess*."

She rolled her eyes and punched his shoulder. He snorted.

He glanced at her then—really looked. She'd changed over the last year. Still Serena, still full of sharp words and sharper eyes, but the angles of her face had lengthened, her cheekbones more cut, the wild black hair always braided now with silver thread before formal events. Her wings, once awkward and oversized for her frame, had grown into something dangerous-looking—sleek, ridged and clawed, powerful. She was nearly as tall as him now. She moved like a sword in a sheath. And she carried herself the way Mab did in court: silent, poised, watching.

It was becoming more apparent that while she had her mother's coloring, her grandfather's wings, and her grandmother's face... it was Edric's personality. Intelligent, scholarly, dutiful.

Mab never spoke to her. Just observed, from across the room, like a naturalist observing something venomous through glass. It was a painful and tragic irony that she was still so focused on hating Serena for lacking her father's appearance that she didn't allow herself close enough to learn that the things she'd loved Edric most for were truly there, living on in his daughter.

Jormunder occasionally tried to tell her this but Mab would not be swayed. She'd determined in those first minutes of life that she wanted nothing to do with this failure of a child and after thirteen years it was ingrained.

"What are you learning now?" Graye asked, nudging the notes she'd been working through earlier.

"Trade policy for the Solace coast," she said without inflection. "Their last envoy hinted at tariffs. I'm expected to hint back tonight, during the fourth dance."

He blinked. "You're negotiating during a waltz?"

"It's how we do it here. Two turns, three words, a smile. *Atta* says that's how Mab always did it. I'm not allowed to fumble." Serena had taken to calling her Mab- not Mother, not the Queen. Just Mab.

He leaned back on his hands. "You won't."

She didn't reply, but her mouth twitched at the corner—barely there, but he caught it.

He sat forward again. "Alright. Teach me one more glyph before we have to go. Something easy."

She picked up the charcoal and drew a smooth shape with three curves, each folded into the next. "This one's for warmth."

Graye furrowed his brow, watching her hand. "Looks like a clover."

"It's meant to look like joined cups," she said. "To hold heat. It doesn't work yet, not for us—not until our power strengthens. But the calligraphy must be perfect. One slip and it becomes a binding sigil instead. And those *do* work."

He raised an eyebrow. "You trying to bind me to the rug?"

"Not yet," she smirked, handing him the charcoal.

He copied it carefully, tongue between his teeth, brow furrowed.

She watched. She always contemplated him with that same fierce intensity, as if he mattered enough to deserve the time. He tried. Because she had all the tutors. All the resources. All the futures laid out for her like a table of knives. And he had Ember dirt, a camp education, and a father who wanted to shape him into a tool.

She tried to teach him everything, as if the shared knowledge would bridge the physical gaps between them.

Languages. Glyphs. Court custom. Names of foreign dignitaries and which words to avoid when greeting a Tides Court matron. The correct tilt of a head when speaking to a

Solace admiral. Even how to bow—not the deep one meant for queens, but the sideways one, Ember-style, when making a point.

He taught her too. Better footwork for close-range duels. A sidestep used in Ember arena fights that disoriented opponents who watched the blade instead of the shoulders. Jokes. How to spit well. How to smile without giving anything away.

"You ready?" she asked, nudging his knee with hers.

He looked at the glyph, then at her. "For the ball? Or for your mother's death glare from across the room?"

"Both."

He grinned. "You look terrifying, by the way."

She bumped his shoulder. "You smell like ink."

"And boredom," he added.

She stood, brushing charcoal from her palms. "We'll be fine."

He stood with her, wings shifting as he reached for his formal jacket.

But before she crossed to the wardrobe, she turned. "Graye?"

"Yeah?"

"I love you." A refrain said frequently on these too-short visits.

He smirked, pulling the jacket over one arm. "I love you, too, Sev. You're stuck with me, remember?"

Four hours later...

The supply closet under the eastern staircase had once held candelabras and ceremonial satchels, but Serena and Graye had claimed it years ago as a retreat when palace life grew unbearable. Tonight it smelled of dust, wax, and a faint echo of dried lavender. One of the old Moon Court banners—folded improperly and shoved behind a stack of gilded stands—now served as a cushion beneath their legs. They were still in formal dress. Still flushed from the warmth of the ballroom. And very much tipsy.

The bottle of wine between them was half gone, balanced carefully on a crate that once held extra lantern oil. Serena's shoes were off. Graye had unbuttoned his collar halfway down and looked gloriously unrepentant about it.

"I swear to the stars," she was saying, one hand gesturing wildly, "he looked at me like he expected me to faint. Like the moment I touched his arm, I'd *swoon*. That's what girls do if they like a boy. I learned that word- swoon."

Graye leaned back against the wall, grin lopsided. "Swoon. Stupid word. Was this the one with the eyebrow? The... Frostvaar one?"

"No—*that* was Lord Velin. He blinked twice during our entire dance. Twice. I counted. This was the Solace Court's youngest cousin. I think he was twelve."

He cackled. "Did he say anything?"

"Oh, yes. He said I was 'becoming.'"

Graye snorted into his sleeve. "Becoming *what*?"

"That's what I asked him," Serena said, eyes alight. "He stammered for twenty seconds, then stepped on my foot."

They both cackled, muffled poorly behind their palms.

The sound of music still filtered faintly through the walls, a distant hum of strings and conversation. But here, beneath the staircase, it was their little world—small, dim, secret. Graye took another swig from the bottle and passed it to her.

She drank, then leaned back beside him with a sigh. "I hate it. I hate the staring. The pretending. The *tone* I have to use when talking about tariffs. I hate the way she watches me, waiting for me to fail."

Graye didn't ask who *she* was. He never had to.

"She didn't speak to me once tonight," Serena added, quieter now. "She just... stared. Like I was a spell that might go wrong or break."

Graye reached over and nudged her with his knee. "Well, you didn't break."

She snorted. "Not yet."

They sat for a while, sharing the bottle in quiet turns, until Serena nudged him again, this time more insistent. "Tell me about *your* Solstice. Tell me about the bonfires again."

Graye grinned, warmth blooming behind his eyes. "Alright, alright. So—last year, Kade tried to build this sled, right? Called it the Ember Fang. He said it could outrun a storm if we got enough speed."

"You sled? On *ice*?"

"On a hill," he corrected. "Mostly rocks. Some snow. Rhune warned him it was going to end in disaster, but Kade kept shouting something about 'speed will keep it balanced.' We tied it to a warhound."

"No!"

"Yes. The poor beast took off like a comet. Kade lasted five seconds. The sled flipped, he hit a tree, and Rhune and I laughed so hard we forgot to catch the dog."

Serena was wheezing with laughter now, half-curled on her side, the wine sloshing dangerously.

"Oh—and the snowball fights." Graye shook his head, eyes distant. "They aren't fights. They're *wars*. We dig trenches. Kade once smuggled salt into his snowballs and nearly blinded a captain. Got kitchen duty for a week."

"I want to be there," Serena blurted immediately, as she always did. "I want to be in the trenches. I want to ride the warhound."

"You'd end up face-first in a tree."

"So?"

Graye looked at her then, long enough for her to notice.

"What?" she asked, brows rising.

He shook his head. "Nothing. Just... you laugh more with me than you do anywhere else."

Serena tilted her head. "Because you're the only person here who treats me like I'm *me*. Not a position. Not a project. Or pitiful."

He didn't have anything clever to say to that. He passed her the bottle again.

She took it, drank, and murmured, "I think your boys are mine now, too."

"Rhune and Kade?"

She nodded. "I've adopted them."

Graye grinned. "They'll love that."

She smiled into the rim of the bottle. "They'd better."

In the silence that followed, they leaned back together against the crate, finery wrinkled, hair undone, the glitter of the court left behind.

Two kids who'd grown into something more—still side by side, still fighting the world in stolen hours and quiet shadows.

That night, Serena, with all the imperious weight of a tipsy- but royal- thirteen-year-old girl informed the royal guards that should Dardani boys by the name of Kade and Rhune ever come to the gates asking for her, they were to be brought to her at once, no questions asked.

The guards shrugged, and said, "Yes, Princess."

CHAPTER SEVEN

THE BITTEREST WINTER

The wind in the Ember camps screamed down from the Frostvaar mountains, knife-edged and relentless, slicing through even the thickest canvas like it wasn't there at all. The Dardani training camps had always been spartan—glory forged through hardship, as the commanders liked to say—but this winter had broken past pride, past bravado, into something meaner. Something feral.

Snow crusted the inside edges of the tents. The firewood stores were gone. The mess pots ran dry more often than not. The nobles had hoarded what little was left—pulling their favored sons into private quarters, guarding food and furs like treasure. For the rest, the sons of farmers, merchants, disgraced bloodlines, and forgotten bastards, there was nothing but what they could steal or share.

Graye, fourteen, sat hunched in the far corner of the tent, arms wrapped around himself, his cloak pressed over his knees. It was barely enough. A thin blanket from his meager Prince of Shade allotment had been thrown over Rhune and Kade, who lay curled together for warmth like animals. Frost clung to the canvas seams above them. Their breath steamed faintly in the cold, too weak to form full clouds anymore.

The ration pack beside him was open. Three small strips of dried meat. A heel of bread, hard as stone. It was all he'd kept from that morning—what he hadn't already passed to them.

Kade had stopped protesting two days ago. Rhune never said anything. Just *looked* at him sometimes. With eyes that didn't judge, but didn't approve either.

Graye didn't care. He wasn't going to watch them starve.

"I'm fine," he'd said. "I've still got the Shade ration scrips; I'm a lord's son. They'll feed me if I faint."

But he *was* fainting. Not fully—just... moments of blackness when he stood too fast. Dizziness when he sparred. Cold in his fingers that didn't go away, even when pressed to his chest. He hadn't told them about the blood he'd coughed up last night. Or the tremor that had started in his sword hand.

The camp was breaking apart. Boys no older than fifteen were stealing from each other, scavenging, prowling like wolves, and stripping abandoned tents for thread. Three had deserted last week. Two had been dragged back by patrols. One of them—Syric, from the Frostlow clan—had collapsed beyond the latrines.

He'd looked like he was sleeping.

But they knew better.

They'd dragged his body outside. Graye had helped. There wasn't even a ceremony anymore. The ground was too hard to dig, and most were too weak to try. They laid Syric beside the others, tucked beneath a windbreak, eyes frozen open to the slate-grey sky. No prayers. Just wind.

That night, Graye wrote the letter by moonlight.

He held the charcoal stick too tight—his fingers were numb, and the pressure made the strokes uneven. But he didn't stop. Not even when the tip snapped.

Sev,

This winter is worse than any we've had. Kade's ribs are visible. They're stripping us down. Took the winter kits for "redistribution," which means the highborns got them. I have a little bit more than most, as Jaryk's son, but we're in training linen, with patched cloaks. There's nothing left to patch.

Rhune hasn't spoken in a day and a half. I can't give them enough. I'm trying, but they're starving. The others are worse. We lost another one today. Just fell asleep and didn't wake up.

I'm scared they won't make it.

I'd never ask if it was just me. But please, if there's anything in the Moon Court stores. Anything at all. Even old grain. We'll eat it.

I'll write you again if I can. But if you don't hear from me, it's not because I didn't want to.

Wherever. Whenever. Always.

— G

He folded it carefully, sealing it with the Moon Court wax token Serena had given him two summers ago, pressed into a ring he wore under his cloak. He didn't cry. But his chest hurt in a way he didn't have words for.

In the morning, when the couriers came through to collect dispatches for the higher posts, he passed the letter along.

And watched it go, pinned with hope to a sack of official reports.

The seal wasn't from the Moon Court.

She recognized it instantly, even before the servant bowed low and placed the bundle of correspondence onto her desk. The black wax gleamed faintly in the firelight, marked with the Shade insignia—not the official one of court communication, but the private emblem Graye had started using three years ago. He'd carved the stamp himself, from river stone, and sent it to her on her twelfth birthday with a note that simply read: *So your letters always know where to go.*

She was on her feet before the servant had finished speaking, the rest of the dispatches ignored entirely.

Her study was silent—curtains drawn, light low, a half-finished scroll on naval tariffs abandoned on the divan. She stood near the hearth and broke the seal with one smooth motion. The parchment inside was creased and brittle, the charcoal faint in places. She read the first line. Then the second. Then all of it.

When she reached the middle, her jaw clenched. By the end, her fingers had curled so tight the page creaked in her grip.

She turned on her heel and moved.

She was out of her study in ten heartbeats, cloak snapped from its hook, boots echoing down the corridor. She did not call for servants, didn't alert her steward.

The main stores for the royal family sat beneath the eastern wing of the palace—a secured floor guarded at all hours, reinforced by spells that sang softly when disturbed. She took the servant's stair. Passed through the training yard. Reached the vault doors in minutes.

The guards stationed outside blinked when they saw her. Straightened. One stepped forward.

"Princess..."

"Move," Serena barked.

The tone wasn't sharp. It was quiet. Controlled. But the look in her eyes stopped him in his tracks. She'd heard her grandfather use that tone hundreds of times and she used it now- Jormunder's authoritative voice, but a siren's cold gaze. He hesitated.

Then stepped aside.

The second guard reached for the seal ledger.

"Your authorization—"

"I am the Princess of the Moon Court, the Heir of Ardaion. My authority," she said before they could open their mouths, "comes from blood, not paper. If you breathe a word of this to anyone but General Jormunder, you'll be reassigned to a snow post in Frostvaar before nightfall."

He did not try to stop her again.

She passed through the threshold and into the vault.

The air was cold and dry. Stone floors. Heavy shelving. Dustless and dim. Everything was organized into perfect military rows—dried goods, emergency rations, winter equipment, alchemicals, medicinal crates. She stood at the center for less than a second before she began pulling what she needed. And after years with the army, she knew exactly what to do.

She started with food.

Not luxury items, not the diplomatic showpieces sent to foreign courts. No. The real things. Soldier-grade rations. Long-keep grains sealed in enchanted linen. Dried meats, heavy with salt and fat. Oats pressed into dense blocks. Tinned fruit. Preserved roots. She found one of the older cheese wheels, wax-sealed and rune-etched for storage during a siege. She loaded it all into a crate without pause.

Then the second crate: winter gear.

Not silks. Not court fashions. *Survival gear.* She selected three full cold-weather kits—fur-lined boots, double-layered cloaks, and thick gloves with warming runes. Undergarments. Heavy wool trousers. Cloaks of mountain weft that would break both wind and snow. She added flintstones, fire-making bundles, and two old survival packs designed for field medics. A third crate followed after that, half food, half additional furs. She did not count. She did not second-guess.

She carried the crates herself.

By the time she reached her tower again, her arms were burning and her shoulders ached from the drag of the third one, but she didn't stop. She kicked the door open with her heel, one foot already sliding it closed again behind her. She didn't notice the trail of snow she left down the corridor. She was stripping off her cloak as she crossed the room to grab rope and sealing wax from her wardrobe shelf.

When she turned back toward the crates, the door opened again.

Elsibetha stepped in.

Her hair was loose, still damp from sparring, braid half-finished down her back. She wore a beaten leather tunic and her hands were bandaged from training. She took one look at the half-packed crates and Serena on her knees beside them with sealing thread in her teeth—and said absolutely nothing.

Serena tossed a winter cloak into the nearest box and reached for the firestarter pouch without glancing up.

Elsie crossed the room.

"What's the crisis?" she asked.

Serena said nothing. She picked up the folded parchment from where she'd set it on the table and held it out.

Elsie took it. Read it. Her jaw set.

She read it again.

"Gods," she said, quietly. Then again, with more venom: "*Fucking gods.*"

She folded the letter, slid it into her belt, and dropped to her knees beside Serena.

She picked up a pair of boots from the stack and tested their stitching. She nodded. "You always talk about them like you've met them."

"I have, through him."

Elsie didn't argue. She stripped off her gloves and started packing. "You've told me a dozen stories. Kade, always grinning. Rhune with his knives and his quiet. Sound like half-trained pups."

"They're his family."

Elsie gave her a sideways look. "And yours?"

Serena said nothing.

It wasn't a moment for words.

Serena packed with the practiced economy of someone who had lived in barracks as much as palaces. She used a wool cloth to pad the food jars and strapped the medicinal supplies into tight bundles using discarded belt loops. She pressed boots heel to toe to conserve space. Her fingers were a blur. Elsie's weren't slower.

By the time they finished, it was nearing midnight.

The crates were heavy. Good. That meant there was enough. Serena pressed her hands to the lids of all three and exhaled once.

Then she stepped back.

Elsie stood. "I'll open the gate."

Serena stood back as her cousin gestured precisely into the air, glowing glyphs showing up like afterimages. She recognized some of them. She'd seen and used mage gates before, moving with Jormunder and the army.

The air shivered.

A final glyph bloomed in glowing lines, curling open like frost spidering across glass. The scent of pine hit them first—cold, dry, and sharp. Mountain wind followed.

The gate opened, revealing a black pine forest in the throes of deep snow drifts and bleak cold.

The gate exhaled cold.

The wind rushed through the glowing circle of carved magic as Serena and Elsibetha stepped into the Ember wilds, the air slicing across their faces like blades. Even prepared, even braced, Serena staggered slightly with the first step onto the packed snow of the mountain slope. The forest here was skeletal—sharp-boned pines rising from drifted snowbanks, their branches stripped bare. Distant howls echoed off the stone. Nothing stirred nearby but wind and ghosts.

She felt it immediately.

The difference between Moon Court winter and Ember suffering.

The air was thinner here. Harsher. There was no veil of civility, no warmth lurking behind velvet tapestries or enchanted braziers. Just the raw, merciless mountain cold, so dry it bit into her skin through the seams of her gloves.

Elsie moved behind her, dragging one crate over the threshold by rope handle. Serena followed, pulling the other two in tandem, her boots crunching over frost-hardened roots. The crates were heavy—more than she should have been able to move alone—but adrenaline lent her strength. She would not leave one behind.

The gate pulsed, the wind catching their cloaks as they stepped fully into the trees. Elsie waved her hand once, severing the tether.

The gate collapsed.

Silence fell.

Only snow and breath and cold remained.

They were already moving before the light faded entirely.

The trail was not well-marked—not even visible to the untrained eye—but Serena had memorized Graye's letters. She knew the rotation patterns. He'd described the southern bend of the low trail where scouting parties were sometimes sent for "conditioning." She didn't know if he'd be on it tonight. But he had to be.

She kept low, following Elsie through the trees, dragging the crates behind her in staggered bursts, muscles burning. Her breath steamed white in the dark. Her wings ached under the weight of her cloak.

By the time they reached the edge of the trail, her gloves were stiff with cold and her jaw had gone numb.

Then—movement.

Three figures.

Far down the trail, hunched and trudging slowly through a shallow drift of snow, too ragged for patrol, too quiet for regular training. Serena stopped breathing.

It was them.

Graye in front—shoulders hunched, his gait uneven. Rhune just behind, his posture taut, head turning slowly, watching for threats. Kade lagged slightly, red hair unmistakable even under the soot-stained hood, arms wrapped around himself, barely keeping pace.

They looked like ghosts.

Their cloaks were wrong—too thin, too short. Ill-fitting. Probably taken from whatever castoffs hadn't been stolen by officers or hoarded by noble sons. Kade's boots looked two sizes too large and stuffed with linen. Rhune's sleeves had been torn and sewn back, but the stitchwork was fraying. Graye's wing-slit cloak hung unevenly, one clasp broken, the wool stiff with frost at the hem.

They looked half-starved.

Gaunt, pale, hollow-eyed. Not training-leanness—*starvation.* Serena's stomach twisted. Her hands tightened around the rope of the nearest crate.

She almost called out.

The words were there—his name, his title, a joke, something. But they stuck. Lodged behind the sudden wave of heat that rose in her chest and curled up her throat. What if they didn't want her here? What if they thought she was soft? She stared at them like they were ghosts, like they might vanish if she blinked.

Her throat closed. For all the years she'd imagined this—meeting them, hugging them, laughing with them—now she was afraid. *What if they don't like me? What if I'm not what they imagined?* She clenched her fists in her sleeves, holding herself back.

She'd never needed to think this way before, to genuinely want someone to like her. She'd never really had a friend besides Graye. Somewhere deep inside her, the first inkling of fear arose that she wasn't good enough. That she might be the things Mab said. That she'd get rejected if she reached out.

Elsie's hand closed around her shoulder, stopping the rise of anxiety and circling thoughts.

Serena nodded. They waited.

When the boys passed around the curve of the trail and vanished into the low grove, she and Elsie moved quickly, fast as wraiths. They dragged the crates out from the trees—far enough off the trail to catch attention, but not so far they wouldn't be seen. Serena tore off her glove, fumbled in her satchel, and scrawled the note with shaking hands.

Wherever. Whenever. Always.

She left the envelope unsealed on top of the largest crate. No names. No markings. She pulled her glove back on and vanished into the trees.

They waited.

The wind picked up again. The sky above them was iron grey, the sun hidden, casting everything in the color of old bones.

Then came the sound—slow boots crunching.

The three boys reappeared.

Graye stopped first. His eyes caught on the corner of the crate where it peeked from the snow, frost already dusting the top. He threw out his arm—an instinctive motion—and the others halted. They already moved like a unit, and he was their leader.

They looked at it like it was bait. Some sadistic training lesson that was going to see them beaten or bloody.

A trap.

Rhune drew a knife from beneath his cloak, his green eyes sweeping the tree line on high alert. Kade simply stared. Confused, dazed, weak.

The three of them began to circle like wolves.

Graye moved in first. Slow. Cautious. When he noticed the envelope, he hesitated. Picked it up.

And read.

He said nothing for a long moment.

Then she heard him exhale.

His hand clenched around the letter, trembling slightly. Not from cold. From relief.

Then came the whisper, ragged, breaking on the wind.

"Thank you, Sev."

The sound of it nearly undid her.

Kade stepped forward, hands uncertain. He reached for the latch on the crate and opened it with a grunt.

Steam didn't rise, but it felt like it should have.

Inside—food. Dense, wrapped in wax. Meat. Hard bread. Honey. Cheese. Blankets. Gloves. Kits. Supplies like none of them had seen in weeks.

Kade dropped to his knees in the snow, half-collapsing beside it, a half-laugh, half-sob escaping his throat. His hands shook as he reached inside, pulling out a pair of boots with laces intact. He pressed them to his chest.

Rhune crouched beside him. No tears. No laugh. Just a single sharp breath. He lifted one of the cloaks, ran a hand across the lining, then spoke, flat and clear, "We need to hide this before anyone comes. I know a place."

"Take the food first," Graye said, voice quiet, eyes still on the letter.

They divided fast.

Not wildly, not with the greed of the starving, but with the urgency of soldiers. Graye stuffed what he could into their packs. Kade pulled his threadbare boots off and forced his frozen feet into the new ones. Rhune passed him gloves. Graye tugged the new cloak on over his shoulders and drew the hood low.

Then Rhune looked up.

"What if they try to take the clothes?"

Graye's voice didn't waver.

"I'll remind them who my friend is. And that I'll write to her. And to Jormunder."

They didn't laugh.

They packed the last of the supplies in silence, vanishing one by one back into the trees, carefully, quietly, coordinated. Serena and Elsie didn't move until the trail was empty again.

Only then did Serena let her shoulders sink.

Only then did Elsie finally speak, voice low beside her. "You saved them. Graye. Your boys."

Serena didn't answer.

She exhaled, slow and steady, watching her breath curl through the pine air—and stayed hidden a little longer. Just long enough to be sure.

Then she turned.

And they slipped back into the trees, Elsie summoning a new gate.

CHAPTER EIGHT

EVERYTHING CHANGED

Spring in the Dardani Camps

The Ember wind carried warmth early that year, sweeping down from the mountains in dry, smoky gusts that rattled the pine needles and kicked dust off the hard-packed training grounds. Snow still clung to the highest ridges in the distance, but in the valley where the Dardani camp lay sprawled across tiers of scorched stone and canvas, it was already warm enough for sweat to slick skin by midmorning.

The three boys, now fifteen, had staked out a corner of the south ring to drill alone—no instructors, no prying eyes. Just the clatter of steel on steel, the stink of oil and heat, and the cocky rhythm of boys beginning to grow into their strength.

They'd traded their wooden swords months ago, the ones they'd used since age eight long since worn and splintered into practice kindling. Now they trained with steel—heavy, unforgiving, loud when struck. The bruises didn't fade as fast anymore. The calluses on their hands had thickened. So had their arms.

Seven years of training had left its mark: lean muscle, sun-browned skin, and the beginnings of real power in their shoulders. They were taller now—Graye fastest of all, his long frame finally matching the wings he'd dragged around as a child, all rangy limbs and honed arrogance. He wore a permanent roguish smirk and sparkle in his green eyes.

Kade had filled out like a brawler, compact and solid, his chest broadening and legs thick from drills. His ginger hair had darkened into an auburn shade and his golden eyes looked like honey. Rhune remained wiry, with black hair, and green eyes, defined not by bulk but by precision—muscle cut close to the bone, a panther's build, all sleek control and quiet dry humor.

They were sweating through their tunics, wings flicking open occasionally to cool off between forms. A few girls from the healer tents had passed earlier, bringing water buckets down from the spring, and the change in all three boys had been immediate—subtle as a landslide.

Kade's stance straightened. Rhune's eyes tracked the movement. Graye had run a hand through his hair and taken his shirt off entirely, claiming it was soaked through. It wasn't.

Now they were back at it—steel blades flashing, circling, swapping partners every ten counts—and talking.

"Well, she smiled," Kade grinned between parries, his blade clanging against Rhune's. "That's not *nothing*."

"She smiled because you spilled water down her front and said it was an accident," Rhune replied flatly, spinning out of the exchange and rolling his wrist to bring his sword back up.

Graye laughed from where he was pacing in a wide circle around them, waiting his turn. "He *said* it was an accident. But his eyes were on her tits the whole time."

"They were not!"

"You glanced four times," Rhune said.

"I counted five," Graye added.

"You two are bastards."

"No argument," Rhune smirked, then feinted hard right and clipped Kade's shoulder. "But we're observant bastards."

Kade hissed and lowered his blade, rubbing the impact. "It's not like either of *you* know how to flirt."

"I don't need to," Graye said with a shrug. "I let them come to me."

Rhune gave him a sidelong look. "Then what? You stammer and offer to show them your new blade oil?"

Graye grinned. "It's good oil."

Kade laughed and dropped onto the rock that served as their gear bench. His tunic clung to his chest, sweat darkening the collar and the curve of his spine where the weight of his wings pressed down. "All I'm saying is, if we're going to be godsdamned warriors, someone ought to appreciate the view."

Rhune snorted and sheathed his blade. "Appreciate it after drills. If you're trying to flex mid-fight, you're going to eat dirt."

"I'll eat it with style."

They passed the water skin between them, their movements loose and easy in that way only boys could be when they'd survived drills, injury, boredom, and adolescence together. There was a kind of comfort in their ribbing, an unspoken rhythm that didn't break even when one of them drew blood or limped home with a bruised rib.

But there was no denying the shift.

Voices were deeper. Smiles sharper. Their gazes lingered longer now when girls passed by, and not just the girls their age. Their bodies were beginning to betray them—shoulders rolling back, jaws squaring, wings twitching with restless heat. They had begun to notice the way women moved, how they laughed, what made them pause. And while none of them knew what to *do* with the attention, all of them wanted it.

Kade pulled his tunic off and flung it over the rock with a sigh. "Tell me again why we can't just sneak into the city, and try to find a brothel?"

"Because the last boys who tried that came back with burns and no eyebrows," Graye said, smirking.

"And because," Rhune added, tightening the straps on his chest piece, "if you can't stand upright after practice, you won't survive tomorrow's spar."

Kade groaned. "So basically, we suffer and try not to get hard every time someone walks past."

"That's the spirit," Graye said, clapping him on the back.

"In the meantime," Rhune smiled, drawing his sword again, "you might want to stop looking like you're ready to propose to every girl who hands you bandages."

"I have a *gentle heart,*" Kade muttered.

"You have a *stupid* heart," Graye corrected, laughing.

They returned to the circle—three half-grown warriors, blades gleaming, limbs strong, full of hunger and arrogance, and that aching, unbearable sense that manhood was around the next corner. That one more spar, one more victory, one more moment would make them everything they were supposed to become.

They swung steel beneath the rising heat of the Ember sun, while pine sap steamed in the air and the season began to turn.

Far away, in the Moon Court, spring crept in quietly—and Serena's siren blood began to stir.

By the time spring unfurled across the Moon Court with its jasmine-laced winds and silver rains, Serena was no longer the slim, sharp-jawed girl who'd shadowed Jormunder across war camps or stood still and silent at Mab's side in court. She was changing—and the realm was beginning to feel it.

She had grown taller over the winter, her limbs lengthening into a long-limbed elegance that was too graceful for her age. Where she had once moved like a soldier's child, all control and readiness, she now glided like her joints were threaded in silk. Her black hair had begun to shift as well, the first hints of indigo surfacing near her temples, the violet arriving next, then faint curls of emerald that shimmered when the strands were wet. No dye, no glamour—just siren blood waking in the marrow.

Her hips had rounded. Her chest, once flat and ignored, now pulled at her tunics. Her waist narrowed. Her posture—though unintentional—drew the eye. Her skin seemed more luminous, her cheeks always faintly flushed like she'd been running. She still spoke with bite and command, but her voice had deepened—no longer the clipped, polished tone of a noble girl. Now it could turn warm unexpectedly, soft and rich as velvet. On more than one occasion, she'd spoken and had a servant freeze, blinking as if stunned, unsure why they'd forgotten what they were doing.

Jormunder noticed.

He noticed when soldiers glanced too long, when young lieutenants grew clumsy and flushed in her presence. He noticed when she passed a row of guards and they stood a little straighter—not out of discipline, but something else entirely. He'd snarled once, openly, and Serena hadn't understood why until that night when she'd heard shouting from his command tent. The next day, they left the army camp.

Two weeks later, she was quietly returned to Ghealach Siorai. Until she learned control, he said. For her own good, and that of the soldiers.

Mab hadn't said a word to her—never did—but her gaze had lingered like frost on glass when Serena passed in a new gown, hair damp from bathing, the streaks of color vivid in the light. The queen had merely narrowed her eyes in silence. Serena had felt that stare down to her bones.

Her magic began to stir—not the studied kind with scrolls and glyphs, but something older. Raw. Instinctive.

The day her blood came, it rained.

She woke in her bed soaked in pain and heat, a low throb behind her navel and a sticky wetness between her thighs. She'd thought, for a breathless second, that something was wrong—until the scent hit her. Not metallic, not sharp, but heady. Cloying. Sweet and rich and wild all at once.

Roses.

Vanilla.

Sea salt and something else—deeper, more primal.

She had panicked. Tried to hide it, scrubbed the sheets, and warded the door with every sigil she remembered from her glyph lessons, but it was *still there.* The scent of her blood hung in the air like a spell.

And it wasn't just hers anymore. It was *siren.*

Serafine had found her in the bathing chamber an hour later—Serafine, cool and unreadable, dressed in black like always, her sharp eyes assessing, not unkind. She said nothing at first. Only set a fresh linen cloth on the basin rim and pulled a satchel from under her cloak.

"We begin tonight," she said. "Shadowdancer training."

Serena stared at her, wide-eyed and bare from the waist down, clutching a robe she hadn't had time to fasten. "*Now?*"

Serafine's lips twitched. "Your bones are strong enough and you've reached the traditional age. The transformation has started. It's time you began learning how to become the most feared thing on the battlefield, and the blade in the dark. As of now, you are a Shadowdancer novice. Your practice gear is on your bed. So is your *sujinn.*"

That was all she said about the blood. About the scent.

Later, it was Elsie who entered.

No knocking. Just a rustle of her cloak as she appeared in the doorway and shut it behind her. She had a bottle of strong wine in one hand, a satchel in the other, and a look on her face like she'd been expecting this moment for years.

"I suppose she told you nothing." She meant Serafine, definitely not Mab, because that answer was obvious.

"She said it was normal," Serena said quietly.

Elsie snorted. "That's like telling someone drowning in fire that it's *just heat.*"

She crossed the room, dropped the satchel on the bed, and sat heavily beside her. Serena was curled under a thick robe, knees to her chest, hair damp and hiding half her face.

Elsie unscrewed the wine. Took a long pull. Then passed it to her.

Serena took it. Sipped.

And waited.

"You're not dying," Elsie said. "You're becoming. This is the price."

Serena's brows furrowed. "The price?"

"The scent." Elsie leaned forward, bracing her elbows on her knees. "Your blood is changing. You're not half-Akyist anymore. Not Dardani. Not even high fae. When your body decided it was time, when the power began to awaken, everything else was overwritten. You're becoming full siren."

"I know that."

"No, you *don't*." Elsie looked at her, really looked. "That smell you noticed? That wasn't just your blood. It was your *invitation*. To males."

Serena swallowed.

"It's addictive," Elsie went on. "The siren scent... you'll smell it on your skin, in your hair, on your breath. But you can't smell it the way they do. Every siren's scent is unique, just like the colors in her hair, but it doesn't matter. To males, it's a drug. A lure, a command. It becomes a need."

"They'll want me?" Serena asked, and hated how small her voice sounded.

"They won't even understand why," Elsie said. "And they won't all know what they're doing. Some don't even realize. That's the worst part. The kindest of them might only... lean too close. Linger too long. Others will be worse. They might try to touch you."

Serena's throat was tight. "Even ones who wouldn't normally want me?"

"Even those. The bitterest of your enemies will heed the siren's call."

She looked down. "How do I stop it?"

"You don't," Elsie said. "It's the scent of your blood awakening. But you *shield*. That's the skill. You use your power to wrap the scent, hold it in, and control when and how it's released. You must learn to do it quickly or you will begin to catch males in the *Thrall*."

That was the truth of it.

Not wrapped in fear, not gentle. Just fact. The Thrall was helpless enthrallment. Males caught in a mindless haze of compulsion and lust- a Siren's power that had nothing to do with magery, just sheer biology.

"You're not prey anymore, Ser," Elsie said, her voice softer now. "You're the predator. The scent is your bait. Your blood will call them. Even the best of them. Even the ones who love you. Even if they respect you. They will lose themselves in it."

Serena's fingers twisted in her robe.

She had always been alone with this body. Rejected for it. Now it was becoming something powerful, but dangerous. Unwelcome, still. Feared.

But Elsie—Elsie stayed.

She handed the bottle back, "It's not easy. It never was. But you've got me and Serafine, our grandfather and Graye. And you're going to learn. It could save your life one day. Imagine being on a battlefield, injured and surrounded, the enemy closing in. You lower the shield and those soldiers closest to you become enthralled with a single breath. Then you order them to defend you- against their own brothers-in-arms."

Serena nodded, slowly.

Outside, the rain fell harder. Washing the scent from the walls, but not from her blood.

Two weeks later...

The guest receiving hall was one of the oldest chambers in Siorai, carved in the early years of the Moon Court and still bearing the original sun-bleached flagstone. The light from the high windows painted long amber stripes across the floor as Graye waited, hands stuffed into the pockets of his travel cloak, wings still half-damp from the crossing, hair windswept. He was taller now, enough that he'd noticed the change in the way the servants addressed him—less boy, more lordling. The wiry strength he'd gained from camp drills had matured into something unmistakably male. His jaw had squared. His shoulders had broadened. And beneath the layers of half-dried clothes and soot, he wore the confident look of someone who knew exactly how good he looked and had begun weaponizing it.

He hadn't seen her in almost half a year.

Not since before the snow. Not since before the crates. And even though they wrote constantly, even though her last letter had arrived two days ago and ended with *You'd better still be faster than me,* he still found himself oddly tense.

He was going to tell her everything. About Rhune and Kade, how they talked about her now like a ghost they'd only half believed in until that winter. How Rhune had said, quiet and sincere, *"I think she saved my life."* How Kade had confessed he wasn't sure he'd have lasted another week without the boots and the food. He was going to say all of it.

The door opened behind him.

Serena swept in.

It wasn't like the other times. Not the mad dashes through palace corridors or the half-wrestled greetings after a long separation. She didn't bound into his arms. She didn't even smile right away. She *walked.*

Glided. Shoulders back, chin up, cloak trailing slightly behind her, fitted leathers molded to her hips and waist. Her siren blood had taken hold, and it *showed.* Her hair—solid black once, now streaked with strands of violet and dark green and deep sapphire—glistened with damp from training, curling at the ends where water still clung. Her skin glowed faintly in the sunlight. Her eyes—once solid grey—now flickered between sea-glass green to stormy blue then back to grey in the light as she smiled.

It wasn't her usual grin. Not crooked, not feral.

It was radiant. Calm. *Regal.*

And it wrecked him.

Graye straightened immediately, his heart suddenly in his throat. He opened his mouth to greet her, something teasing and familiar, but the words snagged on his tongue as she crossed the floor. She was—

Beautiful.

The word hit him before he could stop it.

Not just pretty. Not cute, not fierce. *Beautiful.* And worse—elegant.

"Hello, Graye," she said, her voice rich, warm, and a little lower than he remembered.

Something fluttered in his chest. He covered it with a smirk.

"Took you long enough," he smirked, reaching for easy humor. "Was starting to think you'd outgrown me."

Serena's smile sharpened, a flash of teeth. "Don't tempt me."

He laughed. It came out a little too loud. "I missed you."

That was easier. That was real.

Her expression softened. "I missed you too."

They didn't hug at first. That was the first awkward beat. Then finally she stepped into his arms and hugged him tight.

Normally they flung around shoulders, wings tangling, a full-bodied crash. But now, neither of them moved, both suddenly aware of where their bodies started and ended. Serena stepped back half a pace, and he rolled his shoulders like it was just travel stiffness.

She gestured toward the hallway. "You want to walk? The garden's a mess but there's still sun. Or—"

"I don't care where we go," he said. "Long as it's with you."

She glanced at him sidelong, something unreadable flickering across her face. Her lashes were longer. Her lips, when she pressed them together thoughtfully, looked...

He cut the thought off. Hard.

They walked side by side down the corridor, their steps a little too in sync. The silence was companionable for a few paces, and then... not quite.

Graye cleared his throat. "So. Uh. You smell different."

Her head turned, and she gave him a look that was pure, amused warning. "*Careful.*"

He grinned and held up both hands. "Not bad different. Just, you know. Stronger. Like... flowers?"

"Roses," she said.

He nodded. "Right. Makes sense."

She didn't explain it. He didn't ask. But something about her posture said she was well aware of what it did to people and wasn't sure what to do with this new body. She was worried it might affect him too. Her skin crawled with self-awareness and it made her want to put on more layers, spray some perfume to cover it, take a bath...

"I brought letters," he said quickly. "From the boys."

Her eyes lit. "You did?"

"They wanted to meet you this year."

"Oh?"

"They think they're not good enough."

"They're probably right." It was cheeky, and she showed him a grin that said she was kidding.

He barked a laugh, relief flooding him at the old rhythm. "That's what I said!"

She laughed too. The sound was light, real. It helped. It helped *a lot.*

But they were still off-balance. Every glance lasted too long. Every brush of the arm felt like something more. He noticed the curve of her waist in the way her sword belt sat. She noticed the way his sleeves fit tighter now, how he moved when he walked.

They were trying to keep it the same. To be Graye and Serena, best friends, bonded souls. The boy who once pulled her braids and the girl who once wrestled him into the mud and won.

But they weren't children anymore.

She glanced at him as they reached the courtyard steps. Her sea-grey eyes looked almost blue now in the light. Her voice came softer this time, quieter. Not siren. Just Serena.

"I'm glad you're here."

He looked at her, fully, and answered without hesitation.

"Always."

They stood there, a little too close, not touching, not yet. The wind stirred through the jasmine vines above, and for a moment, the scent of roses and salt and sun-warmed stone wrapped around them both like a spell.

The old world had shifted.

The lake lay wide and still beneath the late afternoon sun, its surface broken only by the rippling wind and the quiet shush of reeds brushing along the bank. Early spring had come to Siorai like a sigh this year, not a storm—warmth curling into the stone walkways, coaxing green buds from the earth, chasing snowmelt down narrow gullies. And for Serena and Graye, it brought with it the familiar itch of freedom—the need to escape corridors, obligations, and eyes.

They'd come to the lake as they always did.

As they *had* always done.

Their boots lay discarded in a tangle near the willow roots, and Graye had flung his tunic over the high stone ledge from which he'd jumped moments ago. He emerged now, water sluicing off his bare shoulders, hair plastered to his forehead, wings dripping. Serena stood at the edge, watching him with a small, amused smile, hands on her hips.

"Tell me again how that dive was supposed to impress me," she said dryly.

Graye grinned, water glinting in his teeth. "You didn't like the splash?"

"You looked like you were being dragged under by your own ego."

"I'm experimenting with flair."

"Try leading with competence next time."

But she was smiling, and he knew she wasn't angry. Her voice held that teasing lilt she reserved for him alone, the one that wasn't quite a laugh but close. He pushed his wet hair back from his face and waded toward the shallows, stopping just short of where she stood.

"Come on," he said. "You're not going to make me be the only one in here, are you?"

Serena hesitated—not because she was shy. She rarely was. But everything had changed.

Two weeks ago, she could've stripped off her shift and dived in beside him, careless as a child. Now she felt his gaze linger when she moved. Now she heard the way his breath caught when she passed too close. She *felt* the weight of her own body in a way she never had before, guardedness. And she wasn't sure if she was guarding herself against his reaction, or guarding him from her.

She sighed and stepped forward.

The cold of the water hit her calves, then her thighs, then her waist. She didn't flinch. Didn't shiver. But the contact made her hair curl tighter, the streaks of color that had bloomed over the past month now deepening visibly with the wet. Siren signs. There was no hiding them. And when she finally ducked beneath the surface, holding her breath for a long, weightless moment, she could almost pretend she was the same.

When she rose, Graye was watching her.

Not obviously.

Not rudely.

But watching.

When she turned to look back at him, water running down her arms, hair clinging to the sides of her face, something in his expression flickered. Thoughtful.

They swam, easy strokes through the slow current. They teased each other, raced to the outcropping where they used to play lookout, and told stories of imagined naval battles. They tossed water, bumped shoulders, and shouted over the sound of wingbeats and spring birds. But every movement now felt slightly weighted—off-angle. His gaze slid a little too low before correcting. Her voice softened a little too much, curling unconsciously into the edge of that siren warmth.

He cleared his throat after a long silence, breaking it with that grin he wore like armor. "Kade thinks we're getting sent out next month. A proper mission. Just border patrol, but still. It means blades out."

"Is that why your ego's so bloated today?" she asked.

"Exactly. I need room to grow."

She smirked. "Heard anything more solid?"

"Just whispers. But our instructor made us drill night patterns. They only do that when deployment's close."

She nodded. "That's something."

Then, quieter, she added, "I had my Shadowdancer novice initiation."

Graye's brows lifted. "Oh tides, already?"

"Serafine says fifteen is traditional. The training is too hard on the bones if you start young, but start too late and you lose flexibility. She calls us the silent certainty."

He laughed once. "That sounds exactly like something she'd say."

"She's not wrong." Serena shifted her weight in the water, voice growing more reflective. "She's ruthless, but she makes sense. Everything's deliberate. Balance, silence, control. She says power doesn't mean anything if it isn't honed. And I have black armor and a *sujinn* sword now. I'll show it to you."

Graye turned slightly, resting his arms on a flat rock, watching her more closely now. "You like it?"

She nodded. "I think I was waiting for it, without realizing it. A way to prove myself. It helps me beat out some frustration and then Serafine teaches me how to still my mind."

Her voice had changed again subtly. That purring softness threaded into it, unintentional, but impossible to ignore. It stroked along his skin like the ripple of heat before lightning. Graye felt his pulse skip.

He glanced away.

Serena followed his gaze for a moment, then looked down at the water. Her fingertips trailed through it.

"There's more, though. Not just Shadowdancer work."

She didn't sound nervous, exactly. But quieter. Guarded.

He turned back toward her. He sensed the hesitation, the awkwardness, and his heart responded to it. "Yeah?"

"I didn't tell you in my last letter because... I don't know. It didn't feel real yet. But it's started. The siren stuff. Not all of it. Not fully. But I feel it waking up."

Graye didn't interrupt. He watched her carefully.

She drew a small circle in the water beside her, watching it spiral. "My scent's... active now. Only a little. It started when I bled. Elsie had to explain it. The blood triggers it. Everything changes."

"You don't smell like blood," he said without thinking.

She looked at him then.

He flushed. "I just mean... you don't smell bad. You smell like—"

"I know what I smell like," she sighed. "Roses. Vanilla. The Sea."

He nodded. Swallowed. "Yeah. That."

She didn't mention what it did. *The Thrall.* He'd heard enough, being around the siren court that he didn't press.

She kept her voice bright. "And the Voice is coming in. Barely. I haven't used it on anyone, not intentionally. But sometimes I say something and people *listen*. Not like before."

He didn't answer right away.

His thoughts were moving too quickly. Trying to remember every time she'd spoken to him lately. Trying to figure out if he'd felt anything strange, anything out of place. But it wasn't wrong. It wasn't bad. It was *her*.

But it also wasn't *just* her anymore.

"Graye?"

He looked up.

She was watching him. Water slid down her collarbone, hair curling around her cheeks, eyes shifting now—grey to green to blue and back again, like the tide.

He smiled. It felt crooked. Part of him wanted to flex and preen, which he stomped into silence.

"I think it suits you."

Her brows lifted slightly.

"The siren part," he clarified. "You don't seem... possessed. Or scary. You just seem... more."

She tilted her head. "More?"

"You know... *more*." He shrugged.

She didn't know what to say to that. So she didn't.

They floated there a while longer, letting the water hold them, letting the air settle between them. Not quite touching. Not quite saying the things that were beginning to form at the backs of their throats.

He waited outside her chamber for nearly ten minutes, leaning against the wall with his arms crossed, pretending to examine the stonework so the passing housemaids wouldn't ask questions. She was usually waiting for *him* in the mornings—hair braided, boots on, smirking like she already had something up her sleeve. But today, the door stayed shut.

He knocked once. Lightly.

Nothing.

Twice.

Still nothing.

Graye glanced down the hall, saw no one, and tested the handle. It was unlocked. Probably shouldn't have been. Probably not appropriate now—not anymore—but they'd never been appropriate. They'd shared pillows and schemes and summers soaked in lake water. No door had ever been closed between them before.

He slipped inside.

Her room smelled like her—moonflower tea, faint vanilla, the salt of fresh soap. The bedcovers were still rumpled. Her window was open to the morning wind. She was seated at her dressing table, facing the mirror. She didn't look up when he entered.

She was in pale silk sleepwear, her hair unbraided, curtain-smooth as it spilled over her back. Her feet were bare, curled slightly under the stool. Her posture was rigid. Her hands gripped the edge of the table. And her reflection—caught in the oval mirror rimmed with pearl—showed tear-tracked cheeks and red-rimmed eyes.

"Sev?" he said softly.

She didn't answer. But her shoulders trembled. Their bond tugged in his chest.

He crossed the room in two strides and knelt beside her, instinct moving faster than thought. His arms were around her before he could stop them, pulling her into the circle of his body as she turned toward him, pressing her face into his chest like she had when they were small. But now there was no awkward elbow jabbing his ribs. No muddy boots. Just silk. Skin. Sobs.

He held her tighter.

"It's okay," he murmured, his hand rubbing broad circles across her back. "I'm here. I've got you."

She shook her head against him. "No, you don't understand—"

"Then help me understand."

She pulled back a little. Enough to look up, her eyes shining with tears, her lips trembling.

"I have fangs," she whispered, then sniffled and brought a finger to her mouth. She used it to lift her upper lip.

"I can't hide them. They won't go back in," she choked. "And I look like a monster."

Then she broke again—soft, helpless sobs wracking her. Her face crumpled like she hadn't wanted to show him, but now couldn't stop. Serena never sobbed. Not even when Mab ignored her or called her disappointment. Not when she came home bleeding from practice.

It shattered him.

His arms tightened again, rocking her, his chin brushing the crown of her head.

"You are *not* a monster," he said, fiercely. "You're Serena. You're my Sev. And you're perfect."

She only cried harder.

He couldn't fix it. He didn't know how. No one had prepared him for this—no drill, no tactic. She smelled like roses and sea wind, and her whole body trembled in his arms, and he felt both protective and completely helpless.

But he kept holding her.

When the worst of it ebbed, when her sobs dulled to hiccups and her arms curled around his middle, he pulled back enough to tip her chin up.

"Let me see."

She blinked at him.

"Graye—"

"I want to see them."

She hesitated. Then, slowly, leaned back. Her eyes flicked away, still red and wet. She opened her mouth, lips parted.

He reached out, gently.

His thumb brushed the side of her mouth, and with care he didn't know he was capable of, he lifted her upper lip.

And there they were.

Not monstrous. Not grotesque. Tiny.

Two little canines, barely longer than what she'd had before, only now tapered into dainty points. Ivory white, clean, elegant—as if her mouth had simply decided to echo the rest of her. They didn't look like they belonged to a beast. They looked... oddly *perfect.* A secret tucked behind soft lips. Just visible enough to catch the eye, to hint. Devilish, if devils could be cute.

"...That's it?" he said.

She scowled. "Don't mock—"

"No, I mean... *that's* what you're crying about?"

Her brows knit. "Yes, because I'm a monster and people will be afraid of me—"

"They're adorable."

She stopped.

He grinned, tilting his head. "I thought fangs were supposed to be terrifying. But you look like you're going to bite *fashionably.*"

She let out a weak, watery laugh. "You ass. You're impossible."

"I'm serious." He tapped her lip, gently. "They're... you. A little dangerous. Very pretty. Kind of smug."

"They are not smug."

"Have you *met* your mouth?"

That got a real laugh. She wiped at her eyes with the edge of her sleeve, cheeks still flushed, but no longer crumpled.

"They don't retract yet," she murmured, embarrassed again. "I can *feel* them when I talk. It's like they don't fit."

"They'll fit," he said. "You just need to grow into them."

She gave him a dubious look.

"I mean that in the *least* insulting way possible."

She sniffed and gave him a tiny pout.

He brushed her hair back from her damp cheek, fingers tucking the strands gently behind her ear. Her face was still wet, but her breathing had evened out. She looked down, then up at him. The rose-vanilla scent still clung to her skin—soft, heavy, dizzying. But he didn't feel threatened by it.

He felt like drowning in it.

And that terrified him in a way no sword ever had.

Because even with her eyes swollen and her lip trembling, she was still the most beautiful thing he'd ever seen. The fangs didn't ruin that. They *highlighted* it. As he looked at them again—those tiny, perfect points—he realized, quite suddenly, that he *really* liked them.

He was still staring when she whispered, voice quiet and cautious, "You're not afraid?"

His hand cupped her cheek.

"No," he said. "They suit you."

He kissed her temple before he could think better of it. And she didn't pull away.

Later that night...

The supply closet beneath the south staircase had always been too large for what it held. A few battered crates, some old ceremonial banners that hadn't seen use in a decade, extra candelabras stacked in dusty rows—and tonight, two noble-born fae slumped on folded velvet with a bottle of stolen wine between them and another one, already empty, rolling lazily against the wall.

The lantern they'd brought with them flickered low, casting honeyed light across Graye's profile as he tipped the bottle back for a drink. It caught in the angles of his cheekbones, the sharp line of his jaw. His black tunic was still buttoned high at the collar, sleek, polished.

He looked like a prince, and he knew it.

Gods, it annoyed her.

Serena sat cross-legged beside him, her gown pooling around her like liquid bronze, cut daringly along the collarbone and tight along her ribs and hips. Her siren figure had become the subject of not-so-quiet court gossip over the last few weeks—*Have you seen her lately? Those eyes? That walk?*—and tonight's gown did nothing to discourage it. Her hair was pinned half-up, streaks of indigo and green catching in the lamplight, and her tiara sat perilously crooked on her head, after shifting there somewhere between the first and second bottle.

Neither of them had bothered to fix it.

"You danced with *six* different girls," she said, voice heavy with wine and mock disdain.

"I needed to keep the court guessing," Graye replied, swirling what little wine was left in the bottle. "If I only dance with you, it'll look like I've already been caught."

"Please," Serena flicked her fingers. "You're not that clever."

He leaned back on one elbow and grinned at her. "Yet you're still here."

She didn't smile back right away. Just took the bottle from him, drank deep, and let her head tip back against the wall.

The room smelled like melted wax and velvet and old wood. And her. Always her. Salt and rose, vanilla, and some darker note he hadn't found a name for yet.

She handed the bottle back, the glass clinking gently against his fingers. "You seemed... off. At dinner."

He was silent a moment, staring at the floor.

Then: "I've been thinking about the mission."

Serena's eyes turned to him, heavy-lidded but clear. "The border patrol?"

Graye nodded once. "I don't think it's training. I think it's preparation."

Her posture straightened slightly. "For what?"

He hesitated. Ran a thumb along the curve of the glass.

"My father's been... shifting coin. Calling in old debts. Nothing overt, just—quiet movements. Rhune heard it first. He's got ears in the Ember camps. But what caught me was something my father said in his last letter. He didn't say anything directly, but it read like code. A *reminder* of what Shade has lost to Mab. A mention of my mother. Of Lyra."

Serena's breath caught.

"Do you think he's planning something?" she asked softly.

"I don't know," Graye admitted. "I *think* so. Or maybe I expect him to. He's lost face since Mab gutted his court after the bond was discovered. He wants something back. Maybe it's political positioning. Maybe it's territory. Maybe he wants to test the waters before a larger move."

Serena was quiet.

He looked at her. "You can't tell anyone."

"I won't," she said immediately.

"I'm not even sure I'm right. I might be wrong. I *hope* I'm wrong."

"But if you're not..."

He nodded grimly. "Then Shade may move against Ember, and I don't know where that leaves me. My father rules Shade. My mother came from Ember. My closest friends are in Ember. But if I *say* something—if I warn someone—I look like I've turned against my own blood. Like I'm hoping to get in good with Mab again by feeding her secrets."

"You *are* Shade's heir."

"Exactly. Shade's court is already half waiting to see if I'll betray them like Mother did."

Serena's fingers curled in the folds of her gown. "If Mab finds out from someone else... she'll burn him down."

"She'll burn *everything*." Graye looked away. "And I don't know what happens to me, or my mother, or my sister if that happens. Maybe we're spared. Maybe we're shamed even more. Or outright executed."

She was silent again.

Then, gently: "What if you told the story yourself? Said you suspected the threat. That you were acting in defense of Ember? That you exposed him to protect your mother's people."

Graye shook his head. "If I'm right, I become the son who took down his own father. If I'm *wrong*, I become the traitor who falsely accused the Lord of Shade. And then I *never* rule."

Serena reached for the bottle again, pulled it from his hands, and drank deep.

"Politics," she muttered. "Utter horseshit."

He barked a laugh.

It was the first time they'd spoken as heirs as well as friends. The first time they truly understood that assassination could be political as well as with a blade- that they had the power to influence outcomes and lives could be lost, destinies determined with either choice. She passed him the bottle. He drained what was left.

They fell into silence, not cold, just heavy. The weight of inheritance wrapped around both of them now—titles, courts, bloodlines. The paths beneath their feet narrow, hardening. The inevitability of the loss of innocence whispering around them.

Graye ran a hand through his hair and muttered, "We should've run away when we were ten. Bought a goat. Dug a garden. Stowed away on a ship."

Serena sighed, leaning her head onto his shoulder. "The goat plan was flawless."

"We could still do it," he said. "Leave all of it behind. Go to the coast, do something crazy like throw the crowns away and raise pigs."

"I'm not touching a pig," she murmured.

"Fine. Goats, then."

"They smell."

He grinned. "You smell."

She elbowed him in the ribs. He caught her arm and held it there. Then his hand reached for hers, their fingers twining, squeezing tight.

They didn't say anything for a long time.

The lantern guttered, casting golden shadows across her skin. Her tiara glinted where he'd fixed it. Her eyes were half-lidded, soft. Her lips slightly parted. And when she turned to look at him again, something unspoken passed between them—warm, dangerous, inevitable.

But they said nothing.

CHAPTER NINE

INNOCENCE LOST

S he had never asked for a debut but it was not up to her. Sixteen was a sacred number for females of Ardaion. For heirs, it was doctrine.

It marked the full awakening of magic. The biological threshold where bloodlines either bloomed or collapsed.

The Moon Court palace was always beautiful—but tonight, her birthday, it had been transformed.

Marble balconies had been draped in silver silk, glowing with faelight and laced with living jasmine vines that shimmered under enchantment. The ballroom had been expanded magically, its ceilings vaulted to mimic starlight, charmed constellations wheeling slowly across the dark. Music drifted through the halls—flutes, low harps, strings thrumming like a heartbeat. It was a night of spectacle, of custom, of status.

Serena stood at the top of the ballroom stairs with her hands folded precisely, wearing a gown chosen by the palace seamstress after a month of argument. It was cut from moonsilk and dyed with crushed pearl and sea-glass—the color of a storm tide. The bodice was sleeveless, fitted to her new siren curves with unsettling perfection, the neckline framed in silver filigree.

Her hair had been braided in front and laced with starlight chains and pale blooms that glowed faintly against the streaks of violet, indigo, and emerald curling behind her ears.

Though her face bore the mask she'd worn since childhood—cool, still, untouchable—she could *feel* the way they watched her.

Every courtier. Every male. Prey in the presence of a predator.

Hundreds of males of every age, from every court, breathing in their first scent of an uncontrolled siren.

Serena didn't just walk like a queen's heir anymore. She *moved* like something older. Something primal. Graceful, effortless, with the unnatural fluidity of a creature that had been designed to lure, to beckon, to enthrall. Something born to rule. Her voice, when she gave her opening greeting to the court, was warm and low—and though it held no overt magic, it stilled the room like the moment before a predator pounced.

The music had already begun when the page whispered her cue.

She did not flinch.

She had been trained for this moment since she was old enough to hold a goblet without spilling it. But as she stood at the top of the staircase and stared down into the throng of nobles, envoys, generals, and scholars, she understood something new: this time, they were not here to judge her lineage or her poise. They were here to taste the power coiling beneath her skin. To inhale it like incense. To determine whether it thrilled or terrified them.

She descended like a queen.

Not fast. Not floating. Just enough grace to suggest she could glide if she wished to, enough danger to remind them that the blood in her veins was older than the palace itself.

Her gown had been chosen by decree—a tailored sheath of ocean-grey moonsilk that clung to her hips and exposed her collarbones, boned in silver and lined in silk. The faint shimmer at the hem caught every flicker of light. Her hair, left mostly down, tumbled in deliberate waves, the tell-tale streaks of siren lineage now undeniable. The tiara was from the treasury, an intricate working of moons and stars, diamonds and pearls, and in the center, a trident rising higher than the rest.

She did not look like a child anymore.

And the court could feel it.

The scent that rose from her skin was no perfume, though she'd bathed twice in mint and powder to try and muffle it. It came from beneath the skin, from the blood—roses after rain, crushed vanilla pods warmed by the sun, and the ache of sea salt in the wind. It was potent. Seductive. It rolled through the ballroom like smoke curling through cracks in a locked door.

She saw the effects immediately.

The ambassador from Ember blinked halfway through a sentence and lost the thread of his greeting. A Solace Court scholar dropped his pen when she walked past. One of the Shade nobles stared openly at her chest for too long before coughing into his sleeve and muttering something about the heat.

Some had been around when Elsibetha went through the transformation and had to learn to shield, but she was the cousin, not the Heir, her debut less important, so many more had not been there. Many courtiers were not as old as Mab, the last royal to inherit the siren abilities. Serena was their first exposure to the unshielded, uncontrolled siren scent.

She bore it with cold dignity.

But inwardly, she burned with discomfort. Not shame—she knew what she was, and Jormunder had taught her to be proud of it. She had earned every inch of power now dripping off her like perfume—but she hated how they looked at her. Not as a scholar, not as a warrior, not as the daughter of Edric and heir to Ardaion. As a prize to be caught, a danger to be avoided.

Some of the lords were hopeful that their sons might catch her eye or even an early mate bond might be triggered. And they plotted how best to use their upcoming time with her in their courts.

Serena kept her steps measured. Her voice was low. She responded to their offerings with the faintest smile, precise and unreadable. Her power was still coming in—rising like a tide—and even the most casual contact with it was disarming. Her Voice hadn't broken loose in public yet, but it was there, always there, humming like a second heartbeat at the base of her throat.

Graye hadn't been allowed to attend, but for her birthday he'd sent her the bracelet that Kriesta had helped him obtain from the Ember shops. For his gift, Serena had sent an ornate dagger with moonstones and the Crowned Crescent etched on the blade, the sigil of the Moon Court.

She meant it as a message that he at least, regardless of his father, was in favor. And she'd sent him a basket of the honeyed moon cakes they used to steal- enough for Rhune and Kade as well- and two stolen bottles of the best wine in the cellar that Graye had once called "mischief in a bottle."

Elsibetha stood near the western columns, dressed in her usual midnight Valkyrie leathers, eyes sharp, arms folded. She hadn't moved in half an hour. She didn't have to. She was already watching every male too slow to disguise his stare.

Serafine flanked the dais, impassive and silent in her veil and black robes. A few of the older courtiers still believed she was only a ceremonial escort. That fiction never lasted long. As was tradition, for the first time in her life, Serena ascended the steps to the top of that dais and sat on the throne. It would one day be hers.

It was large but elegant, set with crashing waves of gold and foams of pearl at the foot and along the sides, tridents at each back corner, and between them, the crescent moon of moonstone, girdled with a feminine crown- a queen's crown.

Serena sat with perfect posture, a neutral expression that never rested long on a single courtier, face framed with the amused detachment of royalty, and sovereign gaze of a siren queen. And in that moment she felt her destiny settle heavy on her shoulders. There would never be a farm with Graye somewhere no one could find them. There was only Ardaion, the crown, the empire.

The nobles applauded. Elsibetha grinned widely, proud of her. Serafine was behind her, the Shadowdancer protector of royalty. Jormunder stayed long enough to see the culmination of the festivities with deep paternal pride and a twinge of painful sentimentality at how alike Serena looked to her grandmother on that throne. Then he disappeared.

Somewhere in the east wing, Jormunder was moving through the palace like a storm. He'd spent the first hour of the evening in rigid silence at Serena's side, watching the nobles approach one by one, his hands always clenched just out of sight. When a minor lord from the Shade remnants had let his gaze wander during his greeting, Jormunder had stepped forward—not enough to interrupt, but enough to *loom.* The lord had nearly dropped his goblet.

Half an hour after that, Jormunder disappeared.

He had had enough of the hungry gazes. Mab had done nothing about it.

"Your blood runs in her veins!" he roared, voice echoing through half the east wing. "You *taught* Elsibetha- ten years under your hand- and you won't give this child even the bare minimum to protect herself? They were salivating, Mab!"

"She is not my student," Mab had growled coldly. "She is a mistake. One I'm not obligated to fix."

"She's your heir."

"She's your granddaughter. Your pet. Keep her away from me."

"She's in danger," he growled. "Her scent is rising. And you *know* what happens when a siren can't shield—"

"She should've died with her father."

The silence that followed nearly cracked the stones. Jormunder left without another word. He slammed the door hard enough to splinter the wood.

Mab glared at it in spite and waved a hand lazily to repair it.

And then she let her rage at being called out by her father get the better of her.

The debut was winding down.

Serena had endured it all, every bow and every veiled comment, every sidelong glance and caught breath. They could sense it on her now—raw magic rising in her like a tide, the unmistakable aura of the wellspring itself coiled with the siren's call. The weight of it had made the evening a drawn-out balancing act. Her shielding was far from complete. Elsibetha had done her best to teacher a little, but the effort of keeping her scent suppressed as she passed among fae males—nobles, warriors, emissaries—had drained Serena completely.

By the time she reached her rooms, she was fraying. Her skull throbbed with tension from the constant awareness of how tightly she had held herself, how every moment demanded perfection. Her dress, tailored in fitted panels, had been suffocating after the third hour. Her skin ached beneath it from how it clung, heavy with sweat and perfume, and still, despite all of it, her scent had broken through. She had seen it in their eyes. The way they lingered. The way they tried not to stare, pupils dilated, and failed.

The moment the door shut behind her, she exhaled. The sound came out shaky, almost a sob, though she hadn't meant it to. She didn't notice that the two guards normally stationed at her threshold were gone. She didn't stop to ask why the wards hadn't chimed when she passed through.

She just wanted to breathe.

She crossed to the vanity, pulled the pins from her hair one by one, and let the black and colored strands fall over her shoulders. The streaks of violet and green caught in the lamplight like oil on water. She was reaching to unfasten the back clasp of her gown when she heard the sound.

A footstep. Behind her.

She turned.

There was a male in her room.

Young. Around nineteen, perhaps. From Ember, she thought—one of the courtly hangers-on from the diplomatic wing. He had been introduced earlier that night, a minor noble's third son. He should not have been here. His jacket was unbuttoned, and his shirt stuck to his chest with sweat. His cheeks were flushed, his mouth half-open, pupils wide. He didn't speak.

He just prowled toward her.

Serena's stomach turned.

She backed up a step. "You shouldn't be in here."

He kept coming.

"Stop," she ordered, her voice firm now, even as her limbs stiffened.

He didn't stop.

His eyes were glazed, distant, glassy with lust and a kind of desperate, breathless awe. She realized then he wasn't seeing *her*. He was following the scent. Her scent. The lure. It had hooked him somewhere during the banquet and dragged him in like a net around his neck. His control was gone. He wasn't thinking.

He lunged.

She tried to dodge, but the gown restricted her legs. He caught her around the waist, pressing his mouth toward hers, panting, murmuring something incoherent about her scent, her beauty, her skin. She shoved at him and tried to get her arm between them, but her elbow was caught in the drape of her sleeve. She twisted, trying to drive her heel into his foot or shift her weight enough to throw him off.

His hand gripped the front of her dress and yanked it upward, fumbling, frantic.

She screamed. "Guards—!"

There was no answer.

Her pulse pounded in her ears. The ballgown wasn't meant for combat—it tangled her legs, caught at her ankles as she thrashed. Her training screamed at her to get low, pivot, and drive her knee into his gut, but everything was off-balance. She couldn't get a grip—the gown was heavy, the corset tight. She couldn't *breathe*. His hand was pushing against her inner thigh now, dragging the skirts higher. She slapped him hard enough to snap his head sideways.

He growled.

Growled.

Her lungs collapsed around a sob.

This wasn't practice. This wasn't sparring or drills or careful lectures about what to do. This was what Elsie had warned her about again and again. What she'd trained for in words but never in flesh. Her scent had pulled a predator straight to her, and her defenses were failing. She could have commanded him with the Voice but her throat was closed tight in fear.

He grabbed her wrist and yanked it down to pin it, his body pressing her back into the side of her bed.

Then she screamed—not for help this time.

Not for the guards.

Not even for herself.

Something inside her broke loose.

The sound wasn't a song. It wasn't a word. It wasn't even the Voice. It was *older*. It was a shriek from her blood, from the power of Ardaion itself, from the wellspring that throbbed beneath the palace stone. It tore from her throat and out into the world like a blade of pure will, slicing through the air with such force it made the lamps shudder on their chains.

And then the male was gone.

He didn't stumble.

He didn't fall.

He *ceased.*

In one heartbeat, he was trying to shove her down.

The next, he was a fine red mist.

It hung in the air, suspended for a long, awful moment like vapor on a still morning—across the carpet, the walls, the canopy of her bed, her dress, her *face*. Drops spattered the mirror. Bits of him decorated the floor in uneven flecks. There was no scream, nobody to cry out, no last breath.

Just silence.

And blood.

And the shaking figure of a girl—no, not a girl anymore—kneeling in the center of it, soaked and shaking and screaming, because the moment the scream began, it couldn't be stopped. It poured out of her in shrieks, and no one came fast enough to silence it. Her hands were covered. Her dress was ruined. Somewhere in the core of her being, something ancient pulsed with vicious satisfaction. *The siren, waking up.*

Her first kill.

And no one had taught her how to bear it.

The blast shook the east wing.

Walls didn't fall in the Moon Court. They were made of stone laced with magic older than most fae bloodlines, bound with silver thread and glyphs etched by the founders of Ardaion. But when Jormunder entered her chamber in full armor, fury like a tidal wave in his wake, the palace *felt* it.

He had come like a storm called from the bones of the realm, rage written into every step, his cloak torn from one shoulder, armor still dusted with blood from the hallway he'd walked through to get here. His wings filled the high ceilings with black shadow. His magic rolled off him in heat and pressure, war magic, old and unfiltered and pulsing with fury. Even the queen's attendants had scattered—without a command, without a scream.

And still, Mab had waited on her chaise with a goblet of pomegranate wine in hand, not even rising.

"I see she found her Voice," Mab said, sipping once, calm and glacial. "Rather loudly, from what I heard."

He didn't speak.

Not at first.

He lifted a hand and shattered the goblet in her hand without touching it. Shards of crystal rained over the marble. Wine dripped down her wrist like blood.

She rose then.

The force of his magic slammed into the walls. Furniture tore from the floor. A mirrored cabinet exploded. Glyphs flared along the baseboards, flickering and breaking under pressure. Mab didn't flinch as one of her portraits crashed to the floor in a burst of gilded frame and shattered glass.

"You lowered the wards," Jormunder's voice was low and shaking with fury. "You *dismissed the guards!*"

Mab's lips curled, not into a smile but something colder. "What's the problem, Father? I did what you asked- I taught her. I gave her incentive to learn and she learned fast didn't she?"

"You let her be *attacked*." The word cracked like a whip. "You exposed her knowing *exactly* what would happen."

"She learned, didn't she?" Mab's voice slipped into a hiss, fangs flashing beneath her calm. "She reacted. She *survived,*" Mab snarled, and now her magic rose to meet his, cold and coiling. "I've ruled for over a thousand years. I witnessed my mother *die* defending this realm. I buried a mate I loved more than my own life. Don't you dare tell me what it takes to raise a queen."

"I will *kill* you."

The words came so quietly certain that the room went still.

For a long moment, neither moved. Neither breathed. Power pressed outward from both of them, ancient, vast, father and daughter caught in a standoff that no one dared interrupt. He meant it. And she knew it.

Slowly, Mab sat.

The chaise was covered in shards. She didn't care. She poured herself a new glass of wine from a decanter that had miraculously remained standing.

"She's yours, then," she said, softly now. "Take her. Train her. Raise her. But do not bring her back to me. I will not look at her."

Jormunder stared at her with a kind of devastation that burned behind his fury. She knew he'd chosen his side.

"You don't deserve her," he said. "You never did."

And then he was gone.

The outer sentries froze when the wind shifted and the silhouette rose from the treeline like something conjured. Not marching. *Striding*. Black steel armor laced with silver runes that shimmered faintly with old power. Wings like storm banners unfurled to full span, trailing shadow where the air should've been still. He did not slow for the challenge. He did not lower his head for diplomacy. No one had seen the Black Dragon walk into Dardani land in over two centuries. Not even to negotiate war.

Now he came alone.

And no one stood in his way.

The first line of guards scrambled to alert their captains. The captains ran to their generals. But it was too late for hierarchy. Jormunder didn't need permission. The camp *parted* around him—soldiers scattering from his path like leaves from fire, veterans stepping aside with clenched jaws and bent heads. Every child raised on war stories knew that gait. That armor. That face was carved from years of blood and steel.

He was legend. He was nightmare.

He was not supposed to be *here*.

Graye stood half-armored, laughing with Kade and Rhune beside a late evening cookfire.

He didn't have to turn.

He *felt* it.

A presence like a thunderhead descending, pressure curling against his lungs.

He turned slowly.

Jormunder stood at the edge of the ring, still and seething. His eyes were like frost under a black sky. His jaw was locked in barely contained rage.

"Graye."

He didn't shout. He didn't need to.

Graye stepped forward, unsure whether to salute, bow, or speak. He opened his mouth. Jormunder raised one hand—*enough*.

"There's been an attack."

Graye froze.

"Serena needs you," Jormunder said, voice clipped. "A male attacked her in her chambers and she killed him. She's not hurt. Not physically. But she's not speaking, eating, or sleeping.

Kade stepped forward instinctively, a growl of fury rising in his throat. Rhune grabbed his arm but stepped forward as well, alert, ready to move on any orders given. Cold rage in his eyes. No one spoke.

Graye's chest rose with a long, shaking breath.

"If she needs me, I'm going," he said.

Jormunder didn't respond. He'd known.

He simply turned and drew the glyph into the air with one armored finger. The gate flared open in a rush of wind and magic, etched in glowing runes old enough to bypass Dardani wards entirely.

"Go."

And then he stepped through. Graye followed without hesitation.

Far away, in a palace soaked in moonlight and dread, a girl waited in silence, locked in a room scrubbed of blood but not memory.

Her general had gone to fetch her soul. And now it was coming home.

Serena's chamber door shut behind Graye with a finality that made the guards flinch—though they did not dare move. Jormunder's threat to them hung in the air like steel suspended mid-swing. No one in the Moon Palace would test it, not with the rage that had radiated from him like a heatwave, scorching everything in its path except the two children he had protected since birth.

The silks of her bedding barely rustled as she sat, upright but unmoving, her legs drawn beneath her, arms limp at her sides. She wore a robe of silk, the kind meant to comfort and soothe, but it might as well have been armor for how distant she looked. Her eyes—storm-grey and rimmed in red—stared into nothing, her face pale and drawn tight with a quiet that screamed louder than anything.

He didn't hesitate. His boots hit the polished stone without grace, still caked in dirt and dust from the Dardani war camps. His armor clattered as he crossed the room in three long strides and threw himself onto the bed beside her, not caring that he was soaked in sweat, grime, and the scent of iron.

He didn't ask permission. He didn't speak. He simply wrapped his arms around her and pulled her into him, locking her against his chest like he could keep the entire world from reaching her if he just held her tightly enough.

She shattered.

Her body collapsed against his like a puppet cut from its strings, her breath tearing loose in a jagged sob that broke something inside him. And then it kept coming—racking, breathless, gut-wrenching sounds that didn't pause, didn't lessen, just wave after wave crashing against his ribs as she wept. She clawed at his shoulders, buried her face into the curve of his neck, and trembled like the grief itself was hollowing her out.

Graye said nothing. He held her.

He stroked her hair—black and wild, still slightly damp from the forced cleansing the court healers had given her. His fingers curled protectively through the strands, his other hand gripping her back, holding her close with the kind of strength that dared anyone to try and take her away again.

Slowly, between sobs and gasped breaths, he coaxed fragments of the truth from her. Not in full sentences. Not even with clarity. Just broken pieces—how the guards had vanished, how the wards had failed, how she hadn't known he was in the room until it was too late. She tried to explain that she hadn't meant for it to happen, that she had sealed her scent so tightly for so long but it had slipped, for a second, long enough for him to smell her blood.

Then the look in the boy's eyes.

That hollow, glazed hunger. The reaching hands. The voice gone slack and empty, speaking without understanding, lust without thought, instinct without soul. The Thrall had taken him. Serena, cornered and afraid, had screamed—with her Voice, and with her power.

The scream hadn't just stopped him.

It had unmade him.

There had been no body to mourn over. No bones left to bury. Just a cloud of blood mist hanging in the air and the high keening of a girl who no longer trusted the walls of her room.

The moment he understood—truly understood—his vision darkened at the edges.

She had been alone.

Mab had removed her guards. Deliberately. Lowered her wards. Deliberately. And Mab had refused to teach how to control her siren heritage. Graye's stomach turned with each new fragment. Pure rage.

Her scent told him everything, or rather, the lack of it. She smelled like *nothing*. No fear. No grief. No sweat or skin or heat. Not even her usual intoxicating rose-vanilla whisper. Only an emptiness so sharp it cut. She had sealed herself completely, shut down everything instinctive and animal and female until she was a void.

Then it hit him.

She wasn't afraid of the male.

She was afraid of herself.

Of the power in her blood. Of the scent she'd barely begun to understand. Of the sheer obliterating violence that had exploded from her without warning. Of what she could *do* now, unintentionally, simply by being alive in the wrong room, with the wrong person.

It wasn't guilt. It wasn't shame.

It was *horror*.

Graye stroked her hair gently, slowly, as if each motion might pull her back from that edge. The once-glossy black strands had started to dry now, tangled from sweat and crying, the faintest shimmer of indigo still catching in the faelight from the sconces.

And as he held her, his mind flashed back.

Back to the morning she woke to her fangs. She'd only been fifteen. She'd whispered, *"I'm a monster."*

He hadn't known what to say back then. Only sat beside her and held her just like this.

Now, the horror was deeper. Real. Lived.

Now at sixteen, she had *killed* someone. With sheer power.

"You didn't choose this," he whispered finally, his voice rasping and low. "You didn't lure him. You didn't ask for this."

But Serena didn't reply. Her face remained pressed into his chest, breath shallow and ragged.

Graye shifted slightly, enough to cup the back of her neck and rest his chin in her hair. He couldn't fix this. Couldn't undo what had happened or take away the image of the blood mist or the stench of raw death that surely still lingered somewhere in her mind. But he could stay. He could hold.

And he could *hate* Mab.

He could let that hatred calcify into something clean and cold and final.

Because the moment Mab went from strategic negligence to calculated cruelty, from silence to active sabotage, she had miscalculated. She had mistaken his loyalty for something bendable, his bond with Serena for something conditional. She had thought he would be grateful. He would play her Shade Court puppet, rising in favor, and becoming the next political tool.

But Graye knew at that moment—with Serena sobbing in his arms and her scent sealed away in terror—that whatever compliant future Mab had imagined for him was gone.

She had lost him.

Forever.

He kissed Serena's head and said "Rest, Sev. You need to sleep. There are guards outside, your room is warded, and I'll stay awake all night. I'll stay right here. Whenever. Wherever. Always."

CHAPTER TEN
INVASION

Delivered by Moon Court courier hawk, sealed in black wax with the sigil of Shade quartered in silver.

Sev,

I'm writing this from a camp just outside the Frost border. The river's swollen from melt and the tents are half-sinking in slush, but Kade insists on calling it "good weather for killing," which is how you know he's lost whatever was left of his civility. Rhune's quieter, as always, though he doesn't sleep much anymore. He's been helping with the strategies lately and the bastard is smart. I don't sleep much either. It's not fear. It's something else. Like waiting for a coin to drop but never hearing the clink.

We're safe—for now. The last skirmish was six days ago. A group tried to cross at dusk near the old merchant road. They moved too clean for raiders, too coordinated for wanderers. Full armor, no colors. No banners. They carried nothing of value and took nothing when they burned the outposts. Just left bodies behind. That's what struck me. They didn't want anything. Not supplies. Not coin. Just control.

We brought down eight. Rhune spotted them first, and Kade and I flanked. It was fast—louder than we wanted, but clean. They were good. Trained. Not like the ones we used to run from in games. Not like the stories. These men had formation, signals, and tactics. We had to kill them to stop them. There was no other way. They didn't speak. Didn't surrender.

We all drew blood that day. Kade with a gut shot. Rhune with a blade to the throat. I took mine from behind. I thought I'd feel something—shame, horror, pride, anything. But I kept moving. Only later did the weight come, hours after the body had cooled. It wasn't grief. Just... a piece of silence I haven't shaken since. I thought about you and how you must have felt.

I keep replaying the way they moved. Their gear's not scrap. It's forged. Not proof, not yet. But the patterns are there, Sev. These aren't random incursions. This is a method. Someone's feeding these strikes with coin, armor, and maps. I'm starting to suspect whose coffers are paying for it.

I won't accuse him—not in this letter, not without proof—but I'm watching. Waiting. And when the name behind the steel is finally spoken, I want you to hear it from me, not from a court crier. I won't lie to you. Not ever.

You'd laugh if you saw me now. My armor doesn't shine. My hair's always half-matted, and I smell like smoke, iron, and whatever soup the Ember cooks call food. I miss you.

I'll be home for festival week if the border holds. I'll bring you something ridiculous—maybe another gryphon feather, though the last nearly got Rhune clawed in the face. You'll like him, Sev. He watches everything. Quiet, but not because he's shy. Because he's measuring things. He sees more than he says. He insisted on being the one who got that feather. Kade's more like me, if I'd been born louder and lacked shame. One day you'll all meet each other.

Until then—hold steady. Watch your back. And if you ever need me, you write me, and I'll come, no matter the cost.

Always, G

The letter had been sent a month before. Before the sky split open over Ardaion's western ridges. Before borders stopped meaning anything at all.

At the time, the warnings still wore masks—armor with no crest, tactics with no flag. Graye's words had been filled with tension, yes, but not finality. He had wondered. Suspected. Even feared. But he had not *known*.

Now, the knowing came with blood. With ash. With the smell of scorched earth and the unmistakable sound of Shade steel carving through Ember soil. There was no longer ambiguity. No more silent games. The Court of Shade had declared war.

It began with fire and shadows.

Not Ember fire—the kind that renews, burns clean, and leaves behind fertile ground. This was a thieving, hungering thing. The kind of fire lit in taverns and granaries, in stables and storehouses. Villages near the border vanished overnight, their inhabitants fleeing into the caves, into the cliffs, only to be hunted there by soldiers wearing black helms and riding hard. There were no demands made. No treaties torn. Shade did not open the war with a declaration.

They opened it with looting. With marching columns. With flame. With consuming darkness that blotted the light and left only the screams of those trapped inside it, their bodies were found mauled by unknown creatures once the darkness moved on.

By the time word reached the capital of Ember, the Dardani war horns were already sounding in the passes. Riders came in threes, armor not even fastened properly before taking flight again. Their messages were grim: Shade had breached the southern ridge, moving not like a raiding force but an *army*—organized, equipped, and aimed directly at the heart of Ember.

Aegin, Lord of Ember, did not wait for council approval. He mounted the high steps of the Pyra Citadel himself, overlooking the redstone terrace where the commanders assembled, and in one breath, called every Dardani flight and every Ember-born warrior to arms. The call rang not as a plea but as a vow: *the capital will not fall. The mountains will not be taken. We are the forge that made the world—let it test us.*

It was the kind of speech passed into legend.

And Graye should have stood beside him.

He should have stood flanked by Rhune and Kade, Dardani pauldrons buckled over his shoulders, weapons oiled and wings stretched wide. He should have answered the call with the loyalty he'd earned over a decade living among Ember's cliffs, training in their passes, learning their rhythms. He should have flown with the brothers he bled beside and earned his name the same way they would. He should have been able to choose his court.

But Aegin didn't give him the chance.

The morning the army formed ranks, when squadrons lined the canyon floor and took to the sky with flames burning across their spear tips, Aegin summoned Graye to the high chamber beneath the Pyra Citadel. Guards stood flanking the doorway, stone-faced, swords drawn—not ceremonial. And in that moment, Graye realized. Before a word had been said.

"You're not going to let me fight," his voice hollow.

Aegin turned from the war table, his expression unreadable beneath the harsh lines of flame-forged light. "No," he said simply. "You're too valuable."

Graye's hands clenched into fists. "I trained beside them. I bled beside them. I know this terrain better than Shade's commanders. I can help—"

"You're the heir to Shade," Aegin cut in. "The only person your father cares about."

Graye's breath caught, enough to betray the crack in his armor.

Aegin stepped forward, his tone hard. "If we put you in the sky, you become a martyr. If we put you in chains, you become leverage."

"So that's it?" Graye spat. "You'll threaten to kill me so he turns back?"

"We won't kill you," Aegin said, but his voice was quiet now. "Unless we must. I've always thought well of you."

The chains were ceremonial—draped gold links meant to signal his status without binding him. But the message was clear to every soldier as he was led through the corridors of the Pyra Keep and placed in the cell overlooking the canyon floor.

Shade touches this capital, and their prince dies.

It worked—at least in part. The main assault line halted, then fractured, splintering as Shade's forces hesitated. Confusion bloomed across the enemy lines. Not enough to stop the war. But enough to let Ember strike first. The Dardani flew like thunder, their wings black against the sun, spears gleaming, fire trailing their blades like banners.

They dropped like meteors from the clouds and split the invading forces wide. Rhune's sword was seen cleaving through two soldiers in one sweep. Half Ember, half Shade, Rhune fought not from loyalty to a court but to his brothers in arms. Kade, reckless and bright-eyed, even as the blood sprayed his armor.

The battle lasted four days.

By the end, the Ember capital had held. The passes remained theirs. The war bands of Shade scattered, retreating toward the basin.

But Jaryk had not come for the capital alone.

While the front lines were mired in chaos, a smaller force had peeled away—fast, surgical, cutting a path toward Ember's inner holdings. Toward the manor where Kriesta, once Lady of Shade and now the longtime guest of Ember, had taken refuge with her young daughter, Lyra.

Graye did not hear of it until after.

They had gone with soldiers- Kriesta under duress, Lyra screaming, both of them gagged and bound for transport through the cliffs. The route was old, a smugglers' path beneath the ridge, long forgotten except by the court who first mapped it. Jaryk himself had been at the rear, ensuring their capture held.

He got no farther than the second bend before the trap sprung.

An Ember mage waited in the shadowed rockfall, determined to end Jaryk's scheming once and for all. No warning. No herald. Just a fire comet, raw and bright and brutal, detonating through the air like a thrown sun.

The blast reached them before they could flee.

The soldiers guarding Kriesta and Lyra were vaporized instantly. So was half the cliff wall. The screams from burned survivors came second.

When the smoke cleared, there was nothing left to retrieve.

Not even bones.

Jaryk survived—shielded by distance, some said by luck, others by a spellbreaker's ward tattooed along his neck. He fled with the remnants of his force, retreating down the canyon without victory, without prisoners, and without the only three people in Ardaion he'd ever kept close enough to name family.

Ember did not chase him.

They didn't need to.

The loss had carved itself into the story already, etched in flame along every inch of the sky above the Pyra cliffs.

And Graye—kept from the field, locked in stone with nothing but silence and a narrow view of smoke trails—learned the truth secondhand.

A courier brought the report. He read it in the dark.

He didn't speak for hours.

When the guards came to retrieve the tray from outside his door the next morning, it was untouched. The gold links had been folded neatly and placed on the cot. Graye sat in the corner, bare-armed, bare-chested, his wings spread and still, his eyes locked on a point far beyond the mountain.

He had not fought.

He had not saved them.

And now Shade was broken. Ember was mourning. Guilt ate at him. He'd kept his suspicions about Shade between himself and Serena, he'd been right, and his mother and sister were dead.

The gate opened in a whisper, not a roar—a ripple through the high air of the Sio-rain peaks, barely visible against the brilliance of the noon sun. The wards shimmered once, then parted, and Elsibetha stepped through first, her boots crunching against the frost-kissed path of the mountain retreat. Graye followed, armorless now, wings cloaked in a long travel coat, eyes sunken but alert. Serena emerged last, her expression unreadable, her dark hair braided with surgical precision, not a strand out of place. Not out of vanity, but control.

Always control.

The cabin stood half-enshrouded by pines and glacier-fed mist, an elegant structure of silverwood and etched stone, its arched windows gleaming with moon-glass panes. It was not large by Moon Court standards, but it exuded power all the same—quiet, old, and mostly unused since the days when Tatiana and Jormunder had brought their two children here for midday swims and long, strategy-filled picnics.

Jormunder had brought Serena and Graye a few times in childhood, summer adventures that seemed a lifetime ago. Now, the cabin had become neutral ground. A holding place for grief. And, perhaps, for reckoning.

Elsibetha scanned them both—her eyes missing nothing, though she said little. "The wards are secure. The enchantments will answer your needs. The pantry restocks by spellcall; don't test the limits or it may think you are unworthy of food. You've three days. The High Court will call when judgment is passed."

Neither Serena nor Graye replied.

Elsie gave them a long look—the kind that tried to unweave their silence—and then, sensing no welcome, nodded once, and vanished into the gate, leaving them with the hush of wind and the groan of pine.

They didn't speak until the front door closed behind them.

Graye walked the length of the main room slowly, taking in the stone hearth, the long lounges stacked with woven blankets, and the tall bookshelves, still dustless from the last enchantment sweep. The warmth from the spring-fed hearth hummed beneath the floor. Beyond the archway to the back terrace, steam curled upward from the carved pool where mineral-rich water still flowed from the mountain's vein.

He looked older than his years. Not with time, but with weight. His wings had not shed their grief-soaked tension. His hands—long, elegant, once clumsy in sword drills—now bore calluses. He had fought. He had bled. But he'd been trapped while his mother and sister burned.

Serena sat down first. Not in a chair, but on the stone ledge by the fire, drawing her knees up as she had done since childhood. Her robes were thick, travel-cut, and still laced. She hadn't unfastened them. She wasn't sure she wanted to.

"Did you know?" she asked after a long stretch of silence. Not accusing. Not soft. Just quiet.

Graye's jaw tensed. "Not then."

Serena looked at the fire. "But you suspected."

"Yes."

She nodded once, slowly. "Why didn't you tell me?"

"I did," he said. "In the letter. I just didn't say it out loud."

She pressed her lips together, not angry, but brittle. "You told me you had doubts. But not that you thought he'd start a war."

"I didn't think he would," Graye sighed. "I thought he'd push. Bribe. Maybe send forces to test the borders and back away. But not a full-scale invasion. He didn't have the forces to pull that off, especially against the Dardani."

A silence stretched between them—sharp, fragile, as if the air itself were afraid to settle.

Serena exhaled. Her voice was a ribbon now, frayed at the edges. "Kriesta died protecting Lyra. That's what they said. Tried to shield her. As if she could. Magefire burns straight through."

Graye swallowed. "I didn't even get to choose a side."

"I know."

"They told me to sit in a tower like a bargaining chip while the people I loved burned."

"I know," she said again, but more softly this time.

He walked to the window. Outside, the mist coiled through the tree trunks. The wind caught the steam rising off the hot spring pool and flung it sideways in silken streams. He stared out over the ledge, at the peaks that framed the valley below. The same view they'd stared at as children. The same slope Jormunder had once pointed to, saying *This is where the high wind comes from—watch the trees bow to it, but never break.*

He turned. "She was more of a mother to you than yours ever was."

"I know. I loved her," Serena whispered.

They both sat for a long time after that, the fire crackling, the scent of snow and mineral spring curling through the space. Eventually, it was Graye who stood and moved to the table where a carafe of water appeared the moment he touched the polished moonstone surface. He poured two glasses.

"She's not doing this out of mercy," he said, handing one to Serena and gesturing around at the cabin.

"No. Mab never does anything for mercy."

"She wants me back under her thumb," Graye muttered, voice like smoke. "You know as well as I do my father will be found guilty by the high court. Mab's playing at being gracious. Giving us this—" He gestured around the cabin. "—so it looks like she's a queen offering sanctuary, not a spider watching two flies tie themselves to her web."

Serena sipped the water. Then said quietly, "And yet here we are."

There was no malice in it. No accusation. Just truth.

He set his glass down, paced a few steps, then stopped beside her. Not quite touching. But near.

"I would've fought for them, Sev. I swear it. For Ember. For my mother. For everything they gave me. But I wasn't given the choice. They made me into a hostage before I could even lift a blade."

"I know. But perhaps it's better this way. You're the heir of Shade, and you were spared fighting against them."

He looked at her then—really looked. At the grey eyes rimmed in weariness. At the faint traces of loss etched into her mouth. At the curve of her spine where she'd drawn herself inward, as she used to after Mab's colder silences.

And he realized—she'd grown more silent again. Not emotionally, not distant. But deeper. More internal.

"I don't think we realized," she said after a while, "when we made our little decisions—sending the letters, asking the questions, *not* telling anyone—we didn't realize how far the ripples would go. We made choices and now we have to live with them."

They stood like that, the air thick with everything unspoken. Regret. Ache. The subtle shift of two children who had grown into their consequences before they were ready.

He reached for her hand.

She let him.

They stayed like that until the sun began to set, the mist turning gold and lavender against the mountain ridges. The warmth of the spring outside beckoned, the spell pool already beginning to glow faintly with bioluminescence as the water rippled against stone.

It would be another hour before they changed and slipped into it. Another hour before she let him see the lines the tears had carved down her cheeks. Before he admitted, quietly, that he dreamed of the blast. He woke to Lyra's scream and vomited.

But for now, they stood in the home that had once belonged to a queen who'd died defending the realm, and a general who'd raised them both to be more than what their bloodlines demanded.

They began, slowly, to let grief do what grief does best:

Draw two broken pieces together, not to heal them...

But to make sure they did not break alone.

CHAPTER ELEVEN

PHILOSOPHIZING

The morning light over the Siorain peaks had the clarity of melted crystal, gold laced with blue and edged in frost. The air was scented with pine bark and old stone, and beneath the wind's quiet hush through the balcony's carved arches, the natural hot springs gurgled lazily in the rocks below.

The second-floor terrace had been enchanted generations ago by one of Tatiana's favored mages—a spell woven into the stone to chase away the mountain chill without dulling the air's crispness or muting the way it carried sound. It had been one of Jormunder's gifts to her, a way to let her take her morning tea outdoors even in the snow.

Now, two others sat in the warmth it offered, wrapped in furs and quiet routine.

They had taken breakfast already, shared wordlessly and without courtly pretense. Now they lay curled together on the oversized chaise—stuffed with down, draped in thick velvet and fur throws, angled toward the rising sun. Facing each other, Serena and Graye sat cross-legged, one of his arms resting against the chair's back, the other raised with concentration as he tried to mimic the glyph she was tracing through the air between them.

It shimmered in his wake—a lock glyph, deceptively simple in concept, but frustratingly intricate in its curves. It required stability of pressure, even tempo, and the ability to direct one's power like a thread through spinning glass.

He didn't have formal training. He had been barred from the mage tower training by Mab. His powers grew almost as strong and fast as Serena's, and yet the knowledge to use them remained at an innate, instinctive level- no advanced, studied magery. Still, his powers with fire and the mind, blinking from place to place, and flinging opponents out of the ring were formidable.

Serena refused to let him fall behind. She taught him. As much as she could. Whatever she was learning, she shared.

Spells. Glyphs. Political theory. War doctrine. Runes and rotations, high etiquette, and the sharp math of diplomacy. How to hold a quill like a diplomat, dance like a prince, and his gaze like a sovereign.

He pressed too hard on the glyph's crescent again. Serena reached out and adjusted his wrist with two fingers—gentle, exact. "Too sharp. It's not a cut. It's a seal."

Graye gave her a wry look. "I thought the point of a lock was to keep people *out*."

"Only if you're a brute," she replied, smirking faintly. "A good lock waits quietly, lets the intruder come in halfway... and *then* denies them. Trap first, wall second."

He drew the glyph again. This time, it clicked softly into the air, and the balcony doors behind them sealed with a whisper of finality.

"Well done," she said, watching the glyph fade. "That would hold even against a half-decent tower-trained caster."

Graye leaned back, one brow arched. "Would it hold *you* out?"

She didn't dignify that with a real answer. Just arched a brow in return, coolly, "Nothing holds me out if I want in."

He laughed, the sound quiet and tired and warmer than most of his had been lately, "says the brute". The laugh faded into a long silence—companionable, unspoken. The kind of silence that didn't need filling. The wind stirred the scent of pine and hot spring minerals through the air. They listened to it as if it carried answers.

Then Serena, in her way, turned the conversation toward shape and consequence.

"You know," she said, lightly, though not without intention, "you'll be a lord long before I ever wear a crown."

He didn't answer. She went on.

"You've never really lived in your court. Shade is a name on your signet, not a memory in your blood. You trained in Ember. You were forged by the Dardani. You don't know the rhythms of the people you're meant to lead, and they don't know *you*."

He remained still, watching her.

"And depending on what Mab does to your father... " she didn't have to say the rest. Everyone knew Jaryk's position was at the brink. "You might not even have much of a court left. Or gold. You could inherit the name of Shade and little else."

He exhaled slowly but said nothing yet.

Serena's voice softened. "So you need to figure it out, Graye. What you feel about the court you trained in for a decade, and the one you were born to. Because whatever Mab decides for your father now, she already decreed *you* would take over once you came of age."

A silence settled over them. Not cold. Reflective.

Graye shifted, drawing one knee up and resting an arm across it. He stared out at the treetops, the misted ridges. His face was unreadable for a long moment.

"I'll fix it," he said at last. Quiet, but certain. "Break what doesn't serve. Reinforce what does."

It was a Dardani answer. Blunt. Decisive.

Serena gave him a dry look. "And what does *serve* mean? Serve *you*? Serve your image of Shade? Or the people who have to live there when your banners are raised?"

He realized she was in one of her philosophizing moods. She could get existential and ponder the meaning of anything but she usually always circled back to power and rulership. Neither of them knew she'd inherited that from Edric.

He turned to her and smirked faintly. "All of it. Eventually."

She huffed softly. "So a benevolent tyrant."

"I prefer *decisive visionary*."

"Of course you do."

She watched him. Saw the shape of the answer settle into his shoulders. "You sound like your father."

At that, his expression flickered—just slightly. The jaw tensed, the mouth thinned. But he didn't look away.

"My father ruled with fear. And ambition and silence. I don't want that. But I *do* think power should mean something. And if we're the ones who carry it—" His voice lowered. "Then we should *use* it. Not sit in palaces and let others rot because protocol says not to interfere."

Serena exhaled, long and slow. "That's the temptation, isn't it? That we know better. That we can fix it. But where's the line between fixing and ruling by force?" She looked at him now, more intently. "Where's the line between power and tyranny?"

He didn't blink. "The line is in the why."

She tilted her head, studying him as he continued.

"My father ruled to *keep*. Your mother rules to *punish*. But us? We'd rule to *change*. And the ones who benefit will know who gave it to them."

Serena studied him, expression unreadable.

"You'd crush Shade to the bone," she said. "Reforge it in your image."

He didn't deny it.

"And if Mab does the same to your father," she added, "does that make her right?"

"No," he corrected. "Because she'd do it alone, for her ends, not the people's."

That surprised her—not because it wasn't true, but because she hadn't expected him to say it out loud. He wasn't wrong. Mab ruled with no voice but her own. She hoarded knowledge. She controlled. She manipulated. She played her games of power from a throne woven with silken blades.

Graye, for all his pride, had always listened. Had always let Serena argue. Had always let her teach. She made him think.

She looked at him then, truly looked—at the calloused hands, the quiet certainty, the boy she had grown with and the man he was slowly becoming.

"You'll need allies," she said softly. "Not just soldiers."

He didn't hesitate. "I have one."

He reached across and took her hand, warm and steady.

"You've already taught me to stand," he said. "Now you'll teach me how not to fall."

"I'll try. But even if you do, I'll always catch you, Graye."

The breath of pine was in the air. Their bond pulsed with warmth, affection, and the familiar fierce loyalty.

And the way their hands fit perfectly together—two pieces of power still deciding what they would shape the world into.

Graye went quiet, his hand still loosely clasping Serena's, thumb absently stroking along the ridge of her knuckle. He was watching her now—more closely than usual. He always did when she went still like this, like she'd dropped out of the world entirely and into one of her thoughts that wrapped like ivy and never had just one answer.

"You're turning it over again," his voice low.

Serena didn't deny it. She shifted slightly in the chaise, not drawing away, but curling more inward, her cheek resting on her bent knee, her gaze angled toward the mountainside where mist clung to the cliffs like secrets that didn't want to lift.

"I've been thinking," she murmured, "about where power comes from. Not just mine. All of it. Yours, mine, the Courts, the towers, the old bloodlines... what we inherit versus what we choose. How to rule well."

Graye tilted his head. "You're never not thinking about that."

But she didn't smile. Not this time.

"Mab trained Elsibetha," she said quietly, "before the wars, before the fallout. Taught her the rites, the songs, the voice control. How to use siren abilities *properly*. What to *do* when the scent slips. All of it. But me?" She gave a short breath of a laugh that didn't touch her eyes. "Nothing. Not one ritual. Not one lesson. Not even a warning. I was trained in what every Heir of Ardaion is trained in—court diplomacy, Battle Magery, the language of law and glyphs—but nothing of *what* I am. Nothing of the sirens."

Graye's brow furrowed slightly. He didn't interrupt.

"She hates me too much," Serena sighed. "I've spent years in the palace, in the mage tower, in the war camps—and I still don't know what it *means* to be a siren. I don't know the chants. I've never danced the rituals. I've never heard the songs of our people around a beach bonfire. Elsie has taught me what she could, but she's just one siren and culturally we're a sisterhood. I'm shaped by it—my voice, my body, the scent—but I'm not *connected* to it."

Graye shifted, his hand tightening slightly in hers.

"I've been thinking of going to the Tides Court," she said. "Mab promised all the courts I'd spend time with them anyway, so why not Tides first? The Mer still keep the old ways. The full-bloods—sirens, nymphs, the sprites that hunt through kelp beds—they still *remember*. They have music. Belief. They don't treat it like shame. I could stay near the water, study under the old speakers, the women who still sing the deep. I just... I need some distance from Siorai. From the blood mist. From what happened in my rooms."

She glanced at him then, eyes shadowed. "I need to understand if I'm dangerous."

"You're not."

"I killed someone, Graye."

"He was enthralled. And he would've—" He stopped himself. She didn't need the rest of the sentence.

"I didn't *mean* to enthrall him. I didn't even *know* the scent had slipped. And if I ever bit someone with these fangs—what happens then? Will I crave their blood? Will I turn mindless as the stories say? What happens if I *like* it? No one's ever told me. I'm an orphan from my parents and my sisters, my people."

Graye was quiet again. Not because he didn't have thoughts. But because he sensed—rightly—that she needed to finish.

"I don't even know if someone could ever love me," the words spoken into the wind, barely audible. "What if the Thrall is always in the way? If my scent or my kiss or my voice mean they never had a choice? How will I *ever* know if it was real?"

There it was—the quiet horror beneath all her command, her precision, her restraint. Not the fear of her power, but the fear that it made her unlovable. No matter how regal she became, how skilled, how composed, none of it would matter if the only intimacy she ever received was a *spell*, not a choice.

It was a deeply buried legacy of Mab's rejection, that fear of rejection. Of not being enough.

Graye sat back, studying her. The girl who had once stolen mooncakes and jumped on a gryphon, who now sat wrapped in ancestral silence, the blood of queens in her veins, the scent of desire woven into her skin like armor she never asked for. He looked at her then not as the heir, not as the weapon, but as the girl who had cried against his chest in silk robes and said *I'm afraid of myself.*

"You're not a monster," he said again, with more weight this time.

"You don't know that."

"I do."

"You've never felt it. The instincts. The way I sometimes feel..."

That made him pause.

There was a flicker in his eyes—curiosity, recklessness, something sharper too. He'd seen the stories and heard the whispers. About the kiss. The bite. The voice. About what it did to males—how it drove them to their knees or into madness. And now, almost seventeen, battle-blooded and golden with strength, part of him wondered what it would be like. Just a taste. Just enough to understand. To *prove* to her it wasn't something to fear.

"Then maybe you should show me," he challenged, almost lazily.

Her head turned sharply. "What?"

"You said no one's ever shown you how to fully control it. How it works. Maybe that's part of it—you're afraid because it's unknown. So make it known. On me."

She narrowed her eyes. "You want me to test it on you? That's..." Her chin was already unconsciously jerking in a negative because it wasn't worth the risk.

He shrugged. "You trust me. I trust you. And maybe it helps to know you *can* stop it. That you won't lose yourself. You won't lose *me*."

Trying to deflect, her voice cooled. "Is this about Rhune and Kade? Want a story to take back? Something about how the heir of Ardaion made you want to rut like a beast?"

He had the decency to flush, faintly.

"Not entirely," he admitted. "But no. This isn't about them. This is about *you*. You're terrified of your power, Sev. And I think it's time you weren't."

She stared at him. Silent. Then, after a long pause, she said quietly, "You don't understand. This isn't like a spell. This is blood-deep, control of mind and body. The Thrall doesn't listen to reason. It turns a kiss into a compulsion. Turns a drop of blood into *worship*. You will *want* me. And what if you fall into it? What if you don't come back?"

"I will."

"You don't know that."

He met her gaze evenly. "You're the only one I'd trust to show me. Let's just try it."

The balcony had never felt so large.

Ten feet of polished stone and charm-forged rails lay between them, but to Serena, it might as well have been a canyon. She stood near the balustrade, back straight but arms folded tightly across her middle as if trying to hold herself together by sheer force of will.

Graye was across from her, near the other edge, hands in the pockets of his trousers, posture easy, a smirk on his mouth, but eyes very much fixed on her. He wasn't naive; he was alert, heart racing a bit but like tides was he going to show it- to let her think for a minute he was nervous or afraid of her. He concentrated on projecting calm.

They had agreed on the distance. She had insisted on it—*at least* ten feet, and even then she wasn't sure it was enough. Her shield had never been partially dropped before. She had never learned the technique, only the brute force method of slamming her power outward to cut herself off from everything. Lowering it delicately, letting the scent seep through in a controlled release—that was something the sirens of Tides taught their daughters. Something Mab had taught Elsie. Not something Serena had ever been granted.

But she was trying.

For him.

To her, Graye's expression was calm, but his gaze was sharp—watchful. He wasn't mocking, wasn't teasing. He wasn't grinning like a boy who thought himself brave. But he also hadn't seen the boy in her room. Hadn't seen the clawing hands, the blood mist. The way the walls and floors had been painted with it.

She had. And it had never left her. But what had never left him was the sound of her sobs against his chest, the way she trembled... the self-loathing.

"You sure?" she asked, voice tight, breath catching in her throat. She hated how small she sounded.

He nodded, gaze steady. "I trust you."

She looked away, jaw flexing. "Don't. Not with this."

Still, he didn't move. "I do."

The words hit something deep in her chest. A bruise or a blessing—she couldn't tell. She looked back at him then, truly looked. He was leaner than he'd been a year ago, hardened by training, bronzed by the Ember sun, and older in his eyes than any nineteen-year-old should be. But there was still *him* in there. Still her boy, her shadow, her twin in everything that mattered.

He gave her a small nod. "Let me breathe it. That's all."

She exhaled—slow, trembling. Closed her eyes.

Not too much, she told herself. *Just a crack. Just enough to slip the scent into the wind.*

She reached inward, to the part of her power coiled behind her ribs. Iron bars locked around the smell of siren. It was bone-deep and older than the palace stone. It was hunger and seduction, moonlight and tide. It was the predator's purr. The siren's lure.

And with a single mental shift—*open*—she let the shield slip.

Graye didn't feel it at first. The breeze brought nothing but mountain air and pine.

Then it hit.

Softly at first. Like the memory of a scent. Rose and vanilla. Musk and sea salt. A whiff of sunlight on warm skin, of moonlit water, of *her.*

Pleasant. Calming.

Then it deepened. The hook buried itself beneath his sternum, subtle and slow. His heart kicked. Breath shortened. Every hair on his arms rose as if she had touched him. Heat unfurled low in his belly, sharp and liquid.

He wanted, *burned,* to cross the distance. To be near her. To *touch* her. It wasn't carnal, not immediately. It was *longing.* As if she were warmth in winter. As if his soul would starve if he didn't get closer. As if he'd do anything, be anything, to make her smile.

But it was becoming *need.* His body was responding. His gaze turned to her lips then lower...

Across from him, Serena's arms had dropped. Her stance had shifted—no longer coiled in fear, but rigid in restraint. She was watching him, braced stiffly as if expecting him to come charging at her.

He knew the line. Aware that if he stepped forward even once, she might panic. She'd never trust herself again if this went too far. And he'd never do anything to make her doubt herself, or him.

But *gods,* it felt good.

"Graye?" Her voice was smaller now. Worried.

He clenched his fists at his sides, focusing on the feeling of fingernails pressing into his skin. Pain helped. A little.

"You can put it up now," he said, voice rough, but calm. Then a tiny bit more forcefully "Sev, put it up."

She didn't hesitate. She *slammed* the shield back into place.

The air cleared, and the scent carried away on the light breeze. The hook was gone. His body shook as if the magic had been a tether cut mid-pull. He kept a smile plastered on his face, panting softly. Sweat beaded at his brow. Every part of him still ached in *absence.*

She didn't move. Still staring, assessing, and the growing length of his silence was pushing her mind to invasion scenarios. *It was too much. I scared him. He's afraid of me.*

But he straightened, breathing harder now, and made sure—*utterly sure*—his voice was even when he said:

"I'm fine. It was strong. But I'm fine."

"You almost—" she started, choked.

"But I didn't."

He crossed to her slowly, and she took a step back as if to prolong the distance, his safety.

When he reached her, he didn't pull her in. Just stood before her. Close. Steady. Warm.

"You didn't lose control," he said. "You didn't let it take me. You chose. You *stopped.*"

She trembled then—not from power, but from fear breaking loose now that the moment had passed.

And when he finally did touch her, it was only her hand, and gently. No heat. No hunger. Just *truth.*

"You're not a monster," he whispered again.

But she didn't believe it.

Not yet.

He was still holding her hand. The air had cleared but not completely. Something of hers still clung to it—like an afterimage on the tongue, like a scent caught in the folds of memory rather than the wind. She stood so still she might have been carved of ice, save for the slight tremble in her shoulders, the taut rise and fall of her chest as if she were fighting back something unnamable. Shame, maybe. Fear, certainly. And more than either—desperation. Not for him, but *from* him, to hold her together.

She'd gone rigid, locked in a full brace, the way she sometimes did after a nightmare, or her mother looked at her too long.

His gaze dropped, and there they were—her fangs. She hadn't noticed them. She never did. Small, delicate, almost pretty in the way deadly things could be—like the curve of a dragon's claw or the shimmer of venom on a blade. They looked charming, disarmingly so. The kind of detail a painter would add to a seductress on a mural wall, some blood myth of beauty and danger.

But he knew better. They were a lie. Those fangs were the legacy of her ancestors—the instruments of power, of the Thrall, of the pull she feared more than any enemy blade. They weren't a quirk of biology. They were the inheritance of a predator. Aesthetics balanced with razor sharpness.

And still, he didn't flinch.

Maybe that was why he said it. Maybe that was why the words left his mouth before he could stop them. Because they were seventeen. Because they were scared. Because grief was still fresh behind his ribs. Because he loved her like he loved his own breath. Because the scent had flooded him and changed him and *hadn't* broken him. Because he still felt like himself, even standing this close to the monster she feared she was.

Because some part of him, reckless and aching, wanted her to stop being afraid because it pained him to see her looking like a bird with broken wings.

"You know..." the grin on his face was old, familiar—half challenge, half invitation, the kind he used to throw at her when they were twelve and he dared her to do something stupid but with all the swagger of a teenage princeling. "You could try kissing me. If you wanted."

Her head snapped toward him, eyes wide.

"What?"

There was too much in that one word. Fear. Horror. Utter disbelief.

He shrugged, the movement exaggerated, casual in the way only young males could manage when they were brimming with adrenaline and still not sure what to do with it.

"I mean, I survived the scent," he said, voice lighter than the thundering beat of his own heart. "Might as well find out what the kiss is like."

She stared. For a moment, she truly thought he was joking.

Because the thought had never fully crossed her mind before. Not seriously. He was Graye. Her friend. It wasn't that she didn't know he was handsome. Or that she hadn't once or twice felt the tension in the air between them and wondered. But this?

A *kiss*?

Her instinct flared. Not the siren's—but the girl's. The panic of proximity. The knowledge, grim and unshakable, that this wasn't a game. That a kiss from her could end everything. That she had instincts but didn't know what to do with them.

"Don't joke about that." Her voice wasn't sharp—but it was strained.

"I'm not," he replied. And there was a surprising steadiness to it.

She took a step back. Not because she feared *him*, but because she feared what she might do. Her fangs hadn't gone away. They were out. Because of this conversation. Elsie had told her that sirens didn't fall for their own abilities. That even with a kiss, some part of the siren was exulting in power, and control- not romance, not lust. Elsie's voice was whispering in her mind with saucy mischief, not realizing her playful comment had sunk its claws deep into Serena's fear, "Remember, Ser... we didn't *just* want them as males...millennia ago they were also *food*."

"I can't," she said to Graye. "It's not like the scent. It can't be blown away on the wind. The Thrall that comes with a kiss is deeper. You taste it- it sinks into you like a drug. And I don't know how to stop it once it starts. What if I want to bite you? What if I go mad and want to drink your blood? What if I ripped your throat out..."

Graye's brow furrowed. But not in judgment- realization.

"You've never kissed anyone," he murmured. It wasn't a question.

She shook her head in one sharp motion.

"Elsie told me about it," she said quietly. "About what it can do. She's had lovers. She said sometimes they want it. They *beg* to be enthralled. And some..." Her breath hitched. "Some don't know what they're asking for. They think it's just intense pleasure. But it's more. It's losing yourself. Willingly. Mindlessly. It's telling a male to slit his own throat and he does it with a smile on his face, just to please you."

Graye stepped forward—*slowly*, carefully.

"And what if I want that?" he asked. "Not to lose myself. But to know what you are, to understand you. And for you to know that I'll love you anyway."

She swallowed hard, her voice barely audible. "I might lose you."

"You'd never lose me."

"You *don't know that*." Her voice was sharp, edged with anxiety.

Her words cracked like a whip in the still air.

But he didn't flinch. Not even then.

"I trust you."

She was shaking now. Every instinct screamed *no*. But some quiet part—older, deeper—was whispering *yes*. The part that wanted to know. The part that ached to not be afraid and to be what she was born to be.

Graye had kissed before. Not often, not seriously—just enough to know the mechanics, the clumsy heat of it, the rush that came from a girl's fingers tugging at his hair, the teasing glint in her eye, the moment where bravado tried to make up for inexperience. Ember had offered its share of opportunity—flirtations at festivals, stolen moments in dark corners when the Dardani weren't looking. But those were the kisses of boys pretending to be men, testing boundaries, earning stories to laugh over with Kade and Rhune around a fire.

This was not that.

This was not about thrill. Not about conquest or pride.

This was Serena.

And this was about *her*—not the idea of her, not the power coiled under her skin, not the danger that came with her bloodline or the scent that still lingered on the breeze like memory.

It was about the girl who still trembled, the one who stared at her own hands like they might turn traitor, who feared what her kiss could do not just to him—but to herself. How much she would hate herself if she ever hurt him. And somewhere in his chest, where the ache of Kriesta's death still sat like a stone, Graye knew this wasn't about daring her into something.

It was about showing her she was still someone who could be *held*. That she was safe, she was loved.

He crossed the last bit of space between them. Slowly. Quietly. No sudden moves, no flash of teeth or cocky grin now. His hands found her shoulders first, grounding her, waiting for a flinch that never came. She let him touch her. Let him pull her gently into the familiar cradle of his arms, the same way he had done since they were little—after nightmares, after Mab's punishments, after letters from courts that made her cry.

She was trembling now. Not with longing. But with the terror of what she might become.

So he did what he always did. He *held* her.

His hand slid up to her temple, threading gently through the hair there—dark as ink, but streaked now with the telltale shimmer of her heritage. Emerald. Violet. Like the deep sea at twilight. Like something royal and unknowable.

He didn't speak. Just tilted her face up with two fingers under her chin.

And then he kissed her.

Just a peck.

Just lips, warm and soft, brushing hers.

Just contact. The most innocent kiss two people could share. And for all that it was simple, it was *deep*. In a way no one else had ever touched him.

Because this kiss meant something.

It was a question, not an answer.

It asked: *Are you still you? Are we fine? Can you love something without breaking it?*

She looked up at him with wide, uncertain eyes—still caught somewhere between fear and guilt, her lips parted just slightly from the kiss, her breathing shallow. The faintest shimmer of something almost like mist clung to her lashes, not tears exactly, but the residue of tightly coiled panic. Her voice, when it came, was small. Wary. Her first kiss and it wasn't romantic, or giddy, but rather an exercise in fear, doubts, and acceptance.

"Are you... alright?"

He didn't hesitate. "I'm fine." And he was, technically. The kiss had been too light. Just warmth and closeness, just proof—for both of them—that she could still be touched without consequence. That she could offer something without losing herself, or taking something from someone else. But it had still been a kiss.

And he wasn't going to tell Kade and Rhune. This was between him and his Sev.

He watched her. He could see she didn't believe it yet, not entirely. Her posture was still stiff, the tension wound in her like wire. But she hadn't run. She hadn't broken.

And he didn't want her stewing in the aftermath.

So he pulled her in again—this time not for a kiss, but to press her firmly to his chest. His arms wrapped around her like he was building a wall with them, something sturdy, something she could hide behind for a moment and remember that she was safe. She resisted for the briefest second, then melted against him with a sigh so quiet he almost missed it. The tension in the bond loosened into warmth.

They stood like that for a minute. The wind tugged softly at their hair. Far below the balcony, birds called in the trees and the scent of pine crept in under the lingering perfume of rose and sea salt.

When he finally pulled back, it was just far enough to meet her eyes again. His voice was gentle but sure.

"See?" he said. "You're no monster, Sev." His cocky smirk was back, with warmth in his eyes.

She blinked at him. Her mouth quirked—barely. Not a smile yet, but the ghost of one. Still fragile, but no longer broken.

Then he nudged her with an elbow, stepping back with that familiar gleam in his eye. His voice shifted, playful, coaxing her back into something that wasn't burdened by bloodlines or terror or power.

"Come on," already turning toward the stairs. "Let's go spar."

She stared at him a moment longer—half stunned, half grateful—then let out a breath that sounded almost like a laugh. Her shoulders dropped, the tension draining out of them like a sluice gate opening. She brushed her hair back, the fangs gone now, and straightened.

"Alright," she grinned, a spark returning to her. "But don't cry when I take you down. I've got new moves Serafine's been drilling into me."

He glanced over his shoulder with a grin. "I thought you were never going to use those *scary techniques* on me?"

She smirked, already following. "Today's your lucky day, Princeling."

And just like that, they were no longer heirs of broken courts, no longer children scarred by blood and legacy. They were just Serena and Graye again—laughing, dueling, daring, always together. Always trying to make the other stronger.

CHAPTER TWELVE

LORDLING

Their three days at the Siorain cabin had come and gone like mist. Three days of uneasy peace—of hot springs and quiet cups of tea, of whispered conversations late into the night. Of aching silence where Kriesta's laughter used to be. Of restrained grief when no words could be summoned at all. Serena and Graye had spent the time circling the loss of Kriesta and Lyra, trying to absorb the shape of their absence, trying to guess what punishment Mab would hand down to Jaryk and what it would mean for Shade, for Ember, for them.

But Mab did not move like the rest of the world. Her strategies unfolded across centuries. Her decisions bloomed slowly, like poison growing in the roots of a tree. They could do nothing now but wait.

On the final morning, Jormunder appeared in the clearing without warning, a dark silhouette emerging through the mountain mist. His wings were folded, his armor gleamed faintly in the sun, and his face was grim. He said little as they packed. There was no warmth in his tone, but no anger either—just steel.

He didn't meet their eyes until they reached the portal stone.

"She's called for both of you."

Serena blinked. "Me too?"

Jormunder nodded once, sharp and clipped. "You and Graye."

Graye flinched, but Serena's voice was quiet, uncertain. "Atta... she's never called for me. She's rarely spoken to me directly. What do I do?"

He looked at her then, finally, his face unreadable but his eyes as sharp and cutting as a war blade. "You stand there. Don't speak until she addresses you. Be calm. Give her only as much as she asks and nothing more. You are the Heir of Ardaion. Don't give an inch."

She swallowed and nodded. He gave no reassurance, no softness. Only the hard truth of how to survive Mab's presence.

They expected to be led to the throne room, where the tribunal of elders would be assembled, where nobles in silver and moonstone would perch in balconies and Ember's grievances would be dissected with cold precision. Where the outcome would be politics as usual.

But that wasn't where the guards took them.

Instead, they were brought to Mab's private office.

That cold chamber at the top of the spire, paneled in pale ash and moonlight stone, shelves of ancient scrolls sealed with the sigils of queens long dead. The room where Mab had once studied, once reigned, and where she and Jormunder had waged their most vicious wars—over policy, over battle plans, and, most often, over Serena.

It was a room Serena had not entered in over a decade. A room she remembered more for its shadows than its light.

Mab stood when they entered, tall and straight as a spear. She wore dark indigo robes traced with silver-thread glyphs that shimmered faintly in the lanternlight. Her hair was bound in braids tight to her skull, her crown absent, though she hardly needed it to look every inch the ruler.

Jormunder remained at Serena's side. Not behind her, not at the wall—but beside her, solid and silent, a presence of authority and protection. His draconic wings were furled, but his stance was unmistakable: he was ready to defend, not just accompany.

Mab's eyes flicked to him. Her mouth curled faintly—not amusement, not affection. Something colder. A sneer laced with bitter humor, as if she knew he'd fight for the girl, and Mab would be the one to lose if he did.

And still, she said nothing.

Her gaze shifted to Graye, then back to Serena. It was the first time in years she had looked at her daughter directly, and Serena felt it—like a knife held to the throat, not yet drawn but promising blood.

That gaze lingered.

Serena did not flinch. Her skin crawled with the old, familiar urge to vanish, to flee, to run back to the Siorain mountains and the safety of distance. But she didn't move. Didn't drop her eyes. She met Mab's stare with her own: solemn, grey, intelligent. The same gaze Mab had seen in the minutes after Serena's birth. The one she had loathed from the first moment it opened.

And still, Serena held it.

Mab studied her, but not with the usual casual disdain of an insect, but one far more calculating, more cunning.

Mab's eyes turned to Graye with the weight of a predator considering a potential threat—or a weapon.

"It seems almost odd," she said, voice like glass stretched thin over iron, "that we've never spoken, though you're bonded to my heir and spent a good portion of your childhood in my court."

Graye did not respond. He kept his expression neutral, respectful, and cautious. The same composure he'd learned in battle, in Ember councils, in the long shadow of Jaryk's punishments. Her icy blue-grey gaze remained trained on him, waiting for even the smallest slip.

"I've heard from Aegin that you are a natural leader," she continued. "Intelligent. Skilled with a sword. And now that you are coming into your powers... strong in them. Exceptionally strong." A pause. "And yet thanks to your father, I have forbidden your training at the university and the mage tower. How do you feel about that?"

There was no flicker in her voice, no signal of what she wanted him to say. Just a blank wall of menace, a test wrapped in false civility.

Graye met her gaze and replied with smooth diplomacy, a perfect answer for a court trained in claws and veils. "I consider myself to be as much a victim of my father's schemes as any other, but it is not for me to question my queen."

She was silent. Watching. A long, sharp silence stretched between them until she finally said, "And if I give you your father's court early, will you be loyal to me?"

Another trap. Another forked path.

"I am loyal to my queen now," he stated, voice steady. In his heart, that meant Serena. It would always mean Serena.

Mab studied him with a calculating gaze, "Twice your father has overreached. The blood bond. The invasion of Ember. He's always been clever and ambitious, powerful. But now his plans have been foiled, his mate and daughter lost. He's licking his wounds yet again. Do you know what else that makes him, Graye?"

He swallowed before answering, choosing his words with care. "Dangerous, Majesty."

Something in Mab's expression shifted. Not surprise—acknowledgment. Approval, perhaps, that he understood things clearly. Her lips curved faintly, a smirk ghosting across her face.

"Dangerous," she echoed, her voice low and curling like smoke. "But you won't be dangerous, will you, Graye? You're bound to Serena. You have a vested interest in the continued success of the Moon Court and Ardaion."

He did not answer. He didn't need to. The bond between them pulsed faintly, troubled, anxious.

Then Mab's eyes shifted. To Serena. And for the first time in Serena's memory, they were not filled with disdain, but with something else—curiosity. Cold and clinical, but genuine.

"Serena," Mab said, her tone still sharp but quieter now. "You have suffered all these years with the longing of one blood-bound. How do you feel about that?"

Serena straightened, spine stiffening with poise learned not from her mother, but from courts and battlefields and a life spent enduring. Her voice was calm. Clear. "I did not choose it, Majesty, but I have never once regretted it."

Mab's face hardened slightly, her tone flattening. "You call me *Majesty*, not *Mother*."

It was a statement. But it was also a question. A trap. A poisoned edge.

Serena did not flinch. She didn't explain. She simply said, "I will call you whatever you wish."

Mab's breath hitched faintly—whether annoyance or approval was impossible to tell. She looked to Jormunder, a knowing curl to her mouth. "You've taught them both to be cagey. Just as well, in a fae court."

Jormunder's expression remained unreadable. But his alert presence was no less thunderous for its silence.

Mab stepped around her desk, the motion a quiet threat. She unfurled two scrolls onto the table with a flourish, the golden seals glinting in the low light. Her quill moved in swift, deliberate strokes. She did not explain.

Only after she'd signed did she speak.

"Graye," Mab didn't look up, "I am moving up the date of your father's retirement as Lord of Shade. You are to replace him as of today. And if you consent to share power with a steward of my choosing until you come of age, I will rescind your prohibition to attend the university and study Battle Magery."

A silence fell heavy.

Graye controlled his surprise. The steward was a warning, and a spy. She would not trust him with full control. Not yet. Perhaps not ever. But he weighed it swiftly. Whoever the steward was, they could hardly be worse than Jaryk had been. Small wins could lead to bigger victories with time.

He inclined his head. Gravely. "Yes, Majesty. I accept the terms."

He did not look at Serena. But through the bond, the flicker of tension rippled between them—concern, surprise, dread. Understanding.

Mab studied Serena now. For far, far longer. The quiet stretched until the silence itself began to tighten like a wire.

"Serena," she said at last. "You are my heir. Now that you have come into your—considerable—powers and proven yourself a true siren of the blood, I have decided to take a more direct hand in your education. It's time to act like an Heir."

Her tone was not maternal. It was not warm.

"I will determine your studies. I will test your abilities. And I will teach you what it is to be a queen. You will take your breakfasts with me. You will begin attending the other courts as an envoy, with appropriate retinue and advisor. You will appear at my side when I hold court."

A pause.

"And... you will call me *Mother*."

The word landed not like a balm, but a brand. She meant it as a leash and Serena felt it, collared to Mab like a debt her mother had come to collect on.

Serena didn't speak. But she didn't have to. Her stillness said everything. She understood perfectly—this was not an offer of affection. This was not love. This was ownership. Control. Reclamation of a legacy Mab had long rejected—until now when it could serve her.

The Heir of Ardaion stood very still. And in that stillness, she knew: her life was about to become far harder than it had ever been.

Mab flicked her wrist and a tiara appeared on the edge of the desk with the casualness of a conjurer tossing a coin, a single trident in the center between sharp spikes. "Put it on," her tone devoid of emotion.

Serena curtsied in answer, her movements graceful, ceremonial. Her steps toward the desk were fluid, and composed. She reached for the tiara and settled it atop her head without hesitation, despite the heavy weight of what it signified. It was not merely a token of appearance—it was a diminutive version of Mab's crossed-trident crown, the design almost a matched set. A message to the room, to the court, to fate itself: the heir had been claimed.

Mab studied her daughter's face. Blank. Measured. Testing.

"Can you summon the spell wings?"

Serena blinked once, her mouth parting slightly before she caught herself. "I have never tried... *Mother*." The word felt wrong in her mouth.

Something flickered in Mab's expression. Not surprise. Something closer to displeasure—though whether it was directed at Serena's lack of initiative or the apparent failure of her mage tutors to provoke such an attempt was unclear.

She stepped forward slightly, voice sharpening. "Center yourself. Push your power down through the floor first and lock it into the wellspring. You'll feel the power rush into you like fire. It will overpower you if you let it. *Don't*."

Mab's posture shifted—the way she peered now was not with maternal interest, but the scrutiny of a queen verifying a relic. A final measure. The test of whether Serena was not merely born of the Binding bloodline, but worthy of it. Whether the girl she'd rejected had, despite everything, grown into what the realm required.

Serena nodded once, tense, then lowered her eyes to the floor, grounding herself. She focused. Drew in a breath. She did as instructed—reaching not upward, but downward. Searching. Not with her hands, not with magic, but with instinct. And she felt it.

The wellspring.

It was not a single source. It was a radiant river, a lattice of life and energy coursing beneath the very bones of the land. It vibrated beneath her, through her, like the humming of a storm waiting to rise.

"Don't just touch it," Mab snapped. "Lock onto it! Drag it up into you!"

Serena flinched slightly. But her fear of Mab, ancient and ingrained, was deeper than her fear of power. She adjusted. No longer tentative, no longer reaching gently—she grabbed. Imagined hands tightened around the stream of energy and yanked it upward with all the desperate command she had.

Obey me!

The words were not spoken aloud, but they burned through her mind with the force of a queen's edict.

It answered.

A flood, a torrent, a sudden invasion of fire and light and pressure that filled her like breath fills lungs after drowning. Her spine arched slightly as the power lit every vein, every artery, every cell. Her eyes glowed, iridescent and unearthly, their hue shifting through sea-glass blues, oil-slick purples, and green-shot greys. Light traced her bloodstream like molten rivers.

She gasped. But she did not fall. She braced against the onslaught, locking down her control of it with the same determination with which she shielded her scent.

Something stung at her neck—the bloodline mark awakening.

Across the room, Jormunder and Graye both felt it. Not just saw or sensed. *Felt.* The sudden wave of divinity that parted the air, thick with command and instinct and something far older than court politics. This was a queen awakening. The air itself seemed to shift under its weight, demanding bow or flight.

Mab nodded once, lips curved in the barest gesture of satisfaction.

"Now," like a general issuing a second order, "focus on your back. Where your wings are. Push the power outward. Imagine the spell wings. You've seen mine. Copy them in your mind—and wear them."

Serena closed her eyes and centered again. Her thoughts turned inward. To her back. To the space around her shoulders. She pushed, not blindly, but with precision. She let the power pool there, bloom outward. She did not expect the wings. She *willed* them.

They erupted.

Not with pain—but with presence. They were not flesh and bone, not the leathery flight-wings of Jormunder. Those had faded with a puff of black smoke as the spell wings were summoned. The spell wings were something else entirely. A manifestation of pure power.

They were enormous. Graceful. Arcing high above her, fanning wide with effortless majesty. Feathered in form but not texture—each one a blade of crystalline glass, thin as paper, glowing from within with pulsing rainbow hues. Light shimmered across their span, refracting across the room in a thousand shifting colors. Walls, floors, even Mab's dark robes lit in scattered prismatic splendor.

The spell wings of the siren queens. The sign of the Binding. The divine signature of a line chosen to wield the heart of the realm.

They moved as if in water, slow and fluid, fanning at rest like breathing. Serena felt them. Not like limbs, but like energy. Alive, conscious, attuned to her will.

She stood at the center of their radiance. But she wasn't looking outward; she was feeling her way inward. The raw power, the sudden access to more power than she'd ever felt. Everything was sharper, more connected to her. She was aware of everything. Some mental construct, something that had felt like chains or iron bars crumpled, snapped wide open, unleashing her spirit.

She'd never been timid. She'd always been bold. But this... this wasn't about being bold. It was about domination and the surety of her absolute divine right to do it. Her face reflected almost none of these thoughts but she flicked her gaze to Mab and her mother caught enough of what she was feeling- the only one who could know what she was feeling- and Mab's eyes sparkled with a cold kind of knowing.

She knew exactly what Serena was feeling. Supremacy. Unbridled power.

Jormunder stared, unmoving, his mouth slightly open. Not in fear—but in pride. The gruff warlord's eyes glittered with joy, with an ache in his chest. Tatiana. Serena.

Graye could barely breathe. This was Serena. *His* Sev. But now—now she stood illuminated, wings stretching like the rising moon, no longer the girl he'd grown beside but the Heir of Ardaion in truth. His throat tightened. He'd never been near Mab as she'd spread hers up high on her dais. But this close he could count every glass-like feather as they glowed and shimmered with shifting light. She looked otherworldly.

Mab stood, hands clasped behind her back, her expression unreadable. But inside, the Spider of Ardaion was spinning a new web. Because this... this was the heir she had denied.

But she'd come to a conclusion. Her duty was still to Ardaion. She didn't have to love Serena, or even like her. All she had to do was train her, to use her. And the boy. Jormunder had taught her a dull sword was useless. A sharp one though...

Mab's voice cut through the air of her study, devoid of any warmth or wonder, as if her daughter had not just summoned the oldest and most sacred magic in the realm. As if spell wings were no more than a tool to be sharpened. "From now on, you will be able to call your natural wings or the spell wings at need. Or dismiss wings entirely. That can be convenient."

Another barked command, "Show me your fangs." Serena felt she was a horse being examined for sale. She opened her mouth and the fangs were there. She looked awkwardly at Mab, which annoyed her. "This is your birthright, this is what you are, Serena. Now..." Mab's fangs bared as her lips curled back and she let out a hiss that turned into a full growl.

Not a normal fae growl or snarl. It was layered, bass rumble layered with a scream like some hunting shadowcat in the mountains. It was vicious and Mab lowered her chin, death in her gaze as she pinned Serena with it. A challenge.

The effect on Serena was decidedly different than on Jormunder and Graye. For Serena, this was pressure to perform, to imitate her mother, and quickly, before she angered Mab. But for the two males that sound triggered something instinctive down their spines, something that made the blood run cold and the back of their necks prickle. Something that told them for all the social order Ardaion had developed, the gentility, they were still *prey.*

Serena swallowed, pulled her lips back, and hissed. It felt odd, unpracticed, and a bit silly... almost like she was toying with Graye, making faces at him. But then her voice dropped into that low rumble Mab had. The feline layering over it didn't come, though she tried. But it was still enough to sound dangerous. Mab said irritably "Practice later until you get it right." An order.

Her tone did not shift, not even a sliver. "I want you to dismiss and call the spell wings three more times for practice. Because when we return to court, you will stand at my side and summon them when I tell you."

Serena obeyed. The wings shimmered out of existence with a thought, then returned, summoned again and again as Mab instructed. She moved with perfect discipline and power under glass. Graye watched the lines of focus in her brow, the flare of raw energy in her posture, and when her eyes turned to him on the third summoning, something else caught his gaze.

The mark.

It gleamed high on the right side of her neck—a new tattoo, etched in radiant silver ink. Not decorative. Royal. The crowned crescent of the Moon Court, unmistakable even through a high collar. Unlike the smaller black sigils worn by Jormunder or Elsibetha as kin to the throne, Serena's mark proclaimed inheritance. Authority. The symbol of a ruler.

It matched Mab's. He stared a moment longer before Mab's voice pulled him back.

"Take Graye to the throne room to stand alongside his father," she said to Jormunder. Her tone sharpened. "The Moon Court's judgment is coming."

Then she turned to her daughter, the air between them knife-fine. "You will walk out with me, behind and to the side. You will stand beside the throne, and you will exactly follow my instructions."

Serena dipped her chin in answer, voice steady. "Yes, Mother." Mab gestured a glowing glyph in the air, floating there for a moment before Serena's clothes changed into a formal gown of sapphire and silver. The colors were the same, the embroidery the same as Mab's, but a younger style of dress. The message was clear- they were now a matched set.

Moments later, without the spell wings summoned, she followed Mab into the throne room.

The court was full, the air charged with expectation. Elders. Nobles. Mages. Advisors. Every seat was filled. All eyes fixed on the dais, on the Queen—and now, the Heir.

Jaryk and Graye stood in the center, surrounded by guards. Serena climbed the steps with perfect grace, then took her place at Mab's side, face a mask of impassive control. The soft rustle of her gown and the click of Mab's boots against the marble floor were the only sounds as they settled into position. The court took in the two royal females with calculation and expectation. This was new behavior and they didn't know what it meant.

Mab did not hesitate. Her own spell wings unfurled.

"Grievances were brought to this court by the Court of Ember after it was invaded by the Shade Court," she declared, voice cool and regal. "This court finds that the invasion was unprovoked and unwarranted. Lord Jaryk, step forward."

The Shade Lord obeyed, stepping forward with his signature, cold one-eyed stare. The other socket remained hollow—Mab's punishment years ago for the blood bond he had dared forge without her leave.

"Lord Jaryk of the Shade Court," Mab continued, "you are guilty of sedition and unlawful acts of war. It was ordered that you should step down as Lord of Shade once your heir came of age, due to your unlawful blood-binding of that heir to my heir. These new acts of war warrant an escalation of that decree."

Then, without breaking the flow of her address, she said low to Serena, voice like the breath of a blade: "*Summon the spell wings.*"

Serena didn't hesitate. They exploded into existence.

Radiant and immense, rainbow-lit and sun-bright, they flared out behind Serena in absolute silence. The court gasped softly—the collective awe of seeing *both* crowned in divine light. Absolute proof that Serena was the Heir of Ardaion, that the Binding lived on in her.

Mab raised her hand, and in it appeared her *sujinn* Shadowdancer blade, obsidian black, curved, sleek, and ancient.

She extended it to Serena with a whisper that only her daughter could hear. "You've trained with Serafine for four years now. Go. Take his head and make him pay for the blood bond, for your suffering."

Serena's eyes widened briefly. For one heartbeat she flicked her gaze from the sword to her mother's face—cold, imperious. Then to Graye, her pulse spiking with panic. And finally, to Jormunder.

He said nothing. Moved not a step. But his silence said enough. This was due. Long due. The general lowered his chin so miniscule everyone but Serena missed it. But she read it well enough: *do it*. In Jormunder's mind, behind his expressionless face- he was reliving his granddaughter's haunted screaming and suffering when Graye had been taken away when they were eight.

But he wasn't only thinking like a grandfather. He was thinking as a strategist and a Prince Consort. Mab might be using Serena now to grandstand, for political theatre, but she *was* paying attention to her. She'd taught her how to draw from the wellspring, to summon the wings. That gown, the matching tiara... that was Mab's silent claim on her daughter.

Serena still struggled with the guilt over accidentally killing that boy in her room. Jormunder reasoned if she was to be a queen- if she was to be a Shadowdancer, a Battle Mage- she would kill again, by choice. It may as well start now, with a roar. Not on a battlefield somewhere obscure but in front of the entire court, wearing the gown and crown, and swinging Mab's sujinn. Mab would continue to be hard, he knew, but this was still Serena's ascension.

"Go, now, Serena," Mab said, her voice silk over steel. "Your first lesson as a siren queen—never suffer your enemies to rise. Sirens do not fear death. *We become it.*"

The weight of the sword landed in Serena's hand like fate itself. Her spell wings fanned slowly behind her as she descended the dais, her gown whispering across the marble. The lights from her wings painted the throne room in fractured color, prisms dancing over stone and skin and blood. Unknowingly, her thoughts were very similar to Jormunder's. She had to do this. For duty. For the eyes watching, including her mother's. *For Graye.*

Mab was weaponizing her daughter, sending dozens of calculated messages across the entire network of the court at once. Every court, every lord, every noble would be watching this and taking a different meaning- a different lesson- from it. And Serena could not botch it. She had to rise, to be the Heir.

At that moment, breathless, expression calm but stormy seas behind her eyes, she made a decision. There would be no more thoughts of the farm with Graye. No more running away. She was going to seize her fate with as much strength as she'd just grabbed hold of the wellspring. She was going to set Graye on his path to lordship. And she was going to rise alongside him. As ever.

She'd been called the Heir all her life. At this moment, she decided deep in her heart "I *am* the Heir. I will *be* the Heir."

She stopped before Jaryk.

He said nothing. He'd gambled and lost.

Serena looked only at Graye.

He met her eyes with calm, unreadable resolve. Their bond was still. She couldn't afford to leak any sort of apology onto her face any more than he could afford any signal of regret or resistance. She'd look weak; he'd look like a traitor.

Serena took a breath to steady herself, just as she'd been trained. Then moved.

The black blade of the Shadowdancers flashed once. Only once.

It was too fast for the eye. Too silent for the ear. Her motion was a perfect shadow—fluid, precise, devastating.

When she stopped, the blade hung at her side again, undrawn in appearance, but Jaryk's body crumpled to the floor, lifeblood spilling in a thick pool at Graye's feet.

She kept her face controlled, regal, resolute. The blow had been flawless, a tribute to Serafine's training. And she hated how, at the sight and smell of the blood, something thrilled inside her. Something that reveled in the kill.

And then Graye's voice in her mind "You are not a monster, Sev." The bond between them flickered, almost like a question: *are we alright?* Another quick exchange of glances between them. The bond settled, calm, and marshaled with an iron will. It wasn't just her ascension, but Graye's.

She turned, unhurried, courtly. Walked back up the dais with the same graceful control. Stopped beside Mab. Took her place, turned, and faced them all. Inwardly she was chaos. Outwardly she was *royal.*

The court was silent. No applause. No words. Only the flickering rainbow of her spell wings behind her.

The Queen had spoken.

And the Heir had answered.

Reflection from Graye

I was born into Shade, but I had never belonged to it.

Not truly. Not in the way the court expected of its sons. I bore its colors—black hair, green eyes, power that curved through shadow like smoke around a blade. But from the moment of my first breath, I was marked by something other. My blood, my bond, my upbringing—none of them belonged to Shade.

I was raised beneath moonlight and sunlight. Nursed in the halls of Ardaion, trained under Ember's unforgiving sun. My mother was gentle, and kind when she could be, but quiet with her grief, as though mourning was something private, not to be shared even with her son. And Serena—Sev was everything. Closest friend, co-conspirator, something indefinable. I don't remember when I started calling her that; Elsie said I'd been trying to call her Ser like she did, but my four-year-old mouth said Sev instead and it stuck.

She challenged me and saved me more than once, but it always bothered me in those early years that while she could be fierce when it came to defending others, she was never as certain when it came to herself. I think when we lost our paradise together at eight, something broke inside her. She learned about loss and loneliness. Jormunder raised her strong, and she was always confident, at ease, laughing around her soldiers, and her adopted family. She could swear and drink godsawful grog while dancing jigs around cookfires with them. She wasn't timid either, no weakling. She saved my life several times. Sev laughed loudly, could get gloriously drunk, and she never refused a dare. I loved her for it. I still do.

She was brilliant, funny, and loyal to a fault. But once she killed that boy, it took years before she fully trusted herself not to accidentally hurt someone.

And with the bond, it was always when one of us was cut, the other bled. I could sense her fear, feel her anxiety, the iron will with which she locked down anything she perceived as too dangerous about herself.

She was a bird in two cages, the palace, and the one she made for herself.

I had seen Shade through the eyes of a stranger when I first arrived. I was eight years old, and my father was still alive, still plotting. Even then, I remember the court watching me. Not with affection. Not even with hope. They watched like they were waiting for a sign—of weakness, or strength, or treason. My time there was brief. Too brief to become one of them. Long enough to understand that I wasn't.

I didn't see Shade again for a decade; I had been training in Ember. By the time I returned to Shade, its pride had been stripped away by Mab's fury, its coffers emptied by war and punishment. Jaryk's name was spat, his deeds remembered only in whispers. And when I walked back through those halls, this time as its new lord, I could feel it—this place didn't want me. I was too polished, too foreign, too tightly leashed by the Moon Queen. Even my title had her fingerprints on it.

But I knew power. I understood what it meant to carry weight, to have eyes watching every step, every word. I'd seen Serena survive it—and wield it. I'd witnessed her become something unignorable. And somewhere along the way, I realized I would have to become that too.

Because she needed me to meet her at her level. To understand her. And one day, she'd need an ally. We'd once wanted to run away and have a farm together; instead, we were going to have Ardaion.

I remember the exact moment I stopped trying to win their trust and started building something of my own. It wasn't dramatic. It came while I was alone, standing in my father's old solar, staring down at his maps and ledgers, the scent of ash and old ink still clinging to the air. I could see his scribbled margins, the schemes that hadn't worked, the power he tried to steal. And I heard Serena's voice, asking me what kind of ruler I wanted to be.

That was the day I buried his legacy for good.

Serena once told me, "There's a reason siren songs are sad. We inspire love, but we don't trust it."

Maybe it's the same with courts. With power. With legacy.

I didn't love Shade. Not at first. I respected it as mine. I didn't try to force it to love me. I simply became the kind of lord it couldn't ignore. It took years.

But in time, I stopped being Jaryk's son. I stopped being the boy Mab spared for political convenience. I stopped being Serena's shadow. I became a lord in truth.

And yet... even now, after all this time, when I walk the halls of my court and feel the silence between the stones, I still wonder if part of me never quite stopped being the outsider looking in. While in her court, Sev was the insider looking out.

CHAPTER THIRTEEN

SCARS

One month had passed since Graye watched Serena take his father's head with a Shadowdancer's blade—a memory burned into him not for its violence but for its absolute clarity. He was the Lord of Shade now, still wearing his power like armor not yet fitted properly. The weight of that moment, the blood pooling at his feet, the cold finality of Jaryk's body collapsing—he carried it in silence, just as his court carried their distrust of him. He hadn't known his father enough to mourn, but he felt his taint.

Shade was a court in ruin. A decade prior, Mab's punishment had stripped it of pride and wealth, leaving its halls darkened and echoing with the whispers of resentment. The recent invasion of Ember had only worsened things, leaving its armies weakened, its coffers depleted, and its banners tarnished.

Now it had a lord who looked every bit a Shade male—black hair, eyes bright and sharp as emeralds—but who had no roots there, no loyalty born from blood or upbringing. They looked at him as an outsider, a lord in name only, and dangerously tethered to the Moon Court through Serena.

Even the smirk that often settled on Graye's lips, arrogant and challenging, was Jaryk's, though no one dared say it aloud.

Graye was powerful, undeniably, and it was whispered not just because of his Shade heritage. His soul was intertwined with the Heir of Ardaion. It made him more than he should have been—stronger, sharper, marked by something divine. But he'd been born in the Moon Court, then trained under Ember's blazing sun with the disciplined Dardani, and lived barely months within Shade's shadowed halls during childhood. He didn't know their ways, didn't speak their beliefs. His only inheritance from Jaryk was bitterness and a name he had yet to fully claim.

Mab had given him a steward to help manage Shade—a leash disguised as guidance, a spy posing as a mentor. Graye tolerated him, though they both knew the truth. It was the price of Shade's earlier betrayal, and Graye had no illusions about the steward's loyalties.

He'd needed allies of his own, trusted ones. And so he'd sent for Kade and Rhune.

Aegin, Ember's lord, had consented easily enough, their relationship friendly despite the dark legacy Jaryk had left. Aegin thought it wise to pursue formal alliance. Kade arrived first, brash as ever, blazing in auburn hair and golden eyes—his flame-born blood a stark contrast against Shade's gloom.

Rhune arrived soon after, quieter but no less imposing, his eyes like emeralds, hair dark enough to pass easily among Shade's nobility. Though his father was a Shade baron, Rhune's mother was Emberi. He seemed strongest with illusions, often able to pass unseen. He had grown more confident over the years, his voice still soft but rarely hesitant now. His strategic brilliance was unmatched—he saw clearly where others stumbled blindly.

Kade, on the other hand, preferred a hammer to subtlety, blunt force to nuanced strategy. Yet beneath his aggressive tendencies was a sharp intelligence, one he employed when necessary. But he had no patience for stealth or subtlety—he preferred confrontations to quiet manipulations. His powers were similar, enough to blast through walls and fling opponents across the room.

Graye dressed them both as Shade nobles. Kade chafed at the dark clothing, tugging at collars and cursing the tight sleeves, while Rhune accepted the garments with his usual quiet dignity; after all, he *was* a Shade noble- though as second-born, his father ignored him. The fact his younger son had allied himself with Jaryk's son didn't win him more favor, either.

With the clothing, they looked the part, at least superficially, but Graye knew appearances alone wouldn't heal Shade's wounds or secure loyalty.

In quiet strategy meetings by firelight, he spoke plainly to his two closest friends: Shade's honor needed to be restored. They needed a symbol to rally around—a victory, a success, something to remind them of pride, strength, and dignity.

Yet even with Kade's blunt strength and Rhune's piercing mind, something else weighed heavily on Graye's thoughts. Serena. One month directly under Mab's eye had to be exacting a toll. He could feel echoes of her tension through their bond. She would be trained harshly, sharpened mercilessly, and forged into a queen through pain and discipline rather than love. He felt it like an ache inside him, the constant pull, her weariness resonating quietly in his bones.

He wanted to see her. Needed to. To speak with her, to remind her she was more than Mab's weapon, more than the creature her mother was intent on shaping her into.

And maybe she could help him understand his place within Shade, his purpose there. He trusted no one more deeply.

Graye stood by the open balcony overlooking Shade's shadow-wrapped capital. The city stretched below, solemn and watchful, holding its breath for signs of what its new lord would become. He glanced back into the room. Kade was pacing, growling over some new frustration. Rhune stood quietly, observing, already calculating moves and countermoves. Neither were Shade-born, not truly, but both had chosen loyalty over blood. Like him, they had grown strong under alien suns, forged in foreign courts.

But first, Serena. Graye reached inward to the quiet place inside him where their bond thrived, the familiar sense of her presence a comfort he hadn't realized he'd missed so deeply. He sent a gentle pulse of reassurance, quiet strength, an invitation to meet.

Whatever Mab had done, Serena wouldn't face it alone.

He turned from the balcony, shadows trailing softly at his heels, as Kade finally threw up his hands, voice filled with frustrated amusement.

"How exactly do you expect them to rally behind us? None of us belong here, Graye. We're not their people."

Graye's eyes glinted sharply, thoughtful and fierce, a promise rather than a boast.

"Not yet. But we will be. And they'll be ours."

The same week...

The breakfast room was bathed in pale morning light, pouring through tall windows framed by heavy curtains of silver and indigo. Serena sat straight-backed at the polished moonstone table, hands folded primly in her lap, her face a practiced mask of serenity. Across from her, Mab's eyes moved like the edge of a blade, dissecting each tiny imperfection.

A month beneath her mother's gaze had worn Serena's patience down to the bone. Mab's expectations were ruthless—her judgments swift and merciless. Every morning now began with some tedious puzzle, logic, or strategy, solved in total silence before Serena was permitted even a bite of food. It was petty cruelty disguised as discipline, and Serena's resentment was growing hotter beneath the surface of careful calm.

After the puzzles came interrogation, relentless and detailed. Bloodlines, historical alliances, and Mab's meticulous theories on rulership and power—spoken as cold commandments. And always, always, the criticisms. *Sit straighter. Smooth your gown. Fix your hair. You're slouching. You aren't learning fast enough. Don't scowl.*

Four hours each day she spent in the quiet torment of courtly study: diplomacy, negotiations, trade routes, contracts, learning how to deliver insults wrapped in smiles. Endless ballroom dancing lessons. Memorizing the traditions, cuisines, and even dialects of other courts. Four hours of Shadowdancer training followed—physically grueling yet somehow easier because at least Serafine's corrections were direct and fair.

Finally, four more hours in the mage tower, deep in theory, runes, glyphs, and Battle Magery. Despite Mab's accusations, Serena *did* learn fast. Her recent testing had revealed powerful affinities for water and air—the abilities of a storm mage. There were wind mages and water mages, but Serena's parentage had given her both. A rare, precious weapon in war.

And that's all Mab wanted—a perfect weapon.

Today, Serena tried hard to remain composed. Graye's latest letter had arrived the night before, announcing he'd visit today. Just thinking of seeing him helped her hold her fragile calm through Mab's morning scrutiny. They'd been discussing Solace Court, but abruptly Mab changed course.

"Tides Court," Mab said sharply, voice brittle as frozen glass. "Tell me how you'd approach negotiations."

Serena's heart quickened, carefully guarded eagerness rising. She hesitated only a moment. "I'd request an audience with their elders, seeking their counsel. If I pay homage to their customs and learn—"

Mab's mouth tightened fractionally. "And then?"

"I'd also pay homage to the Akyist," Serena ventured, mistakenly believing this would soften Mab's demeanor. "My father's people. Edric's people. Surely it would please you—"

But Mab's expression hardened instantly, eyes turning frigid with an anger so sharp it cut through the room. Serena knew immediately she'd miscalculated, badly.

"Please me?" Mab's voice was dangerously quiet, dripping with acid. "You, who never once resembled him—who betrayed his memory from your first breath—think you could please me by paying homage to a people you have no right to claim?"

The words stung deeper than Serena could have imagined. Years of swallowing her pride, her fury, her hurt—all of it suddenly surged upward, unstoppable. Her careful mask shattered, her temper flared, and for the first time, she spoke without thinking, her voice sharp with anger and resentment.

"Perhaps if you'd bothered to teach me anything of who and what I am—if you'd been even half a mother to me—I would know my people and wouldn't have to beg the Tides to teach me my heritage!"

Silence. Instant, absolute silence.

Mab's eyes flashed from surprised to narrowed and dangerously cold in a heartbeat. Her jaw tightened imperceptibly. Serena's heart thundered painfully, knowing immediately that she'd crossed a line from which there was no returning.

Yet Mab said nothing. Not one word.

Breakfast continued in utter silence, tension so thick it was suffocating. Serena barely tasted the food she ate, shame and lingering anger twisting through her stomach like poison. Mab finished first, placing her napkin down with precise, controlled movements. Then, without even glancing at Serena, she rose and exited the room, footsteps echoing sharply on the marble floors.

Serena sat alone for a long, heavy moment, her anger fading to dread. But it was too late—she'd finally let slip years of pent-up bitterness, and now she would pay for it.

Her Shadowdancer training awaited and she was loathe to go. Serafine would see her shaken; her movements would betray her turmoil. But she stood anyway, lifting her chin defiantly. If Mab's cruelty had taught her anything, it was how to stand firm beneath it.

She left the breakfast room, the doors shutting behind her with an echoing thud.

Two hours later...

Nearly two hours into the Shadowdancer session, Serena's muscles burned and sweat dripped down her temples, strands of indigo and emerald clinging stubbornly to her flushed cheeks. She circled Serafine carefully, *sujinn* held lightly but firmly, her breathing disciplined yet heavier than usual.

"You're angry," Serafine said calmly, her eyes focused, observant as ever. "Anger makes you strong, Serena, but it also makes you careless. Your form suffers."

Serena lunged, striking swiftly, but Serafine pivoted effortlessly, the older woman's lithe grace turning Serena's blade aside. Serena stumbled slightly but caught herself, frustration flickering across her face.

"See?" Serafine said, arching a brow. "You're losing your footing because you're fighting your own emotions more than your opponent."

"I know," Serena muttered, resetting her stance. She'd come to deeply respect Serafine, even trust her. She wasn't maternal—Serafine never hugged or comforted with gentle touches—but she was fair, wise, and truthful. Like Jormunder, her presence was quietly reassuring, crusty and dry but reliable as old leather. And like Jormunder, she was lethal.

Serafine sighed gently, eyes sympathetic. "Channel it into focus, Serena. Anger is a storm; you must master it, or it masters you."

But before Serena could respond, Serafine's gaze flicked sharply behind her. Serena turned, following her gaze, heart freezing.

Mab stood there, an unexpected, unnerving presence at the edge of the Shadowdancer training ring. Mab had never once attended Serena's training sessions, never even observed from a distance. Yet now she stood calmly, gracefully spinning a wooden dagger end over tip in her palm, eyes fixed on Serena.

"I've decided Serena will learn about ash wood today, Serafine," Mab announced coolly, voice neutral. "A small cut across her palm should be sufficient. She should heal by tomorrow. You may leave us."

Serafine hesitated only a moment before nodding, bowing her head respectfully, and vanishing silently back towards the palace. Serena swallowed, her pulse quickening with instinctive dread. She turned fully towards her mother, watching warily, dagger still held in her hand.

When they were alone, Mab finally spoke again, her tone deceptively gentle. "You know, what I told her wasn't exactly a lie. That truly had been my intention, to give you a little taste of ash. It was, after all, the weapon that killed my mother. A queen must understand the vulnerabilities of her kind."

Mab continued to calmly toss the dagger as she began moving smoothly toward the weapons rack at the far edge of the ring, eyes distant yet purposeful.

"But then," she said, almost conversationally, "you opened your mouth at breakfast. You dared to put your father's name in your mouth. You dared claim kinship with him when you don't have a wisp of him in you."

Serena's heart pounded painfully in her chest, her mouth going dry, her breathing shallow and rapid. Still, she remained silent, her eyes fixed on Mab's moving figure.

In an instant—faster than thought, faster than sound—there came a savage blur of movement. Serena felt the impact, blinding pain, and she gasped, choking. Suddenly the sky filled her vision, spinning crazily. There was a crunching sound like stone on stone. Confusion overwhelmed her senses as the breath left her in a shocked, strangled cry.

She was on the ground.

She couldn't breathe. Why couldn't she breathe?

She tilted her head down to look, and ice flooded her veins.

An ash spear stood embedded in her abdomen, having plunged completely through, its razor tip anchored deep into the earth beneath her body. Blood—so much blood—pulsed hotly around the wound, spreading rapidly, soaking her clothes, the ash wood ensuring the bleeding would not slow. She clawed helplessly at the earth beneath her, her chest convulsing, desperate to draw air.

Through a haze of agony, she heard Mab's voice, distant and cold as ice, without emotion. "If you bleed to death here, I suppose it's fitting. You do look so much like your grandmother. Perhaps you'll die like her, too."

Her vision darkened at the edges, and consciousness began to slip away like water through her fingers. Mab's footsteps retreated softly, calmly, back toward the palace, as Serena's weakening body shuddered uncontrollably on the training field, gasping, choking, and fading.

As blackness overtook her, a single desperate thought reached out like a plea into the dark:

Graye...

Graye had barely stepped foot into the palace when he felt the first sharp tug on their bond—urgent, desperate, like the grasp of someone drowning. He stumbled, disoriented. It wasn't the usual gentle pull that connected them, that comforting tether he'd known his entire life. This was different, twisted, wrong. Panic bloomed instantly in his chest, and his heart lurched into his throat when he realized the bond was flickering, guttering, fading like a candle in a storm.

He had never known life without that connection—never felt the emptiness of its absence. Now its weakening sent him into instant terror. He was already moving, half-running through the palace corridors, breath ragged as he burst through the nearest exit and took instantly to the air.

From above, the grounds stretched wide and calm beneath him—deceptively peaceful. He scanned frantically, searching, heart hammering against his ribs until he saw her. *Panic.*

Serena lay crumpled at an unnatural angle in the Shadowdancer ring, motionless on the ground. The scene slammed into him like a physical blow. His descent was uncontrolled, and violent, his feet hitting the ground so hard it echoed painfully up his legs. The sound was like a drumbeat, a final pulse, a death knell.

She lay utterly still. Her chest barely moved—each shallow rise more a gasp than a breath. Blood pooled everywhere, saturating the grass, and the soil. The spear rose grotesquely from her abdomen, standing upright, five feet of cruel ash wood gleaming darkly against the sky.

Shock froze him, seized his lungs and muscles, and rooted him to the spot. His vision blurred with horror and grief, overwhelming him completely. It felt like living through the deaths of his mother, his sister, and now Serena—his bond, his soul, his heart—ripped away all at once. The pain paralyzed him. And then he was sobbing.

He didn't care about dignity or strength or lordship. He was losing everything. His chest felt like something was being carved out, his blood cold, his heart beating frantically.

"Serena..." he choked, stumbling forward, falling beside her, voice broken with pleading desperation. "Sev, please hold on, please don't leave me—"

His hands hovered helplessly over the spear, desperate to help but terrified he would harm her further. His Dardani training kicked in—he tried to pull the spear carefully, but it was embedded at least a foot deep into the earth beneath her, immovable. He could do worse damage trying to wrench it free.

Swallowing panic, he did as they'd been taught. He snapped the spear cleanly just above the wound, as close to her abdomen as he dared. He lifted her off it, the wound making a sick sound as it slid from her body. He cradled her carefully in his arms, shaking violently, sobbing openly now, grief and fear making him raw.

She gasped wetly, choking weakly at the movement, and then sagged entirely limp.

For a horrifying heartbeat, he believed she was dead. She was pale, too pale, nearly drained of all color from blood loss. No visible breath, no twitch, no flicker of power. Only the bond—faint, fragile—told him she still held onto life.

He pressed a trembling hand against the wound in her abdomen, desperately pushing basic healing magic through his fingertips. But the frustration tore at him—Mab had denied him formal training at the mage tower, left him inadequate and half-trained, forcing Serena and the Dardani to secretly teach him what little they could.

It wasn't enough. Not nearly enough.

"Please," he gasped, voice broken, hoarse, shattered, tears streaming freely. "Sev... hold on, hold on, don't you leave me. Don't leave me alone—"

His vision swam through tears. Instinct took hold. One moment he knelt in the practice yard, Serena limp and broken in his arms; the next, he blinked and staggered into the healing wing of the palace, screaming for help. He wasn't aware of what he was shouting, the words lost to trauma. Later, he wouldn't even remember.

Healers burst from doorways, three at once, alarmed and urgent. They hurried to meet him, immediately pressing healing glyphs and spells into Serena's body even as he carried her desperately toward the nearest cot. He placed her down with exquisite, gentle care, his hands shaking violently as he stepped back.

Then he simply stood there, swaying, eyes empty and haunted, locked onto Serena's bloodied form yet not truly seeing her. His mind slipped into a numb, hollow place as the healers desperately fought to pull her back from death's edge.

Graye sat beside her in a waking fugue, silent tears streaming down his face, his world narrowed to the faint, flickering bond that trembled uncertainly between life and death.

Two hours passed. Then three. When the first group of healers began to weaken, their magic exhausted, fresh ones were called in to continue the grueling work. Serena's body fought them at every turn—the ash spear had inflicted a cruel and resistant wound, and her blood loss had been devastatingly severe.

Slowly, torturously, the tissue began knitting back together. Color gradually seeped back into her pale cheeks, fragile at first, barely visible beneath the bloodstains, then strengthening bit by bit. All the while, Graye sat in silence, unnoticed and forgotten, slumped forward in a chair beside her cot. He clung desperately to her hand, his fingers trembling with exhaustion and fear, his thoughts chasing endlessly in circles.

She'll be alright. But who did this? Why? What happened? She'll be alright.

Time crawled on, and though the healers labored diligently, there was one wound they could not completely erase. The spear's cruel entry and exit points refused to vanish.

Even when the torn flesh closed over, pink and puckered, a circle-shaped scar stubbornly remained, forever marking the point where the ash spear had nearly taken her life.

By the fourth hour, Serena's breathing stabilized, and her color returned fully to normal. They force-healed her, pushing life energy into her, and guiding her back from the brink. Finally, beneath Graye's aching, red-rimmed gaze, Serena's eyelids fluttered weakly. They opened just enough for a hazy glimpse, pupils unfocused and confused. Her first instinct was to clutch the spot on her abdomen where the spear had pierced her, panic flashing briefly across her face.

Then her eyes found Graye.

He looked utterly devastated, his face drawn and pale, streaked with dried tears. At the sight of her eyes opening, new tears spilled down his cheeks, and he leaned in quickly, pressing his forehead gently to hers, relief and pain trembling through his entire body.

"Sev," he choked softly, his voice thick with emotion, grief, and hope all tangled together, "You're going to be fine. It was bad, but they've healed you. You're going to be fine."

She nodded weakly, her mind still clouded, gaze drifting slowly, uncertainly around the room before returning to him. His breath shuddered, and for a moment he held there, just feeling the faint warmth of her forehead against his own, anchoring himself back to reality.

He pulled back only slightly, just enough to look deeply into her eyes. His voice dropped to a rough whisper, earnest and afraid. "Sev... what happened? What—who—did this?"

Serena's throat felt raw, her voice barely rising above a faint croak as she whispered the terrible truth—the truth that nearly shattered Graye all over again:

"My mother."

Graye went cold. All over. And with that cold came rage. He nearly choked on it. He stroked Serena's hand without ceasing but his mind was elsewhere for the moment. He was so young, with a broken court, and the only power he had was his own. Something icy swept over his heart. A certainty. He was in no position to do anything at this moment. At least, not what he wanted to do. But fae were virtually immortal.

And if it took him a thousand years, *he was going to kill Mab.*

As this truth settled in his heart, a palace steward walked into the room carrying a large covered box. He bowed to Serena and said "Princess" then left the box on the table beside her. She sat up a little bit, grunted with the effort, and laid back down. Graye opened the box and saw a neatly folded formal ball gown, a tiara, and a note on expensive paper.

In an elegant script, it said "*I am told you survived. We have a diplomatic party arriving in three hours. I expect you there.*"

It wasn't signed but it was clear who had written it. Serena stared at it a moment, then wordlessly began hauling herself out of the cot with a grim determination. Graye put a hand on her shoulder and ground out "No... Sev... you can't..." his voice rising with anger and outrage, "*she can't.* You almost died!"

Serena looked at him with the coldest and most determined look in her eyes he'd ever seen. "Yes," she said, "I did. But she *will not* break me." She paused, caught her breath, "Bring me a pain tonic. Prepare another one to take with me."

Years later, Graye would reflect upon that scene and recognize it for the moment that the contentious and nebulous relationship between Serena and Mab resolved with clarity into a battle of wills. It would last the rest of their lives.

CHAPTER FOURTEEN

THE GAME WE PLAY

The court function had been flawless. That was the problem.

Graye had watched Serena through every gilded moment of it—her smile, laughing lightly at courtiers' jokes, offering keen insights during strained diplomatic chatter, moving like a dream carved of moonlight as she danced. She'd stood beside Mab on the dais as she'd been trained, radiant in silver and sapphire, her chin high, voice clear. Not once did she falter. Not once did Mab glance at her with anything other than cool, courteous acknowledgment.

No one in that room could have guessed that hours before, Serena had been bleeding out on the training field with an ash spear through her gut, courtesy of her mother.

Graye had stood at the edge of it all, teeth clenched behind a polished smile, watching the masquerade. He'd never taken much notice of Mab before; she was a thunderstorm that you hid from. But tonight he watched her. The eyes, calculating. The mouth shaped into a regal smile that was a practiced lie. She ruled after her grandmother was killed in battle, after her mother was poisoned by humans. And despite the death of her mate in battle. Those losses in someone else might have caused them to cherish what remained-their daughter. But in Mab, it had twisted into something else.

She wasn't apathetic; she was always focused on politicking and empire-building. And yet Ardaion would not survive with its Heir. Serena was bound to the wellspring and must in turn carry on the bloodline herself one day or all of this would be for nothing. It was as if Mab was painstakingly building a house of cards but was willing to set them on fire for the sake of her pain and rage.

The pain tonic had been Serena's only tell. Halfway through dessert, she'd quietly uncorked the second vial with hands that barely trembled and drank it without a word. No one noticed. No one asked.

Now, back in the stillness of her chambers, she collapsed onto the bed face first in full regalia, her gown rustling like broken leaves as she sprawled across the silks. Graye shut the doors quietly behind them.

He didn't speak. He simply came to her side and began loosening the tight laces of her corset, careful not to tug. His fingers moved gently, unpracticed but familiar with her years-long complaints about how uncomfortable they were. Her skin still carried the scent of copper and power beneath the perfume. This was caretaking. The kind that came after blood and terror and too much composure. He felt as if he was helping an injured soldier remove bits of armor.

She didn't move. Didn't flinch. Just lay there in the aftermath of pageantry, eyes open but distant, like her soul had stayed behind in the ballroom.

He slid the last lace free and let the corset loosen gently. Her breath deepened—not relief, not pain. Just release. He moved to the foot of the bed and unfastened her shoes, easing them off one by one.

When he looked up again, her eyes were on him. Quiet. Raw.

They sat like that for a few long minutes. The moon was high in the windows, painting the silk bedding in cold light. Only then did Serena speak, grimly, her voice muffled against the coverlet.

"Was it bad?"

"It was the worst thing I've ever seen," he said simply.

She closed her eyes.

"I thought you were dead," he went on, voice low, steady but raw around the edges. "When I found you in the ring, you weren't moving. I felt the bond... flickering. Like it might break in two. You were white, Sev. Cold. The spear—" His throat caught, and he swallowed hard. "It was through you. All the way through, stuck in the ground. I couldn't get it out. I had to snap it and lift you off it, and for all I know the tip is still out there buried a foot deep in the ring."

She didn't move, didn't speak. Just lay there, listening.

"I carried you to the healers. Screaming. I don't remember what I said." He gave a weak, humorless breath. "They couldn't stop the bleeding. The ash... it fought them. It was hours."

Finally, she turned her head slightly, her cheek now resting against her folded hand. Her eyes met his, weary and dark. Silence settled again between them. The kind that didn't need filling.

Then, softly, he asked, "What happened, Sev? What led up to it?"

She looked at him for a moment longer, then shifted slowly onto her side, the movement dragging another flicker of pain across her face. Her arm wrapped around her stomach protectively, fingers brushing the edge of the scar as if confirming it was still real.

"I lost my temper," she said, a bitter curl at the corner of her mouth. "At breakfast. I had mentioned my father. A mistake. She baited me—talking about the Tides, the Akyist—and I said something stupid. Said maybe if she'd taught me anything about who I was, I wouldn't have to learn it from strangers. She didn't shout. She didn't even argue. She just... walked away."

Graye was very still.

"And two hours later she had me in the training ring. Told Serafine that I needed to learn about ash wood. I thought she meant a demonstration. She had a little ash dagger in her hand." Serena's voice turned flat, almost clinical. "But as soon as Serafine was out of sight, she walked to the weapons rack, grabbed the spear...Said that my father's name in my mouth was a heresy and if I was going to look like my grandmother, I could die like her, too. Then she just walked away."

Graye's hands curled into fists against the mattress, "Jormunder would kill her if he knew."

Then Serena exhaled, slow and ragged. "She didn't even acknowledge it. Tonight. Not a word. Stood beside me like nothing happened. Not even a glance."

Graye gave a faint, tired smile. "You did the same."

She closed her eyes. "Those are the rules. Don't cry out. Don't get caught. Don't be a baby."

He looked almost disgusted at the parallel and said "Sev...it's not the same thing at all." She looked at him with a strange sort of resolve forming "I'm going to make it the same thing. And she's going to play by the same rules. Starting now."

She sat up, stiff, sore, corset half falling off. For a moment she sat there staring at the bedding, reflecting on some inner resolve. And then he felt that same *whoosh* of power surrounding her like an aura, staggering in its immensity. She'd embraced the wellspring. Her eyes raised slowly to his and they were shimmering and glowing with rainbow hues as they slowly shifted between purples, blues, greens, and golds. The color returned fully to her face, and the tiredness left her. She sat up straight, eyes narrowed in thought, in feeling, in the experience. And then she stood.

Graye spoke softly, carefully "Sev...what are you doing..." But she didn't reply at first. She was coming to a decision. A big one. The corset and dress slid to the floor, leaving her only in a silk chemise. She had not released the wellspring yet and she closed her eyes in concentration. Serena had seen her mother change her gown that day- the day she'd killed Jaryk and been ordered to call Mab *Mother.*

It took her a moment of feeling around the edges of what she wanted to do but once she formed the thoughts, it happened with a weight, a strange tactile sensation all over her body. Graye softly inhaled in a small gasp of surprise. She opened her eyes and looked down at herself. She was wearing a navy dress of light linen. Regal but not restricting, not heavy, and no corset. It was one of her day-to-day dresses.

She released the wellspring and finally allowed herself a small smile, and that smile was everything to him. She'd healed herself more fully than the healers had. She didn't look tired at all, and she'd used her powers in front of him to dress herself. It was an unveiling of sorts, what she could do with concentration.

He began to sense it was alright to smile back at her, that this was something they were sharing, some new undefined and wondrous discovery between them. So he huffed with an amused sound and said more casually than he felt "If you could have done that the whole time, why didn't you heal yourself before the banquet?"

Serena looked at him a moment and said "Because that would have been cheating. As soon as the dress arrived from her telling me to get out of bed and come play hostess, I realized the game we were playing. Playing "don't flinch" isn't the same thing if you heal yourself right after. No, Graye... you take the hit and then you hit back."

He got a little more alert at that because it sounded like the kind of tone she took on when she was about to do something brave and reckless, when her blood was high, and there was to be no backing down.

He started, "What are you going to do?" His voice carried a note of caution as if his instincts were already trying to warn her off whatever it was.

She looked at him the same way she had just before she jumped on the gryphon's back. "I've decided it's time I visited your court, Graye. *Lord Shade.* It's time I met Kade and Rhune. It's time I used what I've been learning. And I'm not going to ask her permission. I'm not even going to tell her. We're going. Now."

"And if she tries anything, I'll tell Atta that she tried to kill me today- in the same way his mate died. But I don't think she'll try anything overt, Graye. Because that's not the game. I'm thumping her. Mab is going to take this hit quietly and plan her next move. Let's see if the Spider flinches."

He was looking at her in a complex mix of being horrified, elated, proud... and nervous. And with that, she gestured an intricate set of glowing glyphs into being that shimmered and hovered in the air as she said "Come hold my hand, and picture somewhere in the Shade court you know well. I've never been there so I have no memory to use. I'm going to gate us." He was already standing, grabbing her hand despite saying "Can you even do that?" And she looked at him, that reckless girl he loved, who could swing a sword and had learned to swear at age nine with soldiers, "*I sure as tides can.*"

The mage gate opened with a rush of energy, a thin shimmer of glowing symbols collapsing around them as Serena and Graye stepped through.

They emerged into shadow and silence.

The room was large, solemn, and unmistakably of Shade—arched windows looked out onto a jagged, mist-drenched skyline, where mountain ridges cut black against the same night sky they'd left behind, but from another edge of the world. Stone walls, carved with faint geometric reliefs. Fae-light lanterns glowed softly from wrought-iron sconces. A large blackwood desk sat near the window, covered in crisp documents, books, and a few scattered training blades. The bed was enormous, draped in obsidian sheets, and at its foot, the only touch of warmth: a thick white fur rug, unmistakably from one of the frost-white ursas of the North. The scent of smoke and cedar lingered, and in the hearth, a fire had leaped to life as if summoned by her arrival.

Serena said nothing at first. She only stood in the middle of it all, taking in the stark elegance of Graye's private chambers. It wasn't extravagant—nothing like the Moon Palace—but it was his. And she was here.

She turned slowly, surveying the space, her eyes catching on every detail—the sword above the mantle, the faded banner on the far wall, the iron-and-leather bindings on the books. A slow smirk curved her lips. Triumph surged through her—hot, heady, electric. Not just for the mage gate, which had shimmered clean and sure beneath her will, but for what it represented.

She'd broken every rule. She'd come here without permission, without informing Mab, without guards or escort or excuse. She'd done it not out of strategy, but desire. She wanted to be here.

And so she was.

Still grinning, high on the flush of power and rebellion, she turned toward Graye and lifted her brows with mock propriety.

"I suppose, technically, I'm required to have the permission of the Lord of Shade to enter his court," her voice lilting with amusement. She tilted her head at him, daring him to rise to it. Graye, who stood there watching her with a look she couldn't fully read—equal parts elation, disbelief, and the kind of awe that made her chest tight.

He chuckled, though a trace of nerves still flickered behind his emerald eyes. There would be consequences, likely. But gods, she was here. His Sev. Not collapsed in a healer's bed. Not playing at diplomacy. Standing in the middle of his room with her chin up, alive, glowing, reckless, and real.

Graye stepped forward, sweeping into a mock bow, hand over his heart like one of the court-trained noble sons they used to make fun of together.

"You do, in fact, require my permission," he said smoothly. "Fortunately for you, I'm feeling generous." She laughed, the first one in a long time. A genuine, mischievous, gleeful laugh. He joined her and they sounded for a moment like the same two children they'd always been for each other.

But Serena wasn't done. She was rebelling and it wasn't going to be sneaking around. It was going to be a tour of anarchy. Flouting every rule and something in her thrilled at it. It was time to play the princess. She started grinning wickedly, eyes flashing with planned mayhem and lawlessness of an almost twenty-year-old royal.

She made a quick gesture in the air and her sapphire tiara was summoned to her hand. She passed it to Graye, "Here, make sure it's straight, and then let's have a tour, shall we?" He grinned wolfishly and leaned in, adjusting the tiara, making sure it was perfectly straight, perfectly level. And while he had his hands lifted to her head making adjustments, on a giddy whim, she leaned in fast and with no warning, and kissed his lips. Just a quick, darting thing, a daring sort of thing, and with a wicked grin that wrecked him she said "I never kissed you back. That day."

He laughed out loud, "Stars, Sev. I like you like this." Her eyes flashed, amused, and he spent just a second trying to read her, to see what that kiss meant. But she didn't look like she was expecting more, and he decided it must have been a simple impulse. Playful. And yet a part of him wished... He stopped the thought before it fully formed. Hard.

He stepped back, having fixed the tiara properly and she grinned at him "Now, the tour. And then I want to meet them." He had no trouble knowing who *them* was. He bowed to her, as elegant as the Moon Court had drilled into him, then stood and held his arm out for her. She smirked again, took his arm, and he found himself escorting the Heir of Ardaion through the Shade palace, Tenebris.

Graye guided Serena quietly down the shadowed corridors of Tenebris, her eyes gliding over polished walls of blackened wood, inlaid with subtle gilt accents catching faint fae light from sconces. The marble beneath their feet, cold and flawless, gleamed underfoot, as did the arched windows casting distorted moonlight onto the stark emptiness.

She noticed immediately how hollow it felt—not neglected, not crumbling, for fae enchantments forbade true decay—but sparse, as though someone had meticulously and deliberately emptied it of warmth, wealth, and life. It had been bled dry of its wealth. Where portraits of ancestors or tapestries of victories should have hung proudly, the walls stared back bare and indifferent. Alcoves meant to hold statues were empty, their velvet pedestals long vacant.

Yet the colors—blacks, whites, maroons threaded with occasional flickers of gold—evoked something rich and quiet, reminiscent of its former glory. The Shade Court had the feel of crisp autumn evenings, the feel of harvests, bonfires, starry skies and soft mists. It was named for the massive trees with their umber and crimson leaves that kept the forests darkened with thick canopy.

Shade had a sense of timelessness which fit their motto, *Watch. Remember.* Its inhabitants particularly adept at illusion magics and stealth. It was clear Tenebris had once been magnificent, a somber jewel among courts, now stripped and left with only its wounded dignity intact.

Barely five minutes into their exploration, they rounded a corner into a wide hall, and Mab's steward appeared with ghostly precision, his silver hair slicked back, posture rigid, every line of him radiating an insufferable air of polite intrusion.

"Princess Serena," he began smoothly, clearly accustomed to royal dealings. "We were not informed you would—"

Serena raised one imperious hand, cutting him off instantly. She fixed her gaze on him, and it was Mab's gaze she wore like a mask—icy, haughty, sharp enough to flay flesh from bone. She played it perfectly.

"This tour," she said coolly, voice dripping with a lifetime of royal entitlement and flawless disdain, "is private, conducted solely between myself and my dear friend, the Lord of Shade. Your services are not needed."

It wasn't a request. It wasn't even a command. It was a dismissal, a royal decree, a rebuke—the kind Mab had perfected. The steward hesitated only the briefest instant, just long enough for Graye to stand taller beside her, shoulders squaring in pride, his lips twitching with suppressed satisfaction. Then the steward inclined his head stiffly, murmured, "As Her Highness commands," and retreated soundlessly into the shadows. She knew he'd report it to her mother and just then she didn't care.

When he was gone, Graye's smile broke fully free, brightening his face like a rare shaft of sunlight breaking through storm clouds.

"Careful," he murmured, delighted, "You almost frightened me for a moment."

Serena arched an eyebrow, the corners of her lips curling slightly. "We've mocked her enough to know what she does and says. All you have to do is look bored and impatient, and act like you're casually weighing whether or not to kill them for speaking to you."

They continued, footsteps echoing down empty corridors, and soon enough they began encountering the courtiers of Shade—figures wrapped in subdued silks and velvets in hues that matched their palace, cautious eyes glancing curiously toward their new, young lord and what could only be the royal heir. Even those who had never met Serena noticed the glimmering crowned crescent tattoo on her neck. Only the royals had that mark, and every fae knew its meaning: *obey me.*

Serena fell seamlessly into her role, her every movement an exercise in grace, authority, and poise. It was sometimes difficult to suppress her amusement with the role she was playing but she had been born a creature of the courts. She inclined her head graciously to each noble, her voice smooth as polished stone, calling some by name—Lord Aravis, Lady Eirene, Master Trystan—effortlessly recalling details from her careful studies. Each encounter, brief but perfectly measured, drew an aura of quiet awe from courtiers who hadn't expected to see the Princess of the Moon Court, Heir of Ardaion walking their halls at night as if she belonged there.

Graye saw the shift clearly, and the subtle change in how they regarded him. In these few short moments, Serena was giving him something Mab's steward never could: legitimacy. His authority grew not because he wore a title, but because Serena chose to stand beside him—unquestioned, regal, and utterly at ease.

By the time they paused before the great doors of the throne room, Graye was almost glowing with pride, exhilaration, and newfound resolve. Serena paused, eyes tracing the ancient carvings on the dark wood doors, before looking back at him, voice softly conspiratorial.

"So," she said, a faint smirk on her lips, "shall we see how much trouble we can stir up before dawn? I'd like to meet them now."

The summons came just before midnight.

Kade and Rhune had been up in the western barracks—Kade oiling his gauntlets, Rhune halfway through a scroll on siege runes—when the messenger arrived, looking faintly apologetic and entirely unsure why the Lord of Shade wanted them now, in the private library, of all places.

Graye hadn't even been expected back. He always spent a full week at the Moon Court once a season, and he'd only departed for it that morning. No one had seen or heard his return.

That alone was cause for suspicion.

Kade muttered, "Think they kicked him out?"

Rhune just raised an eyebrow and followed.

The doors to the library stood ajar—a rare thing. Graye *never* let the staff in there. The chamber was long and high-vaulted, with towering shelves of old tomes, a hearth low with coals, and only three cups laid out on the blackwood table.

Graye stood there already, grinning. Beaming.

And beside him—impossible. Unmistakable.

Princess Serena of Ardaion.

The siren princess. The Heir. The crown jewel of the Moon Court. They recognized right away it was her, for who else could it be? Dressed in a twilight-toned gown that gleamed in the lamplight, her silver-dusted tiara caught every flicker. Her dark hair spilled over her shoulders, and her sea-grey eyes—wide, bemused, slightly anxious—glanced toward Graye as if to say *this was your idea.*

She looked every inch the royal. Not a hair out of place, elegant, but with warm eyes that looked...playful. For males who had spent the last decade training to be warriors, training to be alert to danger, Serena's eyes were what they noticed first. Not haughty disdain but nervous anticipation tempered with genuine warmth and amusement. And she was beautiful.

Graye didn't even pretend restraint. He was beaming, chest puffed. His pride practically glowed. "Kade. Rhune," he said, spreading his arms as if presenting a particularly lavish gift. "Meet my Sev."

Kade, to his credit, blinked and recovered quickly—but not before his mouth opened and closed once like a fish as he turned fiercely red in the face. He attempted a clumsy bow that he'd never been taught and muttered something that might've been *your Highness*, though it came out as more of a croak. He hung back just a bit longer, unsure of where he fit and how close he could get to her before guards might materialize and cut him down.

Rhune said nothing at first. He stood tall, gaze steady, that unreadable stillness falling into place like a second skin—but Serena could see his eyes flicker over her, sharp and assessing, not in judgment, but in growing admiration. As though he was witnessing a myth become real. His bow was silent, slow, polished. With a low, respectful voice he said "Princess." He stood again in a crisp parade rest and simply waited. His eyes never left her.

Graye was practically vibrating.

"Come on," he said, clapping them both on the shoulders and grinning widely. "You've been hearing about each other for years. Time to *talk*. Go, go talk to her!"

Serena, still a little high on adrenaline and rebellion, offered a small, genuine smile. These were her boys. The ones she pretended she knew from Graye's letters, the ones she'd considered worth saving with supply crates hidden in the snow. "I've heard a great deal," she said. "Mostly about rabbits and firewood." She gave them an endearing lopsided grin.

Kade laughed, golden eyes twinkling. Rhune just... smiled. Small. Real. The kind that crept out slow and careful, like something unpracticed. But his eyes, those emeralds, memorized everything.

No one moved. Finally, Graye, frustrated that not enough action was happening said, "Sev... I think you'll have to go to them. They seem to be frozen in place." Kade was grinning and huffed in both humor and agreement, and seemed to be waiting for exactly that. Rhune met her eyes and, with the smallest smile, dipped his chin, then waited as well.

Serena grinned wider as if he'd just given both permission to be herself and go make friends. She'd never had friends except Graye. There were no other children in the Moon Court. Only the elder fae absorbed with magery, diplomacy... her tutors, and Mab's courtiers. She walked up to Kade first and he was a good head taller. He was grinning and watching her with sparkling gold eyes like she was some adorably dangerous thing that he was slightly terrified of but also completely enamored. His wings twitched nervously, feathers ruffling a bit, and he cast an excited glance to Graye as if to say "Look, she's coming to me!" Graye just snorted and shook his head, watching with a massive grin.

Serena smiled at him, taking him in, then right in front of him dipped an elegant curtsy. She said slightly formally, lapsing into what she'd been taught to do, "Kade of Ember, I greet you. I am Serena, Princess of the Moon Court, Heir of Ardaion, and daughter of High Queen Mab of the Fae."

Graye seemed amused by this, too; Serena seldom used her full title outside diplomatic functions but through their bond, he could sense she was a bit nervous and had fallen back on the familiar.

It was just as well because Kade looked a bit awed and it made the moment bigger in his mind. Then on the same impulse Serena had had since she gated from the palace, she leaned up on tiptoe and kissed his cheek. Kade had flinched away at first, not knowing what was coming, prepared for anything except the little peck on his cheek and her beaming grin. Something in him melted on the spot. He shot another glance at Graye, *did you see what she did!* He looked smitten. Graye snorted again.

Serena had moved in front of Rhune. She took in his face, that black hair, those green eyes that were regarding her thoughtfully, curiously, with a small grin that matched hers in warmth. His wings flicked only once but he tucked them tight and sleek against his back again. Serena curtsied again, Graye realizing they had no idea the honor she was giving them- by rank, Serena had to curtsy to no one but Mab.

But this was Sev trying to make friends. His heart ached a little bit at that. For all her training, there was so much about life, real life, she didn't know. She only wanted them to like her.

"Rhune, son of Shade and Ember, I greet you. I am Serena." Rhune's eyes were focused on her as if he couldn't look away, but he made a better show of receiving her greeting, as he said low, but formally, with another bow, "Serena, Princess of the Moon Court, Heir of Ardaion. I greet you and bid you welcome from House Donbaryon." She smiled at him, pleased and the tiniest bit bashful, and moved a bit slower with him.

Graye could see it. Kade was easily approachable, warm, nearly bouncing on his heels. But Rhune was so still, so quiet with just that ghost of a smile and twinkling eyes, she didn't quite know if it was alright to give him a peck as well. But then she was leaning in—again on tiptoe—and placed a light peck on his cheek, catching the faintest trace of bergamot as she drew back. Rhune smiled wider, eyes crinkling at the corners, a slow flush blooming beneath his cheekbones. "Thank you, Princess."

The quickest flash of roses and vanilla flushed the room with the hint of siren, and all three males caught it, but it was gone just as fast. Serena blushed as if she'd let her control slip just for a moment and it was unforgivable; she looked at Graye to be sure it was fine. He smiled back encouragingly and said, "Let's have some food and wine."

An hour later, they'd drawn four chairs around the hearth, close enough for the fire's warmth to brush their boots and flush their cheeks. The high-vaulted library had dimmed to a cocoon of golden lamplight and dancing shadows, the only sound the crackle of flame and the occasional clink of glass. The scent of smoke, aged paper, and red wine filled the air, mingling with the sharp tang of cured meats and the mellow richness of cheese.

A feast—humble by court standards, but generous for midnight—had been laid out on side tables: platters of smoked venison, wedges of sharp white cheddar and soft blue-veined cheese, dried apricots and pomegranate seeds, honeyed nuts, and thin slices of dark bread warm from the kitchens. Her tiara now sat discarded on the mantle above the fire—abandoned without fanfare, like a weapon set down after a long day of battle. Her shoes had vanished at some point—she sat with her legs tucked beneath her, a pillow hugged against her chest, hair falling loose down her back. Her cheeks were faintly flushed from wine.

All of them were smiling.

Graye was mid-story, half sprawled in his chair, gesturing with a piece of bread in one hand and a wine glass in the other. "I swear," he said, laughing too hard to continue for a moment, "the ambassador never even noticed the pig until it was halfway into the feast hall. And then Sev—Sev—just shrugs and says it's one of our traditional blessings from the Moon Court!"

Serena covered her face with one hand but couldn't keep the laughter in. Her eyes sparkled over the rim of her glass, and her voice was low with amusement. "You told me he couldn't understand High Fae."

"He couldn't," Graye said proudly. "But the pig certainly made its point."

Kade was wheezing, doubled over, golden eyes watering with delight. His wings flicked wildly every time he tried to inhale. "I can't—I can't believe you dressed up a pig—"

Rhune sat back in his chair, one ankle crossed over his knee, the flames gilding his cheekbones and the edges of his black wings. He hadn't spoken in a while, but he was watching the three of them with that quiet of his, the sort that didn't intrude but noticed everything. It wasn't cold, that silence. Rhune could seem engaged and amused without saying a word. Every glance, every breath, every shift of energy. When he laughed, it was mostly in silence—a breath through his nose, a tilt of his mouth—but his green eyes shone with warmth. Rhune proved that quiet didn't always mean aloof; sometimes quiet was just quiet.

They weren't acting like warriors tonight. Or nobles. Not like Heirs or Lords or scions of cursed courts. They were just twenty-year-olds with good food, wine, and the shared electricity of something new.

Graye was watching it happen with dawning awareness.

The laughter, the way Serena leaned toward them when she teased. The way Kade's hands kept reaching for the platter closest to her so he could be the one to pass her something, grinning boyishly when she murmured thank you. Kade, for all his brashness, looked a little moonstruck. Like he still couldn't quite believe she was here, in *their* space, dressed like moonlight and laughing with *them*. His eyes lingered just a heartbeat too long. Every time she smiled at him, he straightened slightly, wings twitching at his back as if they couldn't decide whether to puff up or tuck tight.

And Rhune—Rhune hadn't said much at all. He sat relaxed, his wine glass held loose in his hand, and if anyone noticed that he kept Serena's glass full without ever being asked, no one said a word. Serena had caught him doing it, though, and flashed him a smile over the rim of her cup—a quick, dazzling thing, intimate and fleeting. Not the one she gave Graye, either. Something new.

Rhune was always the softly silent one. And yet... even more dangerous. His glances were steady. Weighted. Like he was watching not a girl but a stormfront. He hadn't made a single bold move. Just that wine glass, that nod when she thanked him, that small, almost reverent smile that barely reached his lips but turned his eyes incandescent. It wasn't shyness. It was consideration.

It wasn't overt. Nothing was. But Graye had trained beside these two for years. He knew how they flirted at training camps, at festivals, and in taverns when their armor was shed. And this—this wasn't swagger. This was careful. Tentative. A spark tested at the edges of a flame, not wanting to startle it. Serena noticed both of them. She wasn't immune—Graye could see it in the tilt of her head, the glances she returned. She was aware of the attention, and though a faint blush lingered on her cheeks, she didn't seem afraid of it. She seemed... fascinated.

Graye watched it unfold with a thousand feelings tangled beneath his skin. She was his. He had walked beside her since they were children, had held her hand through death and terror and joy. But now she was here, laughing beside his friends, with something unfolding between them all that he could not predict.

Serena... was glowing. Not literally, though it wouldn't have surprised him. But the siren sheen in her skin, the looseness in her posture, the warmth in her voice—she was *happy*. She was acting, for the first time in years, like a girl rather than a royal. She looked around the room and saw not threats or rivals but *acceptance*. She was letting herself be known, piece by piece.

Graye didn't interrupt it. He let it unfold. But his heart ached a little, too.

Because for all the wine and the laughter and the flickering fire, he understood what Serena had never had before. Friends. Peers. A place where she could lower her guard and not be punished for it.

She wasn't just his anymore.

They'd gotten drunker.

Not slurring, staggering drunk. But loose, flushed, careless. Like overgrown boys who'd lived with the pressure of adult expectations for too long and had finally, gloriously, found themselves unsupervised. And in the presence of a beautiful girl.

The stories were flying now—mostly from Kade, as usual. He had a talent for spinning tales, and with the red wine and crackling hearth, everything was turning grand and golden. He was deep into a boisterous retelling of their early Dardani training—the screaming, the snow, the way the instructors could smell fear like blood. He made it sound absurd and mythic, full of grit and glory. Serena was smiling, wine glass cradled in one hand, her eyes half-lidded in that soft, hazy way that said the warmth had finally gotten under her skin.

Then Rhune cut through the noise like a blade in velvet.

"You're training as a Shadowdancer, are you not?" he asked. His voice was quiet and smooth, but the question landed like a stone dropped in still water. "I have heard that all queens do."

Kade perked up. Blinked. The room got silent for a beat.

"Oh, the Shadowdancers." He gave a short laugh, trying to shake off the sudden weight. "Our trainers mentioned them once or twice. Swore up and down they were real, anyway. Said they'd seen a few take the field in the old wars. Talked about them like war goddesses. Or demons. Hard to say with those grizzled bastards."

Graye didn't say anything. He only sat back, swirling his wine, smugly letting it happen. *Oh, this was going to be fun.*

Serena, still lounging boneless in her chair, gave a small, indulgent nod. "Yes," she said, voice calm and a little dreamy from the drink. "Under Serafine."

Everything stilled.

Kade blinked again, slower this time. Rhune's brows drew together just slightly, his whole body shifting subtly toward alertness.

Serafine.

Even in Shade. Even in Ember. The name was known, had been, for generations.

The right hand of Jormunder, they called her. The female who fought beside the Black Dragon for a thousand years, who danced through enemy lines in the mist and came out soaked in red, never winded, never wounded. She was a legend. One of those ancient fae whispered about in barracks and camps, too old and too perfect to be real. Some said she'd died. Others claimed she had vanished into the mountains or retreated to the sea.

But Serena had just said her name like it was nothing. Like she saw her every week. Like she sparred with her before breakfast. Because she did.

And suddenly—just for a heartbeat—Serena wasn't a girl anymore.

She was something else and it required recalculation.

Rhune sat straighter. Kade just stared, mouth parted, a flicker of awe crossing his face that had nothing to do with royalty and everything to do with fear. The trained kind. The kind born in blood and bruises and years spent watching for predators. The sudden realization that they'd been sitting next to something casually deadly this whole time.

Graye was watching them now, his expression smug as sin. He didn't bother to hide his grin. He could see the realization creeping into their faces and savoring every moment of it. Sev wasn't just a princess. That she wasn't just pretty and kind and politically untouchable. No...she had been trained by the living embodiment of war, by something the Dardani still offered mead to when the wind howled wrong.

He watched them process that—and he smiled ever wider with anticipation.

And then the wine caught up again.

Kade's expression shifted, all that youthful bravado rushing back in to fill the awe-choked silence. He grinned—wide, wolfish, a little cocky. The kind of grin that got him into fights and beds.

"With all due respect, Princess," he slurred slightly, leaning forward on his elbows, "any chance you'd mind showing us a little?"

Graye choked on a laugh, hand flying to his mouth. "You're drunk," he said, delighted.

Rhune didn't interrupt. Didn't scold. Just stared at Serena with sharp, keen interest. Like he'd been watching the stars for years, and one of them had just come down to walk.

Serena's face went through several small expressions as she processed the request. There was no protocol for it so she looked unsure and questioningly to Graye who was grinning like a devil, eyes alight with pure mischief. So... this was a good thing, she rationalized. Graye approved.

She only looked at them, the corner of her mouth lifting slow, dangerous, and curved. Something glittered in her eyes. Not flirtation.

Challenge.

Shadowdancers trained for decades, usually passing from novice to apprentice to full Shadowdancer in a minimum of 80 years. Serena had trained for four years. But four years under Serafine were not four ordinary years.

Siren blood made her fast. Reflexes that didn't come from training. Instincts driven by predator blood and fear. The Dardani style was all muscle and power—broad heavy swords, strong stances, and brute strength. But Shadowdancing was for females, originally a style for courtesan assassins but perfected by the royals as the *elegant* way to kill. Not for strength, but speed. Fluidity. Flexibility. Grace. The movements were balletic, serpentine, sudden.

The oldest forms of it from Morgana's day were described as something like veil dances in the camps of chiefs or at ceremonial fires, but with hidden weapons. The courtesan would dance, tease, delight, and distract the target- and then slash their throats with blades they'd never even seen before disappearing. The style had evolved considerably into a martial art but maintained that lithe dance-like quality. Shadowdancers now could equally be found taking the field of battle in broad daylight or hiding in shadows, silent assassins. Their weapons, the *sujinn* blades, were black, made of sky metal, and almost light as air. Enchanted to be impossibly sharp. They bonded to their wielder and answered to will alone, no scabbard needed. They were not ceremonial weapons—they were built to kill with a flick of the wrist.

Serena set her wine down carefully.

Her fingers were steady as they left the stem. There had been a flicker of hesitation—not from fear, but decorum. She was still reading them, these boys, Graye's boys. Her new friends. She didn't want to make a social slip or show off where it wasn't welcome. But it wasn't fear she read in their faces. It was excitement. Anticipation. Curiosity edged with the thrill of danger. Not fear. Or, if there was any, it was the good kind. They trusted her. And that was enough.

She stood slowly. Not with ceremony, but clarity. Her movements were fluid as she stretched her arms up, loosening her back, letting the folds of the twilight-toned gown sway around her legs. Not armor. Not practice leathers. Barefoot.

She glanced at Graye, her expression casual, but her voice quieter than usual. "Well... I'm in a dress," she said with a dry smirk, tugging a strand of hair over one shoulder. "Usually I'm in leathers. But I can do a little..."

Graye leaned back in his chair, that feral grin already blooming across his face. He knew what was coming. He'd seen it before. He'd sparred with her, year after year, and now only did so because it amused them both. It had been a long time since he stood a chance.

The *sujinn* came to her hand without a sound. One moment her palm was bare, the next the black blade was there—called not drawn. That alone pricked their fascination. The enchanted weapon of campfire stories, of old songs whispered between tents, the kind children dreamed of as they wielded sticks and imagined themselves heroes. To see one was impossibly rare. To see it summoned like an extension of breath—unreal.

Both sets of eyes locked onto it. The sujinn was jet black, utterly matte. It drank the firelight rather than reflected it, like a wound torn into the world. Kade leaned forward unconsciously, wings twitching behind him. Rhune sat still, but his eyes tracked the sword with intense precision.

Serena glanced at Graye, half bashful, half daring. She looked like she might apologize for showing off but wasn't going to. Like she wanted to impress and hoped it wouldn't change how they saw her. For all her power, for all her training, there was still that flicker of uncertainty in her—was she too much? Was she enough?

She took a slow breath. Let it settle. Then smiled—and something changed in her face. That glimmer of playful mischief turned into something sharper, sparkling like starlight on the sea.

She began to move.

It was slow at first. Deliberate. Sword forms meant to focus the mind, to teach breath and control. Elegant arcs, and fluid transitions. Every step placed like a dancer. The gown shifted like water around her, the sujinn blade an extension of her wrist. Where the Dardani might have charged or swung with brute force, she simply... flowed. Graceful. If they were boulders, she was the stream.

Kade's jaw went slack.

Then, without warning, she blurred.

No signal, no shift in stance. Just speed—terrifying, impossible speed. The black blade moved so fast it vanished. Her limbs seemed to defy logic, bending and striking in patterns too fast to track. Each movement was poetry forged in war. Cobra-fast, silent, sure. Kade flinched. Rhune's brows shot up—but he didn't blink. They weren't watching a demonstration. They were watching something lethal.

Then—it ended.

She stopped.

Stood.

Lowered the sword to her side.

Nothing in her expression changed. She hadn't even broken a sweat. There was a long, stunned silence. And then—

Thud.

The top half of the wine bottle tipped clean off and rolled gently across the stone. She hadn't touched the table. No one had seen the cut. The edge was smooth. Flawless. Undisturbed until gravity remembered it.

Graye leaned back, a crooked smile tugging at his mouth, pride lighting his green eyes like a hearth fire—but he didn't look at Serena. He watched *them*.

Kade, still slack-jawed, looked from the bottle to Serena, back again. Rhune was utterly silent, lips parted slightly, that unreadable stare softening into something that looked a lot like awe.

Someone else might have preened after that display—might have smirked, bowed, flourished, bathed in the silence left behind like it was applause. Mab would have. Mab would have drawn the moment out with a predator's grace and smirked, coldly satisfied to be the alpha in the room, to remind everyone why they bowed. But Serena wasn't Mab. And Serena wasn't looking for reverence.

She looked down instead, eyes drifting to the bottle on the floor, to the clean, glimmering edge where it had been severed. Her smile was small. Private. The sort meant only for herself. She wasn't gloating—she was checking. Measuring herself not against them, but against an invisible bar only she could see. Had she done it right? Had the blade been true? Had Serafine seen, wherever she was now, would she have called it... acceptable?

She thought yes. Maybe. A perfect execution. As expected of her.

And yet her posture didn't speak of pride. She stood not like a queen claiming dominance, but like a girl trying to be brave in the face of praise she didn't know how to want. Her fingers still curled around the sujinn's hilt, that black blade still low and angled, not threatening. She turned her gaze up, first to Rhune, then to Kade. That same warmth in her eyes—the one she'd worn when greeting them, when curtsying like it meant something, when pecking them on the cheek.

A heartbeat passed. Two.

Then, quietly—genuinely—she asked, "Would you... like to hold it?"

They didn't move for a beat.

Kade's eyes were wide as saucers, gleaming with disbelief and a flicker of boyish awe. Rhune sat motionless, brows slightly drawn. Not in suspicion, but as if he weren't sure whether it was a trick. A test. Whether touching the sujinn might earn him reprimand or insult, as though to lay hands on something so sacred, so storied, without royal blood or the right oaths, might be overstepping.

But Graye stood, at ease and grinning, the pride still radiating off him in warm waves. He had felt it through the bond—that flicker of self-doubt, the question trembling beneath Serena's calm: *was that too much? Did I do it wrong? Did I scare them?*

He moved to her side, one smooth stride, and wrapped an arm around her waist. His hand settled there gently steadying her. No words. Just presence. Just him saying *I'm here. You're perfect.*

"Well?" he said, cocking his head. "You two going to sit there gaping? The Heir of Ardaion just offered to let you hold her sujinn. I think that counts as bragging rights for at least a decade."

That did it.

Kade lurched to his feet with a grin that barely fit his face. "I'd love to hold it—if you're sure it's alright," then added, far too quickly, "You can hold my sword if you want. I mean— I wasn't... I didn't mean... my actual *sword*. My *real*—"

Graye was laughing before he even finished. "You're such a drelk, Kade."

Kade turned an alarming shade of crimson. "Oh, gods. I'm sorry, Princess..."

She leaned into the comfort of it, the ease of this boyish chaos. Channeling something she'd heard once from Jormunder's soldiers during campfire banter, she cocked her head slightly, eyes gleaming, and said sweetly, "I doubt I'd even feel it in my hands."

There was a beat of shocked silence, then Graye *roared*. Laughter tore out of him as he held his stomach and almost doubled over, tears stinging his eyes, and nearly collapsed against her. Kade let out a strangled sound of horror that quickly gave way to wheezing laughter of his own, his entire face crumpling in sheer, helpless amusement.

Even Rhune cracked—his brow arched in astonishment, but then his lips tugged into a grin he couldn't suppress. He shook his head once, slowly, acknowledging the point. His eyes were full of mirth, warm, and he huffed through his nose several times in quiet laughter.

Serena was grinning too, flushed but triumphant, a spark of confidence rising through her. She liked this. Liked *them*. Liked *herself* in this moment.

She turned and passed the sujinn to Kade with both hands, a formal gesture softened by her smile.

He accepted the sword with wonder, bracing slightly for a surge of magic or weight or some holy resistance—but none came. The grip was smooth beneath his fingers. The sujinn itself, light as air. Deceptively light. So much so that he nearly doubted it was real. That something so delicate could cut through a bottle, a bone, a man. He stared at it, speechless for once, as if holding legend itself.

Rhune leaned in, watching it like it might vanish. Kade turned it gently in his grip, the matte black blade casting no reflection at all.

"It feels like..." he began, then trailed off. "I thought it'd be heavier."

Serena grinned now, truly warming to the fun of it, her cheeks flushed with wine and mischief. She took the severed wine bottle, the cleanly sliced top half long gone, and poured the last of its contents into her glass with a flourish. Then she held up the now-empty bottom half, its raw edge smooth as glass, and extended it toward Kade in silent challenge. Her brow arched, daring, playful.

Kade's eyes widened, caught between thrill and panic. He looked at the sujinn in his hand, then at the glass shard she was offering him like some test of courage or finesse.

Graye, still half-laughing and half-horrified, shook his head. "Careful, Kade," he said, voice rich with mock-serious warning. "It's wicked sharp. Don't cut her fingers off. Or worse."

Serena only smiled wider, her faith unshaken. She didn't flinch, didn't hesitate, just held the glass steady in her palm like it was nothing. Kade looked like he was about to burst from pride and terror. This siren princess, this warrior heir, was smiling at him like she *trusted* him. A mountain of a boy, all muscle and good intentions, he was grinning like a fool now, nerves and eagerness in equal measure as he adjusted his grip and tried to remember every bit of blade etiquette he'd ever been taught.

He took a deep breath, squared his stance like it was the most important move he'd ever make, and carefully aligned himself with the bottle. One hand gripped the sujinn with reverent caution, the other hovering near Serena's, ready to steady the glass if needed—but she didn't budge, didn't flinch. Just eyed him with that quiet, daring faith.

Then he swung.

It wasn't a blow. It wasn't even forced. It was a whisper of motion—like swinging through mist.

And Kade felt it: two barely audible clicks as the blade whispered through the shaft of the bottle—front and back—and then silence. A breath later, a clean ring of glass thudded softly onto the rug. Kade stood blinking, stunned, then beamed so hard it looked like his face might crack.

"Did you *see* that?" he blurted, grinning like a madman. "It just—just *went* straight through! I'm keeping that as a trophy." Still grinning, he bent to pick up the sliced bottle ring, turning it in his hand like it was a treasure.

He passed the sujinn to Rhune next with exaggerated care, still inspecting his prize. Rhune, in contrast, took his time—not to show off, not to perform, but to *understand*. His fingers traced the black blade's matte surface, pausing at each glyph embedded along the metal—glyphs that shimmered faintly like dying stars. He turned the sword slowly, watching the way it absorbed light instead of bouncing it back, and examined the way the hilt had been wrapped—tight, custom, precise.

Serena watched him with a soft, expectant smile, her glass now forgotten on the side table.

"Graye told me you're fast with a blade, Rhune," she said, voice light, inviting.

Rhune's gaze lifted. First to her, then to Graye, who was already smirking like a cat with cream.

"I am... proficient enough, Princess," Rhune replied at last, voice low, modest. Careful.

Serena's eyes glinted knowingly as if she'd already made her own conclusion. "On your guard," she said lightly—and tossed the remaining chunk of the wine bottle high into the air.

Instant focus.

Rhune didn't hesitate. His eyes tracked the glass the moment it left her fingers, green eyes flashing as his body shifted, fluid and immediate. The sujinn snapped upward in a single clean diagonal arc—faster than thought, faster than breath. It was so precise, so efficient, that the bottle continued falling, seemingly untouched.

But when it hit the ground—*clink*—it split neatly into two pieces.

Graye barked a laugh.

Kade let out a low whistle.

Serena's eyes glittered with a kind of appraisal, intrigued, a half smile tugging at the corner of her mouth.

"You *are* fast," she said, her voice soft, breathless, and Rhune let the smallest hint of a grin touch his lips.

Graye appeared at her side, his arm sliding around her waist again, and said to Rhune "She keeps you guessing, doesn't she?" Then, "Sev, it's two bells after midnight. Let's go to bed and pick this back up in the morning."

Rhune stepped forward and handed the sujinn back to her with a low incline of his head. She smiled at him, took it, and let it fade to mist from her hands.

Graye continued, "I don't like the idea of you staying somewhere alone so we'll share. Like old times." Her eyes met Graye's and said, "naturally," with a grin. He smiled back and nodded, then arm still around her, began leading her to the door, calling over his shoulder "See you two at breakfast."

Kade and Rhune looked on as Serena was led out of the room, each with their private thoughts about the princess. They didn't share those thoughts with each other but shared a look before heading to their quarters.

CHAPTER FIFTEEN

OUR OLD PLANS

The next morning, light spilled across the stone floor in narrow shafts, gilding the dark wood furnishings of the chamber with a soft, amber glow. The curtains stirred faintly in the breeze from the high-arched windows, and the coals in the hearth had long since cooled.

On the bed, Graye lay half-curled beneath the blanket, still dressed from the night before. His boots had been kicked off in a trail toward the door, but otherwise, he had collapsed just as he was—exhausted from the day's shock, the return, the reunion, and the appearance of a girl who had, without announcement or ceremony, come to Shade.

And stayed.

It was not the same bed they'd slept in as children, nor the same world. The walls here bore the sigils of a disgraced court. The air smelled not of lotus and history but of cold stone, steel, and cedar smoke. And yet, when he stirred that morning and reached beside him out of reflex, the emptiness told him what his heart already sensed: Serena was up.

He blinked fully awake and found her at once.

Serena sat at the large desk by the far wall. She hadn't noticed him stir. Her head was bent low, one hand curled around a quill, the other steadying a parchment already crowded with writing. Several pages were stacked to her left, ink still drying in crisp lines. She was barefoot, wrapped in a dark shawl over her thin linen underdress, hair pinned hastily at her crown. Her posture was alert, almost hawkish, her brow furrowed in thought as the quill moved with sharp precision.

She was on a mission.

Graye watched her in silence for several minutes, the corner of his mouth twitching in reluctant amusement. She hadn't changed. Or perhaps she had—there was a focus now, an edge of purpose so deliberate it stole the air from the room. Something had hardened in her since Mab's attack, but it was not fear. It was resolve. She no longer moved like someone avoiding danger. She moved like someone who had faced it and now intended to bury it.

Finally, Graye stretched lazily beneath the covers and spoke, his voice rough with sleep. "Whatcha doing, Sev?"

She looked up at once. A grin bloomed across her face, not sheepish but satisfied—pleased with herself.

"I'm helping you become a lord and save your court."

She gestured toward the pile of letters as if they were a siege plan, then turned back to the one in her hand. "I'm going to pay one of my classmates from the university to come here and teach you trade and diplomacy—things you should have learned and weren't allowed. Maybe I'll ask him to teach all three of you together. You, Rhune, and Kade. How to dress, how to speak, how to act the part. You've learned a lot from your time in the Moon Court, but you'd be so much better if you hadn't spent most of your time in Ember."

She tapped the inkpot twice, thoughtful. "Rhune seems to have had courtly training, too, but not enough for my vision. Kade... it'll be good for him. Stefan is good; he's from Solace Court, a second son noble and an ambassador's son. He's had all the right training as the spare but with fewer eyes watching him. And he likes a bit of mischief, so he'll take my coin and think it's fun."

Graye's expression had already begun to shift, amusement thinning into a slow scowl. Of all the things he had expected her to be plotting, a remedial education in lordship wasn't it. She'd come all this way, risked Mab's wrath, defied protocols—and now she was assigning him lessons.

But she wasn't finished.

"I've started making a list," she said, and her tone sharpened as she began flipping through another page. "Things I want to check while I'm here. And people. I'm going to spend some coin, let them see their princess with their young lord, and ask the right questions. They'll feel the Moon Court is directly interested—which might make them more open to cooperation. With you. Not my mother's overseer that she shackled to your court like a leash. *You*."

She pointed to the second sheet now. "And I've started a list of things you need to do. There will be more once I've checked into the status of things. I'm going to play the Princess today, Graye. I'm going to help you get this place in order. By the time we're done, you *will be* Lord Shade."

Graye lay back against the pillow, watching her with a look that shifted between reluctant amusement, despair, and something like awe. He had not learned statecraft. Had not been allowed to. And now he was the inheritor of a broken court, tainted by a father whose legacy reeked of cruelty, failure, and ambition turned sour.

But this—this was what he and Sev had talked about once, deep in the supply closets, whispering over stolen wine: fixing it. Fixing everything. Building something better than what they'd inherited. His mind flashed back to that day at the cabin after Kriesta and Lyra had been killed, and Serena had asked him what kind of leader he wanted to be.

And now here she was. Ink-stained fingers, bare feet on cold stone, planning his reform like it was already law. She had a plan. *Of course* she had a plan.

His chest tightened.

She'd changed. Not softened. But something in her had snapped loose after Mab's spear, and the fear that once shackled her had burned away. Serena had come through death not cautious, but galvanized.

Graye watched her a bit longer, head still cradled in the crook of his arm, eyes half-lidded, the warmth of sleep clinging to him like the remnants of last night's wine. His muscles were slow to respond, mind still fogged with comfort and her presence, but the motion of her hand across the parchment, the way she was cataloging, plotting, organizing—it made sense. Of course, she would come here, sleep for a night in his bed, wake before him, and begin crafting a campaign. That was Serena. She didn't rest. She repurposed.

But as he listened, as the weight of what she was setting in motion began to settle, a thought stirred beneath the haze. Something more permanent than tutoring. More final than a plan. She wasn't just fixing things—she was preparing to leave them behind.

He blinked and turned fully toward her, propped himself up on one elbow. His voice came quiet, rough.

"Sev... you won't be here, will you?"

She stopped writing. The quill paused mid-curve. Then, slowly, she looked up.

"No," she said, softly but with a steadiness that left no room for argument. "I won't."

The words fell like a dropped blade—no drama, no threat, just truth.

"You have some growing to do," she went on, "and so do I. I'm going to leave you in good hands. And with a vision."

She set the quill down and turned her gaze toward the high window, where early light stretched in silver across the floor. The expression on her face shifted—somewhere between longing and clarity, shaped by a hunger he hadn't heard her name aloud before.

"Then I'm going to tell my mother that I've decided to start the duty of visiting the other courts, as she agreed. Tides."

The word hung in the air.

"Something is calling me there, Graye," she murmured. "A longing. Almost like I feel when you're not with me." He could hear it in her voice, that longing.

Her eyes didn't meet his. They stayed on the window, on the sky beyond. Far past the cliffs. Past the forests. Toward the sea.

"Tides is home to the Mer, including older sirens. Ones who never really civilized. And the Akyist. My father's people. I have some stories about Edric—from Atta, from my uncle Rivarin—but not enough. I'm half-Akyist, full Siren. But I don't know myself at all. Not really."

Her hands curled slightly on the parchment in front of her.

"Everything up to now has been about all these trappings of civilization we call society. The courts. The lectures. The politics. But I want to know *what* I am. I want to sing the songs. Dance at the fires. Fly over the breakers like my father did. And I want to remember what we've forgotten along the way. The old ways."

She said it with no romanticism. No illusion. Just intent.

"I'm hoping it will help me make sense of it all," she added, more quietly now. "Help me feel more... whole."

There was a long silence between them.

She looked back down at her pages, jaw tight. "I'll take Serafine with me, and continue my Shadowdancer training properly. And I'll invite Elsie to visit when she's free."

Then, with a quiet bitterness that struck deeper than any grand declaration:

"I'm tired of being the perfect princess trotted out for appearances, Graye. I just want to be *me*."

Her fingers brushed one of the lists—ink still wet, edges sharp. Her voice dropped to a murmur.

"Whoever that is."

Across the room, Graye sat in silence, the space between them now echoing with a different kind of ache. Not grief. Not fear. But the knowledge that whatever came next, they would not walk it side by side. Not this time.

She had decided to find herself.

She contemplated him for a long moment after her confession, as if weighing whether to say the next part aloud. Then, quietly, she did.

"I've always been afraid of the siren parts of myself," she said, not looking away. "Since that boy followed me into my room and I turned him to blood mist. All because I didn't know how to shield properly. And because fear got the better of me."

The words were plain. She didn't soften them. But a note of shame clung beneath the surface, so familiar it was almost baked into her breath.

"I don't want to be afraid," she continued. "I want to master it."

She shifted in her chair, setting the quill aside again, no longer pretending to write.

"But there's more," she said. "Sometimes things... excite me. Violence."

Her voice dropped slightly—not embarrassed, but cautious, as if speaking the truth aloud might alter something fundamental.

"Sparring matches. The fighting. The blood. Sometimes the fangs slip out and I don't know if it's because of their muscles or the blood they're spilling. Or both."

Her gaze drifted to the window again, though this time her thoughts weren't far away—they were coiled tightly around something intimate, something restless and aching just beneath the surface of her skin.

"Sometimes I feel like there's music in my heart, but I don't know the words."

The longing in her voice was unmistakable now. She wasn't just curious—she was aching. Searching.

"My mother taught me how to hiss and growl," she added, "but just to intimidate courtiers. What does it really mean? Does it mean anything?"

Her fingers flexed faintly on the edge of the desk.

"I don't know," she said. "But I want to. The elders will help me. I hope."

There was a faint catch in her breath, not sadness exactly, but the sharp edge of hope's uncertainty. The look on her face was softer than before, gentler. Wistful. And something brighter had begun to flicker beneath it: a growing enthusiasm for the idea. A genuine hunger for understanding.

Graye said nothing at first.

He was still watching her. Still thinking.

How many times had he sat beside her and never realized the weight she was carrying alone? Born with more power than most fae could fathom, raised under the rules and expectations of high fae royalty, only to be transformed into something even more ancient. A siren. With all the instinct, appetite, violence, and magic that came with it.

No guidance. No sisterhood. No elders to shape her. Not even after she'd accidentally killed someone. Not even after she'd broken, bled, and clawed her way back to composure.

This wasn't rebellion. It was reclamation.

Her journey to Tides was not a whim—it was her trying to piece together what had been broken before she ever understood what she was. And suddenly, he knew there was nothing to say but one thing: that he would support it.

He had to.

But before he could speak, she turned and looked at him again. Her expression had changed completely—gone was the wistful distance, the longing for ancient songs. In its place was something quieter, sharper. Her eyes met his, and her voice dropped to a near-whisper.

"Graye..." she asked, "have you ever been with a female?"

The air in the room stilled.

She walked to the edge of the bed, the question hanging between them like breath suspended over cold water.

Graye hadn't moved. Not away, not closer. He simply looked at her, not with hunger or awe, but with the kind of stillness that meant she had his full attention. He opened his mouth to speak but she didn't give him the chance to form a coherent reply.

Her body was bare of armor, bare of courtly masks, stripped down to linen and ink-stained fingers and all the fear she had carried for years. Not of him—but of herself. Of what she might do. Of what she might become if she ever let the siren rise unchecked.

She crawled back into the bed beside him.

Her body settled against his, familiar and unfamiliar all at once. They had done this before—slept curled together after nightmares, shared warmth on cold nights in childhood—but not like this. Not *now*, with twenty years carved into the shape of who they were, and all the unspoken thoughts that had lingered unacknowledged finally pressing close.

Her hands trembled slightly as she braced herself beside him. The instinct to pull back flared—sharp, familiar. The fear. The memory of blood on her skin, the boy pawing at her, the scream that hadn't left her throat for days.

Graye wasn't that boy.

But she was still that girl. Still the siren.

He looked at her. She met his gaze. There were no words.

They had kissed before. At the cabin in a moment of grief and fear. Last night, after her rebellion. But they were tiny pecks. Playful.

The mood had changed between them and it had become heavy with anticipation.

"I want to try," she whispered. "Just the kiss."

He gave the smallest nod, nervous but willing.

Her hand rose first, tentative, resting against his chest. He reached up and laid his over it. Still waiting. Still letting her lead.

She leaned in.

Their lips brushed—soft, hesitant, a trembling breath shared between them. Not a collision. A meeting.

The kiss was slow.

It lingered, questioning.

He didn't grip her. He didn't pull. He just kissed her like she was made of something he didn't dare ruin. She pressed into him more fully, and the second kiss came deeper, her mouth parting just slightly, heat blooming in her chest. His nose filled with the scent of roses, making his heart race.

She tasted him.

And he tasted *her*.

The Thrall flared.

It didn't crash like a wave. It rose slow and hot and inevitable, like something waking from deep within their blood. Graye stiffened almost imperceptibly, his fingers tightening just slightly against her ribs. Serena's breath hitched. He'd always smelled of cedar but now that he was older there was something like sandalwood and leather.

They both felt it—the bond, the pull, that shared tether glowing between them. The soul-slice. The tie forged before they had words for it.

His kiss deepened, lips brushing hers more hungrily now, tongue parting her mouth, breath warm and uneven. She could taste his want. He moaned against her as his tongue slid along hers.

His hands moved.

Slow. Careful.

Along her waist, the curve of her hip, the bare skin beneath her thin linen shift. Awed. Curious.

He kissed her again, mouth open, dragging her under, and the Thrall was in him now—he couldn't feel where he ended and she began. Desire and lust, almost desperate need. Vanilla and honey. The taste was everything. It was *her*. And it made the carefulness falter. He wanted more. He leaned in, pressing more of himself against her, feeling her hand slide along his chest and tease his neck.

His hand slid higher. He shifted and moved fully over her, hips brushing against hers, a knee pressing, trying to settle between her legs—

She caught him.

Her hands rose, gentle but firm, pressing against his shoulders.

"Graye," she whispered.

He stilled. But only barely.

His eyes were wide—dark with something more than want. Need, wild and thick, threaded with the Thrall's insatiable echo. She could feel it in his heartbeat, feel it in the flush of magic humming just beneath his skin. He hadn't meant to lose control. But it was happening anyway. His hips hitched against hers, a silent encouragement to keep going.

She cupped his face.

"I'm not ready," she said softly. "And you wouldn't be able to stop."

He blinked as if surfacing from somewhere deep. No, he didn't want to stop. He was all ache and fire, and she was beneath him...

The magic had begun to recede just slightly as the kiss broke. Enough.

She exhaled. So did he. His forehead dropped to hers, their breaths still twined, chests rising together.

"I wanted to know," she murmured. "Before I go. I wanted to try it."

She swallowed. Ran her fingers through his hair.

He didn't respond right away. Just pressed his lips once more, gently, to the corner of her mouth. His hands still rested on her sides, no longer moving. No longer pushing. But still hovering above her.

"I've thought about it, Sev," he admitted quietly, voice ragged. "For years. What it might be like. If we could be more."

"Me too. And maybe we will be...just not yet. But Graye...what we do have will never change. I love you, and I always will." Serena pressed one final kiss to his lips then rolled to her side, slowly. He let her go.

He sighed, ran his fingers through his hair, trying to clear his head further, and then said softly, with an ache he couldn't quite fully disguise "I love you, too, Sev."

Outside the window, the light had brightened. The morning had fully broken.

They dressed in silence, their movements easy, habitual. But something had changed. Something permanent. He opened the door for her without a word, and they walked side by side down the long hall toward breakfast.

Reflection from Graye

It's been over 100 years and I still think about that year more than any other.

We were almost twenty when Serena came to Shade without permission. No trumpets, no banners. Just her, stepping across the threshold of a mage gate into a court that had nearly forgotten it still had a future. I didn't realize it at the time, but she hadn't come just to see my court or flaunt the rules with Mab. She'd come to build me.

I hadn't realized it at first. I was still tangled in everything we'd just been through—Mab's attack, nearly losing Serena on the stones of the Moon Court. The fear of it hadn't faded yet, not really. So when I woke that morning and saw her at my desk, barefoot, shawl slipping off her shoulder, hunched over my desk with ink on her fingers, she was scribbling furiously. She had pages already stacked beside her. I thought it was just Serena being Serena—more at home with conquest than comfort.

But I'd been wrong.

She was handing me my future. One sheet at a time.

I remember asking her what she was doing. She looked up, grinned at me like she'd just cracked some impossible cipher, and said, "I'm helping you become a lord and save your court."

And she meant it.

She started with Stefan. A week after she left, he arrived—all Solace Court charm and second-son confidence. He had the manners of an ambassador and the teeth of a predator in a silk cravat. Within the first day, I hated him. Within a week, I admired him. Within a year, I owed him more than I can put into words.

He taught the three of us—me, Rhune, and Kade—how to operate in a world that didn't care how good we were with blades or battle lines. He taught us to smile like daggers, to read the unspoken language of posture and pause, and to hear the weakness in a single misused title. I learned how to wield charm like a weapon and law like a noose. I learned how to conduct diplomacy in the morning and financial warfare by dusk.

Stefan taught us how to exploit financial codes, twist laws, and disguise power moves in pleasantries. We learned the art of hosting as a weapon—how the placement of a chair, the type of wine, and how the color of a ribbon could say what you didn't want written. We began to win contracts, rewrite tariffs, and catch smugglers in their own red tape.

But the most important thing Stefan taught me was how to carry a court—not just its demands, but its expectations.

Kade took to the goodwill work—border disputes, merchant crises, and emergencies where strength and sincerity were what mattered. He leaned into the physical roles—military reform, troop morale, infrastructure, and all the goodwill missions to courts that still whispered about my father's disgrace. He was blunt force and banner-smile, and everyone loved him for it.

Rhune...elegance incarnate. Born of a minor house but bred to court life, he needed only polish. Stefan honed him like a blade. Rhune took Stefan's lessons and made them lethal—used his refinement as cover for razor wit, and kept records of every noble's weakness for later.

Rhune was the diplomat, the emissary, the quiet consigliere who could talk a court into surrender or vanish a problem without anyone noticing it had ever existed. Rhune became the man I trusted to sit across from powerful people and make them leave shaking hands without realizing they'd been outmaneuvered. He was also the one who could disappear for three days and return with a problem quietly resolved. He made quiet into power.

And I became what Serena had envisioned. A lord with teeth. Not the son of my father, not the quiet boy tethered to the Moon Court's heir. But a leader in his own right. Strategic. Surgical. Dangerous. But still me. At least in private.

Shade began to change.

Not fast. The coffers were low, the nobility suspicious, the merchants still bitter over what my father had been. But little by little, it shifted. We focused on our people first. Not glory. Not politics. Clean water. Roads. Trading routes. Grain subsidies in bad seasons. And when they trusted us, then we began the business moves—ruthless, brilliant ones. Buying out struggling guilds. Forcing competitors into mergers. Exploiting old laws and rewriting new ones.

But Shade thrived. I began to love my court, my birthright. And it all traced back to that ink-stained morning and the girl who'd handed me a plan.

But Serena didn't stop at diplomacy.

A week after he arrived, so did Master Dewin—an archmage from the Tower. He showed up at my gate with nothing but a walking stick, a battered satchel, and a letter of introduction in Serena's hand. Said she'd settled a 'matter' for him. Wouldn't say what. Only that he owed her, and that she'd reasoned Mab had formally made me Lord, which meant I should be allowed to resume my magery education.

Only now, I had a court to govern.

So the Tower had come to me.

He trained all of us in high magery, not just theory but application—offensive, defensive stealth...pragmatic, and obscure. We could cloak troop movements in ink and code. It was like learning a second language I hadn't known I was missing.

And when it came to the military, she brought in a hurricane.

A month after Dewin, Elsibetha marched in without announcement, threw her travel leathers over the nearest chair, and huffed, "Your military's pathetic. I'll fix it."

And she did. Gods, did she ever.

Once or twice a month she descended like a war goddess, shouting orders, running drills, and breaking every chain of command with nothing but presence and pedigree. But she didn't stop there. When the military was too exhausted to argue, she'd turn to us and teach advanced forms—movements the Dardani never bothered with, footwork meant for terrain we'd never seen.

"If you only fight like a Dardani," she said once, wiping blood from her temple after knocking me flat, "you'll be weak against everyone else."

She was right.

So we trained. We studied. We followed Sev's map to power.

She'd showered the merchant class with coin during her visit that day, walked the markets in a royal gown and her tiara, and asked pointed questions about trade routes, tariffs, and infrastructure. She played a part and looked exactly like Mab the Second. That very specific blend of dangerous curiosity and baleful disdain. Then she'd left, casually mentioning that she would be checking in again—and letting them guess when. That was all it took. The fear of a siren queen was a quiet thing, but it lingered.

I realized that day that all those years of Sev asking me—asking herself—what kind of leaders we wanted to be, and what the nature of ruling meant... she hadn't been existential at all.

She'd been preparing. And when I saw her face —determined, vulnerable, already a world away—I understood.

She was leaving.

She told me she needed to know what it was like before she left. I knew she meant more than the kiss. She meant us.

And I let her go.

PART II: COMING OF AGE

CHAPTER SIXTEEN
TIDES

S he had practiced the words a dozen times in her head—standing before the mirror in her chambers, pacing between her bookshelves, murmuring them beneath her breath as her guards escorted her back from the battle yards. She had even considered the tone. Measured, formal, declarative. The kind that brokered no opening for counterargument. She had built contingencies and planned for interruption. Prepared to threaten.

And yet when the day came, the morning of the mandated breakfast, none of that truly prepared her for the way Mab received her.

The room was still cold with dawn mist, the windows cracked open just enough to allow the scent of the sea to thread through the ivory-paneled dining hall. The servants had already withdrawn. It was just Serena and Mab—silver service between them, gleaming porcelain plates, spoons, and knives glinting softly in the muted light.

Mab ate as she always did: with that exacting, predatory precision. Not a single movement wasted. Not a sound but the scrape of steel against porcelain.

Serena waited until the moment was right—until her tea was cooling and Mab's third bite of poached pear had been sliced. Still, her palms were damp beneath the table, and her spine stiffened as she placed her utensils down, hands folding neatly before her. Her voice, when it came, was calm, pitched for clarity, not confrontation.

She said, "Mother. Years ago you promised the other courts that I would spend time in each of them if they turned a blind eye while the Moon Court enacted vengeance for the bloodbinding."

Mab did not look up. She buttered a delicate wedge of toast and raised it to her mouth, chewing slowly, her gaze fixed on the middle distance. The Queen of Ardaion was dressed in dark amethyst robes today, her crown absent, but her presence no less severe.

Serena pressed on, voice clear. "I mentioned previously that I would like to go to Tides, and that desire has not changed. I plan to send the appropriate letters and leave within the week."

It was not a request. She did not couch it in civility or appeal. She declared it. And she braced.

She had expected a flare of temper. A veiled threat. A rebuke cloaked in frost. She had even prepared her counterstroke—how she would mention the spear, the betrayal, how she would summon Jormunder himself to hear the full truth if Mab tried to forbid her. She had rehearsed the arc of the exchange down to the flare of her nostrils and the set of her jaw.

But Mab only kept eating. Calm. Elegant. Controlled.

Then, softly—almost disinterestedly—Mab said, "Yes, I think you should."

The air shifted. Serena blinked, shoulders tightening. Surprise flickered across her face—just enough for Mab to see. And she did see. She always saw.

Mab looked up at her then, the corners of her mouth curling into that razor-thin smirk Serena had learned to hate more than any shout. "What?" she asked, voice full of cruel amusement. "You thought I'd say no? That we'd argue?" She dabbed at her mouth with her napkin. "Serena... at one point I might have. But I've had an epiphany when it comes to you. Would you like to hear it?"

Serena said nothing. She didn't need to.

Mab leaned back slightly in her chair, fingers steepled now, the voice she used one of slow, almost bored malice.

"You don't matter to Ardaion as long as I'm alive," she said. "And I don't plan on going anywhere. So you will be here for the high days, for the holidays and ceremonies. Otherwise... I don't give a *damn* what you do."

The words landed like daggers. Not because they were new. But because she had finally said them aloud. Had stripped bare the veil of mother, queen, and mentor—left only the bone-deep truth: Serena was her disappointment, a living reminder of her loss. Mab's heart had mostly died with Edric, her mate, but for that one desperate hope that she might see him in their child's face. With Serena's birth, that hope that crumbled and blown away like dry leaves; now there was nothing but bitter duty and the interminable loneliness of the immortal.

Then she added, voice suddenly darker, low, and curling like smoke, "Except for offspring. You know our line is always provided a mate by bond. It is how our line continues with strength, the right male selected by the Binding to contribute to our bloodline. Fail that and you fail Ardaion and your reason for existing."

Her eyes locked on Serena's, and when she spoke again, her voice shifted. A hiss. A guttural warning full of old magic and ancestral weight.

"So remember that while you're out there dancing naked around the flames. You must not conceive your heir with anyone but your mate."

She let the words hang. A threat veiled as instruction. Not because she cared who Serena lay with. But because the bloodline, the Binding, was all that mattered to her.

Serena did not blink. Did not flinch. She sat still, back straight, chin high, and replied evenly:

"Then I will be here for the high days and holidays. And I will not bear a child with a male who is not my mate." It sounded calm, simply agreeing to conditions. And with dignity, Serena said, "As I said... I'll be gone within the week."

Mab did not answer. Just turned her attention back to her breakfast.

Serena did the same.

The next four days of preparation passed with Serena watching over her shoulder, expecting Mab to rescind permission or find another spear. Once or twice, she wondered if her food was safe to eat. But she didn't see Mab again. Serena had not been forgiven for what she'd snapped at her. The breakfasts were canceled.

The Tides Court did not rise from stone-built cities or cultivated hills, but from salt and wind and wings. Spanning a vast coastal archipelago, it was a realm both ancient and fluid—shaped not by conquest, but by tide and time. From a distance, the islands seemed wild, untouched. Towering sea cliffs cut sharply into pale skies, their bases white-washed by the endless battering of waves, their peaks crowned with tangled wildflowers and seagrass. But this was not a lawless wilderness—it was a court carved by magic and shaped by memory.

The great cliffs bore two civilizations. At their bases, where the surf crashed against cavern mouths and narrow inlets, the sea-level caves belonged to the Mer—a collective name for the water-blooded fae: selkies, sirens, nymphs, water sprites, and full-blooded mermaids. No two Mer settlements were alike, for their magic shaped the stone itself. Salt-laced halls curved like shells, glimmering with phosphorescence.

Pools shimmered beneath cut coral chandeliers. Tidal song-magic hummed through the walls, used for everything from healing to storm-calling. These were elegant sanctuaries, carved by ancient hands and sustained by spellcraft so old it whispered still.

Higher up the cliffs, where only wind and wings could reach, lived the Akyist. White-winged and blue-eyed, they were Edric's kin—creatures of cloud and feather, descended from storm and star. Their homes were not crude roosts, but airy sanctums perched in hollows and terraces chiseled into the stone with eerie precision.

Though made of rock, their interiors were softened with sky-colored tapestries, drift-wood balconies, and gilded observation decks facing the constellations. The Akyist were both warriors and scholars, their wings able to bear them for hours over sea and sky. They charted the stars not for poetry, but for navigation, and believed every celestial shift foretold something for those willing to look closely. Their temples were observatories, their battle-halls also archives.

It was Edric, Serena's father, and Mab's younger brother, Rivarin, who first envisioned the Valkyries—an airborne naval force capable of launching from a cliff or sea. There were the Dardani warriors of course, but they were used to mountains, and both scorching heat and freezing snow. Valkyries knew the sea and storms, and were far beyond the normal Akyist warriors. The Valkyries were trained with the Moon Court, including familiarity with its Battle Mages. Jormunder had helped design their tactics, and Elsibetha was counted among their number.

Yet for all its military prowess, the Tides Court was not defined by strategy or conquest. Unlike the other courts—civilized, bureaucratized, gowned and jeweled—the Tides had chosen to remain close to the sea and the sky.

They were not ignorant of the world's customs. Their nobles could spar in etiquette, duel in debate, and navigate Moon Court politics with ease. But they wore civilization like a coat: useful when traveling, discarded upon return. Silks and formalwear vanished the moment their boots touched the salt-soaked stone and warm, white sands. No one in Tides wore shoes unless absolutely necessary.

Life in Tides flowed slower. Here, feast days were marked by bonfires on the shore and ritual duels beneath the stars. Music was the sound of crashing surf and a low hum of harmonized chant. Oaths were taken in sea caves lit by glowing barnacles, or beneath starry skies.

Speakers and storytellers. Tides was community more than court.

Their values remained tribal—kinship, strength, lore, and truth. Decisions were made by council, not decree. Elders led not by law but by wisdom and respect. Song and oral history carried more weight than scrolls. Children swam before they could walk, and every sunrise and storm held omens. The court's dual nature—Mer and Akyist—created a layered culture that revered both ocean and wind, body and spirit, instinct and intellect.

Visitors from other courts sometimes mistook the Tides Court as backward, and primitive. But that assumption rarely survived more than a few hours among the Mer's cunning or the Akyist's penetrating gaze. For beneath the primal rhythm of wave and wind lay deep intelligence, old knowledge, and a sharpness honed by storm and solitude. The Tides Court did not need to prove itself. They did not reject civilization—they simply refused to let it dilute them.

Serena had opened a mage gate to reach the Tides, using Serafine's memory as an anchor—centuries of past dealings offering a reliable location. The Shadowdancer had accompanied her both as bodyguard and swordsmaster, her presence silent but watchful. Before their departure, she had advised that local dress would be more comfortable once they arrived, but protocol dictated Serena appear as the Heir. She had obeyed.

She wore a lightweight court gown dyed in navy silk, its sleeves loose, the skirt parted slightly to allow for movement. Her hair was unbound, the emerald, sapphire, and amethyst streaks catching the light and salt wind alike, broadcasting her lineage even before she spoke. Over it a light silver circlet glittered, dotted with pearls.

The archipelago of the Tides court spread in a crescent behind them—sharp cliffs rising from white sand beaches, wind-sculpted rock and open sea. This was Edric's land, though she had never known it as home. The Mer, the Akyist... her people. Her father's people. And yet who were they, really? What had she inherited from them beyond blood and power?

Nerves gripped her. Her previous interactions with Tides emissaries had occurred within formal settings, all polished courtesies and tailored gowns. She had been warned that things changed when the sea called them home.

Serena's letters had followed proper etiquette. She had not mentioned Mab or her upbringing. She had written that she wished to learn the old ways, to observe and participate, and to understand her heritage. The reply had been polite, neutral. They had agreed to her visit.

Still, as she and Serafine stepped through the gate onto warm white sand, the weight in her chest had grown into dread.

A delegation awaited them: half elder nymphs and a siren, the other half Akyist, their white, feathered wings tucked in ceremonial rest. All were deeply tanned, sea-worn, and powerful in presence. The Mer bore eyes of green and grey, some blue. The Akyist eyes were all blue—starlit and piercing. Serena recognized none of them.

She lifted her chin, steadied her shoulders, and stepped forward. Her smile was warm but controlled, her voice strong and practiced as she dipped her head low in greeting. "Greetings. I am Serena, Princess of the Moon Court, Heir of Ardaion. Daughter of High Queen Mab and Edric of the Tides. My companion is the Shadowdancer, Serafine."

The delegation said nothing. No nods. No words. The silence lengthened uncomfortably, though neither Serena nor Serafine moved. They had been trained for moments like these.

At last, the siren at the front—her chestnut hair streaked with teal and braided with cowrie shells and knotted sea glass—stepped forward. Her voice was low, melodic, but powerful. "So. The rejected heir has come."

Serena's face drained white. Her throat clenched. Her stomach twisted so violently it nearly buckled her stance. Then her cheeks flushed red, hot with shame. She lowered her eyes and stared at the sand. Her voice came small and strained: "I... come to learn..."

She bowed her head fully then, shoulders rigid, the word barely a whisper. Her chest hurt so badly it felt like something vital had been ripped out. "Please."

Another long pause. The silence did not soften.

The siren's tone sharpened. "You're full of shame and fear, girl. What has your mother taught you? Tell me plainly. No pretty words."

Serena did not raise her head. Her lips trembled, but she forced the truth through her throat, each syllable thick with humiliation. "Nothing."

The siren stood watching Serena, her expression unreadable as waves lapped gently against the white sands behind her. A few of the Akyist shifted—subtle, instinctive movements as their white-feathered wings ruffled once, then smoothed. The sound of feathers brushing against feathers was soft but unmistakable, a texture to the silence.

At last, the siren spoke again. "She taught you nothing, but the sea called you home."

Serena, still staring at the ground in mute shame, gave a small nod.

The siren moved toward her then—tall and ancient, but not aged. Graceful still, beautiful in the way only the fae could be: carved from the sea and its legends, not time. Her sea-glass and cowrie shell ornaments clicked softly with each barefoot step. Serena, her gaze lowered, noticing the anklets first—shell and bead woven tight around strong, tan ankles, toes dusted with white sand. Her presence was quiet but immense.

She came to a stop just in front of Serena and inhaled slowly, deeply.

"You're shielding it. Put it down."

Serena's eyes flared wide, panic flitting across her features. Her gaze darted to the figures around her—Mer elders, winged warriors, strangers. Males. She swallowed hard.

"Elder... they'll... the males..."

The siren laughed—a husky, amused sound like wave foam over gravel. "Yes, the males! They live among the Mer and they smell sirens from time to time. It affects them. But they learn to shove it aside. We smack them around until they learn to behave."

That earned a few low chuckles from the Akyist males in the group—deep, rumbling sounds that didn't mock her but acknowledged the truth of it.

The siren fixed her with a stare and repeated, firm and clear: "Put. It. *Down*. We can't know you until we've learned your scent. If you're to be our guest, we have to know you. Put it down."

Serena hesitated, then slowly gave a nod. She drew a breath—deep, steadying—and let the shield drop.

Her scent unfurled immediately: roses warmed by the sun, vanilla on the wind, musk woven with sea salt. It didn't hang heavy in the air—it moved, curling in the sea breeze and stroking across the gathered fae like a beckoning current. Heads lifted. Nostrils flared. But no one moved.

The siren reached out, her fingers calloused but gentle as she cupped Serena's chin and tilted her face upward. Their eyes met.

"The fact you haven't been taught is not your failing, child," she said, voice low, "but that of your mother."

Then she reached into the satchel at her hip—a pouch woven from seagrasses and glimmering threads of pearl. From it, she pulled a carved wooden container, smoothed with age and use. She dipped her thumb into the blue pigment inside, then drew it across Serena's brow in a single line.

"I am Meriden," she declared. "A keeper of the siren stories. Sirens are a sisterhood. But since you've never had a mother... I am your mother now. For as long as you are here, and anytime you return."

She turned then to the delegation behind her. The Mer were solemn. The Akyist watchful. All waiting.

"Do you all hear that?" Meriden said, voice carrying like wind over the open sea. "This child has been floating lost on the currents like flotsam. I found her on the beach, and she's mine now. We will teach her."

As one, the gathered delegation responded without hesitation, their voices united and sure: "We will teach her."

The weight of the moment hung there—deep and sacred, like a vow etched into tide-carved stone.

Then Meriden's face broke into a grin, wide and bright, white teeth flashing like polished pearls against her sun-darkened skin. Her turquoise eyes danced with something warmer now, teasing, kind.

"You can put the shield back up for now," she said, tone suddenly more casual. "They'll all want to meet you. And then we'll find you some proper clothes."

A broad-shouldered Akyist male stepped forward from the gathered winged warriors, the sun glinting off his white feathers and bronzed skin. His bare arms were corded with muscle, and though his age was difficult to determine, the lines around his eyes and the settled steadiness in his movements made it clear he was not young. He bore the confident gait of one long accustomed to command, and the open, easy grin of someone who rarely stood on ceremony.

Serena, still rattled from the dizzying shift from humiliation to embrace—from rejection to being claimed as a daughter—met his eyes with a hesitant, bashful look. She wasn't sure what to expect from this one. He looked nothing like her, but there was something in his energy, his physicality, that tugged at an instinct she didn't have words for.

He stomped to a stop before her and said without preamble, "Serena. I'm Ronan. Edric was one of my best friends, and I miss him greatly. It is a pleasure to finally meet his daughter."

Her throat closed a little, and she shifted, uncertain. "I... don't look like him," she murmured, the words full of regret rather than protest.

Ronan huffed a laugh, a warm, sand-graveled sound. "The things I remember most about your father weren't his eyes or his hair. It was how clever he was. How he loved to laugh. What a flyer he was... Your father was always thinking. We got into a lot of mischief growing up together. Something I've heard you have a talent for as well?"

That earned him a shy, crooked grin from Serena. She glanced down, then back up through her lashes. "Well... yes. I suppose I've had my share of mischief... I rode a gryphon once... "

"There it is," Ronan crowed, booming with laughter. "See? That's Edric!"

Before she could react, he pulled her into a crushing hug, lifting her off her feet as if she weighed nothing at all. The force of it drove the breath out of her, but it didn't frighten her. He smelled like wind, salt, and sun-warmed stone—like the cliffs and waves themselves.

When he set her back down, he kept his big hands on her shoulders and said with unflinching warmth, "And I know he would want me to help look after you. So if Meriden is calling you daughter, you can call me uncle, alright?"

She smiled awkwardly at him, unsure what to say, then nodded, red-faced.

But before the silence could settle, there was a thud in the sand beside them. A gust of wind stirred Serena's skirts as a younger Akyist male landed in a confident crouch, then straightened, grinning from ear to ear. His hair was sun-kissed and tousled, white wings half-flared, catching the late light like sails. His skin was golden and tan like the others, and blue eyes—bright and brazen—sparkled with something utterly shameless.

He walked up, bold as Ronan, and grinned wider. "Father, stop stealing all of her attention and let me meet her."

Ronan rolled his eyes. "Serena, this is Cove, my son. He's about your age and a troublemaker, so don't listen to anything he says."

Serena's cheeks bloomed with color under the weight of Cove's gaze. His grin was the sort that had no doubt gotten him out of trouble more times than not—cocky, charming, and dangerous. She cleared her throat and tried to gather her composure.

"Greetings, Cove. I—"

He cut her off, not unkindly. "Can you fly? We'd heard you could fly, but I don't see any wings."

"Blunt and rude as ever," Ronan muttered and smacked the back of his son's head lightly.

"Yes, I can fly," Serena said, trying to hold her voice steady. "But I have Dardani wings... from my grandfather. And... I guess the spell wings..."

She faltered, aware of how ostentatious they seemed compared to the sleek white wings surrounding her.

Cove lit up, entirely unbothered by her hesitation. "The spell wings! They're like Akyist wings, right? But glow?" His grin widened. "Show us."

He stood there, expectant and teasing, his gaze direct. It wasn't mocking. It was open. Eager. Flirtatious, yes, but not in the way that demanded anything. Just pure, unfiltered curiosity.

"Come on," he coaxed. "Don't be shy."

Serena looked helplessly from Serafine—who raised a brow but said nothing—to Meriden, who watched calmly, and then to Ronan, who only tilted his head as if to say *why not?*

Cove winked at her. He was bold. Boisterous. Too confident by half, and it disarmed her.

Her lips twitched. The wink—arrogant and irreverent—reminded her of Graye. And Kade. And some ridiculous combination of both. She found herself smiling despite her better judgment. Then, gently, she reached inward—toward the wellspring.

They felt it the moment her magic stirred. The air around her shifted, thickened, humming faintly. Like radiance without light. Then, with a shimmer and a pulse, they unfurled.

The spell wings.

They arched high and wide behind her, glasslike and prismatic, translucent feathers catching the sun. Rainbow light spilled across the sand, refracting on the pale stone, painting everyone in waves of color like stained glass. There was no mistaking what she was.

Meriden stepped forward a little, gazing at the wings with something proud and reverent in her face. All sirens remembered the First Matriarch, and that it was they, the sirens, chosen by the Binding to protect Ardaion. Many of their stories passed down included the spell wings, and now here they were in all their glory. Legend made real. Ronan beamed—he had seen Mab's, once—and nodded.

Cove's grin faded into something quieter, something wide-eyed and awed. "They're beautiful," he said softly.

Serena looked away, suddenly self-conscious.

"Come fly with me," he offered, extending a hand like it was the most natural thing in the world. "I'll show you the islands."

Ronan groaned, exasperated again. "Cove, she's still wearing all her fancy clothes. Let her settle in, for the sea's sake..."

To Serena, he added, in a half-grumble, "He may have been excited for your visit."

But Cove only stood there, grinning—golden, radiant, cocky—and still holding her gaze with those piercing blue eyes. Serena smiled again, helpless to stop it, and for the first time in days, her nervousness eased.

CHAPTER SEVENTEEN

MY SISTERS

Meriden had seen to Serena dressing as the Mer did—blousing knee-length trousers and cropped tops, wrap dresses that draped over one shoulder only, all in jewel tones stitched with shells, bits of sea glass, and polished coral. Her black hair had been braided into multiple strands, each decorated with those same adornments, and the look transformed her. Cooler now beneath the island sun, bare feet pressed into white sand, she looked every inch a child of the coast.

She was not used to showing so much skin, not for ceremony or greeting, and the exposure made her blush faintly. But Serafine, composed as ever, observed in silence with a knowing glint in her ancient, violet gaze. Novelties rarely stirred the Shadowdancer, but the subtle amusement in her expression hinted at approval. Change, in any form, was welcome to the fae who had lived too long.

Meriden's cave was part home, part shrine. Its walls had been polished smooth by water and shaped by magic, its surfaces catching the shifting light from ocean waves that reflected through carved openings in the stone. Glowing fae lights lit alcoves lined with shells, books, bottles of pearls, and relics from the sea.

The runes and glyphs painted across the walls were unfamiliar to Serena—not the magery she had studied, but older. Wilder. This was a place of deep memory, alive with scent and sound, with sea winds and the crash of breakers rolling through its open arches. Hammocks swayed lazily in the breeze, and there were soft beds for Serena and Serafine, a concession to the customs they carried from the Moon Court.

Outside, Ronan and Cove waited. Both were barefoot, both tanned and smiling. When Serena emerged—shy despite herself, arms at her sides and face pink—Ronan's smile deepened.

"There she is," he said, approving. "A daughter of Tides. You'll be more comfortable in this; midday can be brutal if the breeze calms."

Meriden gave a final touch to one of Serena's braids and pulled her gently into a one-armed embrace, speaking in a lower, warmer voice now. "You have a couple of hours before sunset. That's when the fires are lit, and the proper welcome begins. Let Cove show you the islands until then."

She turned her gaze to the boy, bright-eyed and barely contained, and added, "Be on your best behavior. Don't take her too far. And don't do anything stupid."

Cove grinned in open rebellion. "That sounds like no fun at all, Meriden."

Ronan sighed. "Cove..."

But Serena, still uncertain yet determined not to retreat into silence, lifted her chin slightly. "I'm sure it'll be fine." Her smile was tentative but real.

Cove brightened instantly. "Alright, Princess. Let's see how you fly."

He stepped out toward the edge, motioning for her to follow, his wings beginning to fan out in the sunlight. Serena's expression shifted, the nerves creeping in again.

"I can't usually summon the spell wings unless I'm locked into the wellspring," she explained as she walked. "So most of the time, I use my Dardani wings. But they're... not feathered. They're like my grandfather's. Draconic."

She hesitated, unsure again—her black, leathery wings marked her like a brand. Among the white-feathered Akyist, they were a glaring anomaly. But Ronan showed no flicker of discomfort. He had worked alongside Rivarin, Edric, and Jormunder to found the Valkyries.

Ronan, noting the hesitation, spoke gently. "To have Jormunder's wings is a gift, Princess. We honor the Black Dragon here." To his son he said, "Cove... they're black, and in this sun they'll heat up faster. Take it easy. Don't let her overdo it."

Cove gave the universal son's reply: a nod that said *yes, no, and I've already stopped listening*. But Ronan let it pass.

Serena exhaled, then summoned them.

In a shimmer of black smoke, the great leathery wings formed—scaled along the ridges, powerful, marked with a subtle iridescence that shimmered like oil. They were immense, dragging shadows across the sand. She stretched them to their full span. The claws at their joints caught the light, capped in ornamental silver.

The others were silent.

Meriden's eyes were steady on the wings. Ronan's face was solemn, respectful. Cove's grin remained, but there was curiosity now, and a flicker of something quieter.

Serena turned slightly, uncertain. "Meriden... why do you think I inherited these instead of Akyist wings?"

The question was old. Older than Serena's arrival here. Older than her earliest memory of Mab's scorn.

"The Binding only knows," Meriden replied at last. "Jormunder was born marked, wings unlike any before or since. And he passed those on to you. The Binding always chooses mates who strengthen the line. Perhaps there's something in those wings that made them worth keeping. They may yet serve you in some way."

She smiled warmly, "Your siren nature overrides all else now, yes. But you are Edric's daughter. Half-Akyist by blood. And Tides knows it."

The answer struck home. Serena gave a faint nod. Then Meriden stepped back, smiling gently.

"Go," Meriden said softly. "Have fun. Be young."

Cove took off with a single leap, wings beating hard, climbing high. Serena glanced once more at Meriden and Ronan, then launched after him, her wings thundering as they rose through the blue.

Together they spiraled upward, the sky vast above and the sea wide below.

From the cliffs, the two elders watched her silhouette rise and follow the boy into the bright horizon.

"Mab has left her half empty," he murmured. "She's got deep wounds, Meri."

Meriden folded her arms and nodded. "Mab wanted Edric back. Grief twisted her. I heard she nearly jumped from the palace ramparts the night he died, before they pulled her back. I think a part of her did."

She reached over and touched Ronan's arm.

"In some ways, this is better," she said. "Tatiana and Mab gave Ardaion polish—but forgot where they came from. We have a chance to give Serena roots, not marble. Did you feel how powerful she is?"

Ronan nodded slowly. "Yes. But I also felt how deep her shame runs. She doesn't think she's enough. That would've broken Edric's heart. He was so proud of the pregnancy. He would have loved her with everything he had."

Meriden's voice, then, was both solemn and resolute.

"Now that's our job."

Cove flew like someone who'd been born into the wind—his body loose, his wings precise, the sea breezes nothing more than a playground for his momentum. Serena was managing, adjusting with each beat of her wings, but she could feel the difference. The Moon Court's skies were calm and inland. This was alive, unpredictable. She adjusted her angle, narrowed her focus, and kept pace.

He slowed for her, glancing sidelong with a knowing look and a half-smile that said he noticed everything—the effort she wasn't used to showing, the way she tried to hide it.

"So," he said over the wind, "what do you think of it so far? Living up to all the terrifying expectations of the wild, savage Tides Court?"

She gave him a breathless, wry look. "I'm not sure yet."

But then her voice softened, the truth slipping past her usual shields. "I was afraid I wouldn't be welcome. Or that I'd be a disappointment."

His expression changed—not surprised, not mocking. Just quiet, and more thoughtful than she'd expected. "That's not how it felt here."

He angled a bit closer, his flight easy, deliberate. "We've been *waiting* for you, Serena. Word spread that you were finally coming. After all these years, after Mab kept her distance and kept *you* from us. Father was the first to say it—he said it meant something that you asked. That you *wanted* to come. That you wanted to learn. That alone earned respect here."

He looked ahead as he banked with the gust. "We don't talk about it much, but after Edric died, Mab cut us off. There were visits promised—your birth was supposed to bind the courts even tighter. But instead, nothing. Not even a letter. Father always thought maybe it was grief. Or pride. Or both." Then he looked back at Serena, steady and frank. "But no one here ever blamed you."

There was silence for a beat, broken only by the wind and the distant hush of breakers against reefstone.

Then he added, voice lighter but still edged with meaning, "My father was near vibrating with pride when your letter arrived. He cleaned the house. That never happens."

Her breath hitched with a laugh she didn't mean to let out, and his grin curved—pleased.

He glanced away briefly, watching the light ripple across the water far below, then back to her. "The old ways matter to us. We thought they'd been buried under marble and protocol. But then we hear the Heir of the Moon Court wants to learn the siren songs, wants to walk barefoot on the sand and fly with us. That's not a disappointment, Serena."

The way he said her name—low, with meaning—made her chest tighten.

"And as for me..." His smile curved slowly, more intimate now, cocky but deliberate. "I'll admit I had expectations too. The daughter of Edric , my dad's best friend? A siren princess who can summon spell wings and walk into a court she's never known like she belongs in both worlds? That's not just welcome. That's... interesting."

He angled into a dive, calling behind him with just a thread of mischief beneath the baritone: "Come on, Princess. Let's see how fast a Black Dragon can fly."

Cove led her back just as the horizon blazed gold, the sky streaked with rose and indigo. Their feet hit the sand with a light thud, the wind still tousling their hair as the last gusts of flight clung to their forms. Serena's cheeks were sun-warmed, her hair tangled from sea gusts, and her grin was wide, eyes alight with the same glimmering mischief that danced in Cove's expression.

Cove looked smug, pleased with himself for the flight, and perhaps more so for her reaction to it. He offered a hand to steady her, though she didn't need it, and grinned as if he'd won something.

Meriden and Ronan exchanged a glance from near the firepit. There was a satisfaction there, quiet but unmistakable. Cove had brought her back smiling. That alone was worth something.

"She's quick," Cove announced, his voice carrying over the sand as he dropped into a casual lean. "Outflew me near the reef."

Around them, the ceremony was taking form. A towering bonfire had been built from white driftwood, now alight with turquoise and jade-colored flames that shimmered like aurora against the night-dark sand. Drums were being arranged in a crescent to one side, their stretched skins painted in spiral motifs, polished bone drumsticks set beside them. Fae lights hovered overhead, casting soft illumination like floating stars. The scent of roasted seaweed, salt-crusted fish, and sweet kelp bread drifted in from nearby fire pits, tended by elder nymphs with sleeves rolled high and laughter on their tongues.

More of the Mer had arrived—nymphs, sprites, other water fae. The Mermaid matri-archs wore one-shouldered dresses in aquamarine and jade, woven from kelp fibers and adorned with shells and gleaming coral. Anklets clinked as they walked, and their hair was braided with bits of polished sea glass and ivory pearls.

The Akyist males wore light trousers, some with open shirts, many bare-chested, their skin bronzed, their wings tucked tight and dusted with sand, while the females wore light dresses or sarongs. None looked surprised by the display of Serena's draconic wings. This was the sea, where lineage bent and magic did not ask permission. And the eyes now resting on Serena were not hostile but curious. She was not merely a visitor. She was Edric's daughter.

A siren. A royal. And newly claimed by Meriden.

Among the Mer, customs were old and enduring. Female-born children remained with the sisterhood, especially if their blood bore traits of water—gills, scaled skin, eyes of sea-glass color, or if their magic transformed them at puberty, as it had with Serena. Such girls were claimed fully by the sea and raised among the water fae.

Boys, though fewer, were just as valued, and often fostered among the Akyist or sent to live as mariners, scholars, or traders. Some joined the Valkyries, rare among the sea-born. Many were the result of unions at festivals such as this one—casual, joyous, and communal. Water fae mated outside their kind to continue the line. The sisterhood raised all children together, which made Meriden's ceremonial adoption of Serena not only fitting, but natural.

Serena stood among them now, clad in turquoise sarong and a white wrap top that left her midriff bare, her braids catching the sea breeze. The blush on her cheeks had not faded, but she did not try to hide it. She looked like one of them, even if she didn't believe it yet. Just a girl of Tides, sun-warmed and wind-tossed, standing at the edge of a welcome long denied but now offered without condition.

And across the fire, Cove stared at her—arms crossed, a smirk on his face. There was a different kind of gleam in his expression now. Not boastful. Interested. Confident, yes, but less playful than before.

Meriden caught it and smiled to herself.

Ronan caught it and groaned inwardly.

The drums began to thrum softly—slow, steady, like waves on stone. The celebration had not yet begun, but it was coming. The sea was ready to remember her.

The drums began to thrum—slow and steady like a heartbeat beneath the sea—and Serena let her wings vanish entirely. The weight faded from her back as Meriden stepped beside her and took her hand, leading her toward the central fire.

The innermost circle around the bonfire was composed entirely of the Mer females, all types of water fae. Some lounged in the shallow tide pools and inlets nearby, letting the surf lap over their legs, their bodies half-submerged beneath moonlight and flame. Most bore fangs like Serena's, though hers remained hidden for now.

But as they reached the fire's edge, Meriden turned to her and murmured, voice low but sure, "Embrace what you are, Serena."

Her smile was kind. Encouraging. And though Serena still met it with wariness—her history with maternal figures a jagged thing—she obeyed. Her lips parted slightly, and she called them forward.

The fangs slid into place. Her blood recognized the moment.

Meriden bared hers in return and loosed a sharp, guttural snarl—not aggressive, but playful, challenging, almost a tease. Her eyes glittered with mirth, and Serena couldn't help it—she laughed, the sound slipping free, and grinned back wide enough to show all her teeth. She didn't snarl. Not yet. But she didn't hide.

The drums softened.

Meriden raised her hand and stepped forward, the sea glass glinting in her hair. When she spoke, it was not in Common, but in the ancient tongue of the sea. Her voice settled into the rhythm of oral tradition—chantlike, lilting, fluid.

She told the story of the Binding. But not the version Serena had heard in the Moon Court archives. Not the one told by kings and queens, by war councils and generals.

She told the story behind the story.

Meriden told of the sirens who remained behind after the queens had risen to power. The sisterhoods who sang the magic into shape each tide, who watched the shores and bore daughters to keep the power alive. She spoke of matriarchs—not crowned but obeyed. Of fangs and blood and scent. Of girls whose bodies burned with the Thrall and who were taught by mothers, aunts, and elders to yield only when they wished, to own what they were.

She spoke of exile and return, of transformation, of how the sea never gave up its own. And Serena listened with wide eyes, barely breathing. No history book had told this version. No Moon Court scroll had ever spoken the names of these women. Serena hung on every detail.

Meriden spoke of the first daughters of the sea, of those who never broke.

She spoke of sirens who bled together, hunted together, healed together. Of the elders who taught girls how to wield the Thrall, how to protect themselves, and how to never be afraid of their hungers. How to snarl. How to smile. How to love.

And then she turned and placed her arm around Serena's shoulders.

"This girl," her voice now in Common, firm, and resonant, "has walked far without a mother. She has lived among stone and silence. But her blood has not lied. *She is ours.*"

She turned fully to Serena now, facing her, and said with ritual clarity, "Serena, you are of the sisterhood. You are of the unbroken line. You are daughter to the sea and sky. While you are here—and anytime you return—you are mine. And by our rites, all who are female-born and bear water magic are raised by all. We do not raise daughters alone. We raise them together."

She looked down at Serena, and with a gentle press of fingers, guided her. "Lower your shield, child. Let them know you."

Serena nodded once, then dropped the shield.

Her scent spread over the gathering like warm tidewater—rose and vanilla and sea salt, lush and unhidden. She felt it uncoil from her like a thread of herself finally allowed to reach others. Serena inhaled—and for the first time, she smelled the others. The subtle layers of sirens interwove into citrus, blossoms, salt, and spice. A current of kinship deeper than language. Nearest to her, Meriden smelled of plumeria and cardamom.

Meriden lifted her arms higher. "We have a new girl-child to raise. My daughter, Serena. Your sister. Welcome her!"

Then she stepped forward, kissed Serena on both cheeks and pressed her forehead to hers.

The drums surged.

One by one, the women stepped forward. Water fae of every kind—Mer with pearl-threaded braids, nymphs in gauzy sarongs, sirens with bite marks still fresh from ritual rites. Each gave her name. Each said, *"Welcome, sister."* Each kissed Serena's cheeks, pressed foreheads, and offered a gift.

Bracelets strung with coral. Anklets made of braided kelp. Shell combs, scraps of shipwreck jewelry, strings of pearls harvested at depth. Tokens of belonging, of bonding, of memory. Serena accepted each one, her hands full, her heart fuller still.

The Akyist stood back—males and females both—watching with calm patience. This part was not theirs. It belonged to the water, to the bloodlines, to the old rites.

But soon they would join. Soon the feast would begin, and the dancing and the fire would burn all night. There would be wine and fruit, fish grilled on polished stones. It was the way of life- pleasure and power, lineage and love, and rituals older than the courts themselves.

And all would dance. All would drink. And yes—there would be pleasure sought and taken. This was the Tides.

CHAPTER EIGHTEEN
SALT AND BLOOD

The music had shifted—no longer the steady, ceremonial rhythm of the inner circle but something wilder, visceral, rooted in bone and tide. It poured from hollow drums and reed flutes and the sharp percussive clack of shells snapped together, layered with hoots, deep-throated cries, and chanting that rose like a storm surge. It had no melody, only movement. The kind of music made not for performance, but possession.

The scent of salt and smoke and faint traces of siren perfume clung to the wind. Though the scents had been shielded once more, the air still carried hints—citrus peel, jasmine, a thrum of magic that tickled instinct. Jugs of wine passed from hand to hand, sourced from across the realm—Solace spiced wine, fiery Ember wine, Shade-dark vintages. There was fruit in abundance: sliced mangoes, moon-plums, tart sea berries. And meat, both roasted and raw, filled the air with savory perfume. The raw fish was marinated in spice, sliced with precision, and layered on broad leaves like treasure on a platter. A siren delicacy.

Serena sat on a gnarled driftwood log near the edge of the firelight, her bare feet dug into the sand, hair half-unraveled from the braids. The fire cast dancing light on her skin as she ate from a carved shell bowl, her fingers nimble and her expression cautiously delighted. She ate with a kind of surprised pleasure, the cool richness of the raw fish shocking but satisfying.

It had a bite of citrus, some brine, and a trace of heat. A dish meant for predators, for those with teeth meant to rend rather than chew. She licked a smear of oil from her fingertip, still slightly flushed from the earlier welcome.

Cove dropped down beside her with a bounce and a grin, hair tousled, sweat shining faintly at his temple. "There you are, princess," he said, stealing a piece of fish from her plate with no shame. "You taste the blood yet?"

She laughed quietly, caught off guard. "It's good," she admitted. "I didn't expect to like it."

"You're one of us now. That means your tongue's got to learn a thing or two," he said, bumping her shoulder with his lightly. His eyes glittered in the firelight, bright and warm. "And your feet."

She raised an eyebrow. "My feet?"

He stood in a single, fluid motion and held out his hand. "Dance with me."

Serena hesitated. Her bare feet curled slightly in the sand, and she gave a small, sheepish smile. "I don't know the songs... or the steps."

Cove leaned in, resting his elbow on his knee, face lit with mischief. "There are no steps. Just your blood and the beat." He stood, held out his hand, and then gave a mockingly scandalized gasp when she didn't move. "You're not scared, are you?"

She opened her mouth, no doubt to protest, but he didn't wait. He grabbed her hand with a warm, calloused grip and tugged.

"Wait—" was all she managed before he hauled her to her feet with a laugh, a soft yelp escaping her as she stumbled into him.

The music surged again—bass rhythm like a crashing tide—and Cove spun her once, carelessly graceful, then tugged her into the blur of bodies around the fire. There were no formations, no pairings that lasted longer than a breath. Just bodies moving, arms lifted, hair flying, hips rolling to the drumbeats. The sand was warm beneath their feet. Serena's skirt fluttered around her thighs as Cove led her into the fray, dancing like it was breath and birthright.

And slowly, hesitantly, she began to follow.

Across the fire, Ronan looked on, arms folded loosely across his chest. His expression was a mix of fondness and exasperation as Cove pulled Serena into the heart of the revel, spinning her around like they'd done this every summer since childhood. Her hair glinted with bits of shell and coral, her sea-toned wraps fluttering with each turn.

"Edric..." Ronan murmured, barely audible over the drums. "I wish you could see this."

The wine had long since dulled the edges of time. The drums were still thundering behind them, and the fire's light flickered dimly over the dunes, but Serena wasn't sure how long they'd been dancing. Her cheeks ached from smiling, her limbs were loose, and her thoughts drifted with the tide. She giggled at something Cove said—she couldn't even recall what—and before she'd fully registered it, he had taken her hand again, lacing his fingers through hers.

"Where are we going?" she asked, breathless, her voice just above a whisper.

"I want to show you something," he said, tugging her along without letting go. His grip was warm, firm, and she followed without resistance, only vaguely aware of how tightly they were still connected.

They crested one of the sandy hills that curved between the beach and the cliffs beyond, and it was there that Serena faltered.

Two pairs of figures were sprawled in the shadows just off the path—water fae and Akyist both—half-draped in woven wraps, their bodies glinting with sea salt and sweat. Moans drifted up like music, raw and unbothered. Hands gripped hair, mouths roamed skin. One nymph arched beneath her partner with a sound of unrestrained pleasure.

Serena stopped short, scandalized.

Her face went crimson, though the moonlight made it hard to tell. "Are they...? Is that—out *here*?" she whispered, shocked. "Anyone can *see*! *We're* seeing!"

Cove glanced back, saw her wide eyes and horrified whisper, and let out a bark of laughter. "What, never seen that before?"

"No!" she hissed, scandalized and still staring, half-frozen in place.

He grinned, clearly enjoying her reaction. "You're definitely from the Moon Court."

"And *you* walk past this like it's normal?" she muttered, stumbling to catch up as he kept walking, still laughing softly to himself.

"It *is* normal," he said easily, not looking back this time. "It's summer. It's Tides. You'll get used to it."

She huffed but didn't argue, not quite trusting her voice. The sounds behind them faded with distance, replaced by the quiet hush of wind and waves as they rounded a bend, skirting the dark base of a cliff. Here the beach grew rockier—less traveled, more wild. Cove led her down carefully, helping her over smooth stones and driftwood until they reached a shallow outcropping where tide pools shimmered between weathered shelves of stone.

It was darker here. Only the stars above and the faint spill of moonlight guided their steps.

Cove knelt by one of the pools and dragged his fingers through the water. A burst of soft blue light shimmered in his wake—bioluminescent algae, glittering like a thousand tiny stars.

Serena gasped softly and dropped to her knees beside him, her scandal and hesitation forgotten. She reached into the water and swirled it with both hands, watching the bright trails flicker outward like magic. Fish darted through the glow, their scales flashing electric.

"Oh," she breathed. "It's beautiful."

Cove didn't answer at first. He just sat back on his heels, arms braced behind him, watching her with a grin that was no longer teasing. Something gentler now, something more intent.

"*You're* beautiful," he said quietly, not expecting her to hear over the waves.

But she did. And her hands stilled in the water.

She turned her head toward him, startled, her hands still trailing faint blue ripples in the water. Her mouth parted slightly, but no words came out. Her brows lifted, her expression caught somewhere between alarm and confusion, as if she'd just stepped into a dance whose steps she hadn't learned.

Because that hadn't been just a compliment.

She wasn't sure what the protocol was. She hadn't been trained for this.

Graye had flirted, yes—but often in that half-sardonic way of his, as though mocking the very idea of flirtation even as he performed it. With Graye, it was layered—habitual, defensive, playful. Sometimes it meant nothing. Sometimes it meant everything. It was Graye.

But this... Cove had known her for mere hours. And yet she could feel the weight behind the words—something sincere, unguarded. Maybe it was just who he was. She suspected that. That Cove existed in that sun-soaked ease, that he spoke what he felt when he felt it. But she also suspected he meant it.

She continued to gape at him, dumbfounded, the sea wind lifting her braids and the scent of salt brushing between them. Her mind scrambled for a response, for the correct posture, the expected line. She came up empty.

Cove grinned, and something flickered in his eyes—amusement, warmth, recognition. He leaned forward slightly, arms still braced behind him, and said with a chuckle low in his throat, "You really don't know what to do with that, do you?"

And gods help her, she didn't.

Cove only watched, the faint light from the tide pools reflecting in his eyes like flecks of sapphire.

He was a stranger. Handsome. Bold. Very, *very* flirty.

And nothing brilliant leaped to Serena's aid—not charm, not poise, not her usual verbal precision. Still blinking at him, a little owlish and entirely uncertain, she asked, "Why...did you say that...?"

The question trailed off unfinished as her gaze flicked—just for a heartbeat—toward the dunes behind them. The unmistakable sounds carried on the warm breeze: breathy, rhythmic, private noises that made her cheeks flame and her thoughts scatter.

Cove caught the glance and huffed a low, amused grin, sensing the trajectory of her thoughts. "So I guess you've never..."

Her eyes snapped back to him, narrowing at the indecency of the question. Her spine straightened with practiced grace, chin lifting in instinctive defense. "None of your concern," she said, reaching for as much regal composure as she could summon under the circumstances.

He laughed outright. "That's a no."

She gasped, scandalized, and slapped her hand through the tide pool water. A shimmering arc splashed across his chest, the bioluminescent droplets scattering over his bare skin like starlight. Cove recoiled, still laughing, the sound boyish and delighted, utterly unbothered by the water or the implication. He wiped a glowing streak off his arm, grinning as he said, "Feisty."

Serena spluttered, struggling to find words. "I guess you have. If all of Tides is like... like... that..." She gestured sharply toward the dunes, where moonlight glinted off the moving forms of entangled bodies, their pleasured cries audible even over the distant crash of the surf.

Cove glanced in the direction she pointed, entirely unbothered. Then his grin widened, lazy and amused. "That?" he said, tone incredulous. "You mean grown fae enjoying themselves under a full moon at a welcome feast? That?"

He leaned back on one hand, the other idly stirring the tide pool beside him, sending ripples of bioluminescent blue shimmering through the water. "You really are from the Moon Court," he said again, not in judgment but mild fascination, as if she were a particularly well-groomed relic from a colder, more austere world. "Don't worry. No one expects anything from you. But if you're staying here, you might want to get used to seeing it. We're fae. We celebrate. We connect."

He glanced sideways, catching the slight furrow in her brow, and added, his voice lower now but still teasing, "And for the record—no. I haven't. Yet."

There was a beat, and then he turned that grin back on her, eyes glinting in the starlight. "Why? You thinking about changing that?"

She gaped at him again, speechless, scandal and disbelief warring in her wide grey eyes. Cove only grinned wider—wolfish, utterly self-assured, as though her reaction was the most entertaining thing he'd seen all evening.

When she finally found her voice, it came out in a splutter. "I... beg your... how dare... What makes you think I *would*... that I'd be willing to... we barely know each other!"

Cove's grin didn't fade. If anything, it deepened with mischief. He leaned back onto his elbows, relaxed and unhurried, the bioluminescent pool casting a faint glow along the edges of his bronze skin. "I didn't say you were willing," he said mildly. "You asked. I answered. That doesn't mean I expect anything." His eyes raked her slowly, not crude but curious.

He paused, then added with mock solemnity, "Besides, I'm not that easy. I like to be wooed. Gifts, flattery, maybe a song or two." Another grin flashed. "You better start practicing. Otherwise, someone's going to snatch me up before you figure it out."

Serena woke to the low murmur of surf and the damp hush of a sea cave, the scent of salt and stone clinging to the air. For a moment, she forgot where she was. The ceiling above her wasn't carved moonstone, but rough limestone mottled with ancient watermarks. No silk curtains fluttered over the windows. There were no windows. Just the hollow light of morning filtering through a distant tunnel and the rhythmic echo of waves breaking on the rock.

Then she remembered—Tides. Meriden's home. The visit. The tide pools. The music. Cove.

Panic flared. Her body moved before her mind caught up, throwing the blankets off. Moon Court discipline had trained her to rise before dawn, to expect summons and tasks and tutors waiting with ledgers and expectations. If she hadn't been awakened, it could only mean one thing: she was already late.

She dressed quickly in a teal sarong, fingers fumbling with the knot, and ran barefoot toward the cave mouth, heart pounding. But the dread that gripped her chest began to loosen as she caught sight of Meriden.

The elder siren was sitting on a low stone bench near the cave's opening, drinking from a smooth shell cup, chatting lightly with a younger female whose laughter chimed like sea glass in the breeze. They were gossiping, carefree, sunlight warming their hair. No urgency. No barked orders. No clock.

"I'm sorry," Serena blurted as she reached them. "I didn't mean to sleep in..."

Meriden only laughed, her eyes bright and unbothered. "Tides doesn't use clocks, Serena. You were tired. And we've got all day."

The younger sprite giggled and poured more tea, entirely unbothered by Serena's arrival.

That was the first clue—that this court moved not by bells or laws, but by rhythm. By tide and wind and instinct.

Then Meriden tilted her chin toward a large conch shell sitting beside her. Pale seagrass had been coiled around its base, and an orchid bloomed from its opening, delicate and deliberate. There was a rich floral scent to it like vanilla.

"That's for you."

Serena blinked at it. "Thank you... it's beautiful."

"It's from Cove," Meriden added, her mouth twitching into a knowing smirk. "He left it at the entrance to the cave early this morning."

The sprite leaned forward, eyes dancing with mischief. "It means he wants to court you."

Serena's hand, half-reached toward the shell, froze. Her expression turned wary, like the gift might bite. "Court me?"

Meriden snorted. "You don't know our customs yet, but that little tide pool trip? That was him making his interest known. And you went. Now the salt-brained boy's going to court you. You may as well take the gift—ignoring it'll just make him more relentless."

Serena lowered herself onto the stone beside them, unsettled. "But what do I *do*... about that?"

The sprite raised a brow, like the answer was obvious. Meriden's voice was gentler now, amused but kind. "Whatever you normally do with boys you like. *If* you like him."

But Serena went still. Not with embarrassment—something deeper. Her body stiffened, her shoulders pulling tight.

Both Meriden and the sprite caught it immediately. The air shifted. The laughter was gone.

"I've never really..." Serena murmured, not looking at either of them. "...let myself do that... I... made a mistake once..."

She didn't elaborate at first. Just stared out at the waves beyond the cave mouth. Her face looked pained, fragile.

Meriden reached for her without hesitation, drawing her in close, settling an arm around her shoulders, and stroking her hair. Serena flinched at first, but the gesture was warm, gentle—maternal in a way Serena had never known. The touch made something in her fracture. Her chest grew tight and her breathing hitched.

"We all make mistakes, my daughter," Meriden said softly.

But Serena shook her head. Her voice was barely a whisper, brittle and trembling. "Not like this... I..."

The tears came without warning. Hot and furious and humiliating. She tried to stop them. Couldn't. She was the Heir. The Princess of the Moon Court. She had cried before only in front of Graye, or Elsibetha. Never like this. It was a weakness. And she couldn't help it.

But now the tears fell, unchecked, and her hands trembled as she tried to speak.

"My grandfather and my mother... they fought. Because she wouldn't train me. She was angry, and she took the wards and the guards from my room." Her voice cracked. "I didn't know how to shield the scent."

The sprite, Mei, had gone very still beside her. Meriden's stroking slowed but didn't stop.

"I was sixteen. A boy followed me back to my room. He was in the Thrall. He... he pulled at my dress, put his hand under it. I was cinched so tight I couldn't fight. He wouldn't stop. He couldn't hear me."

Serena was trembling now, her voice shattering. "So I screamed. And in my fear... something happened. I don't know what I did. But he... he turned to mist. A red mist. Blood. All over me. All over the room. There was nothing left. Nothing." A sob escaped her.

She stared at her hands as if she could still see the blood there.

"I killed him. Because I didn't know how to shield. I *killed* him. It's my fault. I can't... can't let that happen again."

Meriden pulled her close, wrapped both arms around her, and rocked her slowly, protectively, as though Serena were no older than five. No words, no judgment. Just warmth.

Mei took Serena's hand, squeezing it, pressing the tea cup gently into her fingers.

And over Serena's head, Meriden looked at Mei—expression hardening into something razor-sharp.

Rage.

Sisterhood, daughters, mothers... that was the core tenant of the Mer. Mab's failure of Serena was heresy.

Meriden had intended to begin that morning with lessons—glyphs etched into the damp sand, siren phrases whispered between waves, small tests to gauge Serena's untapped fluency. But those plans dissolved like mist the moment the girl broke. There were deeper wounds here than Meriden had guessed—wounds no lesson could touch.

The sobbing had eventually slowed, stuttered, and then stopped altogether, leaving Serena heavy and quiet in her arms, face pressed to her shoulder while Meriden hummed softly, rocking her with the same rhythm she'd once used for her own young. Four years had passed since that night, and yet the memory still clung to Serena like a second skin. No shield could hide it. No title could erase it.

This, then, was why she clung so fiercely to that scent shield. Why she held herself with such rigid control. A predator born too early, left to fend without guidance—powerful, yes, but alone. Untrained. Afraid of herself.

The sprite with the sea-glass grin, Mei, appeared again, carrying a carved bowl filled with a rich chowder, steam curling from its surface. Flakes of fish shimmered among roots and herbs, a small roll of flattened bread resting across the rim like a lid. Mei handed it to Serena without a word, then perched nearby as Serena took the bowl and began to eat in small, careful bites.

Meriden continued stroking her hair, thoughtful. Then she looked toward Mei and said, "Why don't you take Serena for a swim with the others this morning? Show her the lagoon. The water's been so warm lately."

Mei's face lit up. "Of course. It's beautiful in the lagoon, lots of flowers today. We can teach you how to dive for pearls."

Serena, still damp-eyed but steadier now, offered a soft smile. "Thank you, Mei. It sounds lovely."

Later that morning, sunlight filtered down in golden shafts through the canopy above the cove as Serena stepped into the lagoon. The water was warm as bathwater, the color of turquoise and crystal, so clear the sand below shimmered white and undisturbed. Bright fish darted through coral hollows. Green and lavender reeds waved gently near the deeper bends.

Sprites splashed and tumbled around her, nimble as otters, laughing and calling to each other in lilting bursts of High Fae and older siren words that Serena only half-understood. A full-blooded mermaid, sea-pale and silver-eyed, twirled lazily through the water, her hair drifting behind like kelp.

Necklaces of tiny flowers were woven and tossed between hands. Some of the sprites had tucked petals into each other's braids. A few lay on sun-warmed rocks, drying and singing snatches of half-forgotten sea ballads. It was chaotic and playful and utterly unguarded.

Serena hovered at the edge at first, uncertain. She had never been allowed this kind of socializing. Her days had been spent surrounded by soldiers, scholars, mages, dance masters—adults with agendas, not equals. She'd learned etiquette and law, politics and war, but not how to laugh in the shallow, turquoise water with girls who wanted nothing from her but her company.

That kind of loneliness—the kind that creeps in despite full rooms and crowded halls—had never been named. It had just... *been*. Until now.

But the sprites were relentless in the way of happy people. They teased and beckoned, and one splashed her with a perfectly timed arc of water that hit her square in the chest. A few tried to braid her hair. Another slipped a flower behind her ear.

And slowly, uncertainly, Serena began to laugh. And *realized* she was laughing.

It started small. A breathy exhale when one of them tried to climb a rock and fell back with a splash. Then a true laugh, when Mei pretended to offer her a pearl and instead cracked a water lily seed pod over her hand, sending silvery dust everywhere. Then more.

She splashed them back. Dove into the warm shallows. Let her hair be braided.

Not warriors. Not tutors. Not guards.

Just girls.

Just sisters.

That afternoon, after Serena returned from swimming, her mood was lighter. Her hair, still damp, carried the scent of salt, and a crown of flowers—woven by the others—was tucked loosely through the strands. Her pockets bulged with small, glinting pearls. For the first time in days, her step was easy.

Meriden noticed at once and was pleased. She had kindled a small driftwood fire at the mouth of her cave, its orange glow reflected faintly in the hollowed stone around her. When she saw Serena approaching, she smiled and patted the ground beside her.

Serena sat with a smile of her own and passed her a flower, saying softly, "Thank you... for this morning."

Meriden took it, tucked it behind her ear, and smiled. "We're family here. All of us."

She passed Serena a cup of tea, then took a sip from her own. Her voice, when it returned, was quieter. "Serena... I've been thinking about where to start your teaching, and I've decided that to understand anything we do, or why we do it, you need to understand what we are."

She stared into the fire for a moment, then began.

"Long ago, Ardaion was wild and full of wild magic. That's why the Gathering was called. That's why the Binding was created. And your line came to power. You've learned that much. But that's what happened to us. Not what we are."

She took another sip.

"Sirens have always existed in the fae lands. And like anything in nature, there are predators and prey. Sirens have always been predators."

Her expression softened, eyes distant, caught in some old memory.

"With civilization—and with the Binding—we took on a maternal role for Ardaion. Or at least, that's how the first siren believed, when she stepped forward. The Matriarch. The others who had gathered there were males. They were all tribal leaders, and clan chiefs, and they wanted to be the ones to harness the wellspring. Males often seek power, and rarely for the good of all. Their instinct is to dominate.

But while the land fae were fighting their battles between clans and tribes, squabbling for territory, the sirens were already a sisterhood. They were matriarchal, with storytellers and elders; they were maternal, and they understood the power of bonds. We raise our daughters communally. Every child is our child. And our children are theirs."

She stirred the fire with a stick, the embers shifting.

"And when the Matriarch stepped forward at the Gathering, she offered her life instead of her ambition. She was willing to view Ardaion—not just the Mer, but all of it—as her children. To defend it. To die for it, if need be. And that is why the land chose her, and bound her line to this cause. Greater power. Great responsibility."

A flicker of heat danced along the tea's surface. Meriden's gaze shifted back to Serena, not with a challenge, but with something measured.

"I think civilization has done great things for Ardaion and the fae," she said, "but I also think it has caused us to lose part of ourselves. Maybe a part of our souls."

She smiled faintly. "You'd know all about that, wouldn't you? The blood-binding with Graye... But the sea called you to the Tides, and I think it's because you're missing that other part of your soul. Or... maybe it's there, but it frightens you."

She didn't press. Only stirred the fire again.

"Let's go back to the time before the Binding. The primitive land fae, in their clans and small groups, always bickering and waging wars with simple weapons and even simpler magics. They fought over river bends and tree lines. In the lakes, the rivers, the oceans—the water fae were their counterparts. Now sprites, nymphs, naiads... they had a few rifts and scuffles, too. But the sirens always relied on each other. And not just to raise children, but to lift their voices together—to lure their prey."

Her tone shifted—deeper, quieter.

"And our prey, Serena... you know what it was. Fae. Not beasts. Not fish. Not deer in the thickets. Fae males. Everything we are is meant to lure them. Subdue them. No brute strength, no sword or shield. We use scent. Voice. Song. Fangs. Saliva. Blood. The Thrall isn't magic—it's design."

There was no softness in it. Only truth.

"Everything about us is meant to bring them in and subdue them. We don't have males. We don't have brute strength. We have our voice, our scent, our fangs. And we are the most dangerous creatures in Ardaion. No male can resist the Thrall."

She leaned back slightly, and let the firelight catch her features.

"We are the only predators for whom the prey not only comes to them, but also do not struggle. They go to their end with smiles on their faces."

Her voice, for just a beat, was hollow with knowing.

"So when the siren queens came to power over the other fae, it wasn't that they'd become civilized. It was just that the wolves had learned to live with the sheep."

Meriden continued, her tone gentler now, but threaded with iron beneath the words. "The problem is, we're still wolves, Serena. We've learned to build cities, raise armies, and craft wonders. We write books. We etch glyphs so precise they can shift the winds, shatter stone, and hold back death itself. We spend decades mastering magery that used to be nothing more than instinct. We dress ourselves in beaded gowns, wear crowns, dance across marble floors with males who don't know they're already prey."

The flames flickered. Her eyes caught the light.

"But the instincts are still there."

She turned to look at Serena fully now, something hunting in the sharpness of her expression. "Tell me... have you ever found yourself watching a sparring match and enjoying the violence more than their faces? Have you ever felt your fangs nudge their way into view because you smelled the blood? Do sudden movements make you want to bare them?"

Serena didn't answer. She didn't move.

Meriden leaned closer. Her voice dropped low. "Have you ever defeated an opponent and felt a thrill at how they lay on the ground at your feet?"

Serena's breath hitched. Her lips parted slightly—but she still said nothing. Her eyes were wide, not with fear, but recognition. Not ashamed. Guilty. Because she had felt those things. Not always. But often enough.

Meriden's mouth curled into a knowing smile. But abruptly her lips pulled back in a deliberate motion, baring her fangs in a silent, calculated snarl. It was a provocation. Her eyes locked on Serena's with a gleam of challenge, testing her. Pushing her. The gesture was pure predator—no warning, no bluff, just the slow, measured flash of a creature who knew exactly what she was doing and how Serena's instincts would answer.

And they did.

Serena's own body reacted before her thoughts caught up. Her spine straightened. Her shoulders squared. The guilt burned away beneath the challenge Meriden had issued without words. It was instinct. An old one. Ancient, bone-deep. A predator does not shrink from another predator.

Her eyes flashed in response.

And with a jolt, she realized her fangs had slipped free. Not fully—just enough to feel the edge of them on her lower lip as her mouth twitched in the beginnings of a snarl.

Meriden's snarl faded into a smirk. She was still watching. Still nodding.

"That," she said softly, "is what we are."

Then she leaned back and took another sip of her tea as if nothing at all had shifted.

"We're monsters, Serena. But that doesn't mean we're bad."

CHAPTER NINETEEN

SEA AND SKY

Two months passed.

Serena had begun sleeping in the wide-woven hammock slung near the cave's mouth, the sea breeze on her skin preferable to the curtained privacy of the back chamber. Her skin had tanned, sun-kissed, and freckled along her shoulders. Her hair, salted and carrying sun-kissed highlights, now bore more of its natural wave.

She had learned to dive—not the shallow games of pools and riverbeds, but real dives, deep ones, with the pressure tightening around her chest and pearls waiting in the sandy dark. She'd explored a sunken shipwreck with a mermaid named Lisri, who swam ahead like a silver-flanked eel, laughing when Serena gaped at the murals still half intact in the coral-choked hull.

And Meriden continued to teach her the old ways.

They sat often beside the tidepools, or shoulder to shoulder on the broad stone ledge where foam licked the rocks, the elder siren murmuring through her lessons in a cadence older than the courts.

It began with the scent shield—how to refine it, not smother it. How to let a little out when it served, rather than blanketing it in panic or fear. Meriden explained what no one else ever had: that the scent, the kiss, the bite—all of it came from one source.

"The blood," she said one evening, as Serena stirred seawater and crushed hibiscus petals in a carved basin for dye. "That's the heart of it. The origin. Our song, our kiss, our scent—it's the blood that makes them tremble, the blood that perfumes our skin and flavors the taste of our kisses."

She spoke, too, of the customs before civilization. How the sirens once knew each other by scent alone. Breathing in a sister's presence, not hiding it. There had been no males in the sisterhoods, no need for shields. The scent shield had come later—an inconvenience of mingling with fae males in the closed rooms of councils and courts, where enthrallment was unwelcome.

Serena listened. Absorbed. Practiced.

She learned to drop inscribed beach pebbles into the sea, each one bearing a glyph shaped from ancient curves—summoning calls for the water fae. She learned the cadence of tide shifts, and how to read the wind by the hiss of spray on distant rocks. And every night, her voice was lifted into the sea air—she was being taught all the songs of the Tides, one after the other, until they began to come alive in her heart.

Sometimes the Akyist came to hear them—especially Ronan and Cove. But not always. Some nights were reserved for lore kept strictly among the siren sisterhood. Other times, the Thrall-work being taught was too potent, too disruptive to male composure. On those nights, Meriden drew glyphs only Serena could see, and the caves filled with layered harmonies that made the rock itself hum.

But Serena was learning quickly. And more than that—she was *happy*.

For the first time in memory, she wasn't ashamed. She wasn't on edge, guarding against herself or fearing what her body might do. Here, her abilities were understood. Welcomed. The power that had marked her as dangerous elsewhere was normal here, expected. It didn't make her less. It made her one of them.

She was laughing more. Dancing without thought. Singing without fear. And Cove... Cove had not missed a single day. Besotted and relentless.

He found excuses constantly. Carving driftwood charms. Bringing flowers, sand-smoothed shells, and bracelets made of sea glass strung on kelp cord. Her wrists and ankles began to carry the daily evidence of his attention. And though Serena teased, rolled her eyes, and scoffed once or twice, she never took them off.

Sometimes Ronan invited her up to the sea-cliff cave, the one only winged fae could reach—carved into the cliff face with arching stone windows, open to the wind and sea, lit by braziers that gave it a soft, underwater glow. It was Edric's cave once. Ronan had inherited it, and now, he shared it.

He and his mate Mika would serve meals and tell stories, setting out seaweed-stuffed dumplings and glazed rootfish while the wind whistled through the upper hollows. Mika, graceful and flame-haired, braided Serena's hair once with little pearls woven into each knot. She told jokes, whistled the old tunes, and quietly watched the way Ronan was watching Serena.

Because Ronan was seeing it now.

It wasn't Edric's white wings Serena had inherited or his warm golden skin, but the mind—that quick, sharp, strategic way of processing a problem before she even voiced it aloud. The way she listened with full attention and then asked a better question. Her quiet smirks. Her fearless responses to dares—once from Graye, now daily from Cove. The child might bear Tatiana's face, but in every way that mattered, she was her father's daughter. And Ronan loved her for it.

Cove took her flying every morning. Her wings had adapted fast to the gusting ocean winds. She could ride a current now, bank with control, hold her place in a spiral.

He introduced her to the other young Akyist, and they'd glide far out past the kelp beds to watch ships pass, sometimes diving low to call greetings to distant sailors. Once, they landed on the mast of a Solace galleon and traded riddles with a weathered captain who offered dried mango slices in return.

Ronan had stopped trying to dissuade him. The boy was harmless enough. Sometimes, when Cove got especially smug with his flirtation, Ronan would sigh heavily and mutter to Mika, "He gets this from your side."

Mika only grinned and whispered back, "At least he has taste."

One evening, the fire in the cliffside hearth burned low, the flames licking blue-green from sea-salt logs. Serena lay curled in a deep-winged chaise, one designed for the comfort of winged bodies. A throw of thick linen was draped over her knees, her braid half-unraveled. She was grinning, eyes bright, caught in a story Ronan was telling—one of Edric's many dares, back when the male had thought himself untouchable and immortal.

Cove sat beside her. Closer than before.

He had shifted through the entire story, inching slowly. His arm had found its way behind her along the back of the seat, casually. Not touching. Not quite. But there. Present. His parents saw it. Neither said a word. Mika suppressed a smirk behind her cup. Ronan rubbed a hand over his face, exhaling like a father who had already surrendered to the inevitable.

Serena hadn't noticed. Yet.

Ronan had shifted into another story now, the timbre of his voice lowering as he moved from battlefield antics to memories more reflective—about the early days of the Valkyries. How it had started as a thought between brothers-in-arms, sharpened into doctrine through debate and flight. And how Edric had always been the quiet one. The thinker.

"Your father never talked much," Ronan said, his gaze resting somewhere past the firelight. "But when he did, you listened. He wasn't loud. But he was always... thinking. Planning. Solving things no one else had even noticed were problems. He had this way of listening that made people speak more than they meant to. And tides, he loved the stars. He used to fly out alone just to study the sky. Kept charts of where the moons were, the passing of comets, the tilt of constellations... I'll show them to you."

That was when Cove made his move.

His arm, which had hovered at the back of the chaise like a hopeful question, finally settled across Serena's shoulders. Not heavy. Just enough to be undeniable. She kept her face turned toward Ronan, but her eyes flicked sideways—just once, just enough to catch the smirk curling on Cove's mouth. He didn't look away. Didn't pretend innocence. He just smirked and stayed exactly where he was.

Serena sighed.

A long, exasperated sigh that could have come from Ronan himself. But she didn't shove him off.

She let him leave it there.

And for Cove, that was a victory worth more than a hundred flirtatious glances.

The story wound down. The fire crackled. Mika caught Ronan's eye and gave the subtlest tilt of her head, a signal they'd long ago perfected: let them be. They were nearing twenty-one, still quite young by fae reckoning—but old enough to need space for their flirtations.

Cove, picking up on the cue, grinned sidelong. "Wanna go up top and watch the stars?" he asked. "Father's got a telescope."

That caught Serena's attention. Her eyes shifted toward him—interested now, not just tolerant. She nodded once, and that was all he needed.

They took to the sky with an easy leap from the cliff ledge, wings unfurling into the darkening air. The moon was low, still rising, casting silver across the sea like a path of coins. The air smelled of salt and wet grass. They landed on the highest peak of the sea cliffs where the land flattened out in a gentle rise, seagrass rustling around them in the steady wind.

Cove opened the tripod legs and set the telescope on the stone outcrop. He adjusted the angle, found the constellation Edric had always marked as his favorite—Thalas, the sea hunter—and passed the eyepiece to Serena.

She leaned forward, one hand braced on the rock, the other gripping the scope, and her face lit up.

A slow, growing grin spread across her mouth as she looked at the stars blooming sharp and clear in the lens.

Cove looked at her, not the sky.

The wind pulled her braid slightly loose, and a bit of moonlight gleamed off the sea glass bracelet on her wrist—his latest gift, a spiral of deep blue beads and tiny silver shells, worn without comment for the last five days. The fact that it was still there, still on her, made something in his chest tighten and his heart melt a little more.

He shifted closer, slowly. No sudden movements. No jokes this time. Just space closing.

She didn't turn right away. Still watching the stars, her mouth curled slowly into a half-smile—more smirk than sweetness. But the air around her had shifted. She'd felt his gaze, felt the careful way he'd closed the space between them, and something in her, something taut and reluctant and wary, gave way like a tide easing back from the rocks.

"I thought you were the one who needed to be wooed," she said lightly, voice edged with amusement.

Cove blinked—then laughed, quiet and breathless. The sound caught in his throat, boyish and stunned. For a heartbeat, he just looked at her, like he hadn't expected her to remember, let alone throw it back at him.

"That was a *joke*," he said, smile tugging wide. "I didn't think you'd remember."

"I was flustered," she admitted, still not turning. "Not deaf."

That made his grin widen. "I thought I was being subtle."

"You told me someone would snatch you up if I didn't act fast," she said, finally lowering the telescope. She straightened and looked at him fully. "That's not subtle."

Cove tilted his head, eyes bright. "Worked, didn't it?"

She looked at him. The sea wind tousled his hair, and there was a flush across his cheeks now, as if her returned volley had hit its mark harder than expected. He was tall, lean from flight, golden from the sun. His smile was too smug. His fingers were drumming silently on the stone behind her, like he was keeping himself still on purpose.

Serena exhaled slowly, the last of her guarded tension bleeding out.

"Maybe. But I think you like being chased."

He stepped closer. Just one slow step, deliberate, giving her room to back away if she chose. She didn't.

"I liked being noticed," he said, softer now. "By *you*."

For a moment, neither of them spoke. The stars moved overhead. The ocean sighed against the cliffs.

Then—quietly, seriously—Cove asked, "Can I kiss you?"

Serena didn't tease this time. She didn't smirk or dodge the question. She just nodded once, slow and certain.

Cove watched her for only a heartbeat more—just long enough to be sure. Then he leaned in.

The kiss began softly. A brush of lips, tentative and warm, like he didn't want to startle her. Serena responded, lips parting just enough to meet his, the gesture curious, exploratory. Her hand stayed at his arm, fingers flexing against the fine weave of his sleeve. The sea wind threaded through her hair, salt and star-washed, and for a moment it felt like the whole world had narrowed to this single, suspended breath between them.

But then he deepened it.

His mouth pressed more firmly into hers, not demanding, not careless—but sure. It was still gentle, but fuller now, drawn from weeks of half-glances and glancing touches and the careful, patient kind of want that builds when two people know each other well.

Then she pulled back.

Her fingers came to his chest, light, not pushing, but hesitating. Her eyes were wide now, caught between want and warning, her voice a whisper. "The Thrall..."

He didn't move away.

His eyes opened, already watching her, and he didn't flinch. "Yeah. I'll feel it," he said simply, voice calm. "But I've grown up around it, Serena. I won't lose myself to it. And you won't hurt me, urchin."

That last word startled her. She blinked. "Urchin?"

He smirked, still close, still not pulling away. "It's how I think of you in my mind. Prickly. But still kind of cute."

Her mouth parted, half in outrage—but before she could swat him for it, his grin turned shameless, and he kissed her again.

And this time, there was nothing tentative about it.

His mouth found hers with confident pressure, deepening the kiss until her breath caught and her hand moved instinctively to his shoulder. But he didn't grope. Didn't lurch. Didn't paw at her like... *that boy* had. His hands stayed steady, respectful, sure. And that, more than anything, unraveled the knot of fear still coiled beneath her ribs.

She grinned against his mouth.

And then she kissed him back. Because she could.

Not shyly. Not carefully. She kissed him with full intent, and when he made a surprised, delighted sound low in his throat, she kissed him again. And again. Until they were both breathless and laughing and slightly dizzy.

He melted into it.

Gone was the cocky tease. His breath hitched as she caught his lower lip and lingered as if she'd finally realized she was a siren and had chosen to *enjoy* it. The kiss curved and curled, unhurried but intense, and when she finally drew back—just a few inches—he was blinking like the wind had been knocked out of him.

"Stars," he breathed. "I was *not* prepared."

Serena tilted her head, smiling lazily now. "After a month of effort? You didn't have a plan for success?"

"I thought I'd earn a smile," he admitted. "Maybe a little peck. Not this."

She huffed a laugh but didn't pull away. Her hand was still against his chest, warm over the thudding of his heart. Her voice dipped slightly, thoughtful. Still wary of the Thrall.

"You don't feel... caught in it?"

Cove shook his head, steady. "No. I feel *kissed*. And slightly smug."

"You always feel smug."

"Yes, but now it's *earned*."

She rolled her eyes but didn't fight the way he leaned his forehead briefly against hers. Then he tilted his head and kissed her again.

Slower this time, softer—but not hesitant. The kind of kiss that says *I could do this for hours*, and meant it.

When they parted, he eased down into the grass beside her, wings tucked behind him, the curve of his shoulder brushing hers. The seagrass swayed around them in the wind, rustling like a lullaby. Moonlight glazed the contours of her face as she lay back, her eyes reflecting the stars.

She glanced sideways, mouth twitching. "You're going to be insufferable now, aren't you?"

He grinned, broad and unrepentant.

That was answer enough.

But then he shifted, rolling onto his stomach beside her. He propped himself up on his elbows, eyes lingering on her mouth, then her collarbone, then her mouth again. When he leaned down this time, the kiss didn't ask permission.

It picked up heat.

The kind of heat that came from a month of long looks and casual brushes of skin and gifts left without comment. The kind that had time to simmer, to coil low and slow, until now—finally—it could unfold.

Her hand slid up into his hair as he kissed her, pulling him closer, and the press of their bodies turned instinctive—shoulder to shoulder, knee to thigh, lips parting with more urgency. Cove shifted again, settling half over her, his weight braced on one forearm.

His other hand lifted, hovering near her ribs.

He hesitated.

He *wanted* to touch her. Every inch of him wanted to. But he also remembered what she'd whispered earlier. *The Thrall.* He didn't want her to think that was all this was, didn't want her to think he'd lost control. That the way he ached to trace the line of her waist, or the softness of her hip, or the slant of her neck, was some spell at work. It wasn't.

It was *her*.

Her, laughing in tidepools. Her, reciting sea glyphs like they were poetry. Her, serious-eyed and sharp-tongued, smarter than anyone his age had a right to be. Her, finally letting him in.

So he pulled back just slightly, catching his breath, and rested his brow against hers again.

"I want to touch you," he said quietly, honestly. "But not because of the Thrall. And not if you're not ready."

Her chest rose against his. She looked up at him—searching, steady—and she didn't flinch. Didn't pull away.

Her hand slid from the nape of his neck to his shoulder, fingers tightening just slightly, not in warning, but in answer.

Cove followed the pressure willingly, kissing her again, this time slower but no less deep. Her body met his without hesitation, their legs tangling in the seagrass.

Cove's hand slid beneath the edge of her shirt, palm against bare skin now—warm, tentative. Just a male who'd wanted her for weeks and finally had her beneath him, in the dark, under the stars. Her breath hitched, but she didn't stop him. Her body arched faintly into his, wordless.

His mouth trailed from hers to her jaw, then lower, grazing the place just beneath her ear where her pulse beat fastest. He felt her fingers clench in his hair, felt the subtle brush of her hips against his thigh.

Serena made a sound—not a moan, not quite—but something caught between a sigh and a growl. A siren sound. Feral. Female. Pure.

It thrilled him.

She dragged his mouth back to hers with a hand curled tight in his collar, and the kiss deepened again—hotter now, hungrier. It lost its shape. Became rhythm, friction, and breathing.

Her thigh slid over his hip.

Cove groaned against her mouth, hand splaying along her ribs, thumb brushing under her breast. And she let him. She wanted it. She kissed him like something was finally breaking free.

He smelled of the sea, driftwood fires, and the wild ginger blossoms growing in the lagoon. She tasted like honey and heat.

When she finally broke the kiss, it wasn't because she'd had enough.

She just needed air.

They both did.

They lay tangled in the grass, the sound of waves below and the stars above, skin flushed, mouths parted, eyes locked.

Cove ran a hand through his hair and said with a half-cocky, half-dazzled grin, "See... still in control. That... wasn't the Thrall."

Serena's eyes narrowed faintly, her smile dangerous. "No. That was me."

"Serena," he said, breath unsteady, "I really, *really* like you."

She leaned in again, her mouth brushing his ear, and whispered, "Then kiss me again."

She didn't let more happen that night. Not beyond the kisses—the ones that stole her breath and left her skin humming, the ones that made her forget where the sky ended and where he began.

Just the kissing—wild, breathless, laughing between gasps, tangled in seagrass with stars wheeling overhead and the moonlight caught in both their wings. It was the kind of kissing that burned but didn't scorch. The kind that left her flushed and breathless but safe. Trusted.

She hadn't needed to rein in the Thrall.

Cove hadn't lost himself. He hadn't turned greedy, hadn't grabbed or gasped or begged. He'd just *wanted* her, and she'd wanted him. So she kissed him with abandon. With heat.

With the kind of wild, starlit freedom that came from knowing she wasn't dangerous to him. That he wouldn't be twisted into something he wasn't. And she wouldn't hurt him.

It was much later when she finally flew back to Meriden's cave. Her braid was half undone, seagrass still clinging to it in places. Her cheeks were flushed from the wind, or the kissing, or both. Her lips were slightly swollen. Her grin, irrepressible. She ducked inside like someone carrying a delicious secret. Flushed. Lit from within.

Meriden was stoking the coals of the evening fire, still dressed in the loose linen she wore at night, her hair twisted up with a carved pin. She glanced over her shoulder, and one brow arched with wicked ease.

A slow, dry smirk curved her lips. "Seems you had a good evening."

Serena burst into laughter, ducking her head and covering her mouth with one hand. She looked up a moment later, her eyes sparkling like moonlight on open water—no trace of shame, no flicker of fear. Just joy. Giddy, wild, unguarded joy.

She went to sleep that night with the sound of waves just outside the cave and her hand still pressed lightly to her lips, as if remembering each kiss and reliving it again.

The next morning, the sea cliffs were bright and wind-swept, and Ronan was replacing the binding runes of the sky-door on the observatory when he caught sight of Cove striding toward the training perch.

The boy looked... ridiculous.

Grinning at nothing. Hair wild from the flight. Wings tucked but twitching like he could barely keep from launching again. He was whistling. Off-key. And he looked like he hadn't stopped smiling since moonrise.

Ronan leaned on the carved stone column, arms crossed.

Smitten.

There was no mistaking it now. Cove was completely, entirely, and catastrophically smitten.

Ronan exhaled, a long-suffering breath with the faintest edge of amusement.

He knew that look. Knew it far too well.

Cove hadn't just kissed the Heir of Ardaion under the stars—he'd *gotten away with it.* Gotten away with a great deal of something, judging by the boy's grin.

And he wasn't dead. Serena hadn't ended him for his audacity, which meant she'd let him do it.

Cove had that look about him. Stupidly pleased. Whistling to himself, he checked the flight harness on one of the Valkyrie training gliders, wings twitching with restless energy. And that *grin*. That was the giveaway.

Ronan didn't say anything at first.

Watched his son move like he'd just won a war and discovered gravity no longer applied to him. Saw him fumble a knot twice because he kept grinning at nothing. How he snuck a glance toward the path leading down from the cliffs—no doubt hoping Serena might pass by on her way to the tidepools.

And Ronan sighed.

He found himself thinking—not for the first time—what Edric might have said. What the conversation might've been, had he lived to see it.

So, your boy's chasing my girl, huh?

And Ronan would've shrugged, probably. Maybe winced. Maybe laughed. And then they'd have brought out the whiskey.

That night, the salt air was thick with mist and music.

It had been two weeks since that night beneath the stars, and Serena had not slowed—had not once turned back. Her days were full, overflowing. Glyphs inked onto shells. Storm chants carved into her memory. Runes traced in seawater that lingered, glowing, before vanishing beneath the tide. She was learning not just how to use her power, but how to *command* it. Not as a mage forcing the elements into shapes, but as something *of* them, kin to their wildness. She called to the storm now—and it answered.

The songs of Tides had become her heartbeat. The salt, her breath. And every night she stood taller, her shadows lighter, her smile brighter. She took to the rhythms, the stories, and the power as one born to it.

She had friends now. Not courtiers or soldiers who bowed out of obligation, not servants who feared her siren blood, but *friends*—girls who danced barefoot in the sand and shoved blossoms in each other's hair, who teased her about her wings, who laughed when she turned red at the mention of Cove's name. Girls who called her "sister" without ceremony or expectation.

Tonight was the first night they let her lead the songs.

Not as a student. Not as the Heir of the Moon Court. But as one of them.

The driftwood fire cracked and hissed as the sisterhood gathered around, voices rising with the smoke—low and lyrical, some sweet, some guttural. Serena stood at the center, her dark hair half-loose from the braid, her skin sun-warmed and sea-slick, and when she opened her mouth to sing, the sound that came out was pure siren voice.

Old. Wild. Hers.

And they *answered*.

One by one, the others picked up the rhythm. Some clapped, some stomped their feet, some harmonized with high keening wails, others chanted low and rhythmic. The fire flared. The wind rose, stirring waves on the shoreline. Moonlight caught in the water and turned the beach silver, and the whole shore danced with them.

For the first time, she wasn't half-Siren, half-Akyist.

She wasn't a half of anything.

She was whole.

And that knowledge... it settled deep inside her bones, a kind of peace and completion she'd longed for all her life.

Even later, when the fire burned lower and most of the sisterhood had collapsed into laughter and song-drunk lounging, Serena slipped away down a narrow path carved by her own bare feet over the last weeks.

Cove was already waiting—leaning on a rock like he hadn't been watching her all night, like he hadn't looked ready to start a brawl when one of the other Akyist boys had danced too close. But his grin gave him away.

She walked straight into his arms, grinning back, and he kissed her like they'd been doing it forever.

Some silent understanding passed between them—no words, no glances, just the shared heat of a kiss deepening, softening, then breaking with the unspoken pull of what came next.

He took her hand.

They took flight.

Not far—just over the shimmering sea to one of the smaller islets scattered across the archipelago. No torches, no watch posts, no siren voices echoing in the night. Just wildness. A crescent moon above and the hush of wings cutting through the air. When they landed, the sand was pale as bone beneath their feet, the kind that squeaked faintly under pressure, and ahead lay the mouth of a sea cave—open and waiting.

The tide lapped gently at the threshold, slipping in and out like breath, but Serena's breath caught the moment she stepped inside.

Cove had already been here.

He'd lit the place—not with candles, but with living stars. The anemones in the shallows pulsed with a soft glow, blues and greens, speckled across the water like stars scattered on glass. Glow worms reflected off the cave ceiling, dancing with every ripple, every breath of wind through the entrance.

And in the sand, further back where it stayed dry, a blanket had been laid out carefully. At one corner, a small bundle of vanilla-scented orchids spilled their heady perfume into the air, rich and warm. The same flowers he'd given her that very first morning, in the shell.

The gesture struck her silent.

She glanced at him, at his boyish smirk tinged with something bolder now—pride, yes, but something tender too. Possessive in that way only young love dares to be. She blushed, eyes sweeping the space, the intimacy of it, the thought that had gone into every flickering shimmer of light.

He sank onto the blanket, casual as ever, and opened the basket beside him. There was fruit, a slim-necked bottle of wine, and two little cups carved from polished driftwood. She joined him, heart still fluttering from the song, the cave, *him*.

They talked at first.

About the night. About her voice, how it had felt when the others joined in, how it had cracked something open inside her that no one could ever seal again. He listened, fingers toying lazily with the ends of her braid, sipping wine but barely tasting it. Because the taste he really wanted was already sitting beside him.

And she was smiling.

That same grin from the fires. That same light in her face. No longer weighed down by fear of what she was, or who might get hurt.

Just *her*.

The heat built slowly, deliciously. Familiar now, but no less electric. They kissed again—slow, lingering, increasingly greedy. She laughed into his mouth once when he tugged her down with him, lips still pressed to hers, and then the laughter melted into sighs.

The blanket was soft beneath her. His hands were warm, calloused from flight and sparring. Her own slid up over his bare shoulders, over the lean strength of his back, and the kisses turned deeper, mouths parting with every shared breath.

The air grew thick with salt and want, the cave cradling their silhouettes in flickering light. And when he paused just enough to meet her gaze, the question was there.

Serena made a decision.

She wanted him.

Not just the kisses. Not just the stolen moments. She wanted this. Him. Here.

Because it felt right. Because the war inside her—between fear and desire, between instinct and restraint—had finally quieted. Because she could feel, in the way his breath hitched, in the way he held still, watching her, that he was already hers.

And she was his.

Her fingers slid beneath the edge of his shirt, slow, exploratory. The fabric rose as she pushed it up and over his chest, her touch leaving behind a trail of heat across his skin. He sat up just enough to pull it the rest of the way over his head and toss it aside, eyes never leaving hers.

It was a cue he had hoped for—a moment he'd fantasized about. But he didn't move too fast. Didn't pounce. He let her come to him. Let her take the lead, even as his heart pounded hard enough to echo in his ears.

The glow of the cave flickered across them both—over the soft curves of her body silhouetted in the loose wrap she still wore, over the hard planes of his chest as he leaned into her again.

A breathless pause hung between them.

And then it was gone—melted away in the next kiss.

Their mouths met again, hungrier now. His hand slid into her hair as hers found the edge of his belt. Their bodies were flush, the flickering water lights painting the sea cave walls in rhythm with their movements.

Cove's breath hitched as she explored, her fingers trailing over his chest, slow and curious. He watched her as she touched him, his eyes dark with something between awe and hunger. Her lips moved to his neck and nipped lightly as he groaned. When she leaned up to kiss him, he caught her face in his hands, kissing her back deeper, harder, until her spine arched and she sank back onto the blanket.

Her wrap had fallen open. She tugged it off fully this time, a deliberate choice. His eyes dropped and he stilled. She swallowed, nervous for the first time in weeks, until his lips parted and he said, hoarse, "You're... beautiful." His palm skimmed her waist, then up, brushing her breast. She gasped, a little startled at how sensitive it felt, and his eyes flicked to hers.

"You okay?"

She nodded. "Yeah. Just... new."

He grinned a little, nervous, and ducked his head. "For me too."

His mouth found her skin again—kissing, tasting, learning. Down her throat, across her chest, lower still. She threaded her fingers through his hair and let her legs fall open as he kissed across her ribs, his hand stroking the inside of her thigh. He paused once, then looked up.

"Can I...?"

"Yes."

His fingers slid between her legs, gentle, unskilled but eager. She bucked up into his hand, breath catching, and he looked stunned by the reaction he drew from her. He tried again, a bit more pressure this time, circling, and her eyes fluttered shut. She rocked against him until her thighs started to tremble and she gasped "Cove!"

He pulled his hand away and kissed her again. She fumbled with the ties of his pants, got them open, and reached for him. He groaned when she touched him, hips jerking, and she let her fingers explore him—tentative, then more sure as he sucked in a sharp breath and buried his face in her neck.

He repositioned, moving fully between her legs, and pressed against her. They both paused, trembling.

"You sure?"

"I want to."

He pushed forward, slow. She gasped and winced as he stretched her, breathing through it, and he froze immediately.

"Sorry... should I stop?"

"No... keep going. Just slow."

He kissed her cheek and kept easing in, both of them fumbling, adjusting, trying to figure out what angle worked, what helped. Her fingers dug into his shoulders. He was breathing hard, trying not to move too fast, while she adjusted to the burn of it. But then she shifted her hips and he slid deeper, and both of them gasped at the same time.

It wasn't graceful.

It wasn't practiced.

But it was them. And it was real. She relaxed slowly and kissed him.

Cove started to move—slow, shallow thrusts at first, learning the rhythm, learning her. She rocked her hips up to meet him, and that made him gasp again, louder this time, gripping her tighter with a soft groan. Their bodies were slick now, sweat and skin and nerves, their kisses hot and panting.

They found it together.

That place where it started to feel good, then better, then overwhelming. She clung to him as her body locked around his, the first real orgasm hitting her with a cry that echoed through the cave. He followed almost immediately after with a shudder and a moan, face buried in her neck as he released into her, his body shaking.

For a long time afterward, they just lay there. Breathless. Dazed. Wrapped around each other on the blanket while the waves lapped at the edge of the cave.

Finally, he pulled her close and whispered in her ear "Are you alright? Did I hurt you? He kissed her temple and looked into her eyes. She blushed a bit and said "It got better..." and grinned at him, a bit shy, a bit devilish "Did you like it?"

Cove let out a soft, breathless laugh, his forehead pressing to hers. He was still catching up—his heart still thudding in his chest, skin flushed and damp, but her grin undid him. That little spark in her eyes, the mischief layered over the softness.

"Did I like it?" he repeated, his voice low, ragged with leftover pleasure. "Serena... I saw stars."

She laughed, bright and unguarded, and he kissed her again—lazily this time, mouths slanting together without urgency, the shared heat of skin on skin. He rolled to his back, tugging her with him until she sprawled half atop him, one leg tangled between his, her cheek pressed to his chest.

They lay like that, tangled in each other, the faint hiss of waves at the mouth of the cave, the glow of anemones casting faint light across their limbs.

Eventually, she murmured, "You weren't... overwhelmed?"

He tilted his head just enough to catch her eye. "I was. Just not by the Thrall."

She blinked.

He smiled gently. "It was you, urchin. Just you."

Her throat tightened—just for a moment. Then she curled tighter against him, one arm draped over his stomach.

"I still don't know what I'm doing," she said. "With any of this."

"I don't either," Cove replied, drawing idle circles on her back. "But if you're doing it with me, I'll take my chances."

CHAPTER TWENTY

SONGS IN MY HEART

The familiar white slit in the air of a mage gate appeared at the appointed time. Six months had passed and Serena stood on the beach where she'd planned to meet Graye alone. She'd brought fruit, shells, and a little carved box of keepsakes—things she'd intended to share over long walks and private talks.

But when four familiar figures emerged, she stilled.

First came Graye, striding through with the same easy grace she remembered—but the leathers he once wore were replaced by a tailored high-collared coat in dark slate, silver accents glinting at the cuffs. His hair had been combed and trimmed. Even his wings, usually wind-tossed, were neat and folded just so.

Beside him came Kade, his stride a bit more swaggering, dressed in a deep crimson doublet that somehow managed to look both martial and expensive. And behind them—Rhune, sleek, ever watchful, wearing tailored black with a twist of amber in his sash. His hair had been pulled into a bun- formal, controlled. They looked less like boys she'd grown up with and more like princes of Ardaion. Serena's lips quirked into a slow smirk, recognizing Stefan's handiwork.

And then, casually descending last, came Elsibetha. She wore Valkyrie battle leathers, of course—a sash of silver-blue cloth at her hips. She was more familiar with Tides, due to the training. But the set of her mouth was amused, like she was already drunk on sea air and planning her next provocation.

Serena hadn't moved. She was barefoot on the sand, the tide licking at her toes, a red sarong knotted at her hip and barely clinging to her hips, a bandeau wrap of coral-colored cloth around her chest. Sea glass jingled at her wrists, her ankles. Her dark hair had grown longer and was plaited with shells and sea glass, and freckles had bloomed on her shoulder. Her skin was golden. The flower behind her ear was purple, veined in white.

Beside her stood Meriden—serene, hands folded, a wreath of seagrass and pearls woven through her hair. Ronan, quiet and unreadable, gave a low grunt as the males exited the gate, his eyes lingering briefly on Kade's boots with a faint curl of disapproval. And Cove—lean, shirtless, wings damp and half-open, sand drying across his shoulders. He stood near Serena with unmistakable ease, his gaze calm but assessing as the newcomers descended. His hand brushed lightly at her back. He didn't attempt to hide it. Neither did she.

The first person to speak was Elsibetha. "Well. You weren't exaggerating," she said with a low whistle. "You look like a siren now, cousin. And a dangerous one." Serena beamed, taking it as a compliment.

Graye had not said a word. His eyes had locked on Serena from the moment he stepped through the gate and hadn't left her since. The bond between them had gone from excited prior to arrival to taut and expectant, like a drawn wire. He could feel her—feel her happiness, her health, the sunlight deep in her bones. But also... someone else's scent. And Cove standing there, protective.

Graye hadn't prepared for this. Hadn't prepared to see her changed. *Not this much.*

"You brought company," she said, her voice lilting and her smile beaming.

Graye's lips quirked, but it wasn't quite a smile. "Surprise."

She grinned and stepped forward, kissing him on the cheek, then hugged Elsie, then Kade, then Rhune—though Rhune hesitated a heartbeat before accepting it, his eyes flicking between her and Cove.

"I had plans for just the two of us," Serena admitted, pulling back at last. "But I suppose I can forgive you all... if you're ready to lose those fancy boots."

Elsie laughed. Kade grinned, already eyeing a pretty nymph who was eyeing him right back.

Graye said, quietly, "They wanted to join the tour and see you again, Sev."

But his eyes had fallen on Cove again. And this time, they narrowed.

Serena didn't look away. She knew what was coming. But she also knew something else—*she* wasn't the same girl, and no longer apologized for what she was. She was herself now. Her true self.

So she turned slightly, facing them all, and said "I've been looking forward to Graye's visit and now I get to see you all! Let's get you changed into more comfortable clothes and we'll give you a tour, go swimming, and later we'll have a big welcome fire." She was beaming at all of them, and Elsie was grinning right back, mischievous and liked what she was seeing in her cousin. But Graye, Rhune, and Kade were still taking in this new Serena.

Serena could read Graye like a book, even after all this time. And the moment her eyes met his, she felt it—the bond between them straining under the weight of something unspoken. Not anger. Not quite. But tension. Deep and sudden.

She turned her head slightly, murmured something to Cove, and sent him toward Ronan with a soft touch to his arm. Cove nodded, though his eyes lingered on her. Then she turned back, catching up with the four figures making their way toward Meriden's cave.

Inside, the air was cool and damp from the ocean just beyond. Mei was already pressing armfuls of woven Tides clothing into the hands of the visitors, chattering about the fires that would be lit tonight. But Serena didn't hesitate. She moved to Graye's side, took his hand in hers, and without a word, led him to the little back chamber—the one with the stone-framed bed and thick curtains draping the walls.

Once inside, she turned and sealed the door with a whispered word, magic locking it against any accidental eavesdropping. Then she looked at him—her tanned skin flushed from the sun, bracelets clinking faintly at her wrist as she brushed the hair from her face—and tried to smile.

"Ok... what? What's wrong?"

He didn't answer right away. His eyes scanned the room, then her, as if trying to reconcile what he saw with what he remembered. His voice, when it came, was wary. Distant.

"You're different. So different. And I don't mean the clothes. You feel like a stranger."

Serena's smile faltered, lips parting slightly. Then she said, softly, "Well... you do too, in a way. I can see Stefan has been doing his job well."

The silence between them was brittle. Graye crossed his arms, weight shifting as he studied her, still unsure. Then he asked, "And you didn't tell me about *him*. Is it serious?"

She sighed—one of those quiet, tired exhales that said more than words could. "Yes."

Graye's jaw tensed. "So you kissed me before you left... said you wanted to know what it would be like. Then you came here and started sleeping with a Tidelander?"

She flinched. Her eyes dropped to the floor, then drifted to a smooth shell resting on a driftwood shelf nearby. She picked it up, thumb brushing over its ridged surface. "It's not like that," she said quietly. "What I said... it's true. I wasn't ready. If I'd stayed there

I'd probably have never been ready. Because I was *broken*. I was afraid of myself. I was ignorant and terrified I might hurt you."

Her voice trembled just a bit at the end, and she turned the shell over in her palm before setting it back down.

"But I came here," she continued. "That longing I felt; the sea was calling me. Meriden has taught me so much about it. And they accepted me, Graye. They taught me, they cared for me. They're like family but Mab never let them visit. Meriden adopted me as a daughter. And Ronan was my father's best friend. I know so much more about Edric, and the Akyist half of me, not just the siren."

Her eyes found his again, steadier now. "They gave me what I was missing and I healed. And now I feel *whole*. Graye, I told you before I left that I felt like my heart was trying to sing songs that I had no words for. *But now I do.*"

She paused. Then, voice softer: "And Cove... it wasn't like that. We didn't do anything for a long time, Graye. Because I wasn't ready. It was this place, my sisters, Meriden... I learned who I was and I got stronger. It took a lot of growing before I was ready."

Graye stood there, absorbing every word. He didn't lash out, didn't pace, or break eye contact. He just stood—still as stone—but his expression was no longer blank. It was betrayed, bitter, and stunned all at once.

His voice came quiet, clipped. "So you needed to leave to feel whole. And I was part of what kept you broken."

He didn't phrase it like a question.

She gaped, horrified, "No! You are *not* part of it! How could you say that?" It was a stab to the heart.

He glanced at the shell still cradled in her hand, then around the little room. The bed. The folded sarong draped over a chair. Her scent lingering like the sea.

"Do you know what it was like, reading your letters? Trying to picture you here? I thought I'd get to see it for myself. Thought I'd get a few days with you, to feel like we still knew each other. I thought maybe..."

His throat bobbed. His voice was tight, steady by force alone.

"I didn't expect to walk in and feel like a footnote."

Then, a bitter little huff of a laugh escaped him—quick, dry.

"And I sure as tides didn't expect to walk in and realize you're in love."

She flinched.

He wasn't asking. He'd already seen it—in her ease beside Cove, in the quiet way they'd stood shoulder to shoulder without needing to speak, in the way her skin had gone pink when Cove smiled at her.

"You kept that from me," he added, finally looking her straight on. "You told me everything else. Your training. Your glyphs. Your lessons. You just forgot to mention him."

Graye's jaw flexed again.

"Was I supposed to find out like this?"

"Not... like this... but I thought it was better in person, not on paper. I wanted you to see and I thought then you'd understand it, once you were here. And we've never said what we were, what we *are*, to each other, Graye. Please don't let this break us. Don't hate me." Serena's voice was small, pained, and ashamed.

He didn't speak at first. Just exhaled, slow and uneven. Then looked down at his hands, flexed them once, then stilled.

"I know," he said finally. The words were barely above a whisper, rough-edged. "I know we've never had the words for what we are."

His gaze lifted to hers again, dark and searching. "But I thought I meant enough to you to be told. Not find out. Not like this."

He turned away just slightly, enough that the candlelight along the wall caught the furrow in his brow, the tightness at the corner of his mouth.

"And the worst part is," he added, voice low, "you're right. If I'd come here with someone else, you'd be the one furious. You'd be the one saying I should've said something. And I'd be... standing here. Doing exactly what you're doing. Asking you not to let it ruin u s."

He dragged a hand through his hair, visibly wrestling with it.

"But I didn't come with someone. I came to see *you*. With all the hope in the world." His voice broke slightly at the end.

A pause. He looked at her again, softer now. Sadder.

"I don't hate you, Serena. I just don't know where to put this." He tapped a knuckle lightly to his chest. "You've always been here. And now it aches in a way I wasn't ready for."

Then quieter, raw: "What am I supposed to do with that, Sev?"

She stepped up close to him and wrapped her arms around his waist, laying her head on his chest. There were no definitions that could explain them, or what they felt, or what they were to each other. But when one hurt, the other bled.

She whispered, feeling his pain, and said "I'm sorry. Graye, I'm sorry. What do you want me to do?"

He stood rigid at first, every muscle held taut like a drawn bow. But as her arms settled around his waist and her head pressed against his chest, something in him gave—like the tide pulling loose a stone from where it had been wedged too long.

His hands came up slowly, uncertainly, and then curled around her shoulders, then her back. He dropped his chin to the crown of her head. Breathed her in. Not the ocean and sea glass and salt she wore now, but the scent beneath all that. The one he'd known since they were children. Since they'd huddled beneath moonlit windows and drawn battle maps with ink-stained fingers.

He didn't answer right away.

Because what could he ask of her? That she take it back? That she not have healed here, not have found a kind of peace he'd only ever wanted for her? That she break things off with the Akyist?

His voice came eventually, thick.

"I don't know. I don't know what I want you to do."

He swallowed hard, the sound rough against the silence.

"I just... I wanted to be part of the version of you that didn't hurt anymore."

Some ache, a reminder of how she used to feel, unsure, guilty... the monster... began to surface within her. The panic of causing him pain.

Serena looked up at him, pained, but sincere, and said "You *are*. You are in *every* version of me! You could never not be. I love you. I always will. Whenever, wherever. Always." She trembled- something she hadn't done for months.

Graye's breath caught—like her words had struck something in him too deep to speak around. His jaw flexed once, then again, as if holding back whatever answer rose first.

He looked down at her, the light from the cave mouth catching in his eyes, and for a moment he looked very young. Not the polished heir who had strode in with Rhune and Kade, not the poised lord in dark court silks, but the boy who used to sneak pastries into her room and sleep on the floor beside her during storms. The boy who once made her laugh so hard she spilled ink across a royal decree. The boy who had never let her fall.

And yet... she had, hadn't she? She'd been wounded time and again, emotionally, physically...

His hand lifted to her face and hovered there for a heartbeat—shaking, unsure—before he cupped her cheek, his thumb brushing the new freckles along her skin like he hadn't realized they'd be there.

"I don't know what to do with that," he said hoarsely. "Because I want to hate him. And I can't. Because if he made you this... this happy, this strong..." He let out a rough breath. "Then what right do I have to ask you for anything else?"

The silence that followed was thick, humming with grief and love and that terrible in-between neither of them had ever named.

"But I still love you," he added softly. "I don't know how not to."

By the time Serena and Graye stepped back outside, solemn, into the warm, salt-tanged air, Kade and Rhune were in Tides apparel—tan canvas slacks and white shirts like Cove's. Rhune had his buttoned, sleeves rolled to the forearm, but Kade had followed Cove's lead and left his entirely unbuttoned, the sea air ruffling his dark curls and the sun catching against the planes of his chest.

Elsibetha stood nearby in a vibrant purple sarong, her petite fangs visible in a teasing grin, clearly delighted by the casual freedom she'd adopted. Her familiarity with the Tides Court had grown deep through countless visits during her Valkyrie training—training that had linked her closely to Ronan, an old friend of her father, Rivarin. As a result, Ronan had always regarded Elsibetha with the fondness reserved for a niece, just as he did Serena. Which made Ronan's son like an honorary cousin in Elsie's eyes.

Elsibetha's sharp, amused gaze settled on Cove, who had positioned himself conveniently near Serena. Her eyebrow arched in playful challenge as she leaned closer, elbowing him lightly. With a pointed glance toward Serena, Elsie's voice dropped to an insinuating murmur, edged with curiosity and unmistakable familial protectiveness.

"Well?" she prompted, eyes gleaming with sly anticipation. "Care to explain what's going on between you and my cousin? Because from where I'm standing, Cove, it looks rather interesting, maybe even serious."

Cove grinned. His cheeks flushed, but the expression didn't falter. If anything, he looked unrepentant. Proud. His blue eyes sparkled.

"We're together," he said, soft but firm. "Almost two months. It's serious." He paused, "I love her." He was sincere, his face lit with the warmth and awe of young love.

Elsibetha smiled at him—warmth in her eyes, not mockery. She felt a real affection for the boy and had witnessed him grow up on and off the cliffs of the Tides, his swagger tempered by decency, his pride never slipping into cruelty. And truthfully, a little romance might be good for Serena. She was twenty-one now, too long wound tight with duty and grief, and Cove... Cove had a good heart. He'd never hurt her.

But Elsie didn't say any of that. Just nudged his knee again with a smirk and a shake of her head, and said, "Come on, lover boy."

The rest of the day passed in sunlight and salt, six figures weaving through the coastal terrain like they'd never known war or politics. They explored grottoes lit by glowing anemones, dove from cliffs into clear turquoise pools, and flew in loose, tumbling arcs over the waves—some diving low to skim the surface with their hands, others looping high until their wings caught the sun and scattered it like prisms.

Graye was quiet at first. Somber in the way that didn't draw attention, but clung behind his eyes. He didn't speak of it, but it flickered beneath the surface of his every glance. Their bond subdued. Still, when he looked at Serena, he couldn't fault her. Not when she flew like that—wings flashing against the sky, hair streaming behind her, laughter trailing in her wake.

She beamed when she later surfaced from a dive with a pearl in her hand, soaking wet and triumphant, and he smiled back despite himself. He could sense her happiness in the bond. This place was the kind of adventure that he and Sev would have loved as children and yet now, it was complicated.

Cove was with them. Always near Serena. Never possessive, never pressing. Just... there. Present. Warm. Easy to like. He had the kind of grin that made people trust him, and he used it freely—teasing Kade, making Rhune chuckle, nudging Elsibetha into mock indignation. But most of all, he played. With Serena.

They raced each other through the shallows, dove through waterfalls, and splashed like children. At one point, Cove chased her up the rocks and she doubled back, and tackled him straight into the water, both of them sputtering with laughter. He dunked her gently, she shrieked and retaliated, and the fight devolved into chaos. And it was clear, very clear, that they were in love.

Graye watched. That was all he did. Tried to smile. Watched her laugh, and saw her lean into the moment like the weight of lineage had never existed. She was luminous in that sunlight, flushed from flight and salt, and for a second he felt like a stranger.

Because she hadn't done anything wrong.

They had never made promises.

There'd never even been words.

Just the long thread of something unspoken between them, woven from years of glances, of childhood adventures fought side by side, of secrets kept and comfort given. A thousand nights where she was his person, and he was hers, and no one else quite fit into the silence between them.

But now there was someone else in that silence. And the ache—quiet and sharp—made him grit his teeth behind his smile.

Kade, of course, had no such weight dragging on him. He was in his element—shirtless again by midafternoon, climbing rocks like a mountain cat, belly-laughing as Elsibetha called him a reckless fledgling and dove after him anyway.

Rhune was quieter but no less changed—his eyes sparkled with amusement, his smirks came easier, and every so often he tilted his head just slightly, watching Serena with something like private wonder. He didn't interrupt. Didn't intrude. But when she laughed, really laughed, he smiled too—those rare, quiet smiles that said more than words.

Night fell like velvet over the sea, and with it came fire. A bonfire of driftwood, bleached and massive, had been built just beyond the high-tide line—stacked and waiting since morning. As promised, it was lit with a ceremonial spark from the Tides mages, the flames blooming upward in spirals of gold and violet as salt crystals cracked and hissed within.

The drums came next.

At first, only a few—low, pulsing rhythms thudding out like heartbeats in the sand. Then more, until the entire cove pulsed with a sound like the ocean itself had a pulse. Rhythms thickened, layered, shifting with the tempo of feet moving across damp earth. And all around the fire, the fae came.

Mer and Akyist alike.

Sprites with hair like seaweed and eyes full of light. Naiads with shimmering tattoos winding up bare arms. Sirens who wore pearls strung down their backs, and nymphs with shells braided into their curls. They sang first, as was tradition—melodies clear and haunting, the kind of music that seemed to make even the flames lean inward to listen. Their voices moved like water: rising, falling, seamless. Some stood. Others danced in the sand, weaving through the crowd with lithe grace, their motions echoing tides and moonlight.

Then the Akyist males joined in—shattering the trance with raucous joy.

Their songs were rougher, louder, jubilant things. Half drinking song, half hunting cry, full of wild laughter and rhythmic stomps. Their harmonies were shouted rather than sung, layered with howls and the slap of hands on thighs. They sang in rounds, in challenges, in nonsense verses shouted over each other. Someone pulled out a skin of spirits and passed it around. Someone else upended a basket of dried fruit into the air and let it rain down over the drummers.

It was joyous chaos. Music of storm and salt and flight.

And Serena was in the middle of it.

She didn't watch from the edge. She didn't keep to courtly poise. She danced.

Not the formal steps of a queen in training—but barefoot, hips swaying, arms lifted, her laughter catching in the beat. Her hair had come loose in the sea breeze, curling wildly around her shoulders, and her feet were dusted with sand. She moved like water, like fire, like rhythm itself—mesmerizing in the way only a siren could be when unguarded.

She clapped with the chants, twirled with the naiads, and shouted the old verses back at the Akyist who challenged her. Her voice—sultry, musical, unmistakable—rose in one of the oldest sea chants, and the fire leaped higher.

It was impossible not to look at her.

The princess who so rarely dropped her mask. The weapon of the Moon Court, dancing with joy.

She pulled Graye's hands before he could refuse—before he could think. One second he was seated on a bleached log, drink in hand and the thud of drums echoing through his chest, and the next she was in front of him, luminous in firelight, grinning with her whole face. Her skin glowed, sea-damp and radiant, her eyes bright as starlight, and her laughter lured him to his feet like a spell.

He rose.

And she pulled him into the music.

Into the sand. Into the revel.

It caught him off guard—how easily he followed. How easily everything else fell away. The ache. The doubt. The weight. All of it dissolved in the wake of her joy. She twirled, and he twirled with her. She clapped, and he found his hands in motion. Her laughter bubbled again—richer, fuller than he'd heard in years—and he couldn't help it. He smiled. Wide. Real. His eyes only for her.

She was Serena, yes. But different. Unfurling in this place like sea flowers opening to the moon. This was a version of her he hadn't fully known—at home not just with power or duty, but with herself. The Tides had drawn her open, and she was blooming.

He caught her waist, stepped into the spin, and lifted her.

She rose easily into his arms, weightless from memory—how many times had they practiced the Spring Waltz in those endless palace lessons?—and he spun her round and round, her skirt flaring, her hair catching the firelight in streaks of indigo, violet, and emerald.

The crowd whooped and cheered around them, stamping feet and raising hands, their rhythm rising in encouragement. Serena laughed harder, head tilted back, mouth open to the stars.

Graye set her down and she didn't let go—only drew him close again, a second spin already begun.

Across the firelit circle, others looked on.

Meriden, serene and still, her eyes reflecting the flame. She saw a girl who'd been neglected, ignored, abused now finding her light and her power.

Ronan was once again wishing Edric was here.

And Cove.

Cove, who had been laughing a moment before, now stood quieter, watching from the side. He'd only known the Tides side of Serena—the girl who climbed rocks and dove through waves. But he hadn't seen *this*. Not the grace born of palace drills, court dances, and command. Not the history between them. Not the way she melted into Graye's rhythm without hesitation, the way their bodies moved like they'd been choreographed by years. The way they were perfectly in sync. He wasn't jealous, not quite, but he watched with a growing realization that like Graye, he didn't know all of her either.

Eventually, as the fire burned low and the last drumbeats slowed to a steady pulse like a heartbeat winding down, Meriden stepped forward. Her presence was quiet, commanding—not loud, but absolute. Conversation and laughter faded. Feet stilled. Heads turned.

The hush was immediate.

She raised no hand, no voice—only smiled, calm and gracious, the firelight catching in the teal at her temples.

"These are Serena's guests," she said, her voice carrying easily over the night air, "and it is Serena who has brought joy to our cove tonight. So let her lead us now in song."

A ripple of approval passed through the crowd—nods, low murmurs, a few grins from the Akyist males still drying their wings by the fire. But all eyes returned to Serena.

She stood breathless for a moment—windblown and flushed from dancing, curls wild, sand still clinging to her bare ankles. Her eyes found Meriden's and she beamed, truly beamed, a blush blooming across her cheeks. Honored. Seen. Loved.

And eager.

She stepped forward, cleared her throat once, then lifted her voice.

It began softly.

A single note—pure, resonant, perfectly pitched. It drifted across the cove like mist over water, rising like moonlight over the tide. Then another note joined it, and another, forming a melody that none of the visitors had heard before. Not like this.

Not a song.

A *siren* song.

This was no courtly performance. No tavern chant. No lullaby. It was ancient, recalling the wildness of their primal ancestors—older than civilization, older than memory. It struck deep. It reached past flesh and sinew, past heart and bone, and pressed its fingers into the soul with longing.

Graye went still.

The sound wrapped around him like heat, like light, like something holy. It made his eyes burn and his breath hitch. It was Serena, but *not* Serena. It was the wild sea inside her, the legacy in her blood, the inheritance she'd never asked for but now wore like a crown.

He had known her as a seed, yes. But now she bloomed. Not slowly. Not delicately. She *burst* open—glorious and raw and full of power.

Next, Meriden joined her.

Then Elsibetha, her voice lower, smokier, rich with years of shadow and steel.

Then a fourth—Lysane, pale-haired with a voice that shimmered like silver bells through the fog.

Together, the four sirens wove a sound no magic could replicate. Each note a thread, spun from breath and blood and tide. The language was old—older than Common, older than High Fae. Few among the audience, aside from the sirens, understood the words.

But they didn't need to.

Because the meaning bypassed translation. It unfurled like a tapestry of memory and myth. As they listened, images rose unbidden—shimmering in their minds like dreams:

A queen stepping barefoot into the sea.

A prism-winged daughter soaring above a storm. The pulse of the wellspring. The kiss of moonlight on black water. The Binding. The bloodline. The end of one age, the beginning of another.

Kade had stopped mid-swig of something fermented, the drink forgotten in his hand, his usual grin slack with awe.

Rhune didn't move. Not even to blink. Long after the others had looked away or closed their eyes, he kept watching her—expression unreadable, focused on every detail.

Cove watched with a quiet pride that glowed from within, utterly besotted. This wasn't just affection—it was adoration. His Serena, his girl, *his love*, was singing with the ancients. Where she belonged.

Graye couldn't move.

Couldn't speak.

His heart felt too full, too fragile. Not with pain, not with jealousy, but something deeper. Wonder. Something aching and ancient and whole.

He had never seen her like this.

Had never understood—*truly* understood—what she was. Not just his childhood friend, not just the Heir, not even just a siren. She was the sea. She was Ardaion. She was every queen before her reborn.

And across the fire, even as she sang, Elsibetha's mind wandered.

To the east. To the armies. To her grandfather.

Jormunder, who had fought and bled for this realm longer than most of the fae here had been alive. Who had raised Serena with a soldier's precision and a father's pride. Who had named her when no one else would. Who had loved Tatiana so fiercely that even now, in Serena's face, he still sometimes saw her.

And tonight... tonight, she *was* Tatiana.

Living. Laughing. Leading.

Elsie sang through the tightness in her throat, blinking once against the sting behind her eyes.

She only wished he could see it.

As the evening wound down, couples left the firelight to go to the dunes. Including Elsibetha who left with a grinning Akyist male who seemed more than eager. Others sat in quiet conversation or went for late-night swims. Graye had left for a walk along the beach and Serena suspected he needed to be alone for a bit before he came back to her. Kade followed him.

Serena walked over and sat beside Rhune on a log. Her eyes followed the backs of Graye and Kade for a moment and then she sighed and looked at Rhune a bit ruefully. He hadn't had a lot to say, even when he'd been smiling in the lagoon. Not aloof exactly, just quiet, introspective. He focused his green eyes on her and scrutinized her with a deep, unreadable expression for a long moment before saying "It's complicated, isn't it." It wasn't a question.

She knew what he meant and frowned in thought. "Yes, it is. We never asked for it and we grew up with it, so we never had to define it. And even now, we don't know what it is."

Rhune looked at her again, his eyes reflecting the firelight and that fierce intelligence he was known for, "you don't have to know what it is, Serena. You just have to know how it makes you feel."

He waited for a beat as if deciding something. Then his hand went to his trouser pocket and he pulled out a brown and gold feather, distinctive. A gryphon. He passed it to her, studied her face as she recognized what it was, and began to smile.

He spoke low, "A few months ago, I spotted it in the forest. Thought of you. Graye told us about the dare when you were kids." She was still looking down at it and smiling fondly.

But she looked up at him, eyes soft and full of emotion, and said "You brought it all this way? Thank you, Rhune."

The corner of his mouth quirked up in a half smile, eyes lit with something pleased, something warm. He gazed at her a moment longer, and his head dipped in a silent acknowledgment.

CHAPTER TWENTY-ONE

PARADISE LOST

Before sunrise, the shell horns of the Tides Court shattered the archipelago's hush—sharp, discordant, and unmistakably urgent. Their call ricocheted across sea cliffs and through the high sanctums of the Akyist, down to the hidden Mer caves at the waterline. Gulls scattered, cursing the interruption. Sleep was torn away in every hollow and grotto.

Confusion and alarm rippled outward. From the heights, pale-winged Akyist tumbled from beds and hammocks, scrambling to the cliff ledges, wind catching in half-folded wings. Along the foamed rock mouths below, Mer flickered between tidepools and glowing archways, voices raised in a dozen dialects of alarm. Across the wild archipelago, the sound of running feet and shouted questions blurred with the low thunder of surf.

A scout careened in from the sky, landing hard on a narrow ledge high above the sea. One wing was bloodied, his face raw with wind and shock. He barely caught himself before he was scrambling up to Ronan, face agitated and gasping for breath. It was clear he'd flown as fast as he could.

"Warships! At first, we thought it was traders, but there are at least twelve, more coming past the horizon. Humans. Some have reached the northern bay. They've already rowed to shore and they're setting fires. They sent arrows at us the moment they saw us."

For a moment, the only answer was wind and the pounding of the sea.

Ronan's jaw tightened. His voice cut clean and hard through the tumult as he turned to another Akyist male in armor.

"Kerrick, summon every Valkyrie in Tides. Take a company and try to burn the sails of those at sea to slow them down; the hulls too if you can. I'll take more to the landing site to cut them off. The rest need to secure Tides. Go!"

Valkyries broke from their shock, training snapping into place. They launched from the cliffs as Ronan's commands rang out, their wings shearing the wind as they rose to meet the unseen threat. From the higher ledges, Elsibetha flew upward, already armored and braced for orders. She landed near Ronan, breathing hard but steady, every line of her body ready to join the airborne assault.

But Ronan caught her shoulder with one hand, his voice low but immovable. "Spread the word to the Mer. Ensure they are securing themselves and the caves. And then your duty, your only duty, is to protect Serena. Protect the Heir."

For a heartbeat she looked like she might argue, her nostrils flaring with frustration. But then she nodded once, clipped and tight, and launched downward, wings cutting a sharp angle toward the lower beach.

Below, on the pale sand where the cliffs met the sea, Serena stood with Graye, Rhune, and Kade. Meriden was with them, her water-blue robes fluttering in the rising winds, and Serafine stood just to Serena's right, armored and silent, a living shadow of silver and steel.

Elsibetha landed hard beside them and immediately relayed Ronan's orders, her voice tight. She glanced toward Serafine, her tone meaningful.

"We have to get her back to Ghealach Siorai."

Serena's head whipped toward them. "What?! No. I want to stay and fight. They need me... I'm stronger than they are with the power..."

"You are also the Heir of Ardaion," Serafine cut in, calm but absolute. "If you fall, so do we all. This is a surprise attack. We are unprepared. You have no armor, no army at your back. You are still training in Battle Magery. You are still a novice shadowdancer. We have to go and tell the Queen, tell Jormunder. Then we'll return."

Elsibetha was nodding, steel-eyed. But Serena turned as movement caught her eye. Cove, armored and striding down the path from the cliffs, his expression unreadable but resolute.

"No! Cove, no!" she cried. "You're not a Valkyrie. Don't go. Please..."

He walked to her without flinching, cupped her cheek in one hand, and kissed her, quickly, but full of meaning. "I'm just going to help with the defense," he assured her gently. "We need to protect the coast. The Valkyries will be in the worst of it."

Her mouth opened to protest again, but Graye stepped forward, resting a hand on her shoulder. "Sev... I'm going to send Kade back to marshal Shade's army. And I'm sending Rhune to see if Aegin will send the Dardani."

She blinked, stunned, and it came out in a near gasp, "*What?!* You... what are you... Graye, no. Both of you... I can't..."

"I'll stay with Cove," firm but not unkind. "We'll help reinforce the coast until the armies arrive. I'll stay out of the Valkyries' way. But I have to help where I can, Sev. And you have to help where you can, which is telling Mab. And getting the Battle Mages here."

He pulled her into a tight embrace, a long one, then kissed her forehead. "You'll know I'm alright. We have the bond, remember?"

She nodded, eyes brimming, and tried to speak again. "But..."

Elsibetha had already opened a mage gate, its edges shimmering like moonlight on water. Serafine seized Serena's hand and began to pull her gently but firmly toward the portal.

A tear slipped down Serena's cheek as she turned back, her voice breaking as she called out, "I love you." It wasn't clear if she was speaking to one or both males.

Graye nodded, jaw set, grim as steel. Cove gave her a softer smile- brave, reassuring, though his eyes betrayed the anxiety beneath.

Serena looked once, quickly, at Kade and Rhune. "Be careful. I'll be back soon."

Then Serafine pushed her through the gate, and she vanished into silver light.

An hour later, Serena stood in the Moon Court palace, armored and barely concealing impatience with the gears of war. But Mab was the Spider, she was precise. The great war chamber thrummed with tension, Mab at its center, unmoving, a study in barely restrained wrath. She wore no armor. She didn't need it. Rage clung to her like a mantle, cold and perfect, and her silence was more terrifying than shouting.

Around her, the room bristled with war. Jormunder stood in full black plate, face set like carved stone, his wings motionless behind him. He had known war like others knew hunger. He had buried his mate by human hands. And now those same hands had dared an unprovoked invasion of Ardaion. Like Mab, he was ready to kill.

The Valkyrie commander and the Battle Mage General stood at attention, both armed, both silent. Serafine was beside Serena, a sentinel of shadow. Elsibetha remained in Valkyrie armor and like Serena, she was impatient to get back and join the fight with her company.

But Serena wore her armor as if for the first time. It had never been tested in true war. Enchanted leather, not steel, for flight and flexibility, and to avoid drawing the lightning she summoned. She had trained in it, sweated through it, but never bled in it. Not like this.

Her years in the mage tower had honed her spells, her control, her theory. She'd learned incantations that could rupture cliffsides, and summon storms from a clear sky. She had affinities for both water and air, born a storm mage. She wasn't alone in that, but none among the ranks had her access to the wellspring. She could draw deeper, longer, and harder. She could summon lightning nearly without limit. What she lacked in battlefield experience, she could make up for in brute magical force.

Around the war table, advisors murmured, positing theories but no firm answers. No one understood why the humans had attacked. Theories flowed like spilled ink- territory, resources, relics. But Mab listened to none of it.

Her attention remained locked on the military response. She had already dispatched messages to every court, including Solace, their famed healers now on alert. The realm was being raised to readiness, but not yet to war.

At last, Mab's gaze settled on Serena. She stared long and hard, her expression unreadable. She said nothing of the girl who had stepped through the gate an hour earlier, tan from sea and sun, hair still tangled with shells and sea glass. She said nothing of the sarong Serena had shed in haste or the marks of island life still on her skin. Her words came flat and deliberate.

"She's young. She's not finished her training. How good is she?"

Serafine answered before Serena could speak. "Majesty, she has trained for nearly seven years. We continued her instruction while at Tides. She may be a novice Shadowdancer, but I am confident in her progress. She is more than a match for the average soldier."

The Battle Mage General added without hesitation, "She doesn't need a sword. We need her as a mage. With wellspring access, she can summon storms from a distance, sustain them longer, and she won't tire. She is untried but well-trained. Lightning doesn't need precision."

Jormunder's voice followed, low and steady. "She's powerful, yes. I trained her to lead, to think, to strategize. She knows battlefield command. And the soldiers respect her."

Mab's eyes narrowed. The silence in the chamber pressed down.

"Very well," she said at last. "On your recommendations... Serena, you'll be assigned with the Battle Mages. You are too young and untried to take the field as a Shadowdancer. You will remain at the rear for ranged attack only. Away from the fighting."

Her tone sharpened. "You will follow your grandfather's orders. And the Mage General's."

Then she paused, just a fraction, and her gaze lingered on Serena with something more calculating, almost tasting the next words as she spoke them.

"However... if you find yourself cut off, separated from the two of them, you may assume the role of a senior officer and issue orders. But *only then*. Am I understood?"

Serena's jaw clenched, but she bowed her head and said, low and grim, "Yes... Mother."

Mab's stare didn't soften. "Humans killed your grandmother. They threaten your people and your realm. Do not be merciful, Serena."

Serena raised her chin. "I will do as I have been trained. I will defend Ardaion."

Mab looked to Serafine. "Do not leave her side. Her safety, above all."

Serafine nodded once. "Yes, Majesty. My life for hers."

Everyone in that room understood exactly what that command meant. Mab's concern had nothing to do with love. Her interest in Serena's survival was a cold, dynastic necessity. The Heir of Ardaion was not just a daughter, she was a function. A future. The bearer of the siren bloodline bound to the wellspring itself.

And yet... the power had never been meant to be hoarded. The wellspring had been granted to guard, to shield, to hold the realm together. From the first Matriarch at the Binding to Serena now, it had always been given for defense. The true power of the siren queens.

And now Serena would bring it to bear for the first time.

It had only been an hour since the invasion began—since Serena had been pulled through the mage gate to the Moon Court palace—but to those still in the Tides, it already felt like days.

The numbers were worse than they'd first feared. The Akyist scouts had reported at least twelve ships, and now they estimated that no fewer than eight hundred humans had made landfall with the first ship. The coastal villages were burning—set ablaze by the invaders as a diversionary tactic, drawing forces inland while the remaining warships attempted to approach under less resistance. Tides had no choice but to split its defenses—half to the coastline, half to the surf.

And the humans weren't like the scattered pirate bands or smugglers of years past. They were organized. Armored. Their plate was stamped with strange glyphs none of the fae had ever seen—sigils that shimmered faintly when struck, seeming to absorb a portion of every blow, both magical and physical. Fire spells crackled against breastplates and dispersed without effect. Swords skittered across shields with less bite than they should have had. Even the war-trained Valkyries found themselves slowed, forced to abandon standard tactics.

Worse still, the ships themselves resisted destruction. Ronan had ordered fire spells targeted at their sails, but more often than not, flames snuffed out as fast as they caught. Crews tried ripping the sails manually with blades and teeth, but human archers from the decks loosed volley after volley, and many fell before they reached the masts.

Underwater, the Mer fae struck back—racing beneath the waves to batter the hulls with ancient aquatic magics. One ship had gone down—split clean in half by the immense, roiling tentacles of a sea titan summoned from the deep, thrashing under the command of the Mer elders. The wreckage floated now, splintered and slick with blood. Sirens caught dozens in the Thrall, ordering them to turn on their own.

Within the stone-carved sanctuaries of the Tides, the civilian population—winged and water-born alike—was doing all it could to hold the line from within. Akyist wind mages climbed the high cliffs, their arms raised, summoning gusts and storms to try to drive the ships back. But the ocean winds favored the enemy. Natural and ceaseless, they pushed the human fleet forward with relentless momentum, resisting every counterspell thrown against them.

Cove and Graye had taken to the coastline, racing from shore to shore, gathering survivors. Civilians were herded to the great sea caves—vast, glistening hollows with spell-reinforced walls and hidden tunnels for escape. Children and elders were ushered in by the dozen, and wounded tended hastily with whatever supplies remained. Feathers and fins blurred together in flight and water as the people of Tides moved to shelter.

Then, like a blade through silence, a mage gate tore open in the air near the third bluff.

The first ranks of Shade's army poured through. Pennants of red and black waved on the wind.

Kade had returned.

The force was not what it once had been—not after Jaryk's brutal Ember campaign. But those who remained had been well-trained. And at Serena's insistence, they'd spent the last season under Elsibetha's tutelage, learning Valkyrie tactics. They didn't hesitate.

Steel flashed as they hit the ground running, fully armed, their faces grim. Behind them, Master Dewin held the gate wide with runes burning from his hands, sweat beading down his temple. The army streamed out in a disciplined tide—less than a full legion, but focused and formidable.

Kade raised his arm, voice booming over the cliffs. "Second and Third Wings—reinforce the Valkyries in the burning villages. First Wing, with me. Guard the strongholds. Protect the civilians."

Orders snapped like banners. The army split swiftly, half turning toward the inland fires, the other veering toward the cliffs and the sheltering caves.

Smoke curled across the sky now, thick and black, blown inland. Screams carried faintly on the wind. And still, the ships kept coming.

The battle for Tides had only just begun.

While the cliffs of Tides roared with fire and foam, Rhune was already halfway across the realm.

He had *blinked* to Ember, instantly jumping from Tides to a place he knew well.

It had been the place of their training, their shaping. He, Graye, and Kade had learned war there, learned loyalty and fear and cunning. And its Lord, Aegin, for all his brutal traditions, was no fool. He had imprisoned Graye, yes—but he hadn't harmed him. And he'd listened, even then.

Now, as a formal envoy of Shade, Rhune had been granted an immediate audience. He was escorted through the basalt stronghold and straight to the war hall, where Aegin stood bare-chested and barefoot on the smoothed black stone, sparks rising from the volcanic vents at his back.

Rhune gave no preamble. He spoke quickly, describing the human invasion: the numbers, the ships, the coastal fires, the unprovoked aggression. Aegin listened, hands behind his back, his burning gaze unwavering.

Even as Rhune spoke, word came from the Moon Court. A messenger, breathless, bearing Mab's seal. Ardaion's High Queen was activating the courts. She was calling the banners.

She wanted the Dardani airborne. She was sending the mages.

Aegin only nodded once. "Half the force," he ordered. "Ready now."

It took minutes.

Soon after Shade's ranks had begun deploying in Tides, a second mage gate yawned open across the cliffs—wider, darker, rimmed in fire. Umber-colored pennants fluttered in the sea wind, bearing the sigil of Ember- a cleansing flame and sword. Ember's motto was *All May Burn*, and they meant it.

The Dardani came through in waves—winged warriors clad in dark leather and bronze. Five across, they marched and flew in tight formations, their presence a thunder of black wings and rigid discipline. Their battalions gathered swiftly, squads falling into order without a word. The cliffside rumbled under the weight of their boots, and the skies rippled with their wings.

Their captains wasted no time. They shot skyward, smoke plumes guiding their path as they flew to assess the situation with sharp eyes and sharper discipline. Once aloft, they issued barked commands and split their forces with clinical efficiency—one wing diving toward the ships still attempting landfall, the other reinforcing Shade and Tides near the burning villages.

From above, the Dardani became death itself.

They fell on the warships with savage elegance—blades were drawn, wings maneuvering them between arrow volleys, hurling spears into decks, and cracking planks under boots. Some used fire magery to ignite sails when the spells of others had failed. Some dropped smoke canisters enchanted to blind or choke. Their formations were flawless, the result of centuries of highland warfare honed into instinct.

Now, with Ember's forces committed, Rhune wheeled back toward the cliffs—toward Shade's lines—wings beating against the sea winds. He found Graye on the shore near the great sea caves, giving orders to Shade commanders, his eyes scanning every front, every fallback line.

Rhune dropped beside him, armor dark with soot and salt. "Ember is deployed," he said simply. "Where do you need me?"

And just like that, the weight of three courts had come to bear on the Tides. Not enough to turn the tide—but enough to hold it until the Battle Mages arrived.

Half an hour after Ember's forces took flight, the Moon Court arrived.

It began with the sound, an unnatural thrum in the air as multiple mage gates cracked into being, silver-rimmed and wide as rivers. What emerged through them was nothing subtle. The Moon Court came in force, a flood of silver-plated soldiers spilling out in disciplined waves, their armor glinting like blades, their war cries echoing with ancient fury.

They did not shuffle or wait for command.

Jormunder's army did not need marshaling.

These were professionals—soldiers bred and trained for this exact moment, a standing force loyal to the Trident Throne, glyph-armored and pre-assigned to battlefield roles long before this war had begun. They knew the terrain, the protocols, the chain of command. They poured through the gates in screaming columns, then burst like arrows toward the gaps in the lines—Tides, Ember, and Shade all absorbed them instantly, the Moon's gleaming silver and dove-grey punching into the sea-darkened masses like shafts of cold moonlight.

Those with wings took the sky.

The banners came with them.

Silver and navy flags rippled from high poles—crowned crescent moons stitched across their breadth. Wherever the banners flew, morale surged. No court doubted who now held the field. The High Queen had answered.

And at last, the Battle Mages arrived.

They cut through their mage gate with terrifying composure—rows of cloaked figures, their leathers enchanted for flexibility and power amplification. Each one held the gleam of magefire in their palms, ready. The Mage General strode at the front, directing each cluster into place with curt, coded gestures. Fire affinity units to the frontlines. Earth mages to the lower slopes. Wind and water to the cliffs. Healing corps assigned to triage stations near the reinforced caves.

And then came the storm mages.

And Serena.

She wore her armor, the ornate leathers trimmed in silver and blue, the crowned crescent in silver filigree on her chest. Less weight than plate, and safer for those who carried lightning in their veins. She stood among the spellcasters like a comet among stars, her presence unmistakable. The others knew who she was. Some nodded in silent respect. Others only stepped aside.

She'd trained for seven years at the mage tower. She had been drilled, tested, and taught theory and execution. But she had never seen war like this. She had never stood on a battlefield where the dead piled in waves and the air choked with blood and smoke.

But Serena was not afraid.

What rose in her chest was not hesitation but wrath. Pure, undiluted fury. It was instinctive, bred and bound into her bloodline and very being.

Her realm was burning. Her people were dying. Her grandfather's army was bled across the shore, and the boys she loved held swords somewhere in the smoke.

The storm inside her demanded release.

She climbed to the highest cliff with the Mage General close behind. From there, she could see the chaos: ships still advancing through the shallows, the Mer fighting in the waves, the Dardani darkening the sky, and beyond it all, the fire-ruined coast.

The Mage General gave one nod, supervising the Heir and her first engagement.

"Aim for the ships. Strike them down, Princess."

She didn't answer.

She just opened herself to the wellspring.

Power surged through her like a tidal scream. The ancient source of siren magic filled her until her veins glowed faintly beneath her skin. Then she summoned the spell wings—not to fly, but to be seen. They unfurled behind her like living crystals, shimmering in diamond light.

Across the cliffs, across the dunes, across the surf, soldiers looked up and saw her. *Her boys saw her.*

Serena raised her arms and the air obeyed.

Storm clouds rolled in fast and heavy. The skies churned black, green, and blue. Thunder rumbled low like a beast waking. The clouds twisted, clawed, and thickened into a spiraling crown over the sea.

And then the lightning came.

She moved like a conductor—hands slicing through the air, fists pulling downward—and with each movement, lightning answered. Arcs of searing white light cracked down in succession, striking the ships. Wood exploded. Sails ignited. Flames devoured hulls as water and sky conspired to drown them. The enchantments that had protected the human ships could not withstand the Heir.

Serena did not pause.

A fresh ship was nearing land, smaller craft spilling rowboats of soldiers into the surf. They leaped out, armor gleaming, weapons ready...

And Serena struck.

Bolts slammed into the shoreline. Men screamed. Boats shattered. Dozens fell in a single breath, caught mid-motion and flung backward, lifeless on the wet sand. Another strike. Another rowboat was reduced to a floating coffin.

Around her, fire mages launched burning spheres at the larger vessels while wind mages forced the ships back. Earth mages turned shorelines to quicksand, making landings treacherous and destabilizing the footing of approaching troops.

And above them all—she raged.

At twenty-one years old, Serena had never known war. But the magic did.

It poured through her like prophecy denied. She wasn't yet experienced in battle, not the way time would make her, but the Mage General had been right.

Lightning didn't need to be accurate.

And Serena didn't need to be merciful.

CHAPTER TWENTY-TWO
DO NOT BE MERCIFUL

Two hours later, the ships farthest from shore were turning away- keeping just beyond easy reach, sails set north along the coast. Some lingered as if tempted to rejoin the fray, but the message was clear. They were retreating, watched by every sharp eye from the cliffs, harried now and again by Akyist wings or blasts of storm-cast wind. A handful vanished from sight behind the headlands, but scouts had been dispatched to watch them.

Closer in, the battle had left its scars. The ships that had landed first or tried to slip boats ashore now sat burning or wrecked. Hulls were cracked open; decks were split by Mer magics, fireballs, and lightning- flames licking at the charred spars. Those that had made landfall fared little better. The nearest vessels had been overtaken by Tides' defenders, boarded by Akyist and Dardani fighters, or sunk outright by the Mer. The sea was littered with debris and drifting bodies.

Pockets of humans who had managed to land were still fighting, clustered in the dunes and at the charred remains of villages. Their armor still gleamed with strange glyphs, protecting them from the worst of the fae magics, but they were outnumbered, trapped between the battered shore and a sea that now offered no escape. The landing boats had been shattered or burned, and any hope of retreat was long gone. They fought on because there was nothing else left.

The most brutal fighting had raged along the coastal villages set alight in a last, desperate effort to divide Ardaion's defenders and open another front. Smoke and fire had curled skyward, signaling to every court that the invasion was no longer rumor but fact. Of the original eight hundred humans who had pressed for land, only a hundred still fought the Valkyries among the ruins.

Nearly all those who had tried to land by boat were dead, their vessels battered before reaching shore and sunk, bodies washing up with the tide. Perhaps twenty, maybe fewer, had managed to slip into the sea caves, and now they were being hunted.

It was there, in the wet, echoing dark, that Ardaion's defenders converged. The Shade army had taken the brunt of the early losses, having answered the call first and held the line before the full strength of the Moon and Ember courts could arrive. Their numbers were thinned but their resolve had never faltered, and had it not been for the Valkyries of Tides already engaging the enemy, their fate would have been worse.

The Dardani of Ember had been as ruthless as the stories said—every one of them raised for this. Graye, Kade, and Rhune moved among them, side by side in the narrow, slippery tunnels, hunting for survivors. Swords drawn, every sense sharpened by danger, they pressed deeper into the caves. Cove was with them, blade at the ready, silent except for the low signals the Dardani used in the dark.

The fighting there was brutal and close—steel on steel, enchanted blades against glyph-riddled armor, the shouts and cries lost to the sound of the waves pounding the rocks outside. They took no prisoners.

Elsewhere, the Moon Court army did what it had been drilled to do: finish the work with brutal efficiency. They swept the beaches, cut down the last pockets of resistance, and drove the remaining humans out of hiding. The Battle Mages were relentless. Fireballs soared, boulders ripped through the air, waves crashed, and above it all, Serena's lightning fell again and again. Craters marked the sand, and the dead lay thick—mostly human, but all the armies had lost their own.

For all their protection, the human armor and unfamiliar glyphs had only bought time. They had arrived prepared for a massacre, armed with gear mightier than human-make alone could be. But it hadn't been enough. Not against the full wrath of Ardaion.

Another hour passed. The last cries of battle had faded into the crash of surf, the hiss of smoke, and the low, strained voices of those dragging bodies from the sand. Jormunder's orders were crisp and grim—search every ship, even the gutted ones. Scour for maps, scrolls, weapons, and any trace of who had sent them. The Mage General had sent teams combing through splintered decks and bloodied waves, collecting the strange armor shards and shattered weapons still etched with foreign glyphs.

Graye stood apart for a long moment before turning toward his own. Shade's army had arrived first and bled the most. Their strength was spent, and their lands still lay vulnerable. He called for the remaining captains and issued the order: return home, regroup, and protect Shade's coast.

Solace Court healers moved quietly among the wounded. They knelt in blood-stained sand, spoke soft words as they poured salves over burns, straightened broken limbs with power, or closed eyelids with care when they could do no more.

Aegin, having seen the worst had passed, gave his orders too. The Dardani would return most of their force to Ember, but a contingent would remain behind for three days—a precaution against return. His commanders relayed the message and began organizing the pull-back. The soldiers didn't celebrate. They knew better than to call any battle over when ships still lingered beyond the horizon.

Jormunder remained where he always had—on the front, silent and vigilant, with hundreds of Moon Court soldiers now encamped in disciplined rings along the shore. The scent of seawater, ash, and burned flesh mingled with the flickering torchlight as soldiers pitched camp. With the Battle Mages still active, no one would risk trying the inner islands again tonight. Not unless they wished to die screaming.

Near a fire built from the wreckage of a rowboat, the commanders began to gather-Ronan, Meriden, Serafine, the Mage General, Jormunder, captains of Shade and Ember. They spoke low, voices rough with smoke and grief. Maps were unfurled on driftwood, marked in blood and ink alike.

Further down the beach, the people of Tides moved among their own. The mourning would be held at dusk. The bodies would be sung to sea.

The fire crackled, burning timber that had once carried armed men to their deaths. Serena stared into the flames, but her thoughts were elsewhere—flashes of lightning, figures falling into the surf, ships reduced to wreckage. The scent of ozone clung to her skin, mingling with the salt and smoke in the air.

The Mage General approached and spoke in a low voice to Jormunder. "She followed every order. Her control of the storm was perfect. I've never seen anything like it. Legendary."

Jormunder didn't answer right away. He had seen it himself. From the top of the cliffs, her spell wings had flared like glass catching the sun, and casting light over the battlefield as bolts of lightning fell from the black sky. Soldiers had dropped in droves. Ships had buckled under the onslaught.

The power she had drawn from the wellspring had been terrifying. In his long life, he had seen Tatiana wield it, Mab wield it... but there was something different about seeing Serena do it. His beloved granddaughter. This was her destiny, and yet he ached a bit at what she was going through now, what all warriors go through after their first battle. *The reckoning.*

She looked hollow. Not dazed or broken, but drained and blank. Too many lives had passed through her hands today. Jormunder had seen that silence before in others, and he recognized it. Without speaking, he reached a heavy arm around her shoulders. She didn't pull away. Her armor was unmarred, her face clean. The shells in her braids caught the firelight as they swayed gently. She had not been touched by the enemy, but it was clear that the aftermath had left a mark of its own.

Graye arrived from the dark. His steps were steady, but the way he moved suggested exhaustion. Behind him, Rhune and Kade stood at a distance. They wore their own injuries, though none had spoken of them. Graye looked as if he had come straight from the fighting. Blood dried on his hands. Soot streaked his cheeks. Sand clung to his hair. And still, Serena turned the moment he neared.

She turned without a word and stepped into his arms. The bond reflected their emotions, raw and battered.

Graye wrapped her against him at once. Her face pressed to his chest, and he closed his eyes. He'd seen battle but he was well aware she hadn't. He kissed the top of her head and said in a quiet voice. "Sev... you were magnificent." His hand moved along her back in a slow rhythm. She didn't cry, didn't speak right away. It took a few long moments before she whispered, her voice strained and rough.

"So many, Graye. I killed so many."

She didn't lift her head, but the tension in her shoulders told him what he needed to know.

"I know," he said, and his voice steadied. "And if you hadn't done it, more of ours would have died. You saved your people today. This is war. It's terrible. But you did what had to be done."

It happened in the space between heartbeats.

A gasp. Then a ripple of murmurs, tense and startled. Heads turned toward the mouth of a narrow side cave where smoke still lingered, the flames from the battle casting low light across the sand. From the shadows stumbled a human soldier—bloodied, frantic, clutching something in front of him.

It was Mei.

She was crying, small and trembling, dragged in front of him like a shield. The blade he held was pressed to her throat. His other hand fisted in her tunic. His eyes were wide with terror, unfocused, rimmed red as if he had not slept in days. He was sobbing, the sound broken, animalistic. "I just want to leave," he howled. "I don't want to die, just let me go! Let me go!"

No one moved.

The circle near the central fire widened in silence. Warriors stood frozen, hands instinctively reaching for weapons but afraid to provoke him. Every step he took, dragging Mei backward down the beach, made her stumble. She was whispering something, pleading in a voice too soft to carry. Her tear-streaked face turned toward the crowd, and the knife glinted in the firelight.

Then Meriden stepped forward.

Her voice was low, musical, and resonant with ancient power. "*Release her,*" she commanded. The Voice of the sirens poured from her throat, laced with compulsion, with the weight of ocean-deep command.

The man recoiled.

He shook his head violently, eyes darting as if bees swarmed inside his skull. "No! No, no, no," he cried, clutching at his ears. "Get out of my head, witch! Get out!"

The Voice should have worked, but something was interfering with it. Mei began to struggle, sensing his grip faltered.

He didn't let go.

Instead, with a scream of pure madness, he jerked his hand across her throat. The blade flashed. Mei's eyes went wide, her mouth opened—but no sound came out. She collapsed to the sand like a puppet with its strings cut.

The scream that tore through the beach was like nothing Serena had ever heard.

It came from Cove.

He had just rounded the bend from the caves, returning toward the fire. He hadn't seen the entire confrontation but he saw her die. Saw her fall. His voice shattered the night. "Mei!"

Without thought, without hesitation, he surged forward. All instinct and grief.

Serena turned at the sound and froze. Then she saw him sprinting for the soldier. "No!" she screamed, the sound ragged and raw. Desperate. "Cove, stop! No, no, no!"

She shoved away from Graye's arms, stumbling forward, then running.

Her sujinn blade answered her call, flashing into her hand as she moved. She raced toward them, feet pounding the wet sand. The soldier stood over Mei's body, eyes vacant now, wild and gleaming. He saw Cove coming. He raised the knife again, then hurled it.

It struck Cove in the throat.

The boy who had been all charm and firelight and laughter crumpled mid-step, his hands clutching at the wound, blood already spilling through his fingers in gouts of red.

Serena screamed.

It ripped out of her like something primal, something ancient and full of ruin. Her magic roared to life. She didn't stop, didn't hesitate. Her body blurred with speed, a streak of motion across the field. Before the man could react, her blade sang through the air and took his head cleanly from his shoulders. It struck the sand before his body collapsed.

She dropped beside Cove, falling to her knees.

Her hands flew to his wound, to his face. "No! Help! Someone help! Healers! *Atta!* He can't die...." Her voice cracked and shattered. Her hands were covered in blood. His eyes were wide, terrified. He was choking, gurgling. She pressed her hands to his neck, trying to hold it together. "Stay with me. I'm here. Help is coming! They're coming!"

Healers were running, but too slow.

Serena bent over him, sobbing now, shaking as she tried to save him with power, with pressure, with the sheer force of her will. "Please. Please don't die. Don't leave me. I love you, *I love you!*"

But Cove was slipping.

His hand reached for her weakly and touched her cheek. Then it fell.

And Serena screamed.

The first scream was fae.

It tore through the aftermath like a blade, raw with anguish, cracked by pain that was too large for the body it erupted from. Serena knelt in the blood-soaked sand, her hands pressed to Cove's throat, but the bleeding would not stop. It pulsed through her fingers, hot and vivid and hopeless. Her head was shaking, her whole body trembling as her mouth opened again.

The second scream was siren.

It was not a sound meant for mortal ears. It came from her lungs, from her soul, from the ocean-deep echo of a predator queen's grief. It shattered the air like glass. Those nearest her clutched their faces as blood poured from their noses. Several dropped to their knees. One began to vomit.

Serena was still looking at her hands, covered in Cove's blood, then at his body, lifeless beneath her.

She leaned forward, her lips pressing to his, trembling, sobbing. She kissed him like it could call him back. Like love could undo what had just happened. And then she screamed again. And again.

It was unbearable.

Jormunder was already moving. The moment the second scream hit him, he staggered but kept coming. By the time the third scream left her throat, he was upon her, grabbing her shoulders, trying to lift her from the sand. "Serena!" he yelled, but she was feral now. Her grief was white-hot, wild, untamed.

She fought him.

Her legs kicked, her body thrashed, and her fists pounded at his chest. He grabbed both her wrists, holding them tightly, his face contorted not with pain from her blows, but from the sound still ringing in his skull. Blood leaked from his ears.

"You have to stop!" he roared. "You're going to kill someone!"

All around them, fae had dropped to the ground. Mages were bleeding from their ears. Warriors had retreated in disoriented clusters. A few had fainted. Some were dazed, blinking as though waking from a nightmare. Graye had sunk to the sand with a hand pressed to his chest, gasping as if he couldn't breathe, his face ashen with grief he hadn't yet spoken. The bond between them howled through him with every beat of her sorrow.

"I love him," Serena screamed, her voice rasping, ragged, barely coherent. "He can't—he can't— I love him!"

Another scream built in her throat, and Jormunder didn't wait.

He scooped her up into his arms, pinning her tightly to him as she writhed and screamed again. His steps were staggering but determined as he carried her toward Meriden's cave, his bellow rising above the ringing din: "Get one of the mages! Calm her!"

Behind him, Ronan had reached Cove's body. He was on his knees, shouting something no one could hear. Graye could see the horror on his face, the sheer panic as he lifted the boy into his arms and ran toward the nearest cluster of healers, shouting over and over.

But none of it registered through the ringing, the blood, and the silence that followed Serena's scream.

Jormunder had taken her to the back room of Meriden's cave.

She lay still on the low bed of woven kelp and linen, eyes staring blankly at the stone wall. Her body was loose, limp, and nearly catatonic. He had seen her like this once before—when Graye had been taken from her as a child. That same hollow absence in her face. Only now, she was older, and the wound cut deeper. This time, it had been love that was taken.

A healer from Solace had cast the Calm spell, the magical sedative draining the immediacy from her grief just enough to stop the screams. The price had been high—several on the beach had ruptured eardrums, and others were still dazed, shaking.

Cove had not been saved.

Jormunder had been informed of who the boy was. Ronan's son. Serena's first love. And, by the looks of it, a love that had carved itself deep into the marrow of her. Edric's daughter and Ronan's son. It had seemed so natural. So fitting. Meant to be. And now it never would be.

Kade and Rhune had helped steady Graye, whose blood-bound link to Serena had made him collapse under the weight of her grief. He had recovered only enough to rise. Now he entered the room, silent, pale, still slightly unsteady. He crawled into the bed beside her without a word.

Serena didn't move.

Her face remained glassy. Her lips slightly parted, as if caught mid-thought. But she didn't speak, didn't blink. Graye wrapped his arms around her and held her close. She was cold. Her fingers didn't grip his tunic. She didn't even seem to breathe at first.

Then the sobs began.

Sudden, violent, full-body sobs that shook her like a storm wind slamming into the coast. Her breath hitched and caught, choking her as she gasped and cried, the sound raw and broken.

"I loved him," she said, her voice shattered. "I loved him..."

Graye just held her, rubbing her back, burying his face in her hair as she broke apart in his arms.

"We were going to... I thought we'd have a life together. We talked about it. He told me how we'd have our own cave... we'd live above the waves and watch the stars every night. Swim. Fly. We were going to be happy..." She sobbed harder, her voice cracking to pieces. "I loved him. And he loved me..."

There was nothing Graye could say. Nothing that would reach her. He only held her tighter, his face crumpling with silent grief.

An hour later, Meriden entered the chamber.

Her face was tear-streaked, red-rimmed from both the loss of Cove and of Mei, her friend. She knelt beside the bed and touched Serena's hand.

"Serena..." her voice hoarse. "My daughter... we must say goodbye to them. At the fires. We will sing them into the stars, so they will watch over us."

Serena didn't speak. She barely moved. But her eyes flicked toward Meriden, and slowly, she sat up. Graye helped her, lifting her gently by the arms. Her body was heavy with grief. Her face was pale, her eyes rimmed with black circles, and they looked out from a place so far beyond sorrow that it frightened him.

He remembered her just a day before. Laughing. Dancing. Her hair was braided with shells, her siren song lighting the night like moonlight on waves.

That girl was gone.

He took one of her hands, and Meriden took the other. Between them, they led her out of the cave and into the silver-blue night. All along the coast, funeral fires burned. Linen-wrapped bodies rested beside each one. The scent of sea air and ash mingled.

Cove and Mei lay near the largest fire, their forms carefully shrouded. Serena's steps faltered. She stopped, trembling. Then continued. Jormunder looked on from nearby, his own heart twisted. He had seen so many faces like that in his life, but not hers. Never hers. It was a raw, pitiful thing.

She stared at the linens as the rituals began. Words were spoken. Blessings chanted. They passed through her without meaning. She did not hear the rites. Only the echo of Cove's voice, the feel of his arms, the sound of his laugh, the brush of his lips.

Then came the final moment.

The Mer and the Akyist joined in an old spell. They began to chant, their magic ancient, sacred. Slowly, the shrouded bodies began to glow. The glow intensified until it became a blanket of shimmering light. The forms dissolved, lifting into the sky as golden motes. Fireflies of soul-light caught the wind and floated upward. One by one, they disappeared into the stars. Serena moaned in pain, reaching toward the motes before sagging into the sand.

The beach was empty. The sands were bare.

Only grief remained.

The Mer began to sing, led by Meriden, low and haunting. Songs of mourning. Of sea and sky and loss. The sound brought tears to those who had none left. The Akyist stood silent beside them. Some wept openly. Ronan stood still, his face wet, his arms wrapped tightly around Cove's mother, Mika, who sobbed against his chest.

Serena stared upward.

Then she crumpled forward. Graye caught her before she could fall completely, pulling her to him. He sat with her, cradling her, rocking her gently as she pressed her face to his chest again.

Kade and Rhune stood nearby, quiet. Elsibetha watched with her jaw clenched and her throat tight. Jormunder's eyes were fixed on the stars. Serafine's arms were crossed, but her face was streaked with tears.

Grief had come like a tide. It would be a long time before it receded.

Later that night, when the fires had dimmed to embers and the grieving songs fell into silence, the coastline was draped in shadow. Most had slipped into uneasy sleep or sat tucked into hollows beneath the cliffs, mourning in private. The sea whispered now, but the scent of blood and char still clung to the wind.

Serena slipped from Meriden's cave without a sound.

Barefoot, she moved like a shadow between stone and sand, not waking a single soul as she took to the air. The wind caught her, lifting her higher and higher until the beach was a smear far below and the stars stretched wide above. She flew alone to the clifftop above the shore—where the seagrass grew, where she and Cove had kissed for the first time.

She landed in silence. The grass swayed around her ankles, damp with dew and salt. In her mind, she saw him—his lopsided grin, that pleased, arrogant tilt of his head. Heard her own teasing voice: *"You're going to be insufferable now, aren't you?"* And his voice: *"Serena, I really, really like you."*

She walked to the edge.

The cliff dropped sharply, with nothing but open air between her toes and the sand below. Her wings folded tightly. Her toes curled over the ledge. She leaned forward. And for a breath, just a breath, the world seemed still.

Then a hand slid into hers.

Not rough or sudden; just steady. Warm.

Rhune.

She startled but didn't pull away. She hadn't heard him approach. Hadn't sensed him. But Rhune was there, standing beside her, holding her hand as if he'd always known where she would go. The grip was firm.

"I'm not going to jump," she whispered, hoarse. "I just... I don't know what I was doing."

Rhune didn't let go. "I'll sit with you."

He eased down first, legs dangling over the cliff edge. She followed, too tired to resist. Once she was seated, he released her hand but kept his own pressed into the seagrass behind her, close enough to catch her if she moved again.

They sat in silence for a long time.

He didn't speak. Didn't pressure. Just waited.

Then, softly, Serena asked, "Do you think they really do go somewhere? They wait for us?"

She turned her head and looked at him—eyes red, face blank with grief, voice hollow and stripped of everything she'd once been.

Rhune met her gaze steadily. "I don't know. Maybe. We can't know that for sure until we join them. But what I do know is that life here continues in their absence. You are still needed."

"And you are still loved."

She stared at him, then up at the stars.

There was a long pause before he asked, "What will you do now, Serena?"

Her gaze shifted—past the dark beach, past the flickering funeral fires, toward the open sea where the ships had fled.

"Hunt them down," she whispered. "Kill them all."

Reflection from Serena, age 81

I will never forget my time in Tides. Meriden said it was the sea calling me home—and it's true, I felt it. I wonder sometimes if that pull would have been as strong had Mab told me the truth about my heritage, had she raised me on siren lore and traditions the way she did Elsie.

Perhaps it was for the best. Mab would have taught her version, but Meriden taught me the truth: the old ways, the old songs. It healed something deep within me.

Through her, I learned what I truly was—learned to accept it, and most importantly, learned that I controlled it rather than it controlling me. The sisterhood saved me.

I went to Tides like a shattered mosaic, hoping someone could glue me back together. Instead, the sisters gently set the broken pieces aside and showed me how to build something new, something whole.

And Cove...my first love. He wasn't my first heartbreak—that had been Graye when he'd first been torn from me—but what I shared with Cove was freely given, untouched by bonds other than the ones we forged together. It was pure, like his laughter. Like the way he made me laugh. Effortless. Right. His loss is a wound that has never healed.

That wound makes me think of Mab and my father. Were we the same, my mother and I? Did Mab find love once, with a golden Akyist whose eyes mirrored the sea and whose warmth felt like the sun? Did Edric make her laugh as Cove had done with me? Strangely, losing Cove made me understand her more. Not forgive her—but understand. Because I would have done anything to see Cove again, too. To see his smile, to hear him call me *urchin* one more time.

Yet there is no magic to mend a broken heart. Hearts are fragile; they shatter easily, and though we might piece them back together, they are never the same. We simply learn to live with the cracks.

CHAPTER TWENTY-THREE

AFTERMATH

A week had passed since the invasion, but for Serena, time had lost its shape. She moved through the days with a kind of numbness, emotionally flat except for brief, searing bursts of rage that caused glass to burst and parchment to catch fire.

She had spent a day with Meriden, Ronan, and Mika mourning together in the old way, but the pain had not loosened its hold. The Tides felt empty now, hollowed by loss. Every sight, every sound, every taste seemed laced with memory. She could not hear the waves or breathe the salt air without feeling Cove's absence press into her chest. The salve had become the wound.

In the end, she told Graye she needed to be elsewhere. She would spend time with her grandfather and the Moon army. Graye, feeling the depths of her pain through the bond, understood and had returned to Shade, after unsuccessfully trying to get her to come with him.

Jormunder had seen the sense in her wishes. He had always believed in meeting grief head-on, not letting it rot in the dark. She'd recovered from the loss of Graye with the army, and now she'd mourn Cove with it, too.

Serena sat in the Siorai palace with Jormunder, Serafine, the Mage General, and Mab—the five gathered around a wide table covered in the latest battle maps and intelligence. Reports from the coasts were grim—some of the surviving human ships had slipped away into the night, and others were making tentative landings up and down the shore, probing for weaknesses.

The Mage General spoke quietly, paging through sheets of runic notes and sketches of unfamiliar glyphs. The human weapons and armor had been warded—fae enchantments, but not any script the archives recognized. The mages and librarians had been delving into the oldest tomes, searching for any trace, any hint of the source. Progress was slow, and the answers were still out of reach.

Mab's face was unreadable as she listened. But she had already made her decision. A new detachment would be mobilized, Moon Court soldiers and mages, commanded by Jormunder, ready to move at a moment's notice to strike at any attempted landing.

Serena listened as the strategies unfurled, her face a mask. She barely blinked, her gaze fixed on the edge of the map, jaw set, fingers curled tight in her lap. Mab had been briefed; she was aware of Cove's death, of Serena's vengeance, of the siren screams that had nearly brought the cliff down. She had listened to it all, and for a rare moment, the High Queen had seemed reflective. She was well acquainted with loss. Edric, her mother. And she'd known Ronan through Edric. There was a small, hard sympathy for Ronan in her silence, but she spoke nothing of it to Serena.

In private, Mab had said as much to Jormunder. "She's young. She was always going to have some first love. We all do. And we lose them. Now she's gotten it out of the way, she can focus. We lost my mother and my mate to humans, and now she's lost her young love to them too. She'll be motivated."

Jormunder had glared. "Her heart is broken, Mab."

"You think I don't know what that feels like? You do too! You still grieve my mother. Why should Serena be any different?" Mab had looked cold, hard, and resolute.

"Queens don't grieve, Father. We rule."

That conversation was four days past, but Serena knew nothing of it. She came to the war briefings every day and listened without comment, her expression carved from ice.

Today, finally, Mab addressed her directly. "The Mage General and your grandfather have told me you acquitted yourself well, Serena. Storm mages are particularly destructive. And your second beheading..." Her mouth curved in a humorless almost-smile, a pointed reference to the first beheading Serena had performed at her order, the day she executed Jaryk in front of the entire court. "You wish to join the army and the Battle Mages?"

Serena looked up at last, and her eyes were cold, fierce, empty but for a sharp, coiled rage. Her voice was low. "Yes, Mother. It seems I'm rather good at killing."

Mab's mouth twitched, almost a smirk, as she flicked her gaze to Jormunder, silently echoing her earlier words. *See? Motivated.*

"Very well, Serena. You will go with your grandfather's forces. Your role will be at his discretion."

Serena nodded, once, sharply, and returned to her silent study of the maps, the future narrowing to the shape of war.

Months slipped past in a haze of exhaustion and violence. Serena's grief did not lessen. If anything, it crystallized into something colder and more permanent, a layer of ice beneath her skin. She barely wrote to Graye anymore. Her replies, when they came, were brief and impersonal. Eventually, Graye gave up and resorted to seeking news of her through Jormunder and Elsibetha, hoping for scraps of reassurance where there were none. Their bond felt flat, emotionless.

Serena had turned inward, her heart walled off and her expression unreadable. The loss had shattered her heart but sharpened her mind. In the field, she was almost unrecognizable. She was always among the first to rise in camp, strapping on her armor before dawn and going out to train. For hours she sparred with Serafine, the relentless pace of Shadowdancer drills leaving her drenched in sweat, every movement a way to bleed out rage and pain.

When the drills ended, she did not rest. She redoubled her studies in magery, using the isolation of the road as an opportunity for ruthless self-discipline. In her tent by candlelight, night after night, she practiced offensive spells, perfecting the most devastating magics with vengeance in her heart. Sometimes the other Battle Mages joined her for practice, but often she worked alone, her power growing darker, heavier, and more precise.

Unlike most, Serena did not rotate out with the other officers. She was present for every skirmish and every raid, standing at Jormunder's side or taking the field alone when the task required it. She was ruthless, not merely a weapon but a tactician. Drawing on the years of Jormunder's tutelage, she offered commentary on every battle map, proposed alternative maneuvers, and saw the patterns others missed. Shrewd, adaptive, creative. And unforgiving.

She earned a reputation quickly, and not as a royal. The soldiers no longer called her princess. She was the lightning in the night, the winged shadow in the sky. She kept her hair tightly braided, though she still wove shells through the plaits, a small aching piece of her old self and a reminder of what she'd lost, why she was fighting.

Soldiers began to joke she slept in her armor. She never appeared at ease, never without her sword. Rarely smiled. But despite that, the males and females around her learned to trust her implicitly. She was their protector, their avenger. On the battlefield, she was tireless, answering every threat, every incursion, with overwhelming force. Her lightning spells raked the enemy ranks; her swordsmanship grew sharper every day.

Serafine became satisfied that Serena was ready to take the field in smaller skirmishes. Together, the two of them took the field as Shadowdancers, master and novice, black sujinn blades cleaving through human soldiers with a predatory grace that made the others fall back in awe.

Black silk and savagery.

Serena's skill had grown into something that was being discussed around cookfires. Sometimes, in the heat of battle, she reached out a hand and reduced her enemies to blood mist with a gesture, echoing the violence of her adolescence but with a new, deliberate focus. She volunteered for every dangerous mission. She barely slept and rarely ate. Her renown spread as quickly as her skill, and with every engagement, every skirmish, she seemed to shed another layer of the girl she had been.

What remained was purpose and power, memory and pain—driving her forward, night after night, deeper into the war.

A year passed. The war had not ended, only changed shape. The first months had felt like vengeance—hunting down the scattered remnants of the original human fleet, eradicating every beachhead before it could take root. But the skirmishes never ceased. New ships continued to arrive, never at the same place twice, never in numbers so great as the first wave, but always carrying weapons and armor laced with fae enchantment. No one had yet discovered which fae were supplying them.

Each landing was met with brutal force. Serena, Jormunder, and their rapid-response force moved ceaselessly along the coast. They struck and vanished, never giving the enemy time to fortify. Every battle left questions unanswered.

Several times, they captured prisoners, but questioning them led nowhere. Some raved incoherently, maniacal with pain and fanatical resolve, shrieking threats of vengeance and doom. "We will be avenged!" they howled. "Ardaion must fall!" None would speak of their allies. None would, *or likely could,* explain the source of their magics.

Finally, one morning on a sodden, ruined beach, a human commander lay dead with a bloodied message folded in his coat. It was written in a hand almost familiar: the script was like *Hifa,* the ancient dialect of the Moon Court, but not quite. Different enough that it required weeks of careful work at the mage towers to decode.

The answer was as unsettling as it was tantalizing. The letter contained a form of writing not seen since the days of Morgana, the realm's most ancient queen whose name they still knew. The message spoke in riddles, its meaning only half-revealed, but the implications were clear enough: these fae, whoever they were, were not strangers to Ardaion. Some at the war councils began to wonder aloud. Was there a hidden population of fae, some splinter of Ardaion's bloodline, who had left long ago and now returned as enemies? Or had their spies simply been thorough?

Mab, ever watchful, drew her own conclusions. She remembered the oldest stories, the ones that had always unsettled her. She dispatched mages and scouts to the farthest edge of Ardaion's coast—where the Twilight Court had once stood before the land crumbled into the sea and history erased its memory. The stories were few and contradictory. Some said Twilight had tampered with magics too deep, too dangerous, and paid the ultimate price. Some said it had been a magical apocalypse. There were no records, only myths and whispered warnings.

But now, with an ancient language re-emerging, written in a form of high fae un-touched since Morgana's age, Mab felt the prickle of truth hiding beneath the surface. She could not be sure the threat was linked to the Twilight Court. But the pattern, the secrecy, and the evidence were enough to make her cautious—and intrigued enough to send her best mages to investigate the place where Twilight's ruins might still haunt the tides.

By the time Serena turned twenty-two, she had become a figure both familiar and formi-dable to the soldiers of Ardaion. She had been at Jormunder's side since childhood, her earliest memories shaped by the weight of maps, the scratch of quill on parchment, and the harsh lessons of strategy whispered between battles. The soldiers who had once called her "the little general" now witnessed as she came into her own—no longer a child trailing in her grandfather's wake, but a commander in her own right.

Her years at the mage tower and with Serafine in Shadowdancing had honed her into something rare. Though still a novice by the standards of the most ancient Shadow-dancers, under Serafine's tutelage she was already lethal. But it was in magery that she truly shone. Her power was unmistakable, fueled by long years of study and the deep, endless wellspring that marked her as Heir. She could devastate enemy ranks from a distance or turn the tide in close-quarters combat, her lightning a terror to those who opposed her.

Jormunder bore all this with quiet pride and resolve. He had never stopped shaping her for command, always testing her judgment, her endurance, and her will. He made her explain her plans to the commanders and accept their feedback humbly, to earn their trust. Now he decided it was time to see what she could do with the responsibility of true leadership.

He announced it in front of the assembled companies. Serena would have her own command—a new company, drawn not by order or reassignment but by choice alone. Every soldier would be a volunteer. There would be no forced loyalty, only faith freely given. Only those willing to follow Serena as a young commander-in-training.

The flag he unfurled was navy blue, a gold trident and a silver lightning bolt crossed at the center, a crown hovering above them. It echoed the Moon Court flag, but the lightning made clear whose company this was. Mab was the queen of tides and water. Serena was the storm.

He named them the Tempest Company.

By the next morning, thirty fae had come forward—mixed bloodlines, veterans and fresh recruits alike, many soldiers who had known Serena from her earliest years or whom she had saved in the recent skirmishes. Two Battle Mages joined as well, both eager to serve with someone whose power they'd seen at work. These were warriors who had seen her bleed, who had fought beside her, who trusted her not because of her blood, but because of her relentless efforts, her courage, and her brilliance under fire. Around the camp, they were already calling themselves "the Tempests."

The weeks and months that followed proved Jormunder's gamble more than justified. The Tempest Company grew, swelling to a hundred strong by the end of six months, drawing volunteers from every quarter—Akyist and Mer, earth and fire mages, winged and wingless, all those who valued victory and loyalty over protocol or old divisions. They took the field wherever the need was greatest, often deployed to handle the most dangerous incursions, splitting off from Jormunder's main force to respond independently.

Under Serena's command, they did not fail.

Her tactics were careful, often ingenious. She learned from every engagement, analyzed every defeat, and never repeated a mistake. Her power, already extreme, was matched by a determination to protect her own at any cost. Not one soldier in Tempest Company doubted her. She fought with a ferocity that left no room for hesitation, but she also watched over them like a hawk—refusing to lose another soul if she could help it. Serena became an avenging angel of the battlefield.

They followed her not because they had to, but because she was theirs. She had earned it, every step, every scar.

CHAPTER TWENTY-FOUR
STRANGERS

While Serena's reputation and the legend of her Tempest Company grew across the battlefields of Ardaion, Mab remained ruthless in her pursuits. She was not content to simply wage war against the visible enemy. On two fronts, she pressed for answers; one anchored in history, the other scouring the present.

To the west, she had dispatched her most trusted mages to the crumbling coast where the Twilight Court had vanished long ago. They were to study the ancient magics, to sift through rumors and the persistent currents of instability that plagued the land. There, along cliffs that dropped into restless seas, the mages documented zones where power twisted unpredictably and the air itself felt thin, magic thinning like a tapestry with a thread pulled loose. It confirmed what the oldest records had suggested: when Twilight fell into the ocean, something vital in Ardaion's magical network had torn. Power leaked from the realm at that wound, unstable, just as it had been before the Binding.

At the same time, Mab deployed her ships to search the outer waters. She wanted to track the source of the human vessels that continued to attack Ardaion's shores—ships always enchanted, always bearing runes, but never revealing their fae patrons. At first, she believed these were the descendants of those who had once killed her mother, the same humans on whom she had unleashed her infamous campaigns of vengeance, *Mab's Wrath*. She sent spies along the length of those distant coasts, searching for signs of fae magic or even hidden enclaves of fae themselves. They found nothing. No fae, no evidence of enchantment, only wary humans who shied from foreign vessels.

Frustrated but undeterred, Mab ordered her ships farther out, skirting reefs and shoals that had long kept Ardaion's vessels away. Those waters were rarely charted, and known for unpredictable currents, heavy fogs, and spells that sometimes went awry. The rivers and tributaries that would have supported settlement or commerce were absent. There were no easy areas to anchor; it was all dead soil, basalt cliffs and jagged peaks. For generations, Ardaion's fleet had patrolled the other side of the realm instead where there were easy trade routes.

But persistence yielded results. Her captains found an island—a wild, shrouded land off the neglected coast where Twilight had disappeared. The approach was treacherous. Shoals threatened every hull. Mists concealed hidden dangers under the waters, confusing even seasoned navigators. And yet, after cautious probing, Mab's ships found humans living there, clustered near beaches that were relatively safe for mooring. Magic thrummed through the island like a living thing, the same as on Ardaion. Flags were planted near the water with fae glyphs, and yet there were no fae to be seen.

This partially explained why the human armies wielded enchanted weapons and wore glyph-armored mail. They had some contact with fae. What remained unknown was who among the fae supplied them, and to what purpose. It was clear that the island's humans could not wield magic themselves. They relied on the artifacts and vessels left behind, or supplied by hands unseen.

Mab's captains charted the shoals and plotted the mists, but dared not confront the island's defenders openly. The order was to observe and report, not to risk a direct clash that might alert the hidden fae. Meanwhile, the mages at the Moon Court had finished decoding the letter found on the human commander. Its dialect matched records from Morgana's reign, its wording archaic and steeped in references to old alliances, tyrant queens, and lost realms.

A week later the war room at the Siorai palace was heavy with tension, the air thick with the scent of candle wax, old parchment, and the faintest trace of sea wind brought in on the cloaks and armor of those gathered. Maps were spread across the broad table, covered in new notations, ink marks showing the course of ships and the boundaries of tides and currents. The ship captains stood in a loose line, faces tanned, eyes sharp from days at sea.

The mages, cloaked in blue and silver, hovered near their notes and sketches, a hush of speculation running among them. Jormunder peered in stony silence from the end of the table, while the Mage General stood beside him, arms folded, gaze steady. Serena stood slightly apart, face shadowed by the glow of fae lights, while Mab presided over the scene, her presence as commanding as ever.

One of the ship captains began the briefing. Their vessels had found the island off the neglected coast—one beyond the shoals, steeped in mist and threaded with unpredictable magic. They described the treacherous approach, the fae-marked ships moored like silent sentinels along the shore, and the unmistakable hum of power saturating the land itself.

The mages shared their conclusions. The artifacts retrieved from the battles, the language in the intercepted letter, the wild magic occurring along the coast...The loss of the Twilight Court, they theorized, had not simply erased a kingdom from the map. It had torn a hole in the magical fabric of Ardaion itself, a wound that had never fully healed. They spoke of a "leak," or fraying tapestry; a steady draining of power, as if the wellspring that nourished the realm was bleeding out along the coast.

And what if that power was infusing the human island? The humans themselves could not use magic, but they lived surrounded by it, perhaps unaware of its true nature. The mages proposed returning to the island in secret, to determine whether its magic echoed Ardaion's own wellspring... or if something entirely new had been born in Twilight's aftermath.

It was the letter, however, that drew the most speculation. The language was a disused form of ancient *Hifa*, matching the oldest records from Morgana's time. Its dialect and phrasing suggested not outsiders, but kin, fae whose roots lay in Ardaion but who had vanished long ago.

"We believe," one of the mages said quietly, "there are survivors of the Twilight Court. A remnant that escaped whatever destroyed their realm and has been living in exile. We know whoever is supplying the humans are fae and with a dialect still in use that echoes our ancient ones."

Jormunder studied the map, tracing the coastline with a blunt finger. "It still doesn't explain why the humans are being armed, or why they've turned their anger on us. But it's another piece of the puzzle."

Mab's expression was distant, calculating. "If there is a remnant," she said, "then we need to find them. We need to know what they want."

Serena had been silent but alert for the entire meeting but finally spoke in reply to Mab, her tone flat, "What they want is less important than the fact they're doing it at all. They're funding a war without direct involvement. That alone makes them our enemies. Whatever reason they have, it isn't diplomacy." she flicked around the room "And why the steady trickle? Why not a full-scale invasion like the first time, at Tides? This last year has been a war of attrition on their side. It makes no sense."

Jormunder considered her words and nodded, he'd been thinking the same for a while. The incursions had neither stopped nor grown larger. He glanced at Mab, "Serena is right.

What if this is a war by proxy? They supply the humans without getting directly involved themselves. We don't have to know why yet, just prepare for escalations. Send the mages, and figure out if this island is absorbing spilled energy for Ardaion. That may give us more insight."

A week after the council in the palace war room, Serena found herself at sea again, the deck pitching beneath her boots as the ship cut through chill waters. The mission was clear: sail to the human island, skirt the ruins of Twilight's fall, and search for any evidence of a magical leak or signs of fae interference. Mage scholars clustered below with charts, tomes, and artifacts. A handful of seasoned soldiers stood on watch, scanning the horizon, tense and silent.

Elsibetha hadn't needed to come. She was Valkyrie, not scholar or mage, but Jormunder had asked her in secret. He hoped that Elsie, more than anyone, might reach Serena, might draw her back from the edge she'd been living on since Cove's death.

Two days into the week-long voyage, Serena sat on the ship's rail, eyes on the restless expanse of sea, hair whipped by salt wind. She looked gaunt in the sunlight, exhaustion hollowing her cheeks, and the old, restless ache never seemed to leave her face.

Elsibetha leaned on the rail beside her, arms folded, watching the horizon. She let the silence stretch, considering her words. Serena sighed, already anticipating the conversation.

"If you're here to tell me I've been sad long enough, don't bother."

Elsibetha didn't blink. "I wasn't going to say sad. I was going to say something more dramatic. Depression, with rage and a death wish. Possibly masochism."

Serena shot her a glare. "I've had plenty of chances over the past year if I wanted to get myself killed."

Elsibetha shrugged, voice steady. "Sure, if you wanted a quick death. But instead, you're training nonstop, volunteering for every single mission, barely eating, barely sleeping. It's a long suicide while taking as many of the enemy with you as possible."

Serena's voice rose, sharp. "Oh *take off*, Elsie! I'm doing my job. I'm defending Ardaion, leading armies, exploring this godsforsaken coast. Doing everything expected of me. And you're trying to lecture me about it?"

Elsibetha's temper flared. "Yeah, *I am*. Because reasons count. Your happiness counts. Your health counts. I've been answering Graye's letters because he's worried. Our grandfather is worried. The only one not worried is Mab, and you know what that means? When your mother is happy? It means you're suffering. She sees it, and *she's glad*. You're giving her exactly what she wants by being just like her."

Serena's tone went ice-cold, disbelief and fury mixing. "Just like *her*? You of all people telling me I'm like her?"

Elsibetha's voice rose to a scream, raw. "Yeah! Exactly like her. She loved an Akyist and he died. She sentenced herself—and you—to a living hell. And then you go and love one, lose one too. And what do you do, follow in her tides-cursed footsteps. You're just as dead inside as she is *and she's glad of it!*"

Serena's scream tore free. Cove's face rose in her mind, his laugh, and she shoved it ruthlessly away. "You were there! You were there and you saw what happened! I loved him! He loved me. *For me*. Despite the wreck I was. He helped me become something better, and stronger. And I was *happy!* For once in my life I was happy. And now it's ash in my mouth. All of it's gone. I should have known better."

"Because every time something good happens to me, it's taken away. *Every time!* And you know, my mother may be a conniving sea-bitch but she was right about one thing. That day she ordered me to kill Jaryk in front of the court, she whispered in my ear a queen's first lesson: 'Never suffer your enemies to rise. Sirens do not fear death. We become it.'"

"And by the pull of the moon, I will."'

Elsibetha faltered, pain flashing across her face. Her voice, when it came, was gentle, almost lost. "You're not the girl you were, Serena."

Serena's reply was cold as the sea. "That girl has died a thousand deaths and left behind a thousand epitaphs."

Wind hissed through the rigging. Neither spoke again for a long time.

For three days, the ship drifted through tangled mists and uncertain waters, the air thick with the taste of magic and unease. The mages performed rituals on deck and below, seeking the truth of the currents around them, but nothing worked as it should. Spells fizzled and divining rods spun in useless circles. Every scholar and soldier on board could sense the presence of power, but it refused to yield its secrets.

It was on the fourth morning, with fog pressed close and the sun a pale smudge overhead, that something strange and ugly landed on the bowsprit. It resembled an imp, but not quite—its wings were twisted and malformed, its fangs too long, yellow, and dripping with saliva. The crew stilled, wariness prickling along their spines, but imps were rarely bold enough to attack groups.

This one was different.

With a shriek, it lunged at a sailor standing by the rail, its claws raking, jaws snapping. Before anyone could react, the imp's fangs had torn the man's throat open, blood gushing over the boards. Chaos broke loose, soldiers surging forward with swords drawn. It took three to finally run the creature through, its shrieking death cry echoing over the waves.

The sailor could not be saved. He died there on the deck, eyes wide, blood pooling beneath him as the mages gathered around the imp's body. They brought it below for study. Serena stood at the railing, watching the blood being scrubbed from the boards, the sky a heavy lid of gray above.

When she rejoined the scholars and soldiers below, the mages were already dissecting the imp, cataloging its strange anatomy and the residue of twisted magic that clung to it. She listened in silence as they debated, offering theories. At last, Serena spoke softly, voice carrying just enough for one of the senior mages to hear.

"It recalls stories of Ardaion before the Binding. Wild magics, the way things were born twisted, Master Itkan."

He nodded, expression grave. "Indeed, Princess. This is further confirmation that the magics along the coast where Twilight vanished are unstable. But we have been discussing another approach. Our rituals are failing, and artifacts misbehaving. The only anchor we have left is the Binding itself. As you are with us, it seems the most efficient way forward is for you to attempt to lock onto the wellspring from the island. If you can do it, we will know for certain if there is a link. The rest of us cannot access it, and our instruments will not work in this place."

Serena considered in silence, her thoughts turning over the risks and the logic of the proposal. Finally, she nodded. "You're right. It's a logical next step, and it will save us from sailing even deeper into unknown dangers. Elsibetha and I can fly under the cover of the fog, land somewhere isolated, and I will try to sense the wellspring. If there's a connection, I'll feel it."

She glanced at the imp's remains. "Preserve it. I want to show my mother when we return. We'll be back within a few hours."

Serena and Elsibetha moved in silent coordination as they finished preparing on the ship's deck. Each checked the buckles of their leathers and the wards woven into their cloaks, the easy efficiency of veterans who'd long since outgrown the need for conversation. Elsibetha's voice was low and sharp as she tightened the straps on her sword belt. "Don't do anything stupid, Ser."

Serena shot her a withering look, eyes narrowed, but said nothing. She launched herself into the air with a snap of her wings, vanishing upward through the mist. Elsibetha followed a breath later, both gliding high above the rocking ship, climbing until the mists and low clouds swallowed them whole.

The ship was several miles from the island. The fog was so dense that even an enemy ship could have been lurking just out of sight, but the wind was steady and their wings were nearly soundless. They flew in silence, using the cloud cover to shield their approach, scanning the island as it rose from the sea below.

Serena circled, gauging the lay of the land. The island was far larger than she had expected, stretching out in rolling hills and forested ridges to the horizon. Below them sprawled a sizable town—no fae marvel, but a true human city of stone buildings and packed earth streets, the occasional paving stone glinting in the morning light.

Serena kept her altitude, eyes narrowing as she took in the sight. Elsibetha, hovering nearby, watched her cousin carefully, half-expecting Serena to dive straight into trouble. But Serena moved on, as agreed, and led the way toward a lonely stretch of foothills at the edge of the forest.

They landed in silence among the dew-soaked grasses. The moment her feet touched the earth, Elsibetha felt it. "I can feel the power beneath us," she murmured.

Serena nodded, eyes distant. She closed them, reaching with her mind and soul for the wellspring as she had so many times in battle. The response was immediate—a surge of energy roaring through her, lighting her veins and causing her irises to flicker with shifting iridescent colors. She didn't summon her spell wings, didn't risk attention, but opened her eyes to meet Elsibetha's searching gaze.

"This proves it. The island is linked to Ardaion. I don't know how... I saw no fae construction in the city, but perhaps whatever was here has been lost to time. Was this island once part of Twilight? Or has the power bled along the sea to infuse it? I can't tell. But the magic here is part of the Binding. It would not answer me otherwise."

Elsibetha was about to respond when Serena suddenly tensed, her senses wide open to the world around her. "Elsie... there are fae here. I can sense them." Elsibetha didn't doubt her—Serena, tapped into the wellspring, could feel everything in the realm with uncanny precision.

Serena turned slowly, seeing beyond sight, her senses reaching out past the hills and into the town. "They're in the city, among the humans. I want to see what they're doing."

Elsibetha's face tightened in warning. "Ser... we're alone out here. It's too risky."

Serena shook her head. "I'm not going to fight. Just watch. I'll thicken the fog for cover."

She took to the air again, this time lower, angling toward the town's outskirts. From above, she called on her storm magic, weaving a deeper, denser fog from the fields around the city, gradually shrouding the rooftops and streets until visibility dropped to a handful of paces.

There, at the edge of the largest building—a structure with a pointed roof, likely a temple or shrine—Serena and Elsibetha landed softly, pressed low behind the sloping tiles at the rear. They listened, unseen.

Elsibetha edged her head just above the rim, peering down. "They're glamoured. They look human, but their robes are marked with glowing runes."

Below, the townsfolk had gathered in tight clusters around the robed figures. One of the glamoured fae spoke, voice loud and commanding. "The devils from across the sea continue to repel your attacks, but we have come to give you greater weapons, stronger protection from Argainor, God of the Sea! Pray to him and he will deliver you from the devils!"

The crowd erupted in cheers, and their faces turned up in adoration. Serena and Elsibetha exchanged a wary, dubious glance as the glamoured fae ushered the humans inside the temple. Elsibetha frowned. "So... they're playing false prophets, giving the humans magical weapons and protections, sending them to war against us. But why?"

Serena's eyes were sharp and thoughtful. "I'm not sure. They're using the prayers to explain the glyphs—offering up new powers in exchange for faith. I think we should scout the coast further. Either they have their settlements hidden beyond the reach of the humans, or they came from somewhere else entirely. And if that's the case, we need to know where and how."

They flew on, keeping well clear of the scattered villages that dotted the wild coastline. The land grew harsher the farther north they went—jagged black cliffs thrust up from the water, the beaches below narrow and strewn with rough volcanic sand. Human dwellings gave way to wind-bent trees and raw, open wilderness.

Then, as they crested one of the highest ridges, the world changed.

Not a fae city—nothing as permanent or grand—but a temporary camp had sprung up along a black sand shore. Several tall fae ships were anchored just off the beach, their sails black and unmarked, but gold glyphs and runes gleamed all along their hulls, catching every sliver of light. On the shore, rowboats were pulled high above the tide line. Fires burned low in the sand, and near one of them, a makeshift smithy had been set up, the ring of hammers echoing up the cliffs. Fae worked at enchanting and forging weapons, their hands glowing with power.

Elsibetha hovered beside Serena, her words barely more than a breath. "They're making the weapons for the humans. Enchantments."

Serena nodded once, her eyes narrowing, but then something pulled both of them up short—a sensation colder than the wind.

A fissure cut across the air above the water, impossibly bright at its edges. It looked almost like a mage gate, but it was massive, far larger than any Serena had seen, and instead of revealing a view through to the other side, its heart was pure blackness. Not emptiness, but a true void, as if the world itself had been ripped open. The gate gaped out over the sea, its opening descending beneath the surface.

As they looked on, another fae ship sailed through that yawning portal. The prow broke the edge of the rift, passing from the unnatural darkness into the dim light of the misty day. Even as it emerged, a shout went up from the beach, and without warning, a ball of mage fire erupted from the deck, streaking through the mist straight toward them.

Serena and Elsibetha dodged together, wings snapping as the fireball roared past, close enough to burn away a trace of cloud. That was enough. They'd been sensed—if not seen directly, then at least caught by some magical alarm. The air around them crackled, charged with energy.

Serena shouted, her voice barely carrying over the wind. "What in the tides was that?!"

Elsibetha shook her head, already banking away. "We have to get back to the ship. They sensed us—they may send someone after us. They'll know the game may be over!"

Serena was already scanning for pursuit but nodded sharply. "We need to warn the crew. They have to sail for home, now. But Elsie—we need to gate back to Siorai. Mab needs to know now; they can gate whole ships. We can't risk waiting days. We'll reinforce the shields on the ship, get everyone turned around, and then go."

Elsibetha was already angling toward the distant speck of their ship in the mist, her wings moving in quick, urgent beats. "Let's move. If they come after us, we need to be ready."

They raced back across the water, every sense straining for danger. The mists closed in behind them, swallowing the shore, the ships, and the black gate.

Back on the ship, Serena wasted no time. She scrawled a short note onto a leaf of enchanted paper, focusing her will as she wrote: *We found the fae. E and I gating to Mab now. Meet us. —S.* As soon as she finished, the paper shimmered and vanished, slipping instantly through the fabric of magic to hover beside Jormunder wherever he was.

Elsibetha worked with the mages on deck, layering protective wards over the hull and reinforcing the ship's magical shields. Soldiers stood ready, eyes wary on the horizon as they helped turn the ship back toward its outbound course. Serena, drawing on the wellspring, summoned a powerful tailwind to push the vessel faster through the mists. It would not last forever, but it would buy them precious minutes if any pursuit came from shore or sea. She hated leaving them, but Ardaion was at risk, and Mab needed to know what they had found. The crew had warriors, mages, and the cover of thick mist. That would have to suffice.

Barely half an hour after returning, Serena and Elsibetha had briefed the captain and the remaining mages. The wards were set. The ship was underway. With a few words and a careful slash of power, Serena opened a mage gate right from the deck. Through it, the war room of the Moon Palace awaited, lanterns burning above maps and scrolls. Elsibetha checked the ship one last time, then stepped through at Serena's side. The gate closed silently behind them.

They didn't have to wait long. Mab arrived a few minutes later, her presence radiating impatience and authority. Jormunder's gate shimmered open not fifteen minutes after that, and he strode into the chamber, face grim.

Serena began without a preamble, her voice cold and clipped but urgent. "Mother. We located the fae supplying the humans. Elsie and I flew to the island, found a remote part, and I was able to lock onto the wellspring. The power there is Ardaion's, subject to the Binding. But I sensed fae. We tracked them to the human town. They're glamoured, pretending to be priests of a false god—explaining the glyphs as gifts of prayer, and calling us devils. They're building hatred and rallying the humans against us."

She paused only long enough to see Mab's eyes narrow in thought, then pressed on. "We scouted further north along the coast, past impassable ridges, and found several fae ships anchored. They've set up a secret smithy and are forging and enchanting weapons for the humans. But while we were observing, a gate opened above the water—a massive one. It looked like a mage gate, but the other side was pure void. Nothing could be seen through it, and it was large enough to let an entire ship sail through. We were sensed. They sent mage fire in our direction, but it was a blind shot through the fog. Still, they'll know someone was watching."

"We flew back, warned the ship, and turned them for home. Then we gated here."

Serena's expression darkened as she added, "There is more. One of the crew was attacked by an imp—misshapen, unstable. The ship is bringing the body back to study. It happened along the Twilight coast and reminded me of the twisted creatures from before the Binding."

Elsibetha spoke next, voice matter-of-fact. "We did what we could to protect the ship, but this couldn't wait."

Mab nodded, eyes thoughtful, then turned her gaze to Jormunder, waiting for his counsel.

Jormunder stood silent, his hands clasped behind his back, jaw set as he weighed every detail. The undefeated general, shaped by centuries of war, took his time, letting the silence fill the room. When he spoke, his voice was low, measured.

"A proxy war," he said at last. "They're fighting us through the humans, using them as shields and swords both. They glamour themselves, invent a god, and feed the humans lies and hatred. We become the devils, the cause of every loss, every grief. If it were just that, I would understand. But why bother? Perhaps they lack the numbers to confront us directly, or perhaps they simply want to avoid the risks of open war. Their enchantments are strong, but so are ours. Maybe their armies are fewer, or scattered."

He paused, gaze lingering on Serena and Elsibetha. "But the black gate... that's something else. Something outside our history, maybe outside even our lore. Powers that rival our own, or perhaps something darker still. Why fight in shadows and whispers if you possess that strength? Why use the humans as pawns?"

He looked to Mab, the question hanging between them.

Mab's eyes sharpened, the light of calculation flickering in their depths. "That's it. They're sending the humans to us in trickles, *knowing* they can't win. Each attack is doomed from the start, yet they persist. It isn't just a proxy war; it's attrition."

Her fingers drummed once on the table. "They're bleeding the island dry, whittling down its population under the guise of religious war. All the while, they build their numbers and presence in secret, quietly taking over the land. It's not about us. It's about claiming the island and its power."

She glanced at Serena, then at Jormunder, a gleam of cunning calculation in her gaze. "I am sure of it. *Because I want it too.*"

CHAPTER TWENTY-FIVE

WORTH THE FIGHT

Mab's plan was as ruthless as it was simple: continue the strategy their enemies had begun, fighting the humans down bit by bit, until the island was emptied. For Mab, there was no moral distinction between these humans and those who had killed Tatiana and Edric. They were vermin. The only thing that mattered was securing Ardaion's interests—and in this, the enemy's plan and her own aligned.

Any reminders from her council that they still did not know the full strength or origin of the enemy fae were brushed aside. Mab's answer was decisive: the Moon Court would train more Battle Mages, every banner in Ardaion would be readied, and the courts would stand as one. When one was attacked, all would respond. She wanted no court caught unawares.

Jormunder listened to these pronouncements and, with his typical pragmatism, sent Serena and her Tempest Company to Shade. It was a strategic move—Shade was the smallest and most vulnerable court, the most in need of reinforcement—but there was also a deeper, more private purpose. Graye had barely seen or heard from Serena in half a year. Perhaps proximity would bring relief to her rawness, soothing the bond between them, and restore a measure of warmth to her spirit.

Serena had asked Mab, "What about the strangeness of the Twilight coast, Mother? I thought it was a leak we were going to repair."

Mab's answer was cold, unwavering. "It's only a leak if we don't control the island."

A week later, after the safe return of the ship from the Twilight coast and Mab's examination of the imp, Serena's mages opened the first of many great gates. The time had come for her company to march into Shade.

The staging was meticulous. The first through the gate was a herald, Tempest banner held high—navy and silver, defiant against the crimson of Shade. Then came Serena's lieutenants, each leading a column of well-armored, grimly proud soldiers, enchanted weapons gleaming, their faces weathered by war and marked by a fresh pride born of recent victories. They moved with the precision of a force that knew its worth, a company forged by hardship and commanded by someone who had bled alongside them.

Graye, Kade, and Rhune, all dressed in Shade's finery—blacks, charcoals, crimson sashes—stood with Master Dewin and Stefan, watching the parade as it passed toward the wide, flat land where the Tempests would camp. They watched with an odd mix of pride and wonder, seeing Serena's power in the discipline of her force.

When all had passed, the gate shut—and Serena walked through, alone. She was in full battle dress: polished leather armor in silver and grey, the sigil of Moon Court across her chest, hair pulled back in intricate braids save for a single shell gleaming near her temple. She looked older than her years, sharp-eyed, solemn, a quiet force whose every step commanded attention. There was a gravity to her now, the aura of someone who had seen too much loss and become numbed by fighting, the same air that clung to Jormunder after a hard campaign.

Yet when she saw the five waiting for her—Graye at the center, his eyes searching her face—she smiled. It was tired, a little brittle, but real. She crossed the last few paces, gaze fixed mainly on Graye, searching him for signs of forgiveness, of understanding. The uncertainty in her eyes was plain: she wondered if too much time had passed, if too much had changed.

She stopped in front of him, her posture formal, voice pitched to be heard by all. "Lord Shade, I ask leave to establish camp in your court on behalf of the Moon Court."

There was something wry in her eyes, a flicker of humor at the old game of courts and titles. Graye stared a long moment, then huffed, the corners of his mouth lifting. "You have my leave, Princess. Now stop acting like a royal and come here, Sev."

He pulled her in, arms tight, and the bond between them surged—satisfaction, joy, love. The pain lingered too, the ache of grief she tried to hide, but through the bond, he felt the truth: she was glad to see him, and she still loved him. And he loved her, in all her brokenness.

He drew back, pressing a kiss to her forehead. Serena's smile grew warmer, the lines of sorrow eased just a little. She hugged Kade next, who grinned and said, "That is some impressive armor, princess."

Serena gave him a tired smile, then turned to Rhune. He pulled her close, one hand gently guiding her head to his chest for a moment, then letting her go. His voice was soft. "How have you been?" But his eyes, green and searching, asked the real question: *Are you alright?*

Within hours of their arrival in Shade, the Moon Court's presence was unmistakable. Tents rose in perfect lines, pennants streaming silver and navy beside Shade's crimson. Mage lights flickered to life, some warming cookfires, others warding the camp's perimeter. Soldiers of Tempest Company moved with confident purpose, pitching tents, organizing supplies, and swapping news with Shade's sentries. Wherever Serena walked, faces brightened—some with the easy camaraderie of old friends, others with a private, fervent loyalty. She seemed to know them all, greeting them by name, noting who had fresh scars or weary eyes.

At last, her tent was finished—a broad pavilion pitched near the center of the encampment. The interior was a stark blend of luxury and utility: a sturdy bed rather than a cot, its blankets folded with military precision; a small iron stove in one corner, fire crackling beneath a kettle; a writing desk already stacked with correspondence, maps, and battered books; and a round table set with four chairs and proper court silverware, the kind found in royal halls, not battle camps.

Serena stood at the table, swirling a glass of red wine in one hand, her armor still on, but her hair let down at last, the lone shell in her braid catching the lamplight.

When Graye, Kade, and Rhune entered, the cold outside seemed to lift a little. Serena glanced up, offered a small, tired smile, and gestured to the table. "I suppose we have catching up to do..." She looked at them, a spark of the old mischief flickering through her grief. The three took their cue from her—Graye poured the wine, Kade helped himself to bread, and Rhune sat silently, watching her with that attentive calm she'd always found both reassuring and intriguing.

Serena took her seat and began fixing a plate. "It feels like the first time I was in Shade, the night we met." She set a slice of cheese on her bread, then paused and met Graye's eyes across the table. "I know I... haven't been writing. I tried. Several times. But the words wouldn't come. I'm sorry."

She drank, the wine staining her lips. "I know Elsie wrote, and I'm grateful she kept you updated. So tell me what you know, and I'll fill in the missing pieces." Her gaze swept the table, not just Graye but Kade and Rhune too, her tone quietly inviting: not the voice of a queen, but of a friend among comrades, longing for the ease of old times.

Graye leaned forward, his tone quiet but sure. "Just tell us what we need to know, Sev. And what the plan is."

Serena nodded, a wry smirk tugging at her mouth. "I can't tell if that's blind trust or recklessness, Graye."

He returned the look, his smile crooked, familiar. "Both. As always. Everything we ever did was reckless. But we trusted each other."

She let out a breath and raised her glass in a half-toast, acknowledging the old truth between them. Then she glanced at Kade and Rhune. Kade was offering her a gentle, worried smile as if he wanted to urge her to rest but knew better than to say it aloud; Rhune simply waited, his gaze steady, a sentinel, but never missing a detail.

Serena rested her glass and spoke, her voice low, matter-of-fact. "Well, I never knew what Elsie wrote in those letters to you, so I'll just give you my version. Whatever happened with the Twilight Court left a tear in the tapestry of power that covers Ardaion. That corner is so unraveled that magical disruptions and twisted creatures are appearing along the coast. The mages call it a leak. After tapping into the wellspring on the human island, I think it's more like a tether—a direct link. That island's power is part of Ardaion's wellspring. I can lock onto it as easily as I can here."

She glanced around the table, making sure each of them followed. "The dark fae—so called not for their appearance, but for their black sails and the black portal their ships use—are equipping the humans by posing as priests of a false sea god, glamoured to look human. The working theory is that they're using the humans as pawns, letting us do the hard work of getting rid of them. Then, when the island's been emptied, they'll claim it and its power for themselves."

Serena's face hardened as she continued. "Mab has no intention of letting that happen. Not only do these dark fae seem hostile and wield enchantments we don't yet understand, but it would mean an enemy force right on our doorstep. She won't leave Ardaion's back unguarded. The Binding gives us a territorial claim over any power linked to our wellspring. If it weren't linked, it might be a different story. But since it is, Mab claims dominion. *Prior tempore, potior jure*—the older claim is the stronger right."

A faint, tired humor flickered through her as she added, "So, the Spider will keep picking off the humans, no surprise there, until it comes down to a contest between us and the dark fae. Based on the artifacts and notes we've recovered, the current belief is that they're a remnant of Twilight, survivors of whatever catastrophe destroyed the court. We have no idea where their homeland is now; all we know is they use those strange portals, large enough to send entire ships through."

She met Graye's eyes, then Kade's, then Rhune's. "That's why we've reinforced the armies and called the banners. If they can portal warships to the human island, they could portal them anywhere—even to our coasts. We know the shape of the human threat by now. But we know almost nothing about these other fae. Not yet."

Serena's gaze swept the table, steady and direct. "How well prepared is the Shade army?" she asked, her tone all business now, setting aside the weight of old grief. "You've had almost two years to build back up since Tides. The Tempests can handle most human invasions the way they've been coming, two or three ships at a time. But if more arrive, or if the other fae come through those gates, how much are you prepared to face?"

Kade was the first to answer, his voice measured but laced with a hint of pride. "We're stronger than we've been in decades. Stefan's reforms held, and most of the mercenaries who left after the last campaign have returned, better trained, and better armed. We've rebuilt the officer corps. Most of the old commanders who survived now lead the recruits, and Master Dewin's mages have improved our wards and siege defenses. But..." He hesitated, glancing at Graye.

Graye nodded, meeting Serena's eyes. "The truth is, we're better than we were, but we're still the smallest court. Even with the influx of recruits and the Tempests here, we'd struggle against a true massed landing or a force like those fae ships you saw through the gate. Shade can hold a line against the kind of raids we've seen. We can't hold off an entire army."

Rhune's voice was quiet, but there was steel beneath it. "We're ready for a fight. Morale is high, and the people are with us. But Shade can't stand alone. If those gates start opening along the coast..." He left the rest unsaid, but the meaning was clear.

Kade added, "If the other courts respond quickly, as Mab promised, we'll have a fighting chance."

Graye looked back to Serena, the bond settling into a calm between them. "We'll do our part, Sev."

Serena eyed the fire thoughtfully, her expression sharp and calculating. "I know you will," she said quietly. "I don't like how little we truly know about these other fae. My mother assumes that despite their unfamiliar enchantments, they must be an overall weaker force—otherwise, why not attack us directly instead of using the humans?" Her voice dropped slightly, taking on the edge of someone who had spent long hours alone, turning these questions over and over.

"But perhaps they want to avoid a two-front war, against both us and the humans. Or...what if they simply don't care which side wins or loses between Ardaion and the humans? Throwing us at each other means both sides become depleted, worn down, exhausted—until these dark fae sweep in to pick off the survivors. Maybe their goal is to take whichever land is weakest in the end—the island or Ardaion itself."

She shook her head slowly, frustration evident. "I don't like it. And why now? Twilight fell eons ago. What's motivating them after all this time?"

Graye recognized her tone immediately. She wasn't merely speaking for their benefit—these were the questions that had haunted her in quiet moments, questions she'd been wrestling with alone, without answers. Always thinking, always sharp.

Rhune spoke up carefully. "There may be a point of diminishing returns in supplying the humans. Eventually, there may be too few humans left to pose a credible threat, forcing these dark fae to join openly. Or maybe the human numbers fall low enough that supporting them no longer makes sense—then the fae step forward themselves. Either way, their forces will still be fresh, while ours grow weary."

Serena nodded firmly, appreciating the analysis. "Exactly. They'd wear us down over time until we're too weak to resist. Which means we cannot allow it to get that far. We must act aggressively, decisively, at every encounter—no prisoners, no retreat. We wipe our enemies out completely, every time, before conflicts drag on." She leaned forward, her gaze meeting each of theirs with intensity. "My mother's eyes are already fixed on that island, which means direct conflict with these fae is inevitable—either here on our shores or over the sea. If they attack Ardaion, the fewer we allow to escape our shores, the fewer we'll have to fight when we claim that island."

Serena looked at them intently, her voice both assessing and gently challenging. "How far have you come with your magery studies under Master Dewin? I always tried my best to keep Graye at least roughly at my level, but I know it wasn't nearly enough. And now I have almost two full years of constant battle experience with the Battle Mages. It's opened my eyes to how devastating a single mage can truly be—far beyond what any single warrior or even a group of warriors can achieve. The Moon Court has always forbidden the other courts from having their own Battle Mages; all are trained within our own towers, then conscripted for life."

She paused, thoughtful, reflective. "In peacetime, I suppose it makes sense—someone ambitious, like Jaryk, would undoubtedly misuse them. But this is war. We don't have that luxury anymore. I intend to help train you properly for mage combat. Dewin and

Elsie will assist. So," Serena leaned forward slightly, fixing each of them with a probing gaze, "tell me honestly: how much have you learned in terms of basic offensive spells, and what's the true extent of your powers?"

Graye answered first, clearly understanding what Serena was driving at. "Master Dewin has taught us thoroughly, at least in theory and fundamentals. We're all competent in the core personal offensive spells—fireballs, defensive shields, wards, bindings. But we've never had the scale of practice you've experienced in real battles. I've focused mostly on fire and mind magics. My spells are strong, precise, but I haven't pushed them beyond small skirmishes or training grounds."

Kade nodded in agreement. "I've gotten skilled with elemental magics too, particularly fire and earth. Dewin says my precision is excellent, but he's warned I lack the power or endurance that comes with heavy battlefield use. I've never had to sustain attacks for hours at a time, or against overwhelming numbers."

Rhune spoke last, steady, and measured. "My specialties have been defensive enchantments and illusions—stealth and disruption mostly—but Dewin has pressed me to develop my offensive spellcasting as well. I can handle combat magic reliably, but I won't pretend to be your equal, Serena."

Serena was reflective for a moment, staring at the fire. "All of this is a good start. But what you need now is to see battle magic as I've come to know it—raw, devastating, and relentless. Tomorrow, we'll begin drilling. You'll train alongside my mages."

The next morning dawned gray and damp, mist clinging low over Shade's sprawling camp. Serena's orders were brisk and efficient: the Tempest Company was to spend the day with Shade's soldiers, not just drilling but sharing stories, forging camaraderie, and exchanging what they had learned in engagements with the humans. There was laughter and competitive boasting, half a dozen different dialects and banners mingling where there might have otherwise been rivalry.

But Serena herself led Graye, Kade, and Rhune out beyond the bustle of the encampment. They followed a narrow path through the forest—Shade's namesake ancient woods, silent and vast, where the leaves glimmered red and ochre in the damp light, and the air always smelled faintly of rain and moss. Beyond the last of the shadowed trunks, the land rolled open into a plain of low grass and scattered stone—a perfect, safe place for practicing dangerous magics.

Anthra, one of the Tempest Company's veteran fire mages, had joined them, as had Master Dewin, arms full of spellbooks. Elsibetha was absent—deployed with another Moon Court force to Solace, where her expertise was needed among the court of healers. The morning had an edge of hope to it. Proximity to Graye had eased something in Serena, the familiar wound beginning to knit. She looked less haunted; there was light in her eyes, and when she met Graye's gaze, he found himself grinning despite the morning chill. Kade and Rhune were restless and eager, their anticipation palpable.

Serena's tone was firm, but beneath it was the excitement of purpose. "I'm breaking at least a dozen mage tower rules to train you in the way of the Battle Mages," she announced, lips quirking with a hint of her old mischief. "But these are desperate times. If my mother wants that island, she'll need a force capable of capturing it, and holding it."

She turned to Master Dewin. "You've already instructed them in personal defensive fireballs and shields. Today, move on to the battle forms. Teach them fire comets, not just the small orbs. I want them to be able to set ships ablaze. Show them how to expand their shields to protect a unit, not just themselves. And get them used to feeling along a glyph's edges, so they can cut off a ward or barrier at its source. Graye has skill with mind spells; teach him to probe, and the derangement and berserker spells."

Kade stepped forward, a little sheepish. Serena glanced at him. "Kade has an earth affinity, but not a lot of stamina, he says. Focus on quick, effective spells—mud slicks, quicksand, the wider the better, so he can mire a charging force and break their lines. If he gets good at those over the next week or so we might try landslides, too, in case we have to take the fight into the foothills."

Her attention shifted to Rhune. "Rhune's strength is illusion and disruption. I want him practicing large-scale distractions—phantom soldiers, burning wagons, hidden ambushes... whatever can throw an enemy into chaos. And teach him the light-flash spells. He needs to blind them, not just hide himself. Let's have him try disrupting Anthra from casting. No more restricting yourselves to personal magics. Today, you're learning at battle scale."

She stepped to Dewin's side and said under her breath, "My mother will probably not be thrilled if she hears of this, but if she wants to win this *without* training them, she can get her ass off the throne and bleed for once."

That evening, Serena moved quietly among the tents of Tempest Company, weaving through the clusters of Moon Court soldiers as dusk settled into deeper shades of violet and blue. The air was tinged with woodsmoke and the sharp scent of ozone that lingered after a day of magical storms. She paused with each squad, inquiring after their health, inspecting the bindings on a burned hand, and accepting a quick report from a junior officer who was still flush with pride at how his unit had handled Shade's spellcasters.

Every so often, she found a group of Shade soldiers watching her with wary, sidelong glances. Rather than pass them by, she introduced herself—letting them hear her voice, letting them see her not as an untouchable Moon Court princess, Heir of Ardaion, but as a commander who cared. Their tension eased, a few smiles breaking through the uncertainty, and she noted names, faces, and the way even the seasoned veterans seemed to hunger for a steadying presence. Everyone was on edge.

Meanwhile, in the heart of Tenebris, the Shade Court's dark-stone palace, Graye, Kade, and Rhune had claimed a battered table by the hearth in one of the lesser-used studies. The fire burned low and red, the room quiet except for the distant murmur of other officers drifting in and out, but the three of them were unmoving, letting the warmth sink into their aching muscles.

The day's magery had left its mark—Kade sprawled sideways in his chair, eyes half-lidded, fighting the bone-deep exhaustion that came from pushing himself beyond what Shade's training had ever demanded. Rhune sat forward, elbows braced on knees, head in his hands; the effort of maintaining large-scale illusions had left his temples throbbing, a dull ache that no tonic could ease. Only Graye seemed to draw any satisfaction from the ordeal, a stubborn spark alight in his green eyes. He nursed a mug of bitter Solace brandy, gaze lost in the leaping fire, thinking of Serena.

He remembered how she had looked out there, hair plastered to her temples by wind and rain, every movement precise as she called down thunder and reshaped the sky. It wasn't just the display of power that stuck with him; it was the ease with which she had slipped back into the old role—teacher, co-conspirator, the Serena who had once risked Mab's wrath to tutor him behind closed doors.

For a moment, watching her pleased smirk when he'd successfully sent a fire comet sailing through the air, he had felt the weight of years slip away. She had not been wholly remade by grief and war. There were remnants of the girl who had once delighted in sharing knowledge, who had shown him what real power could be.

Graye nursed his glass of wine while Kade said rather mournfully, "I didn't know I could feel so... empty. Like I spent every last bit of my power and half my soul to get through today."

Rhune was massaging his temple and said "Everyone talks about the Battle Mages. And I thought I knew what they could do, but I was entirely wrong. The sheer scale of the spells, and the way they could just keep going without pause. It's devastating. Not just Serena, but Anthra and even Dewin. That is mage tower training, the discipline, and the knowledge. That's why she's doing this. She knows exactly what we lack."

Graye smiled softly, "Sev was always like that. Mab forbid me to have even a basic noble's education, much less advanced magery. And she barred me from studying in the tower. So Sev would quietly send me books with her letters and every time we got together, she'd teach me. She never left me behind. When I became Lord, Mab relented but how was I supposed to study when my court was falling apart? That's why Sev sent Dewin."

Kade smiled tiredly, "She didn't leave us behind either. I'm grateful and I don't think I've ever told her just how much. I thought I'd have a chance to spend some time with her at Tides, but..."

Graye inhaled deeply, then sighed, "Tides. It nearly broke her. Even the name may as well be a metaphor for her life. Something good washes up on the shore, and she's happy, but then the water goes back out again, taking the happiness and even the sand beneath her feet with it. She stumbles, she falls, but just before you think the tide will carry her out to sea with it, she gets back up again."

Rhune looked at him a moment, reflective, inscrutable once more then said "She's a siren, Graye. Have you ever considered that maybe she *needs* to swim with the tides? To follow the happiness where it goes instead of standing on the shore watching it leave?"

Graye watched Rhune with a flicker of something indefinable in his own eyes then said "She's been through too much. It might drown her."

Rhune replied carefully, his tone carrying no inflection "Sirens don't drown, they swim."

An hour later, Serena finally arrived, still dressed in her leather armor. She carried with her bottles of Moon Court wine—Graye recognized the labels instantly—and several sheaves of parchment. The smile she gave them was small, tight, a little warmer than when she'd first arrived but still focused on her agenda. She handed each of them a parchment before sitting, sighing out a tired huff but continuing.

"I've had the enchantments we've seen the humans bearing copied for you. We don't know how to reproduce the effects yet, but we've at least identified which glyphs cause which effects. You'll know if they're warded against certain attacks, if their armor is reinforced, and so on. Then you can adjust accordingly. Lessons learned the hard way." She opened one of the wine bottles and poured herself a glass before passing it to Graye to circulate. He paused over the label, then looked at her, his eyes catching hers and twinkling with a memory. It was the kind they used to steal for themselves, there in the old supply closet. What he always called 'mischief in a bottle.' For a moment, the past shimmered between them; not everything had changed.

He smiled at her and said, "We were saying how the practice today was draining but appreciated."

Kade perked up, voice earnest. "Yes... Serena, it is truly appreciated. You keep looking out for us..." Kade had filled out so much over the years that he was a mountain of a male sitting there in a chair almost too small for him, and yet for all that, he looked almost vulnerable. The words hung there, heartfelt and raw, and Serena almost flinched, as if she refused to let herself feel something that deep. She broke the moment with a flippant, "Someone's got to," and winked at him. Understanding flickered in his golden gaze, and he dropped the subject with a slightly rueful smile and a bob of his chin.

Leaning back with her wine, Serena said, "Honestly, you all impressed me. Battle-scale spells are not easy to learn or maintain, but you are making great progress, and some of my concern for your safety is already lessened. I think it'll be good for your army's morale to see what you can do without us."

She continued, "The soldiers seem in good spirits. I've just come from an internal strategy meeting; Jormunder sent word he's had another attack near Ember, but only one ship. Either their numbers are dwindling or it was merely a probe. Our orders are to remain alert and continue cross-training."

Her gaze settled on Graye. "You're welcome to attend the briefings, you know. You're Lord of Shade now, no longer outside looking in. Or hiding in dim studies." Graye understood her motivation in saying that; it wasn't a pointed remark on his absence or an attempt at political inclusiveness. This was Sev trying to include him in her adventures, wanting him with her. He nodded with an easy smile and said "Then I'll be there."

Later that night, after a stretch of quiet conversation- Serena recounting how the Tempests had really come about, and carefully dismantling the wild rumors that had followed their victories- Kade and Rhune excused themselves for bed, leaving only the two of them in the lamplight.

Graye stood, extended his hand, and said quietly, "Come on, let's go back to my room." Their fingers tangled together, Serena let herself be led from the fading warmth of the fire to the suite she'd once shared with him, nearly two years before, the place where they kissed before she left for Tides. So much had changed since then, and the room bore Graye's imprint now: stacks of books on the shelves, many sent by Serena herself. She smirked at the sight of them, pausing on the shelf where that first battered book on military strategy stood, the same one she'd mailed from Jormunder's encampment when they'd both been learning how to survive the ache of separation.

She spoke softly, almost shy. "I still have the lucky rock you sent me. The one I kept in my shoe. It's on my desk at the palace."

He grinned at her, a familiar warmth in his eyes. Serena gestured, tracing complex runes through the air. Folded nightclothes appeared on the bed, and an extra bottle of wine materialized atop the black desk in the corner. At last, she began peeling off her armor piece by piece. Graye turned away to give her privacy, listening to the muted thud of leather and the whisper of fabric, the unmistakable sound of a cork easing free from the bottle.

When he turned back, Serena stood barefoot in a silk sleeping gown, her dark hair let down, loose and softly wavy from the braids she always wore. She handed him a full glass of wine, keeping one for herself, and moved out onto the balcony. Below, the courtyard stretched out, the dark tree line tracing the edge of the night.

She drank deep, her shoulders tense, the lines of fatigue plain in the lamplight. Graye followed, setting his glass on the balustrade, and slipped his arms around her waist from behind, resting his chin lightly on the crown of her head. They stood there, fitting together as easily as they ever had, the silence alive and gentle.

After a while, Serena spoke, voice quiet and roughened by the weight of all she'd carried. "I've missed you, Graye. So much. I don't know why I stayed away, except maybe because I didn't want to feel anything. And I knew you'd make me feel everything. It's been so easy to bury myself in books and fight until I'm too tired to even dream." She turned in his arms, pressing her cheek to his chest. "But now I'm here and everything that was so raw feels eased, somewhat."

He held her tightly, hands moving through her hair as if to soothe away the last of the ache. He kissed her forehead, voice a murmur in the hush. "I know, Sev. You needed to close it off for a while. I understood that. And it's not like you just sat doing nothing. Look what you've accomplished." He threaded his fingers through one of the violet and emerald streaks in her hair, holding her close. "I felt you sometimes through the bond. Anger, pain, grief. Just flashes. Mostly, I just missed you."

She stayed close, face pressed against his chest, voice muffled and raw. "Do you ever think about our farm? The one we were going to run away to? Potatoes, goats, chickens... Some days there's nothing I want more. Just you and me, in some little shack by a stream." Her fingers curled in the fabric of his shirt, holding tight. "I don't want to let the idea go. But I also can't let go of my need to end this threat. And it's not about defending Ardaion or anything noble." Her breath hitched, words struggling as the memory rose. "I told Rhune that night... after... Tides... I told him I would end the humans for what they did. And I still want to. It's eating me alive."

Serena stayed pressed against him, voice trembling as she spoke. "I keep thinking of what I've done. What I've been doing. What I'll keep doing. Graye, they build me up to be some hero but I'm not. The armor and the banners just legitimize what I'm doing, but if no one else knows the truth—Graye, you do. This is *vengeance*. A reckoning. When Cove died, part of me did too. And I want them to know what it feels like."

Graye held her tight, his hand steady at her back. "No one ever said you had to be noble, Sev. That's always been something that came from within you, a standard you've held yourself to. But regardless of why you say you're doing this, your army believes in you. I believe in you. Because of who you are, because even in the depths of your despair, you care."

She was silent for a long time, the words caught somewhere between confession and fatigue. When she finally spoke, her voice was small. "I'm just so tired, Graye. Tired of it all."

He hugged her tighter, then in a gesture so familiar it felt inevitable, he scooped her up and carried her to his bed. It was an old ritual, a comfort as old as memory itself. He settled in beside her, pulling her back into his arms, her head tucked beneath his chin, his arms anchoring her in the dark. He whispered, "I love you, Sev."

She whispered back, "I love you, too," before an exhausted sleep took them both.

Reflection from Graye, age 108

It had always hurt when we didn't see each other often enough. The bond between us pulled, rubbed raw, chafed. Being near each other was the only relief, the only way to heal, as if the sliver of each other's souls in each of us needed to be near the rest of it to be whole, if only for a while. We'd never gone more than a few months between visits, but this time it had been seven months. The longest. It burned in my chest, in my soul, to the point I couldn't sleep, and could hardly focus without thinking of Sev.

I was always aware of her pain, her loss. It was the dominant emotion at any given time. Sometimes, layered in with it, was fierce determination, or brief flickers of happiness, but never fear. At first, I'd marveled at that—because I'd had enough updates from Elsie to know Sev was actively fighting battles, risking herself constantly. But then I realized what it was: she didn't care if she died. With that realization came another, heavier truth—I understood why she was avoiding me. She didn't want to feel better. She'd made grief her companion and it was the only thing keeping her on her feet.

She'd sent me a letter about Jormunder's orders to reinforce Shade with the Tempests, but I'd received another from Jormunder, too. I guess he wasn't sure she'd bother telling me. That entire morning, I'd been anxious for her arrival. Kade and Rhune too seemed restless—Kade paced, and Rhune stood silent at the window overlooking the field where her army would encamp. I'd sat by the fire, mentally rehearsing all the things I wanted to say, and all the questions I needed to ask. But when she walked through alone, after her soldiers and mages, all of it fled my mind.

Because those things had been meant for the version of her I remembered. What I saw walking up to me was someone who held herself too stiffly, whose eyes looked like they hadn't known real sleep in months, and who was sharp as a hawk. There was a feel to her, even in the air—a sense of danger that prickled the back of my neck. She'd sloughed off a lot of the old courtly ways during her months with the army, and what remained was a blend of the old campaigner Jormunder embodied and something else, something more vicious- the siren peeking through.

Siren eyes are distinctive. I'd learned that not just from Sev, but from Mab, from Meriden, from a few others over the years. Even when they're smiling, they aren't quite seeing you as one of them. It isn't haughty or disdainful; it has nothing to do with rank or status. It's about what they are. Predators. Siren eyes always seem to say, *I see you. I won't hurt you. But I could.*

I had no idea how many hundreds Sev had killed by then, and I didn't want to know. Storm mages aren't discreet—their spells leave entire fields scarred. But the eyes of her soldiers as they marched by were fervent, some looked almost fanatical. They'd all chosen to follow her, with Jormunder's leave, and she'd given them protection, glory, and victory.

My mind flashed back to when we were teenagers, alone at the cabin when she asked, "Is might always right, Graye?" I didn't see that philosophical side of her as I held her in that first embrace. She'd walked alone for a reason—a signal, to me, to everyone: *I am the might. I am the storm.*

CHAPTER TWENTY-SIX
WHEN THEY COME

A month slipped by, marked by the relentless rhythm of war and training. Humans struck near Ember, their ships better warded than before—glyphs woven so cunningly that no mage barrage could pierce the hulls. In the end, it was the winged Dardani who boarded and overran the invaders, blades flashing in the chaos. Jormunder's soldiers fought at their sides, and the battle was won, but not without cost.

Mab moved swiftly, dispatching mages to examine the ship's protections, eager to unravel the mysteries of the unknown fae craftsmanship and, if possible, adapt those enchantments for Ardaion's fleet. The captured vessel was quickly pressed into service for coastal resupply, its resilient glyphs now a shield for Ardaion's own.

Back in Shade, Serena maintained the relentless pace she'd set: Tempest mages rotated through as instructors, training Graye, Rhune, and Kade in battlefield tactics and the endurance required to wield power at scale. Side by side, Shade's army drilled with them, learning to trust in the unpredictable cover of fireballs, mud slicks, and illusions that could turn the tide of a skirmish. They still instinctively flinched at the bolts of lightning and cracks of thunder, but they were getting better about it. Serena's soldiers encouraged Shade's, telling them not to fear the lightning because it meant the Princess was nearby.

Under Serena's orders, the mages worked every afternoon to enchant weapons and armor. There wasn't time or resource enough to give every soldier the layers of glyphs the nobility wore, but every blade stayed sharp, and every set of armor gained at least a basic shield against blunt force or spellwork. They would be harder to injure.

It was all part of Serena's plan—to strike fast, to give no quarter, to finish battles before exhaustion could grind down their edge. She poured herself into it, employing every lesson Jormunder had hammered into her since childhood, every hard-won insight earned in blood and thunder.

Yet even as she worked and commanded, something in her eased. The strain that had etched itself into her features began to fade, day by day. Though still tired, Serena no longer looked brittle and haunted. The curve of her mouth softened; smirks and fleeting smiles grew more frequent in Graye's presence.

The shadow that had followed her since Tides had retreated a little, replaced—not with laughter, not yet, but with something warmer, steadier. Proximity to Graye was a balm, reminding her of old truths even as the world around them threatened to shift and burn.

She spent her afternoons at the cookfires in the camps, sleeves rolled up as she helped enchant battered swords and dented armor, or bent over maps with skirmish reports from every corner of the realm scattered before her. Graye, Kade, and Rhune were almost always there, sharing whatever passed for supper, voices blending with the background of clattering pots and the low murmur of soldiers.

Sometimes their talk circled back to their years with the Dardani- old rivalries, brutal training, small victories, and humiliations. Sometimes it was the memory of Stefan's attempts to transform them into presentable nobles, etiquette mishaps, and accidental insults recounted with wry affection. Other times, Serena shared stories from Meriden, bits of siren history or lore, never quite touching the pain of Tides but no longer skirting around its memory either.

On one particular night, after a long, windblown day, Kade prodded the embers with a stick and glanced at Serena, curiosity plain. "I heard a story about Jormunder when I was a trainee," he said, hesitant, "...that he broke the press in Donridion Pass single-handedly, climbed a hill, started waving the banners, and the enemy just broke and ran. Just like that. Did he ever tell you about it?"

Serena snorted, eyes brightening. "Donridion is one of my favorite bedtime stories. *Atta* used to tell it to me as a little girl. I'd beg for it more than anything else. It's so perfectly him. But the version you've heard... court scribes cleaned it up a lot. They thought the truth was too colorful for a hero's tale."

All three of them sat up a little straighter, attentive, and eager to know the true story.

She leaned in, conspiratorial. "The real story is that the army was packed so tight in the ravine, that nobody could swing a fist, let alone a sword. My grandfather tried to clear some space by buffeting the nearest invaders with his wings, and while he was doing that, he caught one of them right under the chin with the wing claw. The man's head just... came clean off and stuck there, impaled on the claw. He couldn't flick it off, so he just kept fighting with it. That's why they cleared back. He broke the lines charging straight at them with a head stuck on his wing."

She grinned at their stunned faces, warmth flickering in her eyes. Kade's mouth was hanging open in delight. "The banners part is true, in a way. He fought the enemy commander up a slope, wanting higher ground to fight it out. He won, of course. And because he has a dark taste for drama at times, he chopped the commander's leg off at the hip, tied the man's cloak to it like a flag, and stood on a ledge waving the leg over the enemy. He shouted, 'Your commander orders you to retreat!' And, as you can imagine, they did."

For the first time in months, Serena laughed. It was soft and unguarded as she wiped an amused tear from the corner of her eye. She wore a smile that was almost childlike, and nostalgic.

Graye grinned, unbothered by the gore. He'd heard plenty of Jormunder's version of bedtime stories, tucked into bed beside Serena. Kade shook his head, disbelief and a little envy mingling in his voice. "That's the kind of stories he was telling you? And you were, what... eight? Nine? While you were sleeping in his war tent in the middle of an army. That's..." He trailed off, unable to find the right word for it.

Graye's voice was warm, amused. "Oh, he started telling us those stories even younger than that. We loved them."

Kade offered a crooked smile, wistful. "...I'd give anything to hear him tell one himself."

Serena, hearing the longing in his voice, stood and dusted off her hands. "Well... I have one or two of his journals in my tent if you want to take a look."

They'd been camped right outside her tent, so she ducked inside, the canvas flap settling behind her. The others heard the sound of her rummaging; something shifting, a clink of glass, and then a small crash. Rhune, closest to the entrance, instinctively rose and stepped inside. He found her kneeling on the rug, quietly collecting a broken bowl and two heavy books that had tumbled from a narrow, collapsible table near her bed.

"The table's meant to collapse for easy packing, but I guess it wasn't as stable as I thought. There's no harm done, I'll be right out." Her tone was light, and polite, as if to reassure him it was nothing serious.

But Rhune's attention had fixed on one of the books- a battered, leather-bound journal, with what must be Jormunder's distinctive writing on the yellowed pages. It had fallen open and pressed inside, delicate and preserved, was the gryphon feather he'd given her.

Rhune's voice was quiet, almost reverent. "You kept it."

Serena looked at him, warmth softening her features. "Of course. You'd carried it all that way just to give it to me. I haven't thought about it lately, but it's always been here, tucked away, shuffled from one place to the next wherever I go."

Rhune knelt beside her, his fingers brushing over the gryphon feather before he closed the journal, the movement gentle and deliberate. He was close, eye to eye, shadows and lamplight blurring the sharpness of his expression. For a moment it seemed he might say more, but the words caught, unspoken. He rose instead and extended his hand.

She took it, steady and unhurried, holding his gaze for a moment. She searched those impenetrable green eyes, then dipped her chin in quiet thanks before stepping past him and back into the cool air outside the tent.

Once outside, she settled beside Kade, flipping through Jormunder's journal and pointing out entries. Some were marked with rough sketches, and others recounted legendary battles in the old general's blunt, colorful hand. Graye shifted to the other side, leaning in to read with them, the three heads bowed together in the golden firelight. Rhune lingered on the edge, the closed journal with its hidden feather in his lap, his eyes fixed not on the pages, but on Serena. He watched, thoughtful and silent.

An hour later, Graye and Serena went for a walk around the army camp, holding hands as they so often did. Back by the fire, Rhune and Kade remained, the night deepening around them. Kade, without looking up from Jormunder's journal, finally broke the quiet.

"Are you ever going to talk about it?"

Rhune's eyes flicked over, guarded. "About what?"

Kade sighed, closing the book on his lap. "We've known Serena about three years now. And every single time you're in the room with her, you don't see anything else. Now she's been here a month- longer than we've ever been around her- and the way you watch her is getting obvious."

Rhune had gone very still, his face gone hard, unreadable. He said nothing, just stared at Kade with a cold expression that suggested the wrong answer could have consequences. The silence stretched, tense. Kade's golden gaze locked on him, unwavering.

"So what's holding you back? Is it because of who she is, her rank? Or the fact she's been grieving that Akyist? Or maybe because Graye loves her?"

Rhune's stare grew colder, his jaw set. For a moment, it seemed he might say something dangerous, but instead, he stood, voice clipped. "We're not having this conversation."

He picked up the journal he'd been holding, walked to Serena's tent, and left it on her bed. Then he disappeared into the darkness, leaving Kade alone by the fire.

In an eerie repeat of that morning at Tides, when Serena had been wrenched awake by the blast of warning horns, the horns of the Moon Court now sounded through the overcast grey dawn along Shade's coastline. But this coast was nothing like the turquoise shallows and soft, white beaches of Tides. Here, the shore was harsh: rocky, lined with granite boulders and gritty grey sand, the surf breaking where the land dropped off abruptly not far from shore. This meant the invaders' ships could come dangerously close before needing to launch their boats.

The Tempests were already on their feet, moving with the same organized, unhurried speed they'd honed after a year of campaigning under Serena. Their steady efficiency rippled outward, anchoring the Shade army, and in short order, the whole camp was armed and armored, the practiced calm in the air like an extra layer of defense.

Serena, already in her full leather armor, was issuing orders in a voice that cut through the morning fog. They'd drilled for this, mapped every possible landing, and prepared for each contingency. Now three human ships had appeared on the horizon, sails stark against the steel sky. Wind mages stood braced at the shore, summoning a counterwind to slow the invaders' progress. Battle mages climbed onto boulders and sea cliffs, setting themselves for long-range strikes. Beside them, the winged Dardani and Akyist volunteers from the Tempests waited, ready to defend the mages or take to the air to harry the ships directly. Infantry spread out along the predicted landing points, ready for whatever came ashore.

Serena stood atop one of the higher sea cliffs, making herself deliberately visible to both the armies and the oncoming ships. By the time Graye and Rhune reached her, she had already locked onto the wellspring, the magic coursing through her so strongly that her eyes glowed and the spell wings shimmered, vivid against the churning grey sky.

Kade had positioned himself with the Shade army, prepared to use his newly learned earth spells to mire the beachheads in quicksand, making any attempted landing treacherous. Graye was to unleash his fire affinity first, sending fire comets at the ships to set them ablaze, and once they closed the distance, he would reach for the minds of the enemy commanders, trying to incite panic or sow infighting.

Rhune, with his skills in disruption and illusion, was assigned to attack the glyphs on the ships themselves, weakening their magical protections, or if that failed, to conjure visions of impassable reefs and wrecks to steer the invaders toward the most unforgiving parts of the coast.

Having grown up training alongside the Dardani, they were all prepared to trade magic for steel if their power was spent. Already, Serena was calling up a storm of monstrous scale, the black clouds roiling overhead, lightning forking across the sky, and waterspouts lashing at the ships—tearing at their sails, not yet powerful enough to rip them apart but promising chaos with every passing second.

As the enemy ships crept ever closer, the careful strategy Serena had drilled into her forces was bearing fruit. One of the ships already had a mast ablaze, though the flames crawled more sluggishly than expected, hampered by protective glyphs. Another ship drew dangerously near, its crew lowering rowboats etched with shimmering runes meant to deflect both arrows and spellwork. They were angling to force a landing at points more accessible from water than by land. The third ship lingered further out, content to wait while its companions drew the defenders' focus.

Two Dardani warriors swooped down into a rowboat, cutting down the soldiers as they rowed, blades flashing. On the cliffs, Serena unleashed a bolt of lightning, sending it crackling through the humid air. It struck the center of another boat with devastating force, the blast tossing soldiers into the surf. Without ever glancing away from the battle-field, she called over the roar of wind and water to Graye and Rhune, her tone crisp and controlled. "Focus on the landing parties first, but that third ship is smart, hanging back. Don't forget it's there."

On a narrow sandbar, one of the boats managed to disgorge its soldiers. They slogged through the water, only to be trapped by Kade's quicksand, the ground swallowing them to the waist before Shade soldiers descended, blades flashing, cutting them down where they struggled.

Rhune's voice, low and steady, cut through the din. "I've cracked some of the glyphs on the second ship. Graye, try to burn it now."

Without hesitation, Graye hurled a comet of fire at the ship. The deck exploded into proper flames, the fire licking higher as the wards broke. Down the coast, Anthra saw what was happening and cast her own spell. Another column of fire roared to life, and the ship became an inferno. Soldiers began leaping overboard, some dragged down by their heavy armor, others swimming for shore in a desperate bid for survival, the battle raging all around them.

So the battle stretched on for more than an hour. Teams of Akyist and Dardani swooped down on landing parties, harrying them with blades and wind, while the Battle Mages kept up their relentless assault on the ships and the infantry cut down any who made it to the rocky shore.

Rhune, having disrupted the glyphs on the enemy vessels, now turned to illusion. He conjured a wall of fire on a long stretch of beach, and the sight of the inferno sent panicked soldiers crowding together, fleeing straight into the waiting blades of the Moon Court warriors.

Graye, meanwhile, continued launching fire comets at the third ship, which hovered just out of easy reach, but he shifted his focus to the minds of the humans scrambling ashore. Several of them turned on their own, hacking wildly at their companions, and one cluster he sent running off a high sea cliff, their armor dragging them straight to the depths.

The combined Shade and Moon armies could sense the tide turning, bloodlust rising as victory seemed within reach. Soldiers were grinning, adrenaline and triumph spiking through the lines even as the third ship loomed, unmoving on the horizon.

Then, suddenly, far out to sea near the third vessel, a white line appeared across the water, a blade of light so sharp and unnatural it seemed to slice the sea itself. Serena's breath caught, dread chilling her spine. The line widened, spreading until it formed a gaping gate, black as pitch, swallowing light and sound.

Her voice was soft, strained, "By the seas... they're coming. The dark fae." Her next words rang out, sharp and commanding in High Fae, calling for the messengers and the mage commander. The messengers appeared almost instantly, and she snapped her orders: "The dark fae are coming. That is one of their gates. Get word to my mother, my grandfather, and Elsibetha immediately."

The messenger bowed, vanishing at a run. The mage commander arrived, his expression tense. Serena turned to him, her voice clipped and precise. "We don't know what they're capable of, Denin. At least as much as the protections on the human ships, but we haven't seen any offensive spells from them yet. Rest the mages in shifts. Get the healers moving, and patch up anyone who needs it. Let the infantry finish with the humans, and keep the mages ready for whatever comes through that gate. Send a message to the tower for reinforcements, even if it's just students. And be ready to fall back. Our forces here were meant to repel human threats, not these other fae."

Denin nodded, already barking orders and recalling the mages to regroup. Serena turned to Graye and Rhune. "Save your strength. Let the armies handle the stragglers on the shore. We've got a bigger threat to watch."

As they watched from the high cliffs, overseeing the final mopping up of the human remnants below, Serena's voice was quiet, almost grim. "They waited until we were tired. They must be running low on human fodder and now they're ready to test themselves against a smaller force." Her gaze remained fixed on the dark horizon. Even as she spoke, three of the black-sailed ships began slipping one by one through the portal. These vessels dwarfed the human ships, and for now, they stayed frustratingly out of range of even the most ambitious spell.

A scrap of parchment appeared at Serena's shoulder, hovering in the air, and she snatched it with swift fingers, scanning the words. "It's from my grandfather," she said. "It just says, 'We're coming.'"

A strange, tense calm settled over the coast once the last of the humans had been cut down. Only the hiss of the surf, the crackle of burning wreckage, and the far-off echo of orders disturbed the quiet. Serena was silent for a long moment before she turned to Graye, her tone steely.

"Listen to me. You're the Lord of Shade. Even if something happens today, even if we have to give ground and then take it back, we *will* take it back. We won't abandon Shade. And I won't abandon you."

Graye swallowed, jaw set, a shadowed look in his eyes as he surveyed his battered soldiers and the dark forests stretching beyond the beaches. Shade hadn't been his childhood home but it had been his inheritance, and he'd worked hard the last two years to win respect from his court and his people. The prospect of any retreat was bitter, but he understood her pragmatism. After a moment, he answered quietly, "I know you'll do what you have to do, Sev. You always do."

Her eyes searched his face, unsure of the emotion behind his words, and she tried again. She laid her hand on his chest, over his heart. "I won't let Shade fall, Graye."

He covered her hand with his own, squeezing it tight. "Just be careful, Sev." He bent to press a kiss to her forehead, a gesture heavy with unspoken meaning.

Rhune stepped in close, the question clear and direct in his voice. "What do you need?"

Whatever Serena had been searching for in Graye's eyes, she turned to Rhune and snapped back to the present. "Food and drink. There's a lull, and we may be burning through a lot of power today. We'll need the energy."

Rhune nodded, sharp and decisive, and strode off toward the supply tents. Graye turned to Serena. "Come on. If Jormunder is coming, they'll reach the staging area soon."

It was a ten-minute walk down from the cliffs. They could have flown, but Serena wanted to be seen by the soldiers. As they went, she and Graye surveyed the state of their forces. There had been deaths, but not many; the healers were already tending wounds, moving from soldier to soldier with quick efficiency. Battle mages sat on the sand, eating and drinking where they could, faces drawn but determined. Only thirty minutes had passed since the black gate had first torn open. The dark sails of the enemy ships still hung just out of reach on the horizon.

Then, suddenly, a bright white slit of light split open in the staging area. Through the tear in reality came the banners of the Moon Court, bold against the grey morning, and Jormunder himself leading his troops through. They looked a little wild-eyed at having been herded through the portal so quickly, but they moved with professional purpose, driven by Jormunder's relentless discipline. He broke formation when he saw Serena and Graye, striding toward them, issuing orders for the soldiers to march straight down to the beach to reinforce the front lines.

Jormunder stood on a sea cliff, spyglass in hand, measuring the approach of the three black-sailed ships and the last human vessel. The legend of his age, he'd swept back toward the beachfront with Serena and Graye, his sharp eyes taking in the scene: two shattered ships, broken rowboats, bodies floating amid churned foam, and the scattered remains of desperate landings. He needed no explanation. It mirrored every other human incursion Serena had repelled and her tactics had been clean and merciless, just as he had taught her. Even now, the regrouping of mages was managed with near-training efficiency, rest cycles maintained, and readiness preserved. Kade had been taking notes; the Shade army mirrored the Moon Court's doctrine, seamlessly integrating alongside them.

Only those three black ships and the human ship remained. They hung on the horizon, their intentions inscrutable.

Serena finally broke the silence. "We haven't seen their offensive capabilities. Only defensive. And we don't know if what they gave the humans is the limit of those abilities."

Jormunder didn't look up from the glass. "If the humans were meant as fodder, I'm going to assume they didn't receive the full defenses. No point making them too hard to kill. Just difficult enough to tire us out."

There was a crunch of boots on gravel. Serena turned to see Rhune approaching, a shoulder bag slung across his chest. He gave Jormunder a long look, taking in the unmistakable wings and broad build that marked him as the Black Dragon. Jormunder didn't acknowledge him, focused on the ships and the rocky sweep of the beach below.

Without a word, Rhune produced a wrapped parcel from his bag, unwrapped it, and held it out to Serena. Inside was heavy bread, pulled chicken, slices of ham, hunks of sharp cheese, a wedge of melon, and a jug of water. She offered him a tense but genuine smile and began to eat, falling into the disciplined rhythm of a mage at war: *replenish the body, replenish the power.* Rhune passed another bundle to Graye, then opened his own. Both of them ate ravenously, the quick, practiced efficiency of soldiers who never knew when they'd next have time for a meal.

CHAPTER TWENTY-SEVEN

BLACK SAILS

The three ships with black sails completed their passage through the portal, and the rift snapped shut behind them, vanishing as if it had never been. For a short while, the dark vessels and the last human ship lingered just beyond range, the enemy making their final preparations. Serena, watching from the cliff, suspected they were casting last-minute protective spells—the kind that required a caster's active energy, not the passive protection of glyphs. She could sense the prickling pressure of power building across the water, the sense of anticipation like a gathering storm.

Then, the human ship began to angle in, positioning itself as a shield before the three fae ships. The formation shifted, the intent unmistakable: the humans would absorb the first blows, buying time for the fae to unleash whatever they had planned.

On the shore below, Kade was with the infantry, his posture tense, ready for the clash. High above, Jormunder, Serena, Graye, and Rhune kept their vantage point, surveying the approaching enemy. Jormunder made his calculations with a strategist's eye and didn't bother with a call for winds—he knew better than to waste mage strength on a tactic that would likely fail or, worse, be turned against them.

Instead, he ordered the Battle Mages to break into mixed squads, each unit built from a blend of affinities, with disruptors like Rhune embedded within. Each squad was to focus on a single fae ship: bring it down by any means necessary. Meanwhile, the Akyist and Dardani were tasked with boarding the human ship, storming the deck with magic and steel.

The bond between Serena and Graye was a thread of tension, their breaths quickening in synchrony as anxiety and anticipation surged through both of them- worry, rage, and the keen awareness of everything at stake. Graye's hand flexed and unflexed at his side, knuckles pale.

Rhune took in a deliberately deep breath and released it in a controlled exhale, forcing himself to relax. He clamped his hand on Serena's shoulder and let it rest there, pulling her to the present. The effect was immediate; her breathing steadied, and her mind narrowed to the coming battle.

Rhune leaned close and murmured in her ear, his voice low, steady, and warm, "You know you'll have to leave if it gets bad. You're the Heir. If we lose you, the Binding goes with you. Ardaion falls, no matter who wins today. If the time comes, Serena, you go. Back to Siorai. Survive today to fight tomorrow."

She stiffened, jaw set, bristling with refusal even as some part of her acknowledged the truth of his warning. She didn't turn, just answered under her breath, "It won't come to that. I'll drain the wellspring dry before I abandon all of you." Rhune's sigh was quiet, resigned. He let his hand fall from her shoulder but didn't step away, a steadying presence just behind her.

Graye hadn't heard the exchange in full, but he noticed the quiet way Rhune had placed himself beside Serena- bringing her food, offering calm, and reminding her she had a duty that was bigger than one battle. A bitter taste rose in Graye's mouth as the thought struck him, clear and self-reproaching: *I'm angry at him for it, but he's doing what I should have done. What I should be doing.*

A long, raw pause opened inside him. Something in his heart gave way, a wall cracking after years of silent pressure, especially after that kiss two years before, the moment that had shifted everything between them. And in that private, unguarded space, he admitted to himself, "I love her. I always have. But no... I'm *in* love with her. And now... what? We're about to fight for our lives. It's not the time. It's never been the time."

Graye's inward haze fractured as Serena's voice cut through the mounting chaos, sharp and direct: "Graye... you can get into their minds. We need to know what they want, where they come from, why they're doing this... and knowledge of their magery. Can you do that?"

He nodded, fierce and intent. "If you get me prisoners, I'll crack their minds open."

Jormunder turned at that, his golden eyes narrowing with predatory intent. "Then that's what we'll do."

The moment was shattered by the opening salvo from the black ships. Spells hurtled through the air—fire comets, but not the familiar reds and golds. These were blue and black, streaking across the sky before exploding on the beaches in bursts of cold, unnatural flame. Soldiers caught in the blasts screamed, writhing as the flames devoured them, even as they threw themselves into the surf in desperation. The water did nothing; the flames burned, unquenchable.

Serena's gasp was barely audible above the din. "By the gods..."

The Moon Court mages retaliated, sending waves of fire and lightning crashing toward the enemy ships, while water mages summoned colossal surges, attempting to sweep foes from the decks. The attacks struck home, but the dark vessels barely seemed to register the hits. Dardani and Akyist wings filled the air, warriors streaking for the human ship. On deck, the battle was joined in a brutal melee, but the enemy enchantments slowed every advance.

The three black ships pulled up near the shoreline, remaining just beyond easy reach. Jormunder's jaw clenched. "They're not coming ashore. They'll keep pelting us from a distance."

Another volley of blue-black fire comets screamed overhead, forcing soldiers to scramble for cover. Then, drifting after them, came a mist of vivid purple and green, shimmering like dust motes in the sun. As it descended, soldiers caught in the cloud began to choke, clawing at their throats before collapsing lifelessly on the sand. Wind mages rushed to push the poisonous haze back to sea.

Graye unleashed fireballs at the nearest fae ship. Rhune focused on unraveling the glyphs, picking apart the spells at their heart, while Serena's fury sharpened.

"It doesn't matter how large our army is if they refuse to engage directly," she spat. "It's a battle of mages as long as they stay behind those wards. We'll have to go to them."

Jormunder's voice was cold, decisive. "Then we will. Take the nearest ship, Serena. Rip it apart."

Serena reached deep, glowing as she drew on the wellspring, spell wings flaring wide. Power crackled around her, the very air thrumming with energy. She jerked her arm downward; a massive bolt of lightning ripped from the sky, striking the fae ship with a deafening crack. Enemy fae collapsed on the deck, and a jagged tear opened in the black sail.

She was already summoning another. The next bolt was larger still, slamming into the vessel with enough force to blast timbers apart and set the sail aflame. Enemy fae raced about the deck in chaos. Serena was savage in the pleasure she took in the destruction as she realized *'they might outmatch court-born fae, but the Binding is older. Deeper. They weren't ready for the full weight of Ardaion's wellspring focused in one body. They weren't ready for me.'*

Jormunder's voice cut through. "Serena, hold."

Before she could protest, he launched himself from the cliff, wings unfurling. *"Atta!"* she shouted, but the Black Dragon was already streaking toward the burning ship, his great wings pumping hard for speed and then folding tight for a blistering dive. From the air, he located a target, a single fae separated from the rest, and Jormunder crashed into him with brutal force. With ruthless efficiency, Jormunder hauled him up and snapped his leg with a single, vicious stomp, a scream echoing across the water.

But Jormunder wasted no time. With the dark fae trapped in a death grip, he launched himself back into the sky. Enemy spells and arrows battered at his back, but Serena cast a shield, deflecting every strike.

Within mere minutes, he was back atop the cliffs, dumping the captured fae at Graye's feet. Jormunder's eyes were cold and uncompromising. "There's your first prisoner. Tear every last thought from his mind."

How Jormunder had plucked a crew member from the deck- raw power, wings snapping and landing with the force of a battering ram- and the devastation wrought by Serena's lightning brought a strange, uneasy pause to the battlefield.

The black-sailed ships, which had seemed relentless a moment before, now hung back in the water, decks alive with hurried movement and what appeared to be an urgent internal discussion among the dark fae. The defenders, battered but unbroken, stood watchful along the cliffs and rocky shore. Tension crackled through the ranks, nerves frayed by the sense that something greater was being decided just out of their reach.

Meanwhile, Graye worked over the captured fae but his mental shields were proving resistant. The prisoner was wild-eyed, raving and cursing in a guttural dialect—ancient High Fae twisted almost beyond recognition. Even Jormunder, who remembered some words from stories whispered by his father in the deepest reaches of history, struggled to grasp the meaning. The vocabulary was archaic, and the grammar was corrupted.

Serena's patience was already thin. She surveyed the battered armor, its glyphs still faintly glowing, and snapped, "Take his armor off." Her voice brooked no argument.

The soldiers nearby obeyed, wrestling the prisoner on the ground as he kicked and struggled, shrieking in agony when they moved his broken leg. They stripped him down to little more than a tunic, peeling away the layers of enchanted metal and leather until only the sickly, sweat-soaked fabric remained. Without the glyphs to shield his mind, the change was immediate; Graye slid past his mental defenses like water slipping through cracks in stone.

The fae male thrashed harder as Graye probed, his mind invaded by a force he could neither see nor resist. Graye suspected his bond to Serena amplified his abilities and he delved deep. The battle of wills left him spent and shaking, but finally, Graye stepped back, withdrawing with a sharp snap that left the prisoner gasping and boneless, collapsed on the ground. The break in his leg was now an ugly, swollen thing, but his mind was utterly exhausted. He lay there, sweat beading on his brow, no longer struggling—just breathing, each inhale ragged.

Graye looked up, his expression grave. Jormunder listened closely, the lines on his face deepening as Graye spoke. "They call themselves the Soludhi. Their homeland is Soludhus. According to what I found in his mind, they have an oral tradition that says they came from a land of immense power, ruled by a tyrant who refused to honor their way of life. Eventually, some of them began to flee, seeking a new realm. But while they were scattered, the tyrant used their magic to destroy their homeland, leaving them wandering nomads. They finally discovered a new land with a new source of power a few millennia ago and have been there ever since."

Graye cast another look at the prisoner before continuing, "They settled and stayed for generations. But now that power source, similar to Ardaion's wellspring, is dying. At first, spells faltered. Then they lost the ability to cast altogether. Some forms of life there have died out completely, and even among the Soludhi, aging and death have begun to strike at random, immortal no longer."

"They decided to search once more for a new homeland and found the human island, which the humans call Praetia. They saw it was inhabited, so they first ranged further and discovered Ardaion, but found it too populated, its fae too well-trained in magic. The Praeti, the humans, have no such defenses; they were easier targets- easier to manipulate, and easier to fool with a glamour. Praetia is also linked to our wellspring, so it served their purposes."

Jormunder nodded, tracing the logic. "So far that makes sense. But then why attack us?"

Graye's expression was set. "They're cornered. Desperate. They want the island for themselves but don't want to lose more Soludhi than necessary. Their sudden brushes with mortality and failing spells have made them feel vulnerable. The humans attacked them on sight, already predisposed to hating fae, so they glamoured themselves to look human and slowly established a sea god cult, explaining the fae glyphs as gifts from the false god."

"They began with simple spells and tricks that increased harvests or brought in more fish to create believers, and then slowly poisoned the humans against us. The Soludhi claimed their fictitious god desired it, that Ardaion needed to be cleansed of our taint, and that they would be rewarded for their obedience. They armed the humans and sent them to fight us, knowing we could defeat them, and hoping to clear Praetia through attrition-with no loss of life on the Soludhi's side. All the while, they've been hiding, keeping their numbers and strength concealed."

"But there's more. Based on their stories, they've come to believe that we are their ancient homeland. That we're the tyrants, the descendants of those who drove them out."

Serena's eyes narrowed as she considered. "It sounds right, if they were Twilight. There have always been rumors about that court, about dangerous magics and forbidden experimentation that threatened the wellspring. No one knows what truly happened, the records are lost, but it's always been suspected that they were exiled, that a queen forced them out when they refused to stop. Possibly Morgana. And If that's true, they may have destabilized Ardaion's wellspring even as they fled, ultimately destroying Twilight."

"This makes me wonder whether their new wellspring in Soludhus is dying because they continue to misuse it. It might not be the case, but then again it could be. We can't risk it, and we may yet learn more from other prisoners. But if their powers are corrupting or destructive by nature, we cannot allow them to settle on the human island, on Praetia, because it's connected to Ardaion's wellspring."

Rhune's voice was quiet, but certain. "They have likely done that same calculation. They know we won't allow them to have it. They wouldn't just be neighbors but parasites. So they've engaged us in battle because now it's become an all-or-nothing."

The air had grown heavy with the stench of burning pitch and scorched flesh as the lull between attacks finally broke. When the messenger came running, shouting up at the sea cliff, Jormunder's head snapped up, his keen eyes already darkening with suspicion. "General Jormunder! Sir, the queen reports two more of the dark fae ships have attacked Ember. It's a coordinated attack to keep us from relieving each other."

A muscle in Jormunder's jaw ticked, and his wings flared slightly with restrained fury. "They're not stupid then. This lull—" he paused, voice dropping to a low growl, "they're likely communicating with the other ships. Coordinating. Trying to split our strength." Without missing a beat, he dictated a brief message for the messenger to take back to Mab: confirmation of the coordinated strategy, the Soludhi's tactics, and what had been learned from Graye's interrogations.

The reply had barely left the cliff before a barrage of blue and black fire comets erupted from the sea, arching high over the burning hulls and then raining down—not only at the already-scarred beach, but directly at the sea cliff where Serena, Graye, Rhune, and Jormunder were clustered. The first comets struck Serena's shield with a violent roar, blue-black flames fanning out like a living inferno.

Serena's jaw locked, her face drawn in concentration as she poured the wellspring's power through her outstretched hands. "*Atta...* it's taking a lot of power to do this," she ground out, sweat slick on her brow. "I don't think the mages will be able to shield this way. They're going to need something else, something solid. Have one of the Frostvaari mages test an ice wall. We've got plenty of water to work with."

Jormunder gave a sharp nod, relaying the order through a second runner who vanished down the cliff. The blue flames licked hungrily at the shield, then burned themselves out, leaving the rock pitted and the air heavy with the scent of ozone. Serena didn't hesitate, rage blooming fresh in her veins. She drew another bolt of lightning from the storm-wracked sky and sent it hurtling down into the wounded black-sailed ship. The impact split the deck, sending bodies and splinters flying. Some of the Soludhi crew leaped overboard, desperate to escape the carnage.

Jormunder's voice cut through the chaos, his command iron and absolute. "Take them alive for interrogation!" The Akyist and Dardani sprang into action, wings beating as they swooped down over the foaming waves. Dodging mage fire and arrows, they snatched flailing survivors from the surf, dragging them back to the rocky shore. Screams echoed up the cliff as the prisoners were hauled to land, stripped of their enchanted armor, bound in magic-nulling chains, and pinned to the ground to wait for Graye's mind work.

While Serena and the Battle Mages focused their full fury on the wounded ship, Rhune remained locked in his meticulous efforts, unraveling the defensive glyphs on the enemy vessels one by one, his methodical concentration a steady counterpoint to the chaos of the elemental storm.

By the time Graye landed among the new captives, the Praeti ship had been emptied, its human crew cut down by the Dardani in a frenzy of violence. The battered Soludhi ship now sat dangerously low in the water, listing as fire gnawed at its hull. The remaining two black-sailed ships began to pull back, putting distance between themselves and the shore, loosing covering volleys of mage fire but no longer pressing the attack. They were now on the defensive, wary and calculating.

Rhune spoke for the first time in at least half an hour and said with a low satisfied voice, "There. I untied one of the glyphs, Serena. The ship should be able to take more damage now."

That's all it took. Serena turned from Rhune back to the ship, the air beginning to crackle with the tell-tale buildup of power and the scent of ozone. Hairs prickled on the backs of necks nearby. She wrenched her hand down and an enormous bolt hammered into the ship, striking the mainmast which exploded with a concussive boom as wooden shrapnel was flung in every direction, striking crewmembers. The yard, rigging, and sails fell heavily across the deck, disabling it. That ship, at least, would not see its home again.

A cheer went up from the soldiers along the coast.

Chaos descended across the battered shoreline as the blasted remnants of the enemy ship sagged beneath the ruined mast, tangled rigging smoldering amid lightning-scorched timbers. Soldiers along the beach roared their triumph, the battered but unbroken lines of Ardaion surging with sudden hope. But then, like a shadow rolling over the celebration, the concentrated mage fire of the two remaining Soludhi ships honed in on the cliffs—on Serena.

They had seen her power. She was the axis upon which the entire defense pivoted.

Fire comets streaked across the storm-dark sky, blue and black flames twisting with unnatural speed, and then the familiar searing red, all converging on the outcrop where Serena, Jormunder, Graye, and Rhune stood. Serena, eyes wide, screamed above the wind, "Get out of the way, fly!" There was no hesitation—Jormunder swept her against his chest with the crushing strength of centuries at war and launched from the rock, wings snapping open.

Rhune and Graye dove in the opposite direction, skimming the rocks as fire tore the cliff asunder. Graye felt the chill in his blood as the spell fire ate the ground where Serena had just stood.

But high above, the Soludhi had already recalibrated. The lead ship's surviving mage seized on the moment, wrenching a massive boulder from the sea with a word and a savage twist of his will. It arced through the air, a weapon as old as war itself, and struck Jormunder's wing with a splintering crack. The sound was sickening. The wing—so often the standard on the battlefield, feared and revered—folded like wet canvas.

Serena screamed "Atta! Let me go!" panic ragged in her throat, her own power swirling wild in her veins. Jormunder, fighting gravity and pain, managed to release her just in time. She flung herself away, spell wings unfurling with a desperate flash, catching the air and pulling herself upright. She reached for Jormunder, grabbing at his arm, hauling with everything she had to ease his fall. The beach loomed beneath them, with jagged rocks and crashing surf.

From the cliffs, Graye saw it all, agony coursing down the bond as Serena's panic bled into his own heart. He launched himself into the sky, willing his own body to move faster, to be enough. But as Serena and Jormunder angled back toward the sand, another stone ripped through the air—unseen, silent until it struck Serena hard in the head. Her body went limp, spell wings flickering, then vanishing as her connection to the wellspring cut out. She plummeted, falling deadweight toward the churning waves.

Graye screamed *"Sev!"* every muscle burning as he caught her only feet from the surf, the jolt nearly knocking the wind from him. Jormunder crashed into the waves a heartbeat later, vanishing beneath the foam, his ruined wing dragging him under. Dardani, already in motion, dove after him, strong arms pulling him to safety before he could be pulled out by the tide.

On the shore, Graye landed, Serena a limp, bleeding weight in his arms, red streaking from her temple and ear. The bond between them fluttered with the jagged beat of her unconsciousness, panic threatening to break him. "Healer! Now! The princess!" he shouted, voice hoarse with desperation. Half a dozen healers dropped everything, racing to his side, hands already aglow with power.

In the swirl of frantic motion—mages and soldiers pressed tight around their fallen heir—almost no one noticed Rhune. He was a swift, dark streak above the battered enemy ship, sword drawn. His face was carved from ice, every line honed to lethal purpose. With a single, savage arc, he slashed down, severing the head of the mage who'd struck Jormunder and Serena. The body collapsed to the deck, blood pooling between splintered timbers, and then Rhune was gone, flying hard and fast back toward the shore, toward the only thing that mattered: Serena.

Serena was carried to a tent far back in the tree line, healers already surrounding her, the injured but infuriated Jormunder not far behind. His voice broke through the low chanting of the healers, his tone thunderous and agitated. "See to her!" he snapped, shooing at a healer trying to examine his wing.

Serena lay unconscious, motionless on a low cot, a thin trickle of blood matted at her temple. The healers worked over her, voices tense and hurried. One of the Solace healers lifted her head briefly and said, "A small fracture of the skull, General. But we are closing it now. She will wake soon." Jormunder's only response was a silent glare, his great arms folded and jaw set.

Graye lingered at the edge of the tent, suspended in a desperate state between wanting to push through the crowd to reach her and the knowledge that he'd only be in the way. The quiet in the bond unnerved him far more than her bloodied skin; every second she remained unconscious, his fear mounted, tangled with old grief and rage. *Memories of the spear through her...* He forced the thoughts out. The sense of her was still there, faint but present, but it was as if she were drifting in some far-off current, beyond reach.

The flap of the tent whipped aside. Rhune entered, silent, grim, and sharp-eyed. His gaze swept the room, taking in every detail with a soldier's calculation before he crossed to stand beside Graye. Rhune's presence was steady, unwavering; he radiated a singular focus that seemed to sharpen the very air. And rage.

For the first time, Graye truly felt it, felt Rhune's intensity. Not just an undercurrent, but a force. Rhune stood still, his attention nearly tangible, fixed wholly on Serena as if nothing else existed.

Graye turned his head toward Rhune, slow, as the truth crept over him. The flash of understanding became a burning in his chest, possessive and raw. He stared at Rhune, and for a moment it was as if he was seeing him for the first time. The realization twisted inside him, powerful and unbidden. Overwrought and overcome, he struggled to contain it.

Rhune felt the weight of Graye's scrutiny and turned, just as measured. For a breathless span, their eyes locked- two predators, each measuring the other. For a moment, the look that passed between them was volcanic. The tension thickened, suffocating, though neither made a move. Neither needed to. It was all suddenly very clear.

A low growl escaped Graye's throat, instinctive and warning. Rhune did not blink or step back, only coiled tighter, as if preparing for a strike that might or might not come. There was no apology in his eyes.

However, Serena began to stir, hovering at the edge of waking. Two healers turned their attention to Jormunder, leaving two to finish with Serena. Jormunder tried to wave them off, but the eldest healer fixed him with a look and chided, "The princess will want to know you are fine as soon as she opens her eyes, and you know it." He scowled, then relented, giving a curt nod and allowing the healing magic to settle over him. He refused to move from Serena's side.

Across the tent, Graye's low growl cut through the quiet. Jormunder's attention snapped to where Graye and Rhune stood facing one another, locked in a cold, unblinking staring contest, the air between them thick with possessiveness and male fury. He had lived a long time and could recognize it for what it was- young bucks squaring off over a female.

Jormunder's patience wore thin. "Enough! Not here, not now," his tone brooking no argument.

Rhune responded first, turning to meet Jormunder's eyes and dipping his chin before returning his gaze to Serena. Graye, slower to yield, kept glaring at Rhune's profile until Jormunder said, low and firm, "Graye..." Finally, Graye looked at him. In that glance, Jormunder read everything: pain, anger, and a battle not yet over. But he said nothing more.

Serena's voice broke the tension—a faint, slurred whisper. "*Atta...*" At once, Jormunder's focus shifted. He took her hand, sitting at her side.

"I'm here, *Rionna*, my little star. I'm fine. I'm healed," he assured her, the older healer huffing quietly.

Serena's eyes opened fully, taking in the healers gathered around her. She managed a soft, "Thank... you..." and tried to sit up. Jormunder steadied her but didn't hold her back as she swung her legs over the edge of the cot, wincing and reaching for the spot on her skull where she'd been struck. It was still tender.

A healer handed her a small cup. "A tonic to keep the headache at bay, Highness. You are healed, but may still have a little pain for an hour or two."

Serena nodded and drank, grimacing at the taste, then commanded, "Report". It was a little less firm than she would have liked it to sound but the healers knew their business and she was already feeling more steady.

One of the Dardani approached and bowed his head. "Princess. The near ship is listing—we suspect it may be taking on water. There are crew onboard; if they crew as we would with a ship that size, perhaps one hundred still in its decks. You shattered the mainsail, and the sail itself caught fire. They're not going anywhere, but they're off deck, holed up like bobtails in a warren. The other ships have pulled further back. They're still there but out of our range, though we are also out of theirs. We suspect they are reassessing their strategy and perhaps hoping to rescue their crew."

Serena stood, wobbling at first, and placed a hand on Jormunder's shoulder for balance. Her tone was flat and unyielding. "I won't allow a rescue. I am going to make them pay dearly for their hubris. Get a message to my cousin Elsibetha. Tell her to gate here within the hour."

The Dardani brought a fist to his chest in salute and left to carry out her order. Serena offered no further explanation, her face set with a fierce, furious light. She walked out of the tent, each step growing steadier and more purposeful.

Outside, she locked onto the wellspring, drawing strength as she shielded herself. She made her way down to the edge of the beach, searching until her fingers found palm-sized stones among the drift and sand. Behind her, Jormunder, Graye, and Rhune watched in silence, perplexed but wise enough not to interrupt. Graye and Rhune kept a distance between them, tense and trying to watch Serena while trading wary glances. Neither wanted to cause a scene in front of her that would require an explanation.

Once she had gathered what she needed, Serena returned to the shelter of the tree line and sat on the ground. The wellspring continued to surge within her, finishing what the healers had begun. Pain and injury faded as power filled her. She set to work, inscribing runes and glyphs onto the stones, her voice barely above a whisper as she spoke words of power over them. One by one, the stones began to glow, pulsing with magic.

She finally looked up at the three males hovering nearby, their protective presence as tangible as armor. "While I was in Tides, I learned how to create calling stones. Once dropped into the water, they will summon the Mer, any water fae nearby. With their help, and Elsie's, I'm going to empty that ship. It's time they gave up some secrets." Her voice was calm, edged with purpose.

Rising to her feet, Serena gathered the glowing stones and strode toward the shore, glancing up at the sky as it deepened with the coming sunset. The last gold light sharpened the angles of her face, throwing shadows across the encampment.

Behind her, Graye shot another silent, heated glare at Rhune. Jormunder, ever watchful, caught the flicker of rivalry and brought a firm hand down on Graye's shoulder. "Not now," he warned, voice rough with authority. Rhune's eyes flicked from Graye and met the general's gaze with alertness, but unapologetic. Jormunder simply let out a harsh sigh and said nothing more.

Kade jogged over to see them, having finished seeing to the healing and status of the Shade army. All it took was one long look between the three males. Rhune's face was stony, eyes hard. Graye's face almost snarling, his eyes still flashing with barely contained fury. Kade opened his mouth to speak but closed it. What could he say? He'd seen this coming and it seemed every bit as bad as he'd imagined it might be. All that remained was to keep them from killing each other.

Serena was already moving ahead, issuing crisp orders to the infantry. Soon a stack of driftwood was assembled and the fire she kindled burned with vibrant colors- red, green, and blue sparks leaping into the dusk.

From the trees, Elsibetha emerged, having gated into the staging area near Tenebris. She reached Graye, Jormunder, and Rhune first, silent as she took in the battered shoreline. Solace had not been attacked, but here the aftermath was plain. "Gods..." she breathed, her eyes fixed on the enemy vessels. The human ship remained afloat, but the deck was littered with the dead. The fae ship, black-sailed and ruined, floated at an angle. Its shattered mainmast left the sail stretched across the deck like a funeral shroud, no fae visible above.

Elsibetha turned to her grandfather, voice low. "What's she doing?"

Jormunder, who had been silently watching Serena's every move, answered quietly, "She is calling the Mer. Serena is going to sing them off the ship and ensnare their minds. She needs as many siren voices as she can get."

Serena had turned, seen Elsie, and was coming back.

She walked up to Elsibetha and pulled her into a fierce embrace. "We need to ransack that ship for information before it sinks." She opened her palm, showing Elsibetha the glowing calling stones.

A messenger appeared, bowing deeply before her. "Princess. I was asked to deliver a message from the healers down the beach. I regret to inform you that your friend, the mage Adelie, has died of her wounds. She bravely tried to turn aside one of the blue fire comets. She diverted it enough to save the lives of several soldiers, but when it struck, enough of the flames caught on her clothing that she sustained grave wounds. They fought hard to save her, but she is gone. I am sorry for your loss, Highness."

Serena drew in a slow, silent breath, her body going still. A chill settled over her features, her expression freezing into a mask of calm resolve. For a moment she stood fighting an internal battle. Adelie had been young like her, they'd been trained in the tower together.

In a voice quiet and measured, she replied, "Thank you for letting me know. Have them send her body to the mage tower to be entombed with full honors."

The messenger bowed again and withdrew. Serena clenched her jaw, took a steadying breath, and locked away the ache of grief behind walls of cold steel. After a moment, she turned to Elsibetha, her composure restored as if she had not just received news of a close friend's death. "I'm going to call the Mer. Then you and I, cousin, are going to sing those bastards into the water, where our sisters will be waiting."

Elsibetha's eyes widened as understanding dawned, and the three males behind them realized Serena's intent as well. "We will be as the sirens of old, singing sailors to their deaths. May we honor our ancestors," Elsibetha said, a cold light kindling in her gaze.

Serena nodded. "I'm going to go drop the stones along the water. As soon as we sense our sisters, in an hour or two, we will begin."

CHAPTER TWENTY-EIGHT
SIRENS

Elsibetha let Serena walk away, deciding to give her space. Whatever grief Serena chose to display—which was none—Elsie knew, on some deeper level, that her cousin was feeling Adelie's loss. She stood beside Jormunder, watching as Serena's silhouette blurred into the deepening dusk, the last light of the sun fading over the cliffs.

Alone, Serena moved along the precipice, careful not to let any light betray her position to the Soludhi ships offshore. At each chosen spot, she withdrew a glowing stone, whispered, "Come to me, sisters," and let it slip into the depths. She was repeating this for the third time when she heard footsteps behind her and turned to see Graye.

Unaware of the earlier confrontation with Rhune, Serena studied Graye's face—anger and something like anguish mingling in his eyes. She watched him in silence for a moment, then spoke quietly, "I can feel your pain through the bond." It was an opening, granting him space to speak if he wished.

Graye hesitated, weighing what he wanted to say against the weight of the moment. He finally spoke, his voice low and raw. "I hurt because you hurt. Sev... you've grieved so much the last year and more. And I've hated it. I've wanted you to heal and feel happiness again. But tonight you got news of Adelie's death and there was just... nothing."

"I'm used to your face showing nothing. You've been trained to do that. But I didn't *feel* anything from you either, through the bond- you were just flat. The pain is there now but in that moment..."

Serena looked at him, warning flashing in her eyes. "Graye... don't. Don't look at me with those sad eyes. I don't want to be pitied. I don't want to be asked if I'm fine. I will tell you now all that I'm willing to speak about this. No, I'm not fine, my heart is broken, but many other deaths happened today, and many other hearts are broken. So I'm going to continue to do what I was meant to do, what I was born to do and trained to do. Maybe when it's all over I'll give myself a chance to sit down and cry about it."

"But it won't be today."

Still, Graye pressed, "Sev, it's unhealthy not to grieve."

That did it. Her restraint snapped. "*Unhealthy*? You think it's unhealthy to ignore my feelings about one person's death when I have killed *thousands?* I *have* grieved. Every godsdamned day since Tides. And I wish to the moon I could turn it off because then I might have the tiniest bit of peace."

Graye flinched at her tone. "You're twisting my words."

Serena glared at him. "I'm not twisting anything. I'm pointing out the hypocrisy. It took me a while to learn this lesson but I have learned it well. Grieving for the dead is a luxury only those who have nothing better to do can afford. But we're at war, and I *do* have better things to do."

"This is the price for the nobility, the wealth, and the right to rule: the sacrifice. And the only difference between a good ruler and a bad one is whether or not they're willing to pay it."

Half an hour later, Serena and Elsibetha sat beside the driftwood fire, which had grown into a great, roaring pyre. Their hair was braided tightly away from their faces, shells woven through the plaits, a warrior's nod to the sea. They had crushed some of the burnt wood into charcoal, mixed it with grease, and streaked their faces with jagged black lines. The ritual was primitive, but it was what Meriden had taught them.

They did not attempt to hide their fangs as they lifted their voices to the night and began to sing one of the ancient songs learned in Tides. The armies of Shade and the Moon kept well back, aware of the song's potency, watching with a respect born of awe. All understood they were witnessing something not seen in a thousand years, sirens preparing for war. The haunting, beautiful two-part harmony rose and echoed off the sea, reverberating through the trees, weaving power into the darkness.

Jormunder had heard Tatiana sing like this only once or twice in his life. Now he stood unmoving, heart aching with longing for his lost mate, hearing her granddaughters sing the same battle songs she would have sung. Graye stood silent, watching Serena with an almost physical pain, the bond between them numbed by grief and distance, the memory of her sharp words, and the knowledge that she was hurting herself to become what the realm required. His face was drawn, eyes shadowed with sadness and yearning.

A short distance away, Rhune stood like a sentinel, his focus narrowing to Serena alone. He did not dwell on the tragedy of what she was becoming. For him, there *was* no tragedy.

He was in awe. As he studied her—face streaked with black, fangs bared, voice ringing out in the night—he felt a fierce pride take hold of him. She was magnificent.

Kade stood between them, sharply aware of the difference in their moods. Graye felt every pang of what Serena had lost, his protectiveness sharpened by memories of a gentler past and a fervent desire to return her to it. To save her.

Rhune, by contrast, reflected wonder and devotion in his eyes, his stance protective and resolute, but ready to fight at her side. To fortify, to champion.

Kade saw the truth of it- Graye saw her losses, but Rhune saw her strength.

The song grew, rising into a crescendo, and from the darkness of the sea came the answer. A dozen voices, wild and beautiful, called from the waves and the shore. The Mer joined the song, their harmony echoing across the cliffs, each voice threading into the tapestry of the night. Sometimes, out beyond the firelight, a pair of eyes flashed in the water, and soldiers would point or gasp in hushed awe.

It was easy, in the palace, to see a siren adorned in pearls and beaded gowns and believe she was just another fae noble. Civilization bred illusions of safety. They all knew sirens were predators- in theory- but the woman seated across from them with a silver spoon and a silk napkin was always shielding her scent, hiding her fangs, and keeping her voice within the bounds of civility.

Delicate, beautiful, contained.

What stood before them tonight was something else entirely. The darkness was so absolute that the sea and sky became one, but those sudden, glinting flashes near the water's edge were not starlight. They were the eyes of hunters, drawn by the ancient call of their own.

Slowly, the Mer began to converge on the shore, emerging from the waves or gliding along the water's edge. Some lingered in the surf, wild and feral, eyes flashing in the moonlight. Others strode onto the land, each one beautiful in her own way.

Their hair ranged from dark earth tones to brilliant emerald, deep navy, shimmering amethyst, a living tapestry of the sea's palette. Some wore clothing scavenged from ships or woven from seagrass and nets, others barely covered, adorned only with shells and sea glass braided into their hair.

The song continued as they gathered around the driftwood fire, a haunting chorus that wove through the night. One by one, they dipped their fingers into the makeshift grease paint and marked their faces with jagged black lines, joining Serena and Elsibetha in the ritual. The harmony swelled, building until it ended on a single, piercing note, perfectly in unison—a sound that vibrated through the bones and lingered in the air.

Serena did not raise her voice for the armies watching from the distance. This was a Mer ritual, a siren call to arms meant only for their own. She addressed the gathered sisters, her voice steady and cold. "Sisters, the ships with black sails out there are enemies from a distant land. They have misused the wellspring of power in their realm, and it is dying. Now they come to invade us, to steal ours."

"They sent the humans. They have already taken too many lives and must be stopped. The nearby ship is damaged and sinking, but we need to get inside it to learn more about our enemy. There are about a hundred crew hiding away below decks. They know the moment they show themselves, they will die. So we will sing them out instead.

We will use the Voice to call them into the water. Let those in heavy armor sink and drown. The rest—tear their throats out. This is for Tides."

As one, the Mer echoed her words: "This is for Tides."

Without another word, they turned and began wading silently into the water. Their bodies slipped beneath the surface, merging with the darkness as they swam out toward the listing ship, surrounding it with silent, patient menace.

There was an eerie hush along the shore, broken only by the distant crash of breakers and the low crackle of the driftwood fire. The entire army stood tense and silent, every eye fixed on the darkness where the Mer had vanished. Suddenly, a pair of hooting cries rose from the water, wild and triumphant.

Serena stepped forward and let loose a hellish siren growl Meriden had taught her—the unearthly, predatory noise that made fae blood run cold. It was a sound born of ancient hunger, a sound that made prey instinctively recognize its place. Soldiers shifted along the shore, gooseflesh forming on their arms. Serena's growl rumbled low, and then Elsibetha joined her, the two voices melding into something more beast than courtly, more hellcat than highborn.

Some of the Shade soldiers eased back a few paces, fear pricking their skin. But the Moon army, the court of the siren queens, held their ground. This was their royal family; if the sound unsettled them, it would terrify the enemy.

The growls were a signal. Serena launched into the opening notes of a song—not a fae melody, but the pure song of the Voice itself. The sound rippled through the night, woven with longing and compulsion, the kind of music that wound itself around heart and soul.

It sang of heartbreak and lost love, creating in all who heard it a desperate ache to be the one to ease that sorrow, to be chosen, to be worthy. A call to be loved. They would do anything, give anything, be anything.

Just to see her smile. For just one kiss.

From the sea, the Mer and other sirens picked up the song. Their harmony soared, unearthly, impossible for ordinary fae to comprehend. Along the shore, some soldiers began to step forward, drawn toward Serena and Elsibetha, only to be pulled back by their comrades. A few had packed their ears with wax, knowing all too well what was coming.

Then the wind shifted, and dozens of scents unfurled across the sand—familiar and exotic, sweet, spicy, floral. Each siren's unique signature, unveiled at last, shimmered in the night air like iridescence across the water. It was intoxicating, seductive. *The Thrall.* More soldiers faltered, aroused and staggering forward under the pull of song and scent, only to be yanked back by wary friends.

Jormunder stood unmoving, iron-willed, having long ago learned to resist Tatiana's power and the scent of the sirens. He stood as steady as stone. But for Graye, Kade, and Rhune—caught so close to Serena and Elsibetha—the effect was overwhelming. Elsibetha's scent was gardenia and ripe mangoes, lush and sweet. Serena's was roses and vanilla, and something wild and musky. But no matter the top notes of a siren's scent, the bass was raw desire, lust, need. *Bait and hook.*

Kade swore softly, fighting the pull. Graye, glassy-eyed, began moving toward Serena before Jormunder caught him by the shoulder and wrenched him back. Rhune swayed in place, spellbound, Serena's scent crashing over him for the first time. His mask was gone—nothing left but hunger and awe. *Want.*

Desire and longing whipped through the night air, the Voice whispering temptations and the scent curling low in every belly, the promise of sex on the breeze. The song carried on, winding through the ranks and out across the dark water, where the real hunt was just beginning.

A moment passed as the song built, the ship encircled by the Mer. Then came movement—a shifting shadow along the deck, the sound of shuffling feet, and the sudden spark of fae light as a globe floated up over the battered rails. The Soludhi crew began to appear, only one or two at first, some so deeply enthralled they stumbled out like the inebriated.

Others fought against crewmates who clung to them in desperation, trying to keep them inside. But the resistance was short-lived. The song had called them from belowdecks but once out in the open, the scent ensnared them with totality. The slow, uncertain shambling soon grew hungry, then impatient, as the song's magic and the intoxicating scent swept over them. They sniffed the air, eyes glazed, noses lifted like hounds on a trail.

The first to break did not shamble—he sprinted. With a wild, desperate need, he ran to the ship's edge and vaulted into the sea. There was a splash, a gurgle, and then silence. Two more followed, one shoving aside a friend who tried to hold him back. One of them, clad in heavy armor, leaped overboard and vanished beneath the waves without a trace. The song rose higher, sharper, full of longing and sorrow, while the scents drifted across the deck in seductive waves.

One by one, they hit the water. Thrashing and gurgling, one single, sharp scream- but the compulsion was absolute. No one resisted for long.

Serena reached for the wellspring, let spell wings unfurl behind her, and amplified her Voice. The sound grew crystalline, haunting, layered with need and aching loneliness. It reached further and pulled harder. The last of the ship's crew burst from belowdecks, running to the railings, leaping into the darkness, vanishing into the sea—willingly, hopelessly, to their dooms.

Then, silence. The song ceased. The movement stopped. The deck was empty.

From the far side of the ship, a dark-haired siren climbed up, water pouring from her hair and limbs. She called out in the ancient siren tongue, her voice ringing over the water—words only the Mer would understand: "*The sea has claimed them all! For none resist the Thrall!* For Tides!" Wild, triumphant hoots answered from the waves, shouts of "For Tides!" echoing through the night.

The same siren dove back into the water, swam for shore, and came to stand before Serena, who stood with fierce black stripes on her face and the shimmering, prismatic glow of her spell wings. The siren swept into a deep curtsy and declared, "By her pull, we rise!"—the motto of the Moon Court, invoking the moon's dominion over the sea, the legacy of the siren queens.

Serena embraced her, kissed her cheeks, and smiled. The siren said, "Serena, I am Linnae. We will stay until we know what the other two ships mean to do." Her hair shimmered with shades of aqua and gold in the firelight.

Serena nodded. "Thank you, sister. Share the fire with us. We'll bring food and wine. Let our songs teach them fear."

The Mer and the other sirens flowed in around the fire, drawn to Serena, Linnae, and Elsibetha by instinct and kinship. They called for drums, and soon anything that could be beaten or rattled was pressed into service—war drums, battered shields, even empty water jars. A rhythm took hold, rough and primal, and the sirens danced in widening circles, stamping and swirling, their laughter and wild voices riding the night air.

Jormunder sent mages racing to the captured Soludhi ship to strip it for every scrap of information. Others waded into the surf, ropes and magic pulling the battered vessel closer to shore so nothing would be lost to the tide. Every board, every torn banner, every unfamiliar sigil was a clue to the enemy's secrets.

Around the bonfire, the siren songs took on the cadence of old Tides. The drums pounded, echoing out over the sand and water, joined by guttural grunts, hissing calls, and eerie whoops in the ancient dialect. The music swelled as the fire grew, casting wild shadows over Mer faces streaked black, teeth flashing in the flames. They danced, drank, and sang with fangs bared—female warriors, not courtiers, and the war songs reverberated across the bay, loud enough for the black-sailed ships still lurking offshore.

Serena and Elsibetha let the wildness take them, dancing shoulder to shoulder, hair unbound and eyes alight. In the Moon Court, siren celebrations were woven into every festival, but this was different—this was a display of power meant for their enemies and their own. Most of the Moon soldiers kept their distance, not daring to step into the circle, but still clapped along, stomping their boots, howling and hollering into the dark. The revel grew, loud and raucous, a living wall of sound that dared the enemy to approach and dared grief to come near. For Serena, it was catharsis.

The Shade soldiers began to hesitantly join in. It was one thing to know you were ruled by sirens in a distant palace; quite another for those who had never visited the Moon Court to see this visceral ritual. Slowly though, they were drawn into it, purging their grief and fear and feeling the thrill of the victory.

News came from messengers: in Ember, the Dardani and Battle Mages had stormed one of the Soludhi ships by force. Losses had been bitter, but the ship was theirs, the crew dead or taken hostage, and the survivors ransacking it for whatever they could find. The second black-sailed ship on their shores now hung far out, keeping its distance, just as those in Shade had done.

By the fire, Graye, Kade, and Rhune watched the wildness, caught somewhere between awe and unrest. The night throbbed with things unspoken. Then, without a word, Rhune broke away, walking into the forest's shadows beyond the beach. Graye, jaw set, peeled off after him. Kade hesitated, then followed, knowing this confrontation was inevitable.

Once deep beneath the tangled canopy, where the moonlight barely reached and tendrils of mist curled along the forest floor, Rhune stopped and waited. Graye arrived moments later, circling him with the restless energy of a predator. The air was thick with tension—both of them dangerous, both on edge.

Finally, Graye broke the silence. "What do you think you're doing, Rhune?"

Rhune's expression remained unreadable, but a dangerous flash flickered in his eyes. "I think you know."

Graye spat the words. "Why? And for how long? How long have you loved her?"

Kade kept his distance, poised to step in if blades were drawn, but hoping it wouldn't come to that.

Rhune answered quietly, "I felt something from the minute I saw her. When she came with you to Tenebris and we spent that night drinking by the fire."

Graye kept circling, his voice edged with mockery, brittle. "*Felt Something?* You think you know what that means? I've had the bond with her since the day we were born. I've been part of her life from the beginning. I've felt her highs and lows, her grief, and her rage. The gut-wrenching *ache* when she's not with me."

His voice dropped into a low, cold sound, "What could you possibly feel next to that?"

Rhune didn't respond at first, not because Graye's anger cowed him, but because he refused to voice what had been building inside him for years. It hadn't struck all at once—just a slow, undeniable pull, steady as a tide. He let the silence stretch, his gaze locked on Graye's, a challenge simmering there.

Kade's eyes widened as he comprehended the word unsaid, but he held his ground, waiting. Graye read the truth in Rhune's silence. Something fierce and defiant lived in those eyes, daring Graye to piece it together.

And he did. A flash of surprise and fury.

Graye's lips curled in a snarl, a low growl rumbling in his chest. Without warning, he lunged, landing a fist against Rhune's jaw before Rhune could block. Blood welled from a split lip, but Rhune was quick—always quick. Now that Graye had drawn first blood, Rhune was committed.

They crashed together in a blur of fists and knees, falling into the Dardani fighting style drilled into them since they were eight. Punches landed, blocks and holds broke apart, knees and elbows searching for a weak spot.

They grappled in the dirt, rolling, snarling, fists thudding against bodies, grunts and fae growls filling the forest gloom. Kade paced the edge, vigilant, ready to break it up if bones started snapping.

Graye managed to pin Rhune beneath him for a moment, pressing Rhune's fist to the ground above his head. He leaned in close, teeth bared, almost snapping. *"Say it!* Say it, then."

Rhune twisted, driving his fist hard into Graye's kidney, forcing his arm free. "I'm not ready to name it! I could be wrong. We're young, and it's too soon!"

With a burst of strength, Rhune flipped Graye onto his back, locking his legs in a scissor hold. Graye scowled, breath coming harsh. "You look at her like that and then say you don't know for sure..."

They grappled, trading holds, both too winded to speak for a time. Dirt smeared their faces, breaths coming in ragged bursts.

Finally, Rhune growled, "I *don't* know it for sure. I know I love her. I know I'd *die* for her."

The truth, the devotion, that rang in those words provoked Graye even further. Graye snarled, pure animal. "You have *no right* to love her! *I love her.* I have *always* loved her and *will always* love her. We are *bonded*, and you can't break that."

Something broke loose in Rhune then, something cold and feral. He exploded. *"Right?! I should have the only right!* You want the word, fine- I think I'm her *mate!"*

Graye drove his knee viciously into Rhune's thigh, another guttural growl, but Rhune was merciless, pressing on. "You were tied to her by your father's ambition. Your bond to her was illegal, it's *wrong*, never meant to be—and it causes her pain."

He smashed his fist into Graye's jaw, voice hoarse and savage. "And you're so damn busy making excuses for what she is and what she's done that you can't see she doesn't need them! You want to wrap her in silk and tie a bow in her hair. But I am going to hold her crown and hand her a fucking sword!"

Graye was apoplectic and bellowed, "SHE IS MINE!" He punched Rhune in the jaw before he could block it, smashing into his nose, blood running down his face.

Rhune kneed him in the stomach hard enough to wind him, and said in a low, furious hiss, "She is *hers*."

Kade seized the lull to lunge forward and drag them apart, shoving himself bodily between Rhune and Graye. Both were bleeding freely now—lips split, jaws swollen, bruises blooming across their faces and arms, blood staining their clothes.

Kade's voice cut through their fury, sharp and exasperated. "Enough! Enough. You're both acting like it's only up to you, when it's up to her, too. She's still grieving that Akyist. *We're at war*. The enemy is still out there. Now is not the tides-damned time for this. She's not ready—and neither are either of you."

He kept his arms out, blocking them from one another, refusing to give ground as Rhune and Graye glared, eyes wild, breath ragged, pure territoriality crackling between them.

At last, Graye spat blood onto the leaves and muttered, "You're right. She's not ready. She's still in mourning. I can feel it in my chest. But I *will* tell her that I'm in love with her when the time is right. I don't give a godsdamned *shit* about whatever it is you think you have with her. One bond is as good as another. And I won't let you push her to keep fighting when she's never wanted this."

Rhune shook his head, voice cold. "You keep looking backward. Did you see her tonight? *What she did*? Do you see her with her face painted, dancing around that fire? Or do you still see the little girl with a honey cake?"

Kade stepped in again, cutting off whatever reply Graye might have thrown back. "Enough. Both of you, go find a healer before she sees you like this and you have to explain."

Another hour passed as the songs and drums carried on. The armies, emboldened by victory and the wildness of the Mer, began to join the dancing on the beach, mugs of ale in hand, laughter and shouts mixing with the music. The night felt triumphant, primal, as though the old magic itself was celebrating with them.

Then, far out at sea, a white horizontal flash split the darkness—brilliant, silent, and strange. It widened, unfurling into the now-familiar black portal, its edges barely visible against the starless sky. All sound faded to a tense hush as the soldiers and sirens watched, every eye fixed on the distant gateway.

Jormunder's voice broke the silence, commanding and steady. "Get in the air. Hang back, but get close enough to make sure they go through and it isn't some trick."

Two Dardani leaped skyward at once, wings slicing through the cool night air. Suddenly, a flash of light caught Jormunder's attention as a written note appeared, hovering in the air beside his head. He snatched it and read quickly, then announced, "It's from Aegin. The remaining black ship at Ember has gated away."

He peered out over the black water, searching for confirmation in the dark. "We'll wait for word, but it seems they decided the losses were too great to continue. They're pulling back, regrouping."

Serena and Elsibetha, still streaked with feral face paint, joined him, their expressions fierce and watchful as they stared across the sea.

Moments later, one of the Dardani returned, wings beating in the night, and confirmed that the ships were aligning with the portal, preparing to sail through. The other soldier circled high above, keeping watch, too far up for any threat to reach him. Cheers rang out and the revel grew wilder.

Serena slipped away from the celebration once the enemy ships had vanished for good. Around the fire, others were still singing and dancing, voices lifted in triumph, but the exhaustion and anxiety pressed down on her, heavier with every step she took away from the light. The ships were gone. Tension began to bleed out of her, its place taken by grief.

She made her way to the shoreline, seeking solitude, then unfurled her wings and flew to a lonely overhang on the cliffs. There, she sat, legs dangling into the open air, staring out at the black, endless sea. Her body began to tremble, and she fought to keep it at bay, pushing back the tears that threatened to spill over. Her breath came in heaving gasps as she wrapped her arms tight around herself, desperate to hold everything inside. The trembling worsened. She doubled over, head nearly between her knees, and a raw sound escaped—a moan, a keening cry of pain choked back into silence.

Then came the sound of boots on stone, quiet but sure. Someone sat down beside her, warmth pressing close, and an arm slid around her shoulders, pulling her in. It was Rhune. He and Graye had both noticed Serena's absence and set out to find her, but while Graye could sense her pain through the bond—hot and tight in his chest—Rhune had followed his own pull and found her first.

Rhune had barely touched her before. There had been polite embraces, a quick hand clasp at Tides when she'd looked ready to throw herself from the cliffs, but nothing more. The anguish in her cry tonight gutted him though, and instinct overrode hesitation. He whispered, "Come here," and drew her in, cradling her against his chest, arms wrapped tight around her trembling form.

For a moment she stiffened, confusion flickering as she realized it was not Graye's scent, not the comfort she was used to; Graye often smelled of bergamot. Rhune smelled of cedar and leather, and the bonfire smoke. But the strength of his hold and the steady warmth anchoring her broke through the walls. She buried her face in his chest, refusing to cry, but shuddering all over, fighting herself.

Rhune's hand moved slowly, gently up and down her back. He understood without words: a new enemy, the black ships, the shock of unknown magery... the injuries she and Jormunder had suffered, Adelie's death, and the song she had sung—a song that wiped out over a hundred lives in a handful of heartbeats. The songs and dancing that followed—reminders of Tides, of everything she'd found and lost.

He held her tighter, his own heart heavy with understanding, and simply let her break in silence.

Minutes passed, and slowly Serena's trembling eased, her breathing gradually settling, though she still leaned into Rhune's steady hold. Rhune, usually reserved, found himself out of his depth. He had always been the one standing slightly apart, the one who held back, but now all he wanted was to comfort her. That's all he *had* wanted, for years.

The word *mate* echoed in his mind and he flinched inwardly, unsure, almost embarrassed by the enormity of it. It was too serious, too real. He wasn't ready to say that out loud, not to anyone, least of all himself. He'd been too furious before, goaded by Graye and his "right" to her. But now he'd said it out loud, changed everything between himself and Graye, and he felt like a fool. All fae referred to spouses as mates but the Binding... that was *a bond*. That was *Mate*.

He and Serena were both so young, at twenty-two, too young for most to consider marriage. From what he knew of the Binding, its bond didn't manifest until a male was older and had developed into his full potential. A male was selected by the ancient spell for what he could bring to the bloodline. Usually, it didn't begin to take hold until after fifty years or more, and by then, it was undeniable—a force, a certainty, a near-compulsion.

What he felt now was nothing so dramatic. Just nudges. A persistent pull. A quiet, unspoken urge to watch over her, to help, to do anything in his power to make things right. Of course, he was attracted to her—how could he not be, with those streaks of color in her hair, those shifting sea-grey eyes, the impossible beauty and danger of a siren? But it was more than that.

She had always been there for them—for Graye, Kade, and himself. She had saved them, fought for them, and believed in them. She never looked down on them, never treated them as lesser or unworthy. She was kind, fierce, generous, and loyal to the last. She had sent Dewin, Elsibetha, and Stefan to help salvage Shade, and had defended them today with everything she possessed. He loved her for all of it, loved her in a way that he couldn't define with words. It was just that quiet, insistent tug in his soul, always there, always drawing his attention to her, urging him to notice, to care, to act. And now, to fight for her.

Did he have a claim on her? He'd only recently started naming it, only experimentally, to see how it fit. Maybe he was completely wrong and it was just some stupid infatuation that didn't mean anything. And maybe everything she'd done, she'd only done for Graye. *Was* he wrong? Was he a total fool? An ache of denial formed in his chest.

Serena shifted, burying her face more deeply into his chest. The trembling had stopped but she was still silent. Should he do something? Say something? But she did instead.

"It's so hard. All of it." Her voice was muffled against him, "I was supposed to stay in Tides and keep learning my heritage. I was supposed to go to the other courts and spend time with them. I'm still an apprentice Shadowdancer. I could spend years more studying at the mage tower. I'm supposed to still be learning. We all are. You three are supposed to be studying with Dewin and Stefan, not... this..."

Rhune kept rubbing her back and whispered in a soft, warm whisper, "Things rarely turn out the way we plan, Serena. We're measured by our deeds, not our meant-to-be's. And by that measure, you have been incandescent."

She slid her arms around his waist but kept her face buried. Her fingers began unconsciously moving in the same steady rhythm up and down his back and she asked "Are *you* alright?" He felt that tug again—warmth blooming in his chest, tightening his throat. She cared enough to ask about him. There was the slightest hint of roses and vanilla on the wind though her hair smelled of the bonfire. He closed his eyes for a moment, absorbing it.

"Yes. I'm fine..." and then his heart, his body, his control... his everything betrayed him because he ducked his chin and placed a kiss on her forehead before his mind caught up to what he was doing. Because she cared. Before he could stop it. And he froze, not knowing what to do. Had he overstepped? Had he spoiled whatever this was?

She didn't move for several heartbeats and he wondered if she'd even noticed. But then she lifted her face finally, inches from his, and looked at him. Really looked. Her eyes were full of strain and hurt, exhaustion. Her face was still streaked in the black grease paint but it was smudged.

Savage, but vulnerable. He just studied her, memorizing everything as he always did.

She lifted her lips to hover near his and he froze. Not even breathing. Heart pounding in his chest.

But she blinked several times, as if becoming more aware of what she was doing, and slowly leaned further back from him, whispering, "Thank you."

Slowly he nodded, maintaining eye contact. Then trying to spill out even the smallest bit of what he was feeling and thinking, "Serena, anytime you need... *anything*... I'll be there."

"I know."

Serena landed back on the beach, boots sinking into the damp sand as she stalked toward her tent, intent only on finding silence and solitude. Graye intercepted her, worry etched across his face. "There you are, I was looking for you, Sev..." But as he took in her bleary, red-rimmed eyes and the black smudges on her cheeks, his tone softened. "Let's get you to the tent. You need to rest."

She nodded, silent, letting him take her hand and lead her through the camp. The Moon Court tents glowed softly with lantern light, muted voices drifting between them. Serena stumbled inside and collapsed onto the edge of her cot, fingers clumsy as she tried to unbuckle her armor. Graye knelt beside her, helping her out of the battered plates and leather straps, setting each piece aside with care.

When she sat, still and hollow, staring at the ground, she tried to speak—"Graye, I..."—but shook her head, unwilling to find words, unwilling to explain. He understood. He pressed a glass of chilled wine into her hand and then fetched a damp face cloth before sitting beside her.

"Sev... I know it was bad today. All of it. But you did what you had to do. And now you need to rest."

He reached for her chin with lifelong familiarity and began wiping her face clean with the cool, moist cloth. She submitted, eyes closed, and let him tend to her.

After he'd finished, she drank the wine in three swallows, voice barely above a whisper. "Yes... I just want to rest." She pulled down the blankets, crawling under them still in her sweat-soaked underclothes, shivering from exhaustion. Graye climbed in beside her, fussing with the covers, tucking them around her until she was warm and safe. Then he pulled her close, letting her curl into his chest the way she always had, since childhood.

Serena nestled in, breathing him in, the comfort of home settling over her. Graye ran his fingers gently through her hair, soothing the last of her tension until her breathing slowed, her body finally relaxing.

He pressed a soft kiss to her forehead, and whispered, "I love you, Sev." But she'd already fallen asleep.

CHAPTER TWENTY-NINE
VENGEANCE

A grey dawn broke over the war camp, illuminating scenes of devastation and ruin. Enormous craters pitted the sand, some edges turned to glass by the heat of battle. Here and there, a few Soludhi bodies had washed up with the tide—casualties of those lured overboard by the siren song. The human vessel still rocked in the surf, largely intact, while the captured Soludhi ship had been towed into the shallows. Soldiers had hastily constructed a floating boardwalk to connect it with the shore, enabling teams to scavenge and study the enemy craft.

There were few bodies from the Moon and Shade Courts. Lives had been lost, but the mage fire had burned hot and swift, leaving either the healable or the ash. Of the surviving Soludhi ships, there was no sign. They had vanished through the portal—whether back to the human island of Praetia or their fae homeland, Soludhus, none could say.

Serena slept deeply for only five hours before Jormunder entered her tent. He found her and Graye curled together as they had so often since childhood, the memory of them as newborns clinging to each other surfacing and softening his stern features. But they weren't children any longer, and he wasn't sure where last night's tensions between Graye and the other boy were going to lead. He stood over them for a moment, then bent close and whispered, "Serena. My shining star. We need you up to receive a delegation from your mother."

Serena twitched awake, shifting beneath the covers as Graye stirred beside her. She nodded, voice rough with sleep. "Alright, Atta. I'll be there in five minutes." She began to throw back the blankets and Graye blinked, groaning, still heavy with exhaustion.

"I'll find us some breakfast, Sev," he mumbled, already rolling to his feet.

Serena washed her face, stepping behind the changing screen to pull on fresh underclothes. The routine was so familiar it took only moments before she was out again, pulling on her ornate leather armor and running a comb through her hair before braiding it and tossing it over her shoulder. She left the tent, jaw set, shoulders straight.

Jormunder waited for her just outside, his face unreadable. Beneath one of the ancient trees for which the Shade Court was named, a group of senior Battle Mages, army commanders, diplomats, and royal advisors were gathered, their expressions a mix of tension and anticipation.

Jormunder leaned down and whispered in her ear, his tone cryptic, "Don't give anything away when you see her."

Jormunder led Serena to the assembled group, standing just long enough to watch each of them bow—murmurs of "Highness" and "Princess" following her steps. At the center of the gathering stood Mab herself. Jormunder's warning echoed through Serena's mind.

Mab was wrapped in glamour, potent and complex; Serena doubted anyone else could see through it, except perhaps Jormunder. The power coming off her mother was unmistakable, locked onto the wellspring and rippling across the sand. Her face flickered like a desert mirage, wavering between her true form and that of a scowling blonde stranger. Mab rarely left the palace, and after the assassination of her mother, Tatiana- particularly in a time of war- she often travel disguised.

Jormunder gestured toward the shoreline, voice crisp. "Serena, take the Ambassador ahead. I'll follow with the rest." Serena nodded, and Mab detached from the group, moving to walk at her side.

They strode through the wreckage toward the battered ships. Serena pointed out items of note as they walked. "They used a mist that caused a choking death, but the wind mages could push it back. And fire comets that burned blue and black, flames that wouldn't die even underwater."

Mab listened in silence, her expression unreadable as they passed the ashes of last night's bonfire.

Serena went on, her tone steady. "Once the ship was disabled, there were about a hundred dark fae—the Soludhi, as they call themselves—holed up belowdecks. I called the Mer. About two dozen answered, including five sirens, led by one called Linnae. We surrounded the ship and sang them into the water."

At that, Mab's head snapped to the side, eyes narrowing as she studied her daughter, sharp and appraising. "You sang them to jump..." Her gaze was so piercing it felt as though she could see through Serena's skin. "Meriden taught you well."

Serena nodded. "We made a fire, painted our faces, and sang. We left none alive." She bared her teeth—not in threat, but to underscore her words, fangs catching the morning light.

Mab regarded her for a moment, unreadable, then shifted topics, "I saw your standard in the camp when we gated into the staging grounds."

Serena turned, chin raised, her voice slightly defensive. "The Tempests were named and created by my grandfather. He designed the standard."

Mab snorted, a sharp sound. "I am well aware. He informed me. I told him I would allow it, on his recommendation. I decided having a toy army under your command would either teach you to lead or be your downfall. Your victories are mine; your losses, yours."

Serena met her eyes, cold and unyielding. "Then I hope your victories have pleased you."

A smirk twisted Mab's mouth, the glint of challenge in her gaze. "Do you hate me, Serena?"

Serena watched her for a long moment, gauging the shifting currents of Mab's mood, then answered, voice measured, steady. "I don't think about you enough to hate you."

Mab laughed, low and sardonic. "A few years ago, you would never have spoken so boldly to me. You walk a fine line, Serena. Having a spine is expected of an Heir—you may be High Queen one day. But you are still the Heir. Be careful."

Serena's reply was flat, the hard light in her eyes unwavering. "My grandfather did not raise a fool." The words were carefully chosen, a pointed reminder that Jormunder, not Mab, had raised her.

Mab heard the barb. She bared her fangs in mild rebuke, a silent dare. Serena didn't rise to it, her expression unchanged. Mab turned, flicked her gaze to the ship, and said, "Take me to the ship."

They stopped beside the Soludhi ship on the rough boardwalk, gazing up at the glyphs carved along the rail. Serena pointed to several, her voice clipped with focus. "That's fire protection, and this one looks like general damage protection. That much has been discovered by the tower, based on the human ships."

Mab said nothing, her eyes moving over everything, sharp and calculating. She was too well-trained, too old and shrewd, to betray any reaction. But Serena could sense her mother's mind working: this was her territory, and she would not let the insult of an invasion pass unstudied.

On deck, a path had been cleared through the wreckage so the cabins could be accessed. Splintered wood from the mainmast—destroyed by Serena's lightning—had been swept aside along with the tattered black sail. Near the center of the deck, a gaping hole yawned down to the levels below.

Mab glanced at Serena, one eyebrow arched. "Your work, I presume."

It was less a question than a statement. Serena nodded. "They were well warded. It took repeated strikes, even locked into the wellspring. Maybe five before the mast finally shattered."

Mab's brow lifted in silent appraisal, but she pressed on, unwilling to rely on anyone else's account. She moved with the quiet certainty of one who had learned war and magery from the best—Tatiana and Jormunder, her parents, and the master mages of the tower.

They ducked into the captain's cabin. The walls and doors were etched with more glyphs, none familiar to Serena. The magical artifacts, books, and maps had already been taken away by mages and scholars, bound for deeper study. Mab trailed her fingers over the linen of the captain's bed, frowning. "I don't recognize the fabric. Some crop we do not have here."

Without another word, she turned back toward the deck, her tone brooking no delay. "I want to see the prisoners."

Back on shore, the prisoners were shackled with magic-nullifying chains, held apart from the bustle of the camp. Their clothing was unlike anything worn in Ardaion—marked by enchantments and glyphs no scholar had yet deciphered. One of the Soludhi prisoners, eyes wild with fury, caught sight of Mab and began to rant, shouting in a guttural, bastardized form of ancient *Hifa*. Mab did not flinch, did not react to the torrent of rage, but listened, parsing the tangled language with cold focus.

Serena observed in silence before offering, "Graye has strong mental abilities. He was able to break into their minds once the chains suppressed their magic. Much of what you've seen in the reports was the result of his work."

Mab's gaze flicked to Serena. "A valuable skill. He's proving his worth, after all." Her eyes lingered darkly, then added, "And I heard he was using tower-level spells, too. I wonder, Serena, how he learned those..."

Serena met her mother's look with measured defiance. "I made a strategic decision to train him in a few ranged, battle-scale spells. Not everything—there was no time. But he contributed greatly to our victory because of it."

Mab was silent, watching her for a long moment. Then: "He'll be useful to me, then."

Serena schooled her features to blankness, refusing to give away any reaction.

Mab strode to the male prisoner who had shouted at her. With surprising strength, she locked her fingers around his throat, her power surging into him. The male thrashed and screamed, his body lighting up with a silver tracery of veins and arteries as Mab delved deep—into anatomy, into power, searching for secrets. When she released him, he collapsed unconscious, breathing but spent. He would still be examined for what he knew.

Mab turned back to Serena. "Their power feels similar to our own but not quite. It may be they are a surviving remnant of Twilight, but we cannot be certain yet. However—" she gestured to the prisoners and their glyphs, "if their magic is akin to ours, I see no reason why we can't master their glyphs and these new spells ourselves."

Serena replied with careful caution. "If they were the reason for Twilight's doom, and the failing of their homeland's wellspring, it could be tied to how they wield their powers. The spells may taint their magic, corrupt it."

Mab shrugged, already thinking ahead. "The tower will discover the truth. But you have named one of the reasons for my next orders. Come. We're going back to Ghealach Siorai for a proper council meeting."

While Mab's entourage toured the wreckage along the beach and the ruined ship, Jormunder stood at the edge of the treeline, where the forest gave way to sand, watching it all. His expression was unreadable, reflective. That was when he spotted Kade among the Shade forces.

He started walking.

Jormunder had taken note of the red-haired young male before—one of Graye's two right hands. Dardani by training, Ember by blood, and someone who carried a glint of admiration when he looked Jormunder's way. Hero worship, perhaps. That wariness in his eyes now, trying not to look startled as the Black Dragon himself approached, confirmed it.

Jormunder gave a short nod. "Walk with me." His tone was gruff but not sharp. His face was schooled to something that wasn't friendly, but mild enough not to intimidate outright.

Kade ducked his chin quickly. "Yes, General."

They walked into the cover of the trees, quiet, the sounds of the beach receding. Jormunder stopped once they were far enough for privacy, then turned. "You're friends with Graye. One of the two Dardani boys he trained with. The ones Serena took an interest in when you were still boys."

Kade nodded. "Yes, sir. My name is Kade. Born in Ember. Here to serve Graye with Aegin's permission."

Jormunder nodded once. "You look Emberi. The red hair. But the other one... black hair, green eyes."

"Rhune, sir. He's half-Shade. Noble on his father's side, Dardani on his mother's."

Jormunder's eyes narrowed slightly. "What can you tell me about him?"

Kade hesitated a breath, sensing the weight behind the question. "He's quiet. Smart. Second-born, so he was sent to train with us in the camps. He's fast with a sword, faster with his mind. Graye uses him as a diplomat by day and a knife by night. He's strong in magic—illusionist, and a gifted nullifier. We haven't been allowed in the Tower, but even without that training, Rhune's... sharp."

Jormunder chewed on that, rearranging mental pieces. Then his tone shifted. "And why were they growling at each other in the healing tent?"

Kade stiffened. "Well... I... wasn't there, General. I can't be certain."

Jormunder gave him a skeptical look. "Kade. I was there. They looked ready to kill each other. I stopped them, but I knew that wasn't the end of it. So I made sure I'd hear if anything more came of it."

His gaze sharpened. "So I wasn't very surprised when both of them showed up at the healer's last night. Beaten black and blue. Cracked jaw, cracked rib, split lips, black eyes. What I want to know is why. And you know."

Kade paled slightly, caught between his loyalty and the weight of the question. He swallowed, then said slowly, "They both love Serena."

Another silence. Another pointed stare from Jormunder.

Kade faltered, then continued. "Graye's always loved her. You know that. But he's in love with her, too. Has been for a long time. And Rhune... Rhune's loved her since the minute he saw her. When we were eighteen, nineteen...Never said anything. Never acted on it. But when she got hurt, Graye saw it. Felt it. That's when it all came out."

He sighed, decided to let it all out. "Rhune said he wasn't sure yet, that it was too soon to say for certain. But he thinks... he might be her mate."

Jormunder went still, absorbing that.

"That would do it," he said at last. "That would provoke Graye."

He ran a hand over his face, voice low, as if thinking aloud. "I wondered if this would happen. And how it would work if it did."

His gaze grew distant. "Graye is blood-bound to her. A piece of her soul fused into him, and vice versa. Illegal magic, his father's ambition. That kind of bond doesn't fade. It's a tortured existence. A hunger —for the other person, but also the missing piece of soul. They're never whole again. The closest they come is staying near each other."

He looked down, lips tight. "And then... the mate bond. It isn't like everyday love. The Binding requires the siren line to keep growing stronger and to improve itself. The bond selects males with something the bloodline needs. And when it does, the pull begins. A soul tether. Just as irrevocable."

Jormunder shook his head, exasperated. "So now Graye has a sliver of her soul. And Rhune may be tied to the rest of it."

He exhaled hard. "Jaryk's ambition continues to spoil everything."

His eyes narrowed again. "Kade. It's true they're young. And she hasn't been herself since Tides. But assuming Rhune's suspicion is correct... is he a good male? Is he worthy of her?"

Kade didn't hesitate. "Rhune is honorable. He's loyal and smart. He'll stand by her no matter what comes, no matter how long it takes or how difficult. But... so would Graye."

He added the last part because it needed saying. He'd grown up with Graye. Heard his stories. Knew the depth of feeling behind every 'Sev' he uttered.

Jormunder pressed his lips together tightly. "I know."

The delegation gated back to the palace at Ghealach Siorai, the air still heavy with the scents of smoke and brine from the battlefields. Mab had ordered Graye to accompany them, and Jormunder had tracked down Rhune, commanding him to attend as well—he wanted to weigh the young Dardani for himself.

Now they all sat at the massive stone council table, under the arched glass and moonstone of the great hall. Around them gathered two dozen diplomats, the Lord of each court, senior mage scholars, the Mage General, Jormunder, Serena, Elsibetha, Mab, Graye, and Rhune. Spread across the table were seized weapons and armor, tracings of unfamiliar glyphs, battered spellbooks, and maps marked with enemy routes and magical zones.

The chamber was a cacophony of voices—private debates, emotional arguments, speculation and fear simmering beneath the formal words. But when Mab rapped a polished quartz orb on the council table, the sharp echo cut through everything. The conversation died away. All eyes turned to her as she slowly swept her gaze across the room, taking the measure of each court and their leaders.

"We have not faced a threat like this since my mother was assassinated here in this very palace." Her words were cool and clear, each one weighted with authority. "The following things are certain: Ardaion's wellspring is bleeding across the channel, saturating the human island. The Soludhi homeland's wellspring is failing. They have deluded and sent humans against us for more than a year, and now they have risked open war, attacking our shores and displaying unknown magics."

She paused, her stare sharp as a blade. "We suspect they are a lost remnant of the Twilight Court, and we suspect the fall of Twilight and the subsequent collapse of their current wellspring may be tied to these unknown magics." She took her time, meeting every gaze in the room. "It is the suspicion that their magics may be corrupting which concerns us most gravely. I would not want a hostile people settling on an island so close to Ardaion under any circumstance. But an island bound to our wellspring—inhabited by a people who may have corrupted theirs? That cannot be permitted. At best, it would be a staging ground. At worst, a poisoned wellspring."

She paused for dramatic effect, letting the weight of her words settle. "Therefore... we will seize it first. Occupy it. Wipe out their toehold on the island and deny them access to a source of power. If they want to continue attacking us, they will have to do so from their failing land. Perhaps their dying realm will help us end them—and the threat they pose—once and for all."

For once, heads nodded in rare unanimity. It was in their best interests to fight with everything for Ardaion, or they might find themselves looking for a new land with new power, like the Soludhi. No one who had seen the devastation on the beaches doubted the necessity. This, after all, had been the point of bringing the delegation to the battlefield.

Mab continued, voice low and dangerous. "They staged smaller, unpredictable human attacks to spread our forces thin along the coast, then struck two places at once, gating in with no warning. They hoped to pick us off piecemeal, perhaps test their magics against ours. We suspected they were hoarding their strongest spells, and we were right. But..." Her lips curled into a devilish smile, the tips of her fangs just visible. "...they did not plan for Battle Mages. And they could not withstand the power of the Heir of Ardaion."

At that, Serena turned her head sharply, uncertain what Mab meant but doubting it was genuine praise.

Mab continued, voice calm and calculating. "Serena—as my Heir—is powerful. She drew on the wellspring during the battle and was able to substantially damage the ships, as we all saw, despite their protections. She and the Mer also sang half a crew into the sea, compelling them in the oldest of ways. It was an ingenious solution." She let the compliment hang in the air just long enough. "For the past year, she has established herself credibly as the commander of the volunteer force known as the Tempests."

There were nods of agreement from around the table. The Mage General gave Serena a rare smile, and one of the army commanders inclined his head in her direction. Serena did not return the gesture, her posture a disciplined neutrality.

Jormunder, seated beside her, had caught Mab's undertone just as swiftly, and with a deceptively casual motion, he rested an arm along the back of her chair, claiming space. Shielding. Watching. This was a performance. Not genuine praise-*justification*, for what was to come.

Graye's expression was wary, brow drawn as he shifted slightly in his seat, eyes locked on Mab. Rhune remained unreadable, as always, but he was listening—watching not just Mab but everyone, from the lords at the corners of the table to the way Jormunder had moved. His gaze flicked to the tracings of glyphs and the maps, then back to Serena.

Mab resumed, tone shifting slightly. "We cannot allow them to keep dividing our forces on their terms. If we continue to respond reactively, they will maintain the advantage. I propose we divide our forces in the manner of our choosing. One force will launch a counter-invasion of the island. The other will remain here, on Ardaion. It divides us, yes—but it divides them more. And they are further from home."

Jormunder gave the faintest nod. That much, at least, had been expected. But Mab wasn't finished—and even he didn't predict the blow that came next.

"The Tempests have been a good test of Serena's leadership," Mab said, voice still cool, almost conversational. "While I have the lords of all the courts gathered, I am choosing this moment to expand her command. She is to be given a proper army. The Princess's Army." She let the words land. "It will be formed of volunteers from every court. Should volunteers prove insufficient, I will order conscription."

She turned, sharp and deliberate, to Serena.

"You have proven yourself capable thus far, Serena. Your new orders are to take your army and invade the island. We are not keeping the human name, *Praetia*. From now on, it is *Skaera*—an old word for Twilight. And that is what you are to re-found. The Twilight Court."

A ripple of reaction moved around the room—some startled, some murmured with swift calculation. Taking Skaera was one thing, establishing a court was another. That implied not just military occupation but a change in Ardaion political structure. Mab continued before anyone could interrupt.

"Remove the humans. Eliminate the Soludhi dens hidden among them. Establish a defensible stronghold. They cannot be allowed to use or poison our wellspring." Her voice dipped slightly. "Elsibetha will command the Moon's army here in Ardaion—responding wherever needed by gate. General Jormunder will retain supreme command of both armies, moving between Ardaion and Skaera as he deems appropriate."

The table broke into side conversations, advisors whispering to lords, some already scribbling messages to dispatch.

At Serena's side, Jormunder's jaw was set. He had expected a battlefield. He had not expected *this*. Mab was sending Serena, at only twenty-two, to hold the island, defend the wellspring leak, and establish a new court. Not just a court, but reviving Twilight, with all the rumors and myths that came with it. And Mab was doing it with the cold calculus of knowing that Serena *could* do it- with support- but it wouldn't be easy.

Graye was staring at Serena, tense with something he couldn't mask. It felt like a trap to him. Rhune's focus had locked to her the moment the command was uttered. Neither spoke. They were both waiting for her reaction.

Serena kept her face blank. As she had been trained to. But she was already mulling the enormity of the command. Not just the invasion or defensive stronghold. The humans. Humans who had killed her grandmother, her father, and Cove. Humans who didn't know it yet, but were under a death order from Mab and she was the one to carry it out. Abruptly her mind flashed back to that day at the cabin with Graye.

"Is might always right, Graye? What kind of leader would you be?"

"I'd break what doesn't serve, and rebuild it better."

"So a benevolent tyrant. But where's the line between fixing and ruling by force? Where's the line between power and tyranny?"

"The line is in the why, Sev."

Jormunder broke the quiet that had crept over them. "Majesty," he said, voice calm but edged, "would it not be preferable to keep the Princess here? Near Siorai? For her safety.

If anything were to happen to her—" he didn't need to finish the sentence. The Binding was understood.

But Mab was ready. "She will have an army at her back. And the wellspring on Skaera can be accessed as easily as here. She can gate back if desperate. I will remain here, holding Ardaion's power. She will hold Skaera's. That way, both are secured by our line."

Then Mab's voice dipped, almost purring as she glanced at Serena, then between Graye and Rhune. "Though you make a good point about the end of our line, Father. We might all sleep better knowing the next heir could arrive soon. The Binding must continue, after all."

Her lips curled at the corner. Not a smile. A provocation.

In that instant, Jormunder developed a calculus of his own: this was another chance for Serena to prove herself to Ardaion. The Tempests, and now Twilight. He was going to help her. And when she finally ascended the throne, her name would be legend. His granddaughter, Tatiana's legacy.

Serena did not look away. Did not flinch. But in the silence that followed, the air in the council chamber felt very, very thin.

Moments after the council broke up, the great chamber was a flurry of messengers, lords relaying orders to their standing armies, rallying volunteers who would answer Serena's call. Any who chose to follow her knew what they were agreeing to: invasion, occupation, the defense of an island with no guarantee of return. They would do it willingly, bound by loyalty and the lure of a cause larger than any one court.

But Serena herself remained seated at the long council table, motionless, her thoughts running in too many directions to rise just yet. Graye moved quietly to her side and took her hand in his, threading his fingers through hers.

"It'll be alright, Sev," he murmured. "Jormunder's been training you for this since you were eight. Remember how you'd move map markers and tell the commanders what you'd do?" He tried to coax a smile, but his voice was gentle, steady. "You'll have a veteran force who want to follow you. And he'll still be there if you call. You know he'll come."

Rhune had positioned himself by the window, watching the palace grounds, though his ears were tuned to every word. His mind was already leaping ahead—supply lines, deployment, politics, the details of command.

Serena spoke softly. "I know from the army's standpoint it'll be alright. I can use what I've learned from the Tempests and just scale it up. Atta will be there for advice. So will

Elsie, if I need her. It's the rest of it, Graye. Wiping out the humans. Establishing a new court. The ethics."

He leaned closer, nodding, truly hearing her. "You're philosophizing," he said, not unkindly.

She nodded, and he kissed her temple, long familiar with the way her mind worried things until she made sense of them. He squeezed her hand. "We'll figure it out together."

Serena shook her head, almost sadly. "Shade needs you, Graye. You have your court to defend. Kade and Rhune can't do it alone. The Soludhi could come back tomorrow and try again. But... I want you to visit. Promise me you'll come when you can. Not just for the bond but so I don't feel so far from home."

She made no mention of Mab's pointed comment about heirs. Perhaps she meant to brush it off as just another barb, insignificant compared to the orders she'd been given. But Graye had caught it, and so had Rhune.

While Graye was talking with Serena, Jormunder was making his way through the palace corridors, catching up to Mab in her private study. He closed the door quietly behind them, wasting no time.

"What are you doing? And what do you know?" His voice was blunt, edged with frustration and paternal warning.

Mab had anticipated this confrontation and his protectiveness. She met his gaze, unruffled. "What I am doing is defending my realm with the resources I have at hand. I am taking the island before they can tighten their grip, before they taint Ardaion's wellspring. Serena can access the power there—no one else can, except myself. She'll have the army in front of her and can cast at range with minimal risk. You raised her in an army camp, for tide's sake. You trained her to do this. Do you doubt yourself now?"

Jormunder's growl was low, tired. "I know what I taught her. And I know she's good. It isn't her mind I worry about, but her heart. Can't you see how worn thin she is?"

Mab scoffed. "Her heart? What I saw today was that she looked me in the eye, stood up to me, and didn't cringe. She was hard, cold—she killed hundreds yesterday, with fang and song, with pure power." There was a flicker of something in her voice—pride, or something dangerously close to it.

Jormunder caught it and raised an eyebrow. Mab rushed to correct herself, "Don't mistake me. She's a weapon. And I'll wield her like one. Besides, you'll go with her at first, to ensure a good start. I'm hardly throwing her to the wolves."

He said nothing, knowing even his deep love for his granddaughter didn't change the truth. Serena was an asset as much as a princess. And she was a future queen.

Mab slouched insouciantly into the leather chair behind her desk, turning coy. "As for what I know... you have your eyes and ears, Father. I have mine. Graye and the other boy got into a fight over Serena—bad enough to crack a rib. Graye is a known quantity, but I had a dossier compiled on Rhune." She glanced over at a stack of papers.

"Second son of Baron Eirich of Shade. Sent to the Dardani camps, where he met Graye and Kade. His mother, Reina, is Dardani, but she's got Emberi powers—she can summon hellfire. She'd have been useful in the tower. So far, the boy is counted lethal with a sword, and proved himself a talented illusionist after Serena had Dewin train them behind my back."

She scowled slightly at the memory. "Field reports mark him a tactical prodigy. A strategist. Talented enough to barter trade deals with a silver tongue by day, and handle espionage or even sabotage by night. He's part of why Shade's coffers are filling again."

Jormunder realized, with some chagrin, that Mab had beaten him to what he'd meant to investigate himself. She smiled sharply, "So... why would he fight Graye, his lord, over her? Younglings being young? He doesn't seem the type to act on impulse. Maybe I should be asking you what *you* know, Father."

Her small, knowing grin said everything—she suspected the truth. Jormunder gave her the truth, plain. "I got some details out of Kade, the Emberi. He hedged. He's loyal to their triad. According to him, Rhune doesn't know for sure. He hasn't claimed her, hasn't told her. He's the type to wait until it's certain and they're too young to be sure."

"But Serena took a head wound in the battle, and he couldn't help himself—he had to be with her in the healer's tent. I was there. He didn't take his eyes off Serena. Didn't say a word, didn't need to. HIs face said everything. Graye was there too, sized up Rhune rightly, and it led to blows. She's still grieving the death of the Akyist boy. So they're both circling her, a waiting game."

Mab tapped a painted nail against her fang in thought. "Uncertain times. It was no lie that a child would secure the line—and could be kept safe here in Siorai while her mother continued to fight. If Serena had been beyond healing, the line would have ended. Yet I need her in this war, the wellspring power, or it's all for naught anyway. If we lose to the Soludhi, we lose Ardaion. Maybe even the wellspring."

Mab looked out the window a moment, thoughtful, "Her age is largely irrelevant. She's an adult with access to a palace full of staff. She'd hardly be struggling to raise a child alone in some hut. But she can't have an heir without certainty. The Binding is explicit. So we wait. It may be years more. But that doesn't mean we can't take some steps."

Jormunder's frown deepened, wariness prickling at his spine. Mab rolled her eyes, exasperated. "I simply meant Graye has proven valuable, the mental interrogations. I could enthrall them, but to what end, when we don't share the same language? In their minds, however, Graye understands them, directly shares their thoughts. I intend to keep him nearby for that; he can help expand our knowledge of the enemy."

"But if he's in love with Serena, and he's not her mate, then he's a distraction. A liability. She needs her mate determined by the Binding, not her old playmate. Rhune will go with her. I'll name him aide-de-camp. Perhaps proximity will provide clarity."

Jormunder's look could have melted steel. "Fine. Graye stays, Rhune goes. He proved himself yesterday as capable in a fight. But Mab—you *will not* interfere further than that. I loved your mother. You loved Edric. Give Serena the space to find love, too."

She shrugged, expression unrepentant. "I'm not opposed to her finding love. But she's a queen in waiting. Duty first, duty always."

Mab straightened in her chair, arranging herself with a queen's composure before summoning Serena and Rhune. Serena felt that old, brittle defensiveness flicker through her—a bracing for any cruelty that might follow. Rhune, called for reasons he could only guess, masked his uncertainty with the calm, neutral expression that had long been his armor. When they entered Mab's study together, Rhune bowed low, Serena curtsied with practiced formality, and then offered a bland, "Mother."

Mab did not respond at once. She let the silence stretch, weighing Rhune with her gaze, comparing the dossier to reality. He was tall—naturally lithe, but honed by the brutality of Dardani training. A full six inches above Serena, with an elegant face, blue-black hair, and striking emerald eyes that flashed with the sharp intelligence her reports had promised.

He moved like a courtier, effortlessly poised. Which, Mab supposed, was expected: a noble son, refined by that clever little diplomat from Solace. But there was an edge beneath that—courtesy layered atop a dangerous capacity. Her informants had been thorough;

she knew what he was capable of. Knew also that he'd beheaded the mage who'd attacked Jormunder and Serena before flying to the healers tent.

She stood, circling him in a slow, appraising orbit. Handsome, but not soft. Stern. As she drew near Serena, Mab's hand darted toward the dagger at her waist—a deliberate, rapid movement, pure theater. Not a threat to Serena, not truly, but a test. Serena, with Jormunder watching, held her ground without so much as a blink.

But the gesture hadn't been for her. Mab observed Rhune, and saw what she wanted: he flinched—barely, almost imperceptibly—but his body moved not away from danger, but toward it. *Toward Serena.* Instinct to protect, even against the High Queen herself; a move that, had it been real, would have spelled his end.

Mab smoothed her skirts and resumed as if nothing had happened, though the glint in her eyes betrayed satisfaction. It was an indicator, if not conclusive. Serena wore the mask of a bored heir, unimpressed by whatever game was being played. Rhune, now fully alert, studied Mab with the wary sharpness of a duelist.

At last, Mab spoke. "Rhune, of Donbaryon House. I have witnessed the Shade Court's rebirth under Graye's rule and have taken note of your part in it. You have been... effective. Lord Aegin thinks highly of you."

Rhune inclined his head, perfectly polished. "I serve as I am able, Majesty."

Mab's mouth quirked into a predatory half-smile. "Then you will serve the Crown during our campaign against the Soludhi. You are hereby seconded as aide-de-camp to the Princess for the Skaera campaign and the re-establishment of Twilight. Your blend of steel, diplomacy, and tactical acumen makes you well-suited for the role. And you have known Serena for some years through Graye, have you not?"

"I have, Majesty. I would be honored to serve the Princess in whatever capacity she requires."

Mab nodded, satisfied. From his place in the corner, Jormunder checked Serena for any flicker of reaction, but she was as still and trained as ever—revealing nothing, least of all before Mab.

Mab turned to her. "I trust you have no objections?"

Serena finally answered, her voice cool. "No, Mother. I have faith in Rhune's abilities. More importantly, I trust him."

"Good," Mab replied, content with the web she was weaving. "When we are done here, see that he is given armor and a sword befitting his new rank."

Mab sent for Graye next, keeping Serena and Rhune where they stood. He arrived quickly, having hovered nearby, worry etched deep by a lifetime of witnessing Mab's cruelty. Graye took his place on the other side of Serena, bowing to Mab with careful formality.

Mab regarded him for a long moment—this time, not as a puppet, nor as Jaryk's son, nor the inconveniently and illegally bound male, but as Graye himself. He was attractive in the Shade way: dark hair, green eyes, a face usually touched with a cocky smirk—but not today. He stood close to Serena, almost too close, projecting possessiveness and protection, his gaze cold and wary as he watched Mab.

Subtly, he brushed one finger against Serena's hand—a fleeting gesture almost no one would have noticed, but Mab saw it. She was attuned to every power dynamic in the room. Yes, she thought, Graye loves her. He would fight for her, would throw himself between Serena and Rhune if it came to it. And if Rhune truly had the mate bond, that could not be allowed.

Mab adopted the serene face of a ruler, concealing her calculations behind a mask of calm authority. "Lord Graye, your assistance in interrogating the prisoners has allowed us to bypass the language barrier in Soludhi speech and writing. Your work has been invaluable." She let the praise hang for a breath, just long enough to read his face, then continued, "For this reason, we will continue to rely on your abilities for the war effort. As a reward for your service, Shade's trade contracts with the Moon Court will be restored, and you may continue your Battle Mage training without the requirement of serving in our army." It was a bribe and a leash both.

Mab's voice remained even, but the intent behind her next words was crystal clear. "I know you likely had entertained thoughts of accompanying Serena to Skaera, but Ardaion needs you here. Your skills are indispensable, and your court cannot be left leaderless. In anticipation, I have already seconded Rhune to serve at her side, in your place. As one of your trusted seconds, I know you will be relieved."

She allowed herself a small, predatory smirk—sharp enough to cut. *In his place.* The jab was felt by all. But it was nothing but logical, nothing overtly hostile. Polished cruelty—Mab's specialty.

Graye's expression faltered, struggling to mask a flash of anger and pain as the blow landed. But with no recourse, he bowed slightly, "You are both perceptive and generous, Majesty." His hands were tied, but he turned to Serena and said, "I will visit you as often as our bond requires, and as often as it pleases you, Princess. You will need to be strong for what lies ahead." It was a message for both her and Mab: *I will not be gotten rid of so easily.*

Serena smiled at him, warm and sincerely, feeling the undercurrents of the room but ignorant of the depths of the stakes. "I will look forward to your visits, Lord Graye."

Mab's eyes cooled further, sharpening for just an instant before she slipped on a faint, false smile. "Then everything is settled. Serena, the courts have three days to raise your army. You will use that time with your new aide and your grandfather to plan the invasion. You may all go."

Serena nodded, curtsied, and departed, the two young males trailing her, exchanging silent glances.

When the room was empty, Jormunder remarked, "You tied that up neatly," his voice edged with grudging pragmatism.

Mab's eyes glittered. "I learned from the best." A reminder that, whatever she had become, Jormunder had shaped much of it. He simply nodded, a tired frown tugging at the corner of his mouth, and left the spider to her web.

CHAPTER THIRTY

FAREWELLS

Serena turned to Graye as they left the room, her expression softening, a worried frown settling in. "Graye... I know that wasn't what you wanted to hear in there, but she's right—I told you as much. You have a court that still needs its lord. And you can interrogate our enemy."

"You can do more in that capacity than as one mage on the field. And now that she's allowing you to train, not just at the tower, but as a Battle Mage with no obligation... take it. Grab it with both hands and train hard, every minute you get. Fortunes—and her moods—change with the tides. If she's going to use you, use her for everything you can get."

She reached for his hand, squeezing it. Graye sighed, pained acceptance flickering in his eyes. "I have to equip Rhune for his new position. Mother's orders. Meet me tonight at our usual drinking spot, alright?"

A smile broke through, warmth and love threading across his features. He flicked a glanced at Rhune before he leaned in, kissing her cheek. "Of course. See you tonight, Sev." The secret meeting place, the kiss, the nickname—all genuine, but also a message for Rhune. *She's mine.*

Rhune remained expressionless, his mind fixed on the coming campaign, not Graye's silent challenge. He followed as Serena led him through the Moon Court palace—his first time in its halls. He missed nothing, every detail adding to Graye's stories of their childhood. Serena moved quietly, occasionally pointing out rooms, artifacts, or old paintings. In the armory, after instructing the staff to fit Rhune with the best armor and weapons for royal service, she finally turned to him, studying his face.

"You're so hard for me to read sometimes, Rhune. What do you think of my mother's orders? You probably wanted to stay in Shade with Graye and Kade. I guess it's selfish to say, but... I'm glad you're coming. I know I'll have *Atta*, the commanders, Elsie... but the day-to-day would feel lonely without someone I know." She abruptly scoffed at herself. "I sound childish, talking about loneliness when we're at war. As if that matters. But this is the biggest thing she's ever asked of me. I'm nervous, and I can't fail."

Rhune was silent for a beat, weighing how much to reveal. He'd already decided he was going with her when Mab had announced her orders at the council table. There was no version of that story where Serena left without him. Mab's orders had been a surprise but convenient.

At last, he said, "I think... I couldn't be happy in Shade, not knowing if you're safe. I'll work every day to see you succeed." He drew a breath, his chest tightening with emotion he was trying to keep hidden, then took her hand. "You will never be alone, Serena. And I won't let you fail."

Rhune changed into the unfamiliar Moon Court armor: dark grey with the Crowned Crescent sigil etched across the chest, fine black filigree marking him as royal staff. The fit was elegant, the craftsmanship finer than anything he'd worn before. The armor shimmered faintly—enchanted to absorb minor damage—and a mastercrafted sword hung from his hip, its scabbard matched to the set. The blade bore an Ever-Sharp glyph: it would never nick or dull, no matter the use. Around his waist was a deep navy sash stamped with the Tempests' trident and lightning sigil—a subtle, unmistakable signal. He was Serena's staff. Not Mab's.

He looks good in it, Serena thought, realizing perhaps for the first time in a very long time that he was rather handsome.

His Shade armor had been fine—lordly, practical, well-kept. But this... this was Sio-rai-forged. The difference was visible even to the untrained eye. Serena smiled slightly. "It suits you."

He returned a small smile of his own, understated as ever.

Serena hesitated, clearly weighing something in her mind. "We once had a tradition in my grandmother's era," she said softly at last, "back when battles were frequent. It fell out of practice during the peace, but perhaps it's time to revive it: Fidelity glyph tattoos. They were used to confirm identity—especially among those who acted directly on behalf of the Crown. Armor can be stolen, glamours cast...but these glyphs can't be falsified." Her gaze darkened slightly. "The Soludhi have proven adept at glamours, enough that they were able to spy on us before launching attacks."

She bit her lip. "I thought perhaps since we're invading enemy territory, it might be wise to bring the tradition back." She touched the silver glyph at her throat—the mark of the Heir of Ardaion, which had appeared the day she'd first embraced the wellspring and summoned her wings. "Besides," she added, suddenly a little shy, "I already bear mine."

When Rhune gave no immediate answer, uncertainty flickered in her eyes. "If you'd rather not, I understand—"

"No," he interrupted gently, calm and certain. "It's wise. I will be your representative, near you daily. If it helps keep you safe—if it can't be counterfeited—I accept."

A flicker of surprise crossed Serena's face, replaced by quiet delight. "Very well. To prove you are who you claim to be..." she said, a playful note entering her voice, "what happened the first night we met?"

Rhune offered another one of his rare smiles, dry and understated. "As I recall, there was heavy drinking, followed by you throwing a wine bottle at me."

A startled laugh escaped her, bright and genuine. "Not *at* you. *Up*. I'd heard you were fast and wanted to see for myself."

It had been too long since he'd heard her laugh so freely; it tightened something deep in his chest. His smile warmed, his voice lowering with amusement, emerald eyes glinting softly. "And did I impress?"

"Oh...I suppose," she teased, smiling even wider.

Rhune huffed quietly, utterly charmed by this rare glimpse of her, so genuine, so unguarded. Then Serena stepped closer, close enough that his breath caught.

She was still smiling, still near. Beautiful.

His pulse quickened as she raised a hand toward his throat. "Are you sure?" she whispered. "I can remove it later if you hate it."

He had grown distracted by her nearness, by the subtle, enticing scent of roses and vanilla. "Very sure," he murmured, breath quickening more than he liked. She didn't seem to notice or perhaps chose not to.

She turned her attention fully to his neck, her finger tracing a cool, precise path along his skin as the glyph took shape beneath her touch. He remained perfectly still, scarcely daring to breathe.

He'd replayed their embrace after the cliffside battle countless times. Now she was close again, her touch branding him in a new and permanent way. As she focused intently on her work, his gaze involuntarily shifted to her lips. He knew the legends of siren kisses—sweet as honey, seductive, enthralling...

She was so close.

Her hand lowered, but she didn't step away, carefully inspecting the small black glyph at his throat: the Crowned Crescent, marking him irrevocably as hers. He exhaled slowly.

Finally satisfied, she looked up into his eyes, a smile of quiet pride and something deeper on her face. "Perfect."

Kade had arrived a few hours later, drawn by news of the queen's orders and Rhune's imminent departure with Serena. He and Graye had both frozen as the pair approached, Serena in her now-familiar silver-filigreed armor, and Rhune beside her, cutting a striking figure in the Moon Court's livery. But what drew their eyes—what neither of them could ignore—was the tattoo now visible at Rhune's throat. A black Crowned Crescent. It was smaller than Jormunder's and Elsibetha's but still noticeable. He looked... elevated.

Kade's gaze flicked over Rhune, methodical, missing nothing—each buckle, each glyph.

Graye's stare lingered longer. His jaw clenched.

That armor wasn't just a uniform. It was a symbol of everything Mab had done to cut him out. To keep him from accompanying Serena. Rhune and Serena looked like a matched set now and he hated it.

He told himself Rhune would take care of her. That Rhune would die trying if it came to that. And yes, the bastard was talented. Talented enough to contribute meaningfully to the invasion, even to the establishment of a new court. But none of that dulled the salt in the wound.

For over a month, he'd seen Serena daily in Shade. Trained beside her. Planned beside her. And now, just like that, she was leaving again—leaving his life, save for the visits the bond required. It ached in his chest. Enough that Serena caught it.

Her eyes flicked to him, a brief frown forming. "Rhune's armor and tattoo mark him as my man," her voice neutral but deliberate. "He's to be trusted and granted access to any part of Siorai. Kade, I thought you two might want to explore the palace or the city, maybe the mage tower—while Graye and I share a private ritual. Food and drinks are on my tab."

Kade smiled warmly at her, genuine, though fully aware of the tension humming beneath her words. "Thank you, Serena. I'd like that. Everyone talks about this place, but it's beyond anything I imagined."

Rhune dipped his head, offering her a small, private smile. "We'll try not to get into trouble. I'll see you in the morning."

Then he and Kade turned and walked off, their boots echoing against the polished stone.

Serena turned to Graye, looped her arm through his, and said softly, "Shall we?"

A dozen minutes later, they were tucked into their familiar supply closet, the one they'd claimed long ago. Six bottles of a very good vintage waited for them. The blankets and pillows they'd once used were still folded neatly in a corner. They spread them out and sat cross-legged on the floor, back in the one place the world couldn't find them.

Serena took the first pull from the bottle, long and bracing. "You know... hiding away in here, I could almost forget that my mother is sending me to invade a hostile island and wipe out an entire population."

Graye huffed, annoyed. "I don't like it, Sev. I know you were trained for this, I know you can do it. You've done amazing things with the Tempests—they're famous. But that's a company, not a tides-damned army. And that was defense, not invasion. How do we know she's not setting you up to get killed? Maybe she just sees you as a future martyr."

He took his own angry gulp from the bottle.

"Because she's giving me the army. Not just the company," Serena replied evenly. "And she's not leaving me to sink or swim—Atta has the authority to supervise. If she wanted me dead, she'd forbid him from coming. She'd send me out with the Tempests alone, set me up for failure."

Her voice cooled, calculating. "She's made a tactical decision. The Soludhi are unknown. Their magic is powerful and unpredictable. If she waits, they pick us off in clusters up and down the coast. If she acts now, she forces them to consolidate. Forces them to fight on two main fronts. We'll be divided too, yes—but we have access to the wellspring. And once I clear the nests of them off Skaera, they'll be limited to whatever they can carry from Soludhus. Mab is retaking the advantage and using me as a threat they can't afford to ignore. It's strategically sound."

Another drink.

"I'm terrified," she admitted. "But I won't be alone. I'll have seasoned commanders. Jormunder will still hold overall command. And Rhune will be with me—"

Graye scoffed. A harsh, bitter sound. "Yes. Rhune. Handpicked by your mother. As my replacement."

Serena frowned, the lines between them suddenly sharp. She still didn't know the truth. Not about the fight. Not about Rhune's suspicion. "Graye, you two have been tense since yesterday. What happened?"

He didn't answer right away. Wouldn't. Couldn't. Not yet. Not while everything felt this precarious. Finally, he muttered, "We fought. Haven't made up yet."

Serena studied him for a moment longer, "We'll be leaving in a few days and there's no telling when we might see each other again. Make up with him before we leave. You may regret it if you don't."

The drinking continued. Two bottles each, now, and the edge was off—the world felt blurry, safe, insulated by the stone and the quiet of their hiding place. They leaned together, backs pressed to the wall, hands clasped, Graye's thumb tracing slow, lazy circles over Serena's knuckles. The silence between them had grown companionable, words no longer necessary for the moment.

At length, Serena broke it, her voice a little thick with wine but carrying a defiant note of hope. "I'm not going to let this get all depressing. This... this is a chance, Graye. To do what we've always talked about. To do things our way, for the right reasons. A fresh start. A brand-new court we can shape the way we want..."

There was something in her tone—optimism, fragile but fighting, the "we"—that drew him. It wasn't the fatalism he'd seen in her for so long, nor the cold, pained glare she'd worn walking through the mage gate. She was dreaming again. Trying, as ever, to claw her way back from the brink. No matter how many times she was kicked down, Serena always stood up again.

"I love you, Sev." He said it plainly, stripped of artifice, stripped even of the safety of habit. He meant it fully, every word.

She smiled and replied as she always did—warm, heartfelt. "I love you too. Whenever. Wherever. Always."

But he shifted closer, catching her gaze, the wine making him bold, unguarded. "No. I mean—Sev, I'm *in love* with you. I think I have been for years, but everything always felt muddled between us—the bond, our history, everything. It took me a long time to sort it out. I planned to wait because I knew you weren't ready. I wouldn't even be telling you now, except you're leaving again. I won't be there to hold you if you're lonely, hurt, or afraid. I won't be there, and it's killing me. Serena, *I love you*."

He was already close, and she hadn't moved away. She remained still, suspended between the haze of wine and the sudden weight of his confession.

Heart thundering, the bond roaring in his blood, Graye leaned forward and kissed her, softly at first, careful and uncertain. She hadn't moved. He tried again, slower, lingering. For one sweet, breathless moment, Serena kissed him back. Yet even as she did, he felt her holding herself carefully in check, restrained—gentle, unwilling to push him away but unwilling to let things go further.

"Graye..." she whispered. "What you said... you're right. I'm not ready. I can't. Not yet, and certainly not now, when I'm about to leave again. I love you, with everything I am. But I can't."

He exhaled heavily, the ache sharp, the acceptance painful. "I know. I know, Sev. But I couldn't let you leave without telling you."

She reached out and kissed his cheek—soft, loving, final. "You are my other half, Graye. Write to me like always. Visit me when you can. And when this war is over, meet me here, in our closet. Then we'll figure everything out."

He sighed again and gathered her into his arms, holding her close. For just a little longer, the entire world narrowed to the two of them, safely tucked away in the only refuge they'd ever truly shared.

The next few days passed in a blur of activity as volunteers from the other courts began arriving, drawn by Mab's call, their lords' reports, and the renown of Serena and her Tempests. Shade, still battered and wary from recent attacks, sent just fifty—a small but fiercely loyal band, all with something to prove. Solace contributed a corps of one hundred: healers, diplomats, and scholars of law, the latter intended to help establish the new Twilight Court. From Tides came two hundred Valkyrie-trained Akyists and fifty Mer, including two sirens, shimmering and dangerous as moonlight on water.

But Ember sent the most. The Dardani were spoiling for vengeance after their shores had been attacked, and the prospect of invasion held more allure than holding a defensive line. Four hundred Dardani arrived, with another hundred fire fae and thirty Frostvaari in tow. All told, over nine hundred volunteers joined the three hundred original Tempests. Mab, unsatisfied with those numbers, committed one hundred Battle Mages from the tower—an unprecedented show of force—and five hundred veteran Moon Court soldiers, swelling the Princess's Army to nearly eighteen hundred.

They began calling themselves "The Gale".

Some, like the Solace contingent and the Frostvaari, had never seen active fighting against the Soludhi. Many of the Dardani had never met Serena, but word of her and the Tempests had spread through tales carried by their kin who had fought on the shores of Shade. Rhune proved an unexpected boon—half Dardani himself, his polished Moon Court armor and reputation in both Shade and Ember marking him as a native son, someone they could trust. He moved through the ranks quietly, offering a warrior's pride and subtle leadership, a figure who belonged to both Serena's world and theirs.

Jormunder took command of the sprawling staging grounds in the fields beyond Ghealach Siorai, raising Serena's tempest banner for all to see. All volunteers wore navy sashes with the trident and lightning bolt, proud to advertise their loyalty to the Princess, the storm mage. The original Tempests, now seasoned, were awarded golden lightning pins for their collars and promoted into senior roles, guiding the new arrivals, training them in Serena's methods and ethos.

Serafine, who had been stationed in Tides when Serena was sent to Shade, returned and assumed the role of bodyguard at Jormunder's request.

Every day Serena was among them—circulating, walking the lines, sitting beside Jormunder in strategy meetings. Rhune remained at her side: quiet and steady, always prepared with reports, maps and messages, and ensuring she took time to eat, no matter how relentless the schedule. He recruited a trusted informant from Shade to serve as a windreader—someone who could read the winds of rumor, plot, and discontent before they ever broke the surface. Gossip, threats, and opportunities: all passed through Rhune's hands before reaching Serena.

Meanwhile, Graye was kept busy with endless rounds of prisoner interrogations for Mab. Kade was sent back to represent Graye in Shade while he was away, a task normally assigned to Rhune.

Most of the Battle Mages and half the Dardani had already been sent ahead by ship—the rest of the army would be gated to Skaera as soon as a beachhead was secured. The ships were not mere transports, but weapons: Mab intended to hunt the Soludhi fleet, not just defend the shore. There would be no more waiting for attacks to come—this time, Ardaion would break their enemies' ships, and crush their fleet outright.

On the eve of the army's departure, Mab summoned Serena and gated them both without explanation to the wild Moon Court coast, to a craggy outcrop high above the surf. Waves pounded the black rocks below, spray catching the wind and shrouding them in brine and foam. At the edge, Mab raised her hand: a gleaming gold trident appeared in her palm, its tines wickedly barbed, the shaft engraved with runes and ancient glyphs that seemed to pulse with power.

Mab looked from Serena out toward the endless, turbulent sea, her voice sharp and cutting like the wind whipping the cliffs. "I would end them all if I could—the humans. They took my mother. They took your father. They took the boy you loved. And now another enemy seeks to claim everything that is ours."

Her voice softened just enough to become something deeper, more ancient, as though every past matriarch spoke through her. "Our line stretches back to the first Matriarch—the one who was willing to sacrifice herself to forge the Binding and give us a future. That is our true purpose, Serena. Not courts or laws, not art or palaces. Survival. A queen and an heir, joined to the wellspring, fighting to keep Ardaion alive."

Mab turned, fixing Serena with eyes as cold and hard as tempered steel. "You have two duties now—only two. Fight, and when the time comes, birth the next heir. These duties alone give meaning to your life. Fail either one and Ardaion falls."

A blunt honesty resonated within Mab's words, her tone absolute. "I doubt I will ever come to love you, daughter. But succeed in this, and you will earn my respect."

Serena met her mother's fierce gaze and accepted Mab's truth, her own eyes sharp with resolve. "I understand, Mother. I will not fail."

Mab peered deeply into her, assessing her very soul, and finally gave a slow, deliberate nod. "You called on the old ways once already, sang those sailors into the sea. This is another, one that has slumbered far longer. We will wake it together. It answers only to a siren queen. It will know you by your blood and obey you through the trident." Her voice turned reverent. "My mother taught me to summon it when I was young, and now I teach you. Hold the trident with me."

Together, they planted the trident's shaft deep into the stone, both gripping it tightly. Serena felt Mab's intent surge into it, a torrent of ancient will and unrelenting power. The trident began to hum, vibrating with barely contained magic, glyphs burning gold against the darkening sky. Mab's voice echoed forth with the commanding resonance of the siren Voice, shattering the quiet:

"*Awaken.*"

At first, only silence followed—a tense, deafening emptiness. Then the ocean began to churn violently, waters heaving in a chaotic boil. A deep bass groan rolled forth from the abyss, shaking the rock beneath Serena's feet. Vast shadows writhed beneath the waves, immense shapes uncoiling, rising inexorably toward the surface.

Tentacles burst forth, enormous as ancient oaks, slick and barbed, towering impossibly high until they loomed above the cliffs, their hooked tips cutting the air like blades. Below the writhing mass, a colossal face slowly breached the waters—flat, armored, primeval—with a single enormous eye opening, amber-gold and ancient, its pupil constricting as it fixed upon the queen and her heir.

Serena's blood turned to ice, breath locked in her throat.

Mab's lips curled into a savage, predatory smile, fangs gleaming in exultation. "The Kraken," she whispered, almost reverently. "It has not been awakened for over a thousand years. We will use it to shatter their fleet—and then send it back into the depths. Now, prick your finger. Let your blood touch the sea. It knows me already; it must learn you."

She handed Serena a dagger etched with runes. Serena took it and pressed the blade into her thumb until blood welled bright and red, her heart pounding with adrenaline and awe. Reaching her hand over the cliff's edge, she let droplets of blood fall, spiraling downward into the foaming sea. Immediately, an alien consciousness brushed against her mind—vast, ancient, unfathomable—tasting her bloodline, acknowledging the Binding.

Mab nodded again, her gaze fierce and satisfied. "Good. Channel your will through the trident, and it will answer your summons. It will obey your commands. Bring their fleet to ruin, Serena. Break every last ship they possess."

A day later, word arrived: the mages had sped the ships swiftly through the mist and perilous seas between Ardaion and Skaera. They'd found a harbor cloaked in heavy fog, its waters deep and calm, opening onto a broad floodplain large enough to hold the entire army. The hour had come.

The Princess's Army stood assembled on the wide fields beyond Ghealach Siorai—row upon row clad in enchanted armor, weapons gleaming, supplies stocked and ready for a long campaign. Tension coiled through the ranks, a potent blend of fear, determination, and restless courage.

At Serena's side, Jormunder stood silent and steady, his immense presence lending weight and gravitas to the moment. This was her army now; his quiet strength was enough. Rhune stood just behind her, hands clasped behind his back, outwardly composed, though beneath the facade his nerves crackled like lightning before a storm.

Serena drew deeply from the wellspring, feeling the power surge through her veins. She unfurled her spell wings wide, cascading prisms of dazzling light scattering beneath the sun, casting rainbows across the soldiers' awed faces. A fierce, thunderous cheer erupted from the assembled warriors.

She raised her voice, magic amplifying her words to reach every soldier, clear and resonant across the gathered host.

"Armies of Ardaion! We face an enemy of parasites. They have poisoned their own wellspring, allowed their homeland to die—and now they come to steal ours. Unprovoked, they brought their war to our shores. Today, we take the fight to them. We are the gale they cannot withstand, the storm they will not survive. Ever Victorious!"

A mighty roar exploded from the ranks. Fierce, defiant, unstoppable.

Then Jormunder stepped forward, drawing every eye as he spread his immense draconic wings, black as midnight and terrible as legend. His voice thundered like the breaking storm:

"By her pull!"

From two thousand throats the ancient answer crashed forth, reverberating through earth and sky:

"We rise!"

At their battle cry, the waiting mages on Skaera's distant shore unleashed their spell. With a shattering crack, a mage gate tore open before the army—twenty paces wide and rippling with magic. Beyond it lay Skaera: mist-wreathed plains cloaked in shadow, an unknown land awaiting conquest.

The army moved instantly, orderly columns twenty abreast, one hundred rows deep, passing steadily into the waiting gate. Within the hour, the entire force would stand upon enemy soil.

Jormunder turned, voice steady, deep, and sure. "I'll go ahead to oversee the camp. Say your farewells, then join me there." Serena nodded once, and he was gone through the gate, vanishing into the mist.

Rhune stepped to her side, alert and protective, his hand resting upon the pommel of his sword. Leaning close, his whisper was meant for her alone: "You can do this." For a brief moment, she wondered if he meant the invasion or the farewells.

Then Elsibetha was before her, tears glimmering unshed in her cousin's eyes. "Be safe, cousin," Elsie breathed, voice trembling slightly. "I know you will be. I know you'll have protectors, but I still worry. Write me often. I'll visit whenever I can. I love you."

Elsie hugged her fiercely, and Serena pressed a tender kiss to her cousin's cheek as she stepped back, wiping hastily at tears.

Graye approached next, the bond tightening painfully between them, already aching with impending separation. Without a word, he drew Serena tightly into his embrace, breathing her in, etching every detail into memory. Serena pressed her face into his neck, her voice a trembling whisper:

"I love you. I will always love you. Visit when you can. Write every day."

His chest ached fiercely, throat tightening as he whispered into her hair, "I will, Sev. I promise. I love you."

He kissed her forehead gently and brushed her cheeks softly, and Serena quickly wiped away a solitary tear; an iron will holding the rest back, refusing to yield further.

From her distant vantage, Mab watched in silence. Serena met her mother's gaze steadily and pressed a fist firmly to her chest. Mab's expression was carefully unreadable, but she inclined her head slowly—a gesture of quiet acknowledgment. She had already said all she needed to say.

Serafine moved silently into place at Serena's side, ever the Shadowdancer—blademaster, guardian, mentor. She offered only a low, calm, "Highness. I am with you."

Serena swallowed hard, her heart beating rapidly as she watched her army march steadily into the gate, stepping into uncertainty and war. Unbidden, the image of the Kraken surged into her mind—the writhing, monstrous tentacles, the primal, golden eye gazing up from the abyss. Ancient, merciless, summoned by blood and will.

I may not have been a monster, Graye, she thought quietly, heart heavy and resolved. *But I fear I am about to become one.*

End of Book One

Appendices

The Courts of Ardaion

Moon Court The High Court of Ardaion, home of the Siren Queens. Neutral and sovereign, the Moon Court stands apart from blood feuds and alliances. It serves as arbiter and metes out justice. Its crystalline palace rises from forested hills and silver pools, a seat of ancient governance and magical law. Scholars, mages, and nobles gather here to shape the realm's fate. Unlike the other courts which mostly speak Common, the Moon Court predominantly uses ancient High Fae, or *Hifa*. It is less about pretension and more about practicality- the most ancient of the fae tend to live in Ghealach Siorai, having gravitated there as they became elevated to senior positions in the High Court. They simply opt to speak in the language of their youth rather than adopt the newer Common. To speak the Moon's tongue is to speak authority.

Ember Court Forged in fire, the Ember Court rules the volcanic heartlands where molten valleys and black cliffs birth warriors, not diplomats. The Emberi are fierce, black-winged, and shaped by heat and trial. Above them roam the Frostvaari—nomadic iceborn clans who answer only to mountain winds and winter steel. Together, they are blaze and blizzard, the crucible and the cold.

Solace Court From the salt-soft shores to the flowering plains, the Solace Court is known for healing, diplomacy, and cultural grace. It houses air fae, physicians, and negotiators who value connection over conquest.

Shade Court Beneath star-choked skies and crimson leaves, the Shade Court listens while others speak. Masters of illusion, memory, and quiet power, its people guard truths buried by time. To be seen by Shade is to be known more than you wish.

Tides Court The Tides Court commands the oceans of Ardaion. Its white-winged Akyist soar above the storms, while the Mer rule beneath. Here, wave mages call tempests and salt-warriors ride them. Tides governs what no land court can hold: the ever-changing sea.

◻ **Twilight Court** *(Lost)* There was once another court—Twilight. It gleamed brighter than any, until it fell into the sea, drowned by its ambition. Now, its name is spoken only in warning. Its magic bleeds still from the depths, corrupting slowly what should have remained buried.

The Age of Foundation

Civilization did not come with the First Binding. It came after—slowly, uneasily, and not without blood.

The queen's line had calmed the wellspring, tethering wild magic to a living anchor. But the world beyond her blood still fought, raided, and carved borders with teeth. They did not kneel. They did not call her sovereign. They watched her as one watches a star falling into the sea—distant, untouchable, dangerous.

Yet where her bloodline lived, the land responded. Rivers held. Crops grew. Storms returned to their seasons. The first to come were cautious. Then opportunists built around her, not for her. But they built.

Ghealach Siorai, City of the Eternal Moon, rose from fire circles and dust. Glyphs were carved into doorways. Magery evolved from survival to permanence. A city took shape—not just of stone, but of will.

They called it the Moon Court. Not for the sky—but for the sirens who bled by the moon, who bent tides with song. The matriarch had carried the moon in her blood. So did every daughter after. The name honored them—and warned others.

The queen did not rule. She didn't need to. The land ruled through her. Each generation bore one daughter. The Binding selected her mate from any court—chosen for strength, not love. The bloodline was designed.

Civilization followed not law, but gravity. Tribes formed courts, drawn to Ghealach Siorai's endurance. Most collapsed and rose again. But over centuries, Ardaion stabilized. The Moon Court remained unallied. Unassailable.

From that city came magery.

Innate magic lived in fae bones—elemental, instinctive, untaught. Magery could be taught. Glyphs, once crude, became language. Basic runes brought light, locks, and wards. Advanced magery—complex, ritual, unforgiving—created enchantments, death-halting elixirs, and weapons that never dulled.

Towers rose. Not temples. Schools. Affinities emerged—fire, water, earth, wind, frost, healing. But not all mages belonged in towers.

So the Moon Court built something new: Battle Mages. They trained in glyphs, tactics, and elemental warfare. They moved in unison, adjusted mid-battle, and shattered enemy lines before blades were drawn. Then they healed their own.

No other court dared try.

They were why the Moon Court's war cry was not a promise—It was a fact.

Ever Victorious.

Siren Queens of Ardaion: Morgana

It was Queen Morgana, third of the line, who made that permanent.

She governed not for power, but for survival—establishing law, structure, the mage towers, and doctrine. She kept the Moon Court neutral, a high court: diplomatic when possible, lethal when not. Siren rule was fair—but never soft.

And when human raiders came, Morgana rode with her army. Struck by an arrow to the throat, she died on the field.

Before sunset, her daughter rose. And the land did not shudder. Because the line remained unbroken.

Siren Queens of Ardaion: Tatiana

If Morgana forged Ardaion into form, Tatiana made it permanent. She inherited a realm shaped but still raw—its courts drawn, its borders held, but its identity uncertain. Morgana had laid the foundation. Tatiana built upon it—not with reverence, but with the certainty of a queen whose bloodline had been chosen by the land itself.

Tatiana ruled with precision. She was no figurehead, but the living tether to the wellspring—the conduit through which all fae magic remained balanced. Yet her power went beyond biology. She had vision. She knew the realm could no longer afford to react. Ardaion was consolidating. It needed a spine.

At her side stood Jormunder, her mate and equal. He was no ceremonial consort, no silent shadow at court. The Binding had chosen him—a Dardani warlord born with draconic wings: massive, serrated, clawed at the joints. Most Dardani bore feathered black wings. No one knew why Jormunder's were different—a quirk of magic, perhaps. A throwback to the wilder, more unpredictable powers. It didn't matter. They called him the Black Dragon, not in fear, but in recognition. His wings were made for command.

And command he did. A ruthless general and exacting strategist, Jormunder knew how to dismantle a campaign before it reached the field. He was a legend, undefeated. He and Tatiana moved as one—her vision, his execution. Their bond was open, fierce, and deeply in love. She named him Prince Consort not for title alone, but function—placing him above all other lords and empowering him to serve as envoy in her name.

Tatiana formalized their dynasty. To Ardaion, she and her daughter were Queen and Heir. To the courts, they were the Queen and Princess of the Moon. The first, a truth of blood. The second, a truth of diplomacy.

Her reign was efficient and unyielding. Jormunder crushed rebellion, enforced Morgana's borders, and swept away any threat to internal unity. When conflict stilled, the realm turned inward. Culture bloomed. Cities rose. The Moon Court became not just the center—but the apex.

Ghealach Siorai evolved into more than a capital. Its engineers, mages, and marble-shapers transformed it into a marvel. Curved structures followed magical geometry; towers shimmered with glyph-etched stone; light poured from faeglass and enchanted crystal. Under Tatiana, the fae aesthetic was born—graceful, supernatural, and unmatched.

Tatiana and Jormunder had two children. Mab, the elder, inherited the Binding and was groomed to rule. Rivarin, her brother, chose the military.

While Mab trained in the palace as the daughter heir, Rivarin trained in the skies. Along the coastal cliffs of the Tides Court, he partnered with an Akyist commander: Edric, a quiet, brilliant tactician with white wings and sharp eyes. Edric, who became Mab's mate and greatest love.

Tatiana's reign might have endured for centuries if not for the fear she inspired across the sea. Her end did not come from within. It came from humans.

Thus Mab came to power.

Terms

Atta: High Fae honorific meaning grandfather. It's what Serena calls Jormunder.

Drelk: Slang for Idiot

Ghealach Siorai: "Eternal Moon". Pronounced GAHL-ukh SHEER-ee.

Glyph: A precise, magical symbol used in formal complex magery. Glyphs are linguistic in origin, like characters from a magical alphabet, and must be combined correctly in spells or enchantments. Their appearance is usually intricate. They require training to interpret and are often used in scrolls, wards, or magical formulae.

Mate Bond: The bond created by the Binding after it selects a male for his ability to improve or strengthen the line of siren queens. This is the queen's Mate, and he becomes a Prince Consort. Jormunder and Edric were both Prince Consorts, though after Tatiana was killed, Jormunder preferred to use his rank, General. Colloquially, all fae tend to use the term *mate* to mean spouse, but there is no bond.

Rune: An ancient, primal mark infused with elemental or ancestral power. Runes are often carved or burned into weapons, armor, or stone, and their meanings are inherited or instinctual, not read like language. Their appearance is simple; often straight lines easy to carve. They resonate with raw magic, often specific to a race or culture.

Shadowdancing: An ancient martial art practiced almost exclusively by the royal women of the Moon Court, Shadowdancing blends balletic, fluid, unpredictable movement with close-quarters combat, illusion, and speed. Shadowdancers use agility, misdirection, and the manipulation of darkness to evade, strike, and confuse their opponents, often weaving spells seamlessly with physical techniques. Mastery requires decades of discipline; the art is as much about reading intention and controlling fear as it is about a blade or spell. Once feared and nearly forgotten, Shadowdancing has been revived as a symbol of Moon Court heritage and deadly grace. Training begins at age 15 due to the intensity of the training- it is too hard on young bones that are still hardening from childhood.

Sigil (Magical): A personal, conceptual symbol, crafted to represent a specific force, being, or intent. Sigils are usually used in ritual magic to channel will, summon entities, or bind energy. Their power comes from intention and design, not language or ancestry.

They are often customized by the mage for a specific purpose when a glyph is too generalized, and are sometimes one-time use.

Sigil (Heraldic): A symbol or emblem that represents a house, court, military unit, or noble bloodline. Heraldic sigils are visual identifiers used on banners, armor, documents, and seals to convey status, allegiance, and legacy. They follow traditions of color, shape, and symbolic meaning rather than magical function.

Sujinn: The swords of the Shadowdancers. They are slightly curved with a matte black blade that does not reflect light. Made of sky metal (meteorites) and forged only by master smiths in Ghealach Siorai. They are honed to be razor sharp. They are also enchanted with glyphs for Lightness (reduces weight), Ever-Sharp (takes no damage), and Recall (creates a lifelong bond with the Shadowdancer which allows them to summon it to their hand at will). All sujinn are property of the Crown due to their value. Students train with unbonded swords until they progress from novice and apprentice to full Shadowdancer, which generally takes about 80 years. At that time, they are then bonded to the sword with the Recall glyph. Upon their death, the sword reverts to ownership by the Crown's treasury.

PREVIEW OF BOOK TWO

Twilight: Book Two of The Trident Throne Trilogy

They walked down to the beach, letting the waves lap at their feet as they strolled along the shore. Serena glanced out over the darkening sea, her thoughts drifting—wondering where the Kraken was, what it might be doing beneath those distant waves. But she turned back to Rhune and asked, "How far apart can we get while you still hide us?"

Rhune's mouth curved in his small, dry grin. "Best not test it," he replied and pointedly tightened his hold on her arm.

She huffed, amused. For a fleeting moment, her face fell. She recognized the note of flirtation—the same easy, teasing manner Cove had once used. His face flashed unbidden in her mind: that first night in Tides, his laughing, "I like to be wooed. You'd better get started or someone else will snatch me up." Her heart twisted with pain, and she shoved the memory down, burying it beneath everything else. Rhune, perceptive as always, surely noticed, but he only continued walking at her side.

A few steps later, he stooped and retrieved a large sand dollar from the wet sand. He passed it to her, saying, "My mother showed me one of these once. If you crack it open, there are tiny little things inside that look like birds. She said they were wishes, and you should throw one into the sea if you want it to come true."

Serena studied the sand dollar, her interest piqued and the ache momentarily distracted. She whispered, "Did you ever wish for anything?"

He smiled, a touch of mystery in his eyes. "If you tell, they won't come true."

IslaMelysin.com